# The Blue Tamarisk

## D'Angel Moon, Volume 4

Mick Daley

Published by Silver Eggheads, 2024.

THE BLUE TAMARISK

**First edition. October 20, 2024.**

Copyright © 2024 Mick Daley.

ISBN: 979-8227280374

Written by Mick Daley.

# Table of Contents

Dramatis Personae - In order of appearance .............................1

THANKS ..............................................................................4

1 | An Inch of Gold ...........................................................6

2 | A Thousand Pairs of Eyes ........................................ 13

3 | The Enlil Effect........................................................ 17

4 | Tangerine Believers.................................................. 30

5 | My Mother's Second Cousin ................................... 38

6 | Starlit Realms........................................................... 46

7 | Bamboozled .............................................................. 60

8 | Weft and Weal........................................................... 67

9 | Mere Women ............................................................ 77

10 | The Ecology of Souls.............................................. 80

11 | The Lady of Damp Shadows .................................. 94

12 | Sweetmeat ............................................................ 100

13 | The Limits of his Experience ............................... 105

14 | Get a Room........................................................... 111

15 | Dimity Pocket ...................................................... 124

16 | No Paradise .......................................................... 131

17 | Juche .................................................................... 138

18 | Mansplaining........................................................ 148

19 | An Unfamiliar Wing of the Hospice.................... 160

20 | Egress to the Stars ............................................... 170

21 | A Shambles............................................................ 179

22 | Gone .................................................................... 186

23 | Gutta Percha ........................................................ 192

24 | Groot Verkeerslicht............................................. 201

25 | One Way Traffic.................................................... 205

26 | Your Spears are Carried off by the Wind.............. 208

27 | Ever Becoming...................................................... 214

28 | The Rampaging God............................................. 225

29 | A Commotion in his Pants................................... 229

30 | Cold Flesh .......................................................................231

31 | The Data will be Galvanised.........................................237

32 | As Above, so Below .....................................................247

33 | A Fulcrum of Cosmic Energies....................................255

34 | Antimatter....................................................................261

35 | Horse's Legs and a Woman's Breasts .........................265

36 | Mere Theatrics.............................................................272

37 | All the Demons in Creation ........................................283

38 | A Golden Compass .......................................................288

39 | Stone Trees and Flower Mountains .............................295

40 | D'Angel Moon...............................................................300

41 | Sifting Through the Ashes ...........................................304

42 | Wax Batteries................................................................308

43 | War Stories....................................................................310

GLOSSARY ........................................................................311

# Dramatis Personae - In order of appearance

BOOK ONE
Inanna - Sumerian goddess.
Grudoff - a Transylvanian coachman.
Lt-Colonel Sebastian Lafayette Chance - Irish.
Bejikereene Beruvoskii - innkeeper, Cristañan.
Olaf Beruvoskii - innkeeper and philosopher.
Mitke - urchin of the Eagles Nest.
Old Rugel - retired miller of the Eagles Nest.
Kalyenka Menschkievr - Moravian artist.
King Gustavus of Cristaña.
His son King Roland.
Proko - hapless young thief.
Petrov Morlulian - his cousin, an equally.
Lazlo - baker of the Eagles Nest.
Black George - Cristañan bandit chief.
General Manfred Von Teufel - Prussian hard man.
Kaiser Eitel Friedrich of Prussia - knife collector.
Dr Zegher Botghert Vehemple - Physicist. Dutch.
Baron Codrût Ancoulsis - Wallachian scholar
Enlil - Sumerian god.
Marduk - Sumerian god.
Duke Ferrapont Gennadi Galitzyn of Petrograd
Vania de Mezzanotte - Italian writer.
Don Enrico de Mezzanotte - her father.
Zosha Kuznetsov - Russian
Carlo Guilani - Genoan doctor.
Doctor Adhira Amordule - biologist, Indian.
BOOK TWO
Crown Prince Eitel Humbert of Moravia.
Julie Brown - American opera singer.
Colley Macready - English impresario.
Tibor Liszt - Hungarian impresario.
Bujar - Armenian bodyguard.
Alfonso Zithembe - musician. African American.

Veronica Almonado - Cosmician. African American.

Cesáire Devurrier - engineer. French.

Joâo Rodriguez - Hospice defender. Portuguese.

Caliph the Padishah Must Čelebi - Turkey.

Mullah Nasreddin - his Chief Mullah.

Kulan Pulynyuu - Pitjantjatjara ethnobotanist.

Sándor Petöfí - Poet.

Lajos Kossuth - Hungarian politician.

Abd al Alim - Turkish war elephant.

Fat Ursula - Transylvanian madame.

Lord Algernon Cockwattle - English.

Zhāng Sān - Vietnamese Dream Engineer.

Prince Dmytro Vyshnevetsky - Ukraine.

Commander Hieronim Nekanda Trepka - Polish.

Matthew Weiss-Brown - Julie Brown's father.

Madeline Brown - Julie's mother.

Doctor Augustine D'Angel - Persian.

Rilka Arud - Norwegian biochemist.

Gustave Courbet - artist, French.

President James Buchanan - 15th US President.

J. B. Henry - the President's private secretary.

Cora Scott - swamp creature.

Jian Cong - Chinese Shefu, or sorcerer.

General Yaklovev - Serbian war criminal.

Léon Carvalho - Parisian theatrical agent.

Madame Eusapia Bisson - French medium.

BOOK THREE

Ernesto D'Angel - Italian merchant.

Princess Shirin Azarmidokht - Persian princess.

Hafiz - Persian poet

Jimmy Jella - Pitjantjatjara rock star.

Abu Zayd al-Balkhi - Persian archeologist.

Sarantsatsral Yargui - *Natugai* of the Mongolians.

Galyna Black Otter - the *Znakharka* of Ukraine.

The Völva Yrsa - a Nordic priestess.

Nefu - Egyptian guide.

Baast - Egyptian goddess.

Menahem Ziyuni - a Kabbalistic scholar.

Al-Baladhuri - Persian alchemist.

Babak, his servant.
Dastur Rashin Shanahnaz Shahzadi - Zoroastrian.
Major Mengele - Prussian artillery commander.
Vidyadhishananda Subramuniyaswami - a monk.
Azriel - a Qliphoth demon.
Veronique - Hospice nurse.
Noxolo - baby girl.
Zithembe - her brother.
Gilgamesh - King of Uruk.
Ea-Nasir - his assistant.
Neocoles - *Lịmmûm* pioneer.
Chederlaomer - his business associate.
Bo Bae - Korean student.
Bitgaram - her brother.
Jae Won - Korean graphic artist.
Ermengarde of Occitania - *troubaritz*
BOOK FOUR
General Lazare Hoche - French soldier.
Lieutenant Deaglán Laghles - Irish soldier.
Gilbert du Motier - the Marquis de Lafayette.
Madame de Lafayette, his wife.
Anastasie de Lafayetter, his daughter.
The Grófka Kalyenka Žerotín - Moravian.
Kalyenka Minskovna Javakhadze - Russian.
Kalyenka Musatei cā Vlach - Wallachian.
The Karageorge - Serbian freedom fighter.
Aiwass Khonsu Ra Hoor Khuit - Sephiroth.
Bebop - Australian environmental activist.
Groot verkeerslicht - gigantic automaton.

# THANKS

THIS BOOK BEGAN IN JEST. The D'Angels were a slip of the tongue in performance by Bones Tain, became a shared joke with Leigh Ivin, blossomed in its own subterranean strata and emerged as a short story which gradually evolved into the cosmic gothic thriller which has occupied me for the past five years through plague, bushfire and flood. My longtime collaborator and publisher Adam Bell provided the epistemological infrastructure which sustained me throughout.

I especially thank my editors Tanya de Lys Mandorla, Paul Carey, Bianca Joy Symonds, Therese Murphy and Tessalie Parker.

My heartfelt thanks to all the many people who have sheltered, encouraged, cajoled or consoled me during the course of this long and obsessive project.

To Ann Daley, Kate Daley and Grant Bedford, Narelle Butterworth, Annabel Daley, Steve Perry, Evey and Isabel, Ian Wakeling and Naya Crookshanks, Mark Ford, Sam Fiddian, Nicola Collins, Scott Bennett, Charlie Barker, Mark McCartney and Jo Ferrari, Mark Savic, Naomi Takita, Darren Bridge, Sarah Jones, Craig Lawler and Jo Collings and Tim Somerville.

In Ireland and the UK: Dave Virgin and Clare, Rohan and Alex Healy, Nev Swift and Hazel Kenny, Michael Kiernan and Monika Bakanovaite, Matthew Jennings and Karen McLaughlin, Katie West, Mike West and family.

Jimmy Willing, whose artistic integrity is a beacon.

Aidan Ricketts and Adele Wessel for legal and ethical advice.

Especial and precise cachet to my occult adviser Paul Carey, without whose arcane knowledge and unparalleled imagination I would not have been able to envisage the aberrations and liberties I took with this highly scientific field.

Daniel Landinski's brilliantly playful translations of Hafiz allowed me to contemplate the poet as a complete character and thence prosecute some kind of understanding of the Great Work and the divine beauty of quantum entanglement. The great mysteries will never be the same again.

The translations of various scholars provide insight into the poetic sensibilities of a distant age and their authentic awe of the divine.

*The Hymn to Enlil* first translated by George Aaron Barton in 1918, later translations by Thorkild Jacobsen, Miguel Civil and Joachim Krecher.

Excerpts from the *Rig-Veda* translated by Ralph T.H. Griffith in 1896

Black, J.A., Cunningham, G., Ebeling, J., Flückiger-Hawker, E., Robson, E., Taylor, J., and Zólyomi, G., *The Electronic Text Corpus of Sumerian Literature* (http://etcsl.orinst.ox.ac.uk/), Oxford 1998–2006.

Inanna Spoke Anonymous, c. 2000 B.C.

from The Cycle of Inanna: The Courtship of Inanna and Dumaz Akkadian; trans. Diane Wolkstein & Samuel Noah Kramer

Imants Tillers, 'Locality Fails', *Art + Text*, no. 6, June 1982

To my literary exemplars Terrence McKenna, William Gibson, CJ Cherryh, Tolkien, Steinbeck and Elmore Leonard.

# 1
# An Inch of Gold

There were dragons of course, the stone statues favoured by all dynasties. There were water features in abundance and succulent leaves of the money tree, framing arrangements of tables and chairs in accordance with the principles of *Qi*.

Jian Cong the Confucian *Shefu* had not neglected to display a profusion of painted epigrams either, noted Ancoulsis dryly. Banners bearing proverbs in Chinese characters were deployed around the courtyard, which appeared to constitute a space carved out of quantum reality as much as it existed in the *Gēttīg*.

Ancoulsis had just arrived at this rendezvous, as arranged. Though he could not have said exactly where it was located in geomantic terms, the dream map he had been furnished with relied on precise mathematical coordinates.

The place had physical dimension certainly, situated on an eminence in what must be the Altai Mountains, going by the Siberian fir trees below and a giant ibex cropping the shoulder of an opposite summit. In the distance, just visible were the plains of Mongolia. A freezing wind scoured the terrace, but though Ancoulsis was attired for Bombay summer his eidolon suffered no discomfort.

His physical body was seated in the room at Watsons Hotel, breathing deeply, eyes closed. The culmination of a ritual had reposed him thus, after summoning the requisite energies to project his soul across the *Mēnōg*.

He had learnt long ago that ritual was the key to astral projection. It prepares the psyche and in Hermetic terms, 'opens the temple'. The foundational principles instilled by centuries of study enabled him to build that ritual, drawing a circle in chalk upon the floor, placing the idol of Enlil within it as a fulcrum. River stones from the Himalayas were arranged in a mandala, guarding him at north, east, south and west, for Ancoulsis knew only too well that using these powers was a process fraught with mischief.

Thus he had made gestures in patterns which reverberated in the astral plane, invoking his spirit to enter the ceremony. Scented candles on the perimeter of the circle provided sensory anchors, holding connection with the *Gēttīg*. His body was the crucible in which these elements came together, circular breathing to compel a trance state and send energy along his spine, propelling his astral body outwards. It was focussed on the mountains by a talisman, given him by Jian Cong a decade earlier.

They had met briefly in Belgrade, when the *Sarhang* invited Ancoulsis to discuss the potentiality of an alliance. That ill-fated discussion had not lasted long and afterwards, in the drawing room of a hotel, Ancoulsis was approached by the Confucian *Shefu*, who wordlessly handed him a small package and hurried from the room. Later Ancoulsis opened it, to reveal a silver model of a *siheyuan* house. He'd recognised it as a talisman, indelibly linked to the *Shefu's* elemental energy. He wondered briefly why the man would give him this precious item, but dismissed it as a ruse, many of which he'd faced since his early days of Hermetic revelation.

Decades later, the night after his tryst with Vania in Watson's Hotel, Ancoulsis experienced a lucid dream in which Jian Cong displayed a scroll inscribed with a *siheyuan* ideogram, whose *fántǐzì* inflection connoted deeper meanings. Ancoulsis intuited that Jian Cong was inviting him to a secret meeting. Accordingly, next evening he placed the talisman in the centre of his magik circle, beside the idol of Enlil.

With both talismans in place he was able to invoke an astral chariot that swept up his eidolon and carried it through a blizzard of metaphysical topography. Ancoulsis found himself gazing out on the

Mongolian steppe. He sat on a bamboo *yi* chair and pondered the ibex. The absence of his host was of a piece with the abstract nature of his invitation.

"*Fashionably late*"thought Ancoulsis.*This intriguer at least has*" "*a sense of style*"When the *Shefu* did arrive, it was with a theatrical plume of smoke and the roar of an offstage dragon. Jian Cong emerged from behind a silk partition, tugging his robes into place and staring sternly at his visitor as he strode down the stone walkway into the garden where Ancoulsis sat.

The two men's eidolons faced each other in appraising silence, before the *Shefu* lit a long-stemmed pipe and the scent of clove tobacco filled the air.

"Your promptness is appreciated," he said eventually. "*Yī cùn guāngyīn yī cùn jīn, cùn jīn nán mǎi cùn guāngyīn.*"

Ancoulsis cocked his head, mentally translating; "An inch of time is an inch of gold, but an inch of time cannot be purchased for an inch of gold."

He almost guffawed. "Folk wisdom, or the price of treachery?" he said, learning forward. "Surely you didn't ask me here to lecture me on horology, Cong *Zǐ*?"

The *Shefu's* upper body remained erect as he relaxed into a chair opposite Ancoulsis. "Your Western understandings of time are deficient, but it is only pertinent aspects of commerce I am concerned with at this moment."

"Excellent," said Ancoulsis. "Practical matters are all I am concerned with also."

"As to your other remark, I do not consider myself a traitor," said Jian Cong. "I have been placed in an unfortunate position by my colleagues in the Entheogen Academy, who insist that all must be sacrificed to honour their juvenile ideologies. They have allowed themselves to be deluded by the notion that Hermetic philosophies comprise the one true understanding of the Cosmos. They imagine that their manipulations of science should go unchallenged and predispose me to follow suit.

"But I am from Zhōng Guó, an ancient culture whose antecedents make a mockery of Western philosophies. They cannot and will not understand that their foolish tropes do not concern the Middle Kingdom."

"Precisely the situation I find myself in," said Ancoulsis. "Cosmic prerogatives cannot be sacrificed to erroneous notions of the common weal."

Jian Cong extended a long forefinger from the bowl of his pipe, pointing at Ancoulsis who instinctively made a warding gesture with his left hand.

"Instead I have decided to temper their strategies," said Jian Cong. "It is my duty to prevent them from sacrificing humanity to false philosophies."

"I have tired of attempting to dissuade your *Sarhang* from his follies," said Ancoulsis. "But he and his charlatans are set firmly on their cosmic delusion."

"*Shi de*," said Jian Cong. "This is why I gave you the talisman. I could see that you would understand my point of view."

The *Shefu* stood, waving his pipe in the air. "I know that you do not use psychedelics, as do the woolly-headed savants of the Entheogen Academy. Entheogens are indiscriminating. They open the user up to the universe, vulnerable to malign energies. The Hospice Seers cannot be allowed to promulgate such doctrines to the world! In opposition to their folly I plan to open an academy of Wuism; Chinese Magik, the most potent of all, focussed on specific aims, to counter this *feihuā*!"

Jian Cong cocked an eyebrow at Ancoulsis, who remained immobile. The *Shefu* resumed his seat, smoothing out his robe. He cleared his throat. "I will not proffer refreshment. Your eidolon would not appreciate my *Gôu Yinjing* wine."

"Yes, animal penis would be wasted on my jaded palate," said Ancoulsis. "In any case, I prefer we cut to the matter you invited me here for. Forgive me, *Shefu*, but I have no patience for the elaborate parsing of agendas. I would be indebted if you will speak plainly. The spell I have enacted will not last long and my spirit is already stretched, having travelled this far."

The *Shefu's* eyes widened in annoyance. "Conversation is a matter of appraising one's correspondent, deciding whether or not one intends to carry out the matters discussed."

Ancoulsis waved a hand dismissively. "Just so, I have been paltering with men these six centuries past and found that actions count for a thousand conversations."

Jian Cong gestured and a vision prism appeared, suspended in the space between them. It showed a heavy-laden steam train labouring through rocky desert. Emblazoned on the cars were logos in Mandarin characters, which Ancoulsis recognised as the branding of Jian Cong's family business.

The *Shefu's* voice-over followed the train into Tajikistan, where it stopped, disgorging its cargo. "The Silk Road has been since ancient times the preeminent source of trade between East and West. Fear of losing that market kept the Western Empires in check, for they knew it would cripple their economies. Now that the navies of European pirates control all trade routes, the Silk Road has been rendered obsolete. I intend to redress that situation."

A bowl of rice wine materialised in Jian Cong's hand. He took a sip. "I wish to come to an understanding with you as regards our mutual agendas. I am aware of the ambitions you hold for your Balkan League. In light of the geopolitical history of this region, I consider your strategy wise. Accordingly I am willing to override the proscriptions of the *Sarhang* of the D'Angels, which have no jurisdiction over the imperatives of the Middle Kingdom, and to support your Balkan League, in exchange for a vital concession."

"Please elucidate," said Ancoulsis. The fingers of his right hand flourished, making geomantic shapes to sustain his eidolon's presence.

"My family has vital connections in mining and transportation," said Jian Cong. "I request that you appoint them as your partner in the building of a rail road and the delivery of goods to your Balkan League. In short I am making a business proposal. You must understand this is not a venal intervention. I am expecting no enrichment from the transaction."

"Of course not," said Ancoulsis smoothly, as his left hand began the dance. "The agendas of a *Shefu* must by definition exclude mere financial benefit. Do not fear. The Seven Tribes of the Balkan Leagues will honour your family and the historical eminence of the Silk Road. Furnish me with the details of the company and I will ensure they oversee a Chinese rail connection with the Balkans."

Jian Cong inclined his head.

"In recognition of this I shall also require a small service," said Ancoulsis.

"Name it," said Jian Cong.

"I ask only that when the *Limmûm* invasion through the Skein comes to a head, I be quietly admitted inside the Hospice. I must be on hand to properly finesse the events I have set in train. The fate of the Balkan League depends upon it."

Jian Cong inclined his head. He deposited his rice wine on a bamboo table. "The talisman you possess will fulfil that duty. I shall furnish you with a vision map of the appropriate entrance to use."

"Then we have come to our agreement." said Ancoulsis, bringing his hands together. "We can arrange the details via visionary conference. Now I must depart."

"One moment," said Jian Cong. "There are further nuances to discuss. When you enter the Hospice the Entheogen Academy Seers will be immediately alerted to your presence. I may be forced to join them in confronting you and give the appearance of resisting your incursion."

"Of course," said Ancoulsis. "Continue the charade. The important thing is that I gain access at the crucial moment. I will take care of your colleagues."

"Very well. You will find your access. But from there you will be on your own."

Ancoulsis nodded curtly. "That is a circumstance with which I am only too familiar. Now if it please you, I shall return to my body, ere my astral connection begins to fray."

Jian Cong rose and bowed. Ancoulsis returned the courtesy, closed his eyes and enacted a power word. He was instantly flying through the *Mēnōg,* returning to the hotel room in Bombay. He felt his body close around him like a familiar bath robe, smelt the incense burnt during his ritual and prepared to end it. But at that moment there was a knock at the door. On a previous occasion an impudent servant had entered unannounced to clean his room. Ancoulsis could not allow that to happen again.

Though feeling somewhat muzzy-headed from his astral jaunt, he forced himself upright and answered the door.

"Go away," he commanded the manservant. "I am not ready for cleaning."

"*Mujhe bahut khed hai mahoday,*" the fellow apologised, head bowed as he back away. At that moment Ancoulsis remembered a breakfast appointment with Vania and quite forgot to reenter his chalk circle and complete the ritual, reabsorbing the cosmic energies he had unleashed. They were left to ferment in the ethers, with his cosmic signature all over them.

# 2

# A Thousand Pairs of Eyes

Proko had been feeling increasingly uneasy in the confines of the metal chamber, its ascension making his throat constrict and his mouth water. As it slowed to a stop he fell to his knees and vomited on Black George's boots. The bandit chief retaliated with a savage kick that slammed Proko into the floor, where he lay hearing voices and seeing visions.

"Lick it off, *glupan*," snarled Black George and with the hoots and howls of demons filling his head, Proko scarcely noticed his own tongue writhing over his tormentor's boots. This kind of mental static was a phenomenon he was accustomed to in everyday life, but now that he was inside the lair of the *tougrak* the hallucinations had trebled in intensity.

When the door slid open Proko vomited again, lurched to his feet and followed Black George out into a corridor. Its walls were covered with plants and weird murals that shifted and crawled and followed him with a thousand pairs of eyes. He flinched as a drooping lichen stroked his head.

The voices intensified as they progressed along the corridor. Proko saw himself as if in a mirror, a bent and wizened little man, hobbling through a forest of demons that scorned and reviled him. That image devolved further, his face sloughing from the bone, eyes drooping in their sockets, a miserable aspect of rotten flesh and congealing blood. He screamed in anguish, but only a drooling sound issued from his cracked lips.

Things got worse from there. Proko heard an insectile buzzing and stared, horrified at his hands. He could see through the mortifying flesh, watch blood whizzing through his fragile veins. That somehow led to a vivid memory of his wife Alžbêta, face

13

wrinkled in misery, bleeding from the mouth after he struck her one morning for burning the porridge.

Proko was standing in the kitchen of their filthy hut, jug of sour wine in hand, screaming at her for his myriad afflictions. He hit Alžbêta while the children shrieked from the doorway, begging him to stop, but there didn't seem to be enough blood, so he hit her again.

"What are you doing little man?" growled Black George. The wife beater was sprawled on his back on the oddly textured floor, making a high keening noise. Black George kicked him, but his heart wasn't really in it.

Black George had felt strange too, ever since they'd entered the *tougrak* lair. Adrift in this stinking, vermin-infested pile he felt assailed by indeterminate emotions and the vague premonition that something dangerous was afoot. The walls were unstable - they wobbled when he looked at them and threatened to close in when he looked away. Bizarre, terrifying secrets leaked out of them, whispering voices threatened with indistinct, coded warnings.

Visions kept blinking into his head. Strange capering villains with pointed toes like jesters, giggling wickedly as they performed ludicrous dances just out of eyeshot. He yelped. One of those clowns had zoomed in, uttering some reptilian edict as its ghastly eyes bored into his.

More images jumped unbidden into his head. Himself as a slim, handsome adolescent, beating insensible a burgher's son who called him a Jew; Fat Ursula gurgling her life out through her chubby throat, after he stabbed her with the biggest kitchen knife he could find. Petrov Morlulian, Proko's cousin, choking on the crude noose Black George strung him up with. Black George giggled, finding himself sexually aroused.

There were other victims, too many to count. They crowded around him, clamouring for attention. That didn't bother him too much, once he'd reasoned they were mere phantoms. No memory stuck him with a knife yet.

He glanced over at Proko. The wife beater was crawling along the corridor, body contorted, eyes blank, face a rictus of extreme distress. Black George twisted his chain, causing the wife beater's legs to deform further, though interestingly the evident pain did not bring him to his senses.

"Who are you? What are you doing here?"

A voice pulled Black George out of his reverie. He looked up. A slight man, lightly bearded, wearing spectacles and a white coat stood before him. Black George smiled and took a step forward, hands open.

"Ah, my friend, this madman here is in need of a doctor. I am seeking directions to the Dutchman's laboratory. Perhaps you can help us?"

The annoyingly neat and unflinching fellow eyed him suspiciously. "Do you have any identification? Are you a tradesman? You look like a gypsy vagabond. How did you get into the Hospice?"

Black George halted, smiling. His eyebrows levitated, perplexed at the *tougrak*'s unmannerly behaviour. "Good sir, I am shocked. I am a guest in your house, invited by our mutual friend. Will you not help me? I merely want for directions."

"Which mutual friend is that? Identify yourself, sir." The bespectacled milksop backed away and seemed about to shout for assistance. Black George darted forward, grabbing him by the lapels. His knee crashed into the *tougrak*'s groin. A series of rapid punches to the face and the man was sprawled on the ground, gagging. Black George whipped out a knife and kneeled on his narrow chest.

"I look like a gypsy, eh?" he purred, blade stroking the man's pale cheeks. "Ah, my friend, such rudeness is unfortunate. But perhaps now you will answer my questions, eh?"

He hauled the *tougrak's* head up by his hair. Cracked spectacles fell and tinkled on the ground. Black George placed his dagger point against an eyeball.

"I don't have a lot of time," he hissed between clenched teeth. "So. Tell me professor, where is the Dutchman's laboratory?"

Shaking, drooling blood, the man spat teeth and tried to speak. Black George shook him violently. "What, fool?" he shouted.

"I, I do not know what floor the Dutchman works on," the man quavered. "Please, I do not know."

With a casual jab and a popping sound, the knife of Black George punctured the *tougrak's* eye and plunged into his brain. White ichor spattered the bandit and he flung the dead man's head against the wall. He stood grinning, wiping his hands on his tunic.

"We didn't see eye to eye on that one, eh Proko?"

But Black George heard a howl and turned to see Proko blundering away, chains clashing as he disappeared around the corner.

# 3
# The Enlil Effect

Kalyenka sat at the *Sarhang's* table, watching him. His eyes were open, but their glazed aspect indicated he was still operating somewhere deep in the *Mēnōg*. He blinked, shook his head, and his brown eyes focussed on Kalyenka.

"There," he said. "I have restored the lens, temporarily at least. I have also planted several false leads into the *Gēttīg*, to distract the *Ljmmûm* from our hiding place. If they evade those decoys and locate us here, we are in real trouble."

"You said they'd never find us," said Kalyenka and despite her eidolon self felt her armpits prickling.

"I was sure of it," he said. "The Skein must be further advanced than I thought. Using it the *Ljmmûm* have roughly established my geographical and epochal location. If they knew exactly where it was they would have flushed us out already. Instead they are only able to meddle with my connection to the *khutiverse*. That tells me they are operating on subjective time, which means the Skein is close enough to the Hospice to influence matters."

Kalyenka glanced uneasily at her painting. "What does that mean exactly?"

The *Sarhang* frowned. "As the Skein has no *khuti* component, it runs on subjective time. If they can use it to infiltrate the Hospice, they will obliterate the objective continuum within and in that case, for reasons too complicated to explain, they will surely find my Riemann node and force me to flee."

"What happens in that case? Are we in danger Augustine?"

Standing abruptly, the *Sarhang* approached the painting. He indicated a golden archway, beyond which could be seen a boiling turbulence.

"I will send you immediately to the Centre of the Atom, a safe refuge. I will be obliged to go deeper into the *Mēnōg*, where I will be unable to assist in the defence of the Hospice. We are in a precarious situation Kalyenka. But my tale has had the desired effect. Your painting is resonating through the Cosmos."

Kalyenka's gulped. Her last image had depicted a grey cloud obscuring the earth. "I am amazed my work has such cachet. It has never before attracted such attention."

"Nevertheless it has become of paramount importance to our investigation," said the Sarhang, returning to his seat. "With that in mind we are going to examine the continuum of Hoche, the Revolutionary French general with whom it seems you have some interconnection."

"This really is otherworldly detective work, isn't it?" said Kalyenka.

"Why yes. The lens provides the best method for unscrambling this cosmic thriller. Now Kalyenka, look."

*The lens resolves into the interior of a humble cottage. Kalyenka peers intently into that other-world, which seems more vivid than what she remembers of her own. She sees a blue-coated soldier standing by the door of a cottage opening onto a narrow village street. Through it she glimpses wounded troops slumped in the dirt, a dog begging from a weary sergeant, pipe clamped into his mouth, singed black shako leaning on his head. The stink of decaying bodies, gun smoke and faeces fills the air, somewhat leavened by the smell of coffee and fried onions from inside the cottage.*

*The Sarhang's voice intrudes. "It is May in what you know as the year 1797. We are seeing through the eyes of Lieutenant Deaglán Laghles, an aide de camp to General Hoche. His army is encamped in the Belgian village of Sayn. Look, do you see Hoche there? Not the sleeping fellow, the officer to his left."*

*General Hoche stands scowling over a map, spread on a table in a room cluttered with wooden chests, canvas bags, muskets and sabres piled against a wall. Another officer is sprawled on a chaise lounge, snoring softly.*

*Hoche's uniform is crumpled and dirty, a bandage around his left bicep. His face is prematurely aged by stress. Furrows angling down the forehead make a sharp vee around the bridge of his nose.*

"That is Hoche?" *said Kalyenka.* "I do not understand. This is not the man I loved in Cristaña. He looks nothing like Chance."

"Yes, this intrigues me also," *said the* Sarhang. "Let us keep watching to see how it resolves."

*A rap at the door is answered by the sentry, who admits an elderly man leaning on a walking stick. Though poorly dressed and frail, his bearing is proud, eyes vital and intelligent. He peers intently at Hoche as the sentry closes the door behind him.*

"Good afternoon sir. My carriage has been stopped by soldiers. I requested to speak to their commanding officer. They sent me here."

"Who are you?" *Hoche snaps, eyes straying back to his map.*

"I am Gilbert du Motier, the Marquis de Lafayette, late of Olmütz gaol."

"Lafayette? Mon Dieu, *you have aged. You are dressed like a ragamuffin. What are you doing here?" demands Hoche irritably.*

*Lafayette bows.* "Forgive me. I am enroute to Paris after release from a Prussian jail. My carriage was obliged to detour around an Austrian army."

"I defeated that army yesterday at Neuwied," *says Hoche, glowering at this nobleman whom he, like many others, suspects of being a Loyalist sympathiser. He well remembers Lafayette's speech attacking the Jacobins before the Assembly in Paris, his denunciation by Robespierre and subsequent flight from Paris.*

*"You have the advantage of me sir," says Lafayette. "I do not believe we have met. I have been a prisoner of the Austrians and the Prussians for five long years."*

*"Then meet General Lazar Hoche," that officer replies. "I have the honour to be Commander of the Army of the Rhine. I am preoccupied at this present moment, organising the pursuit of the Austrians."*

*"But have you not heard?" says Lafayette. "First Consul Buonaparte has signed an Armistice with the Austrians. The Hapsburg Emperor has capitulated."*

*"At last," says Hoche. "How come you by this intelligence?"*

*"I was told by the the odious Major Arco, commandant of the jail at Olmütz, yesterday, upon my release."*

*"You are on intimate terms with a Hapsburg officer?"*

*Lafayette shakes his cane like a sabre. "By no means. He merely informed me that his country was no longer at war with France. Nor am I obliged to stand trial by you sir. Now if you will allow me to depart, I must urgently return home."*

*Hoche bristles. "You must await my pleasure sir. You will remain in this house as my guest, until I can ascertain your credentials."*

*"Credentials? You recognised me yourself. I am a confidante of the First Consul and a staunch republican. I commanded the National Guard at Versailles and was a signatory to the Oath of the Tennis Court!"*

*Hoche folds his arms. "And there are some who say you assisted the King in his attempted flight to Varennes, that you are still close to the counter-revolutionaries."*

*"And I tell you they are liars - that I defeated these nobles on the Day of the Daggers, that I am a loyal soldier of the Revolution."*

*"Yet you will understand my caution in this matter," says Hoche archly.*

*Gilbert du Motier, Marquis de Lafayette, draws himself to his full height and raps the point of his cane upon the wooden floor. "I object most strenuously, General. You impugn the honour of a former commander of the Army of the North, a recipient of the medals of the Avenger of Liberty and the United States Society of the Cincinnati. I tell you that my wife and daughters await me in yonder carriage and demand you let us leave for Paris at once."*

*"Nonetheless you will humour me," says Hoche, unsmiling. He gestures impatiently toward the host of the chimera lens, who stands by the parlour door, sipping a mug of bitter coffee.*

*"Meet my aide de camp, Lieutenant Deaglán Laghles of the Irish Revolutionary Army," says the general. "He will remain with you in this cottage, awaiting my return."*

*Lieutenant Laghles, host of the chimera lens bows, showing long legs and cavalry boots. The Marquis de Lafayette leans on his cane with a furious glint in his eyes. "You have discomfited me Hoche, and I shall not forget it, when I speak to the First Consul."*

*"Be that as it may. You shall await my return." Hoche has one hand on the cottage door when it opens suddenly.*

*Hoche steps back as three women enter the cottage, followed by a pale young man. The Marquis takes the oldest woman by the hand. "My wife, Madame Lafayette, my daughters Anastasie and Virginia. My secretary, Felix Pontonnier."*

*Hoche has been scowling with annoyance, but catching sight of Anastasie he stands straighter, a crooked smile spasming across his face. He bows.*

*The women regard him dispassionately. "What is the manner of this imposition?" demands Madame Lafayette.*

*Her husband taps her forearm. "Patience my love," he says and turns to Hoche. "Sir, you behold a family so loyal to France that they chose years of misery over abandoning the pole of their liberty. There are none more devoted to the cause of the Revolution."*

*"You are testing my patience, Marquis Lafayette," scowls Hoche, but his eyes stray to tawny-haired Anastasie at least once too often.*

*The Marquis stamps. "We both fight the same war sir! When a man who is deeply impressed with a sense of the gratitude he owes General Buonaparte, and who is too ardent a lover of glory to be wholly indifferent to him, connects his suffrage with conditional restrictions, those restrictions not only secure him from suspicion, but prove amply that no one will more gladly than himself behold in Buonaparte the chief magistrate for life, of a free and independent republic!"*

*"Fine words indeed sir, but I must let my own judgements sway me," Hoche retorts. "You arrive in the aftermath of battle and tell me in the same breath that peace has been signed. And you have it from your jailer sir! Forgive me if your tale sparks my incredulity. No sir, you shall wait till I corroborate this fantastic story. Sit and be patient."*

*With that Hoche is gone out the door. The soldier places himself before it, musket held at rest. Lieutenant Laghles indicates the chaise lounge, vacated by the officer who has hurried off after his general.*

*"Please Marquis," Laghles says. "Rest. Our general has not slept and is a little irritable. Once he has satisfied himself we are not to be surprised by an Austrian counter-attack, I'm certain he will hear you out."*

*"Merci, Lieutenant," says the Marquis haughtily and composes himself upon the lounge. Anastasie and Virginia retire into the adjacent parlour and resume an apparently interminable card game, laughingly imploring the sentry to take a hand. From the viewpoint of the lens it seems that Laghles too is quite taken with the man's daughters.*

Kalyenka blinked out of the chimera lens and stared at the *Sarhang*.

"This is all very well, but how does Hoche come to be Chance?" she demanded. "And how can I possibly have been intimate with the man? I would have to be, what, ninety eight now?"

"I confess I have no answer to that, Kalyenka," the *Sarhang* said. "It cannot have escaped your notice that you are exceptionally well preserved. I believe that is a side effect of having come into contact with the idol of Enlil. Your *apeira* is affected retrospectively. That is to say, your *khuti* is enhanced by the circumstance to the point where you will always be perceived as young for your age, right up to the point where you expire, as your mortal frame runs out of juice."

Kalyenka scowled in exasperation. "But if I am to make love to Chance and he is to become his own father or great grandfather or something, then I am what, his great grandmother?"

"No, no, the Enlil Effect cannot achieve that kind of mischief, I am certain. It is a confusing intersection we are faced with, but it will be resolved. We must follow this *apeira*, to see what transpires."

*In the chimera lens Lieutenant Laghles observes Madame Lafayette retire outside to the cottage privy. It is a sordid affair, but as she loudly remarks upon her return, no worse than the sewer at the jail. Her robe is grimy and the panniers dangle absurdly, but the Marquess carries herself with enormous dignity. The Marquis joins her on a chair by the fire. "At least we are freed of that Prussian hellion, Major Arco," he observes.*

*"Must have been a hellish time," remarks the Irish Lieutenant.*

*"Indeed," says Lafayette. "Worse for the womenfolk than for me of course. Poor Felix had it badly too, did you not my lad?"*

*The pale young man is sitting on a camp chair by the fireplace, huddled in a greatcoat several sizes too large. He smiles, but his greasy hair and sickly complexion give the lie to it.*

*"He is ill, poor man," says Lafayette. "All the more reason we must be allowed to return to France, that Felix may find proper medical attention."*

*"I will fetch him some brandy," says Laghles.*

*A dirty mirror occupies one wall of the parlour where Lafayette's daughters sit playing cards. As Lieutenant Laghles passes it his eyes meet his own reflection. Kalyenka gasps.*

*"It is he!" she exclaims, for the man exactly resembles Chance.*

*"Ah," says the* Sarhang. *"The connection is made plain."*

*Kalyenka stares at this man called Laghles. Though he wears a French uniform, he is exactly the man she knows as her darling Chance, down to his bearing and the way he smiles. She feels that it is just as the Sarhang said, that his tale is alive. As if it were a theatrical play that has somehow strayed into her life and is resolving in front of her.*

*"Except for the small matter of his name," says Kalyenka sharply. "Why do I know this man as Hoche?"*

*At that moment the door onto the street opens and Hoche himself appears, red in the face. He strides into the cottage, accompanied by another man in drab breeches and tailcoat. Outside a squadron of horse artillery are streaming by. The rumble of wooden wheels and clatter of hooves fills the room. Hoche hurls the door shut. "Laghles!" he shouts.*

*"Yes General," says the Irishman, hurrying back into the map room. Hoche pours himself a cup of wine and nods at Lafayette.*

*"You sir, are free to go. You will be given safe passage to Paris."*

*Lafayette stands slowly, leaning on his cane. His daughters abandon their card game and rush to his side.*

*"I apologise to you sir, and hope you will forgive my inclemency," says Hoche. He gestures at the civilian, whose eyes coldly assess the Marquis.*

*"This is Monsieur d'Herbois," says Hoche. "An envoy from the First Consul. He will accompany you to Paris with an escort of hussars. Despite the Treaty the First Consul has signed, you are still in a region of hostilities. There are marauding deserters who would not hesitate to apprehend a carriage full of beautiful women."*

*The younger ladies blush, but Madame Lafayette stares severely. "Enough talk young man. Anastasie, Virginia, put away those damned cards and gather your things. En avant!"*

*Lafayette bows stiffly. Taking his wife's arm he limps to the door, followed by his daughters. As Anastasie passes, Hoche steps forward and addresses her quietly. "I beg of you mademoiselle, one moment? I know we have not been introduced but I, I have seen you from afar, once,* in Paris two years ago. Because of the emotion that I felt then, I feel compelled to ask. Will you allow me to call on you in Paris when I return?"

Face colouring, Anastasie glances in confusion at her parents. Madame Lafayette passes her eyes over Hoche as though he were a cossack. The Marquis stares briefly before he gives a slight nod and continues on his way.

When they are gone Hoche takes Laghles aside. "Mon Dieu, what a marvel. I saw that woman once and my world was stolen from me. She is the air of my life. I tried to ask her to dance, but I was interrupted by a damn Prince, the cousin of Talleyrand. And now she appears here, in the midst of war. It is truly singular."

Hoche shakes his head, but his stress lines seem less prominent and his eyes are alight. "So, my Irish friend. The First Consul's envoy, that cold-eyed bastard Monsieur d'Herbois, has orders for me, as well as Marquis Lafayette. I am to lead an invasion force to dispel the British from your homeland."

"Congratulations," Laghles says flatly.

Kalyenka wishes she could see the expression on Laghle's face. Hoche put a hand on his shoulder.

"Do not be downcast my friend," he says. "You have an entirely different task. You are to travel east to the principality of Cristaña, wherever that may be. I am told that its people are on the brink of revolution. You are to do what you can to foment it. You are to wear my uniform, posing as me. It is the ideal subterfuge. British spies will never suspect that the real Hoche is leading an invasion of Ireland."

"Sláinte," says Laghles bitterly. His hands occupy centre focus of the lens as they tip a prodigious serving of brandy into an earthenware mug and apply it to his mouth. Kalyenka revels in the taste.

"Of course," said the *Sarhang* as the chimera lens vanishes. "I have just now followed Laghles' *apeira*, at a speed you could not endure. The officer you meet at the ball in Cristaña is indeed

Lieutenant Laghles, posing as Hoche. You have quite an energetic liaison with him. But some unearthly interference interrupts your lovemaking. Afterwards Laghles is captured and tortured by British secret police, but escapes and reappears in Paris some time later."

"Dear god," Kalyenka whispered. "Is this really happening?"

"Of course it is my dear," murmured the *Sarhang*. "Pay attention, please. Before he sails for Ireland, General Hoche calls on Anastasie de Lafayette. She agrees to see him upon his return, but it is Laghles who visits, after his escape from British spies. He informs Anastasie that Hoche has died of consumption.

"A romantic attachment grows between Laghles and Anastasie. They have an intense affair before Laghles joins Buonaparte's invasion of Egypt and is killed at the Battle of the Pyramids. Anastasie bears a son in secret and sends the child to the Foundling Hospital in Dublin.

"The boy suffers horrific abuse at the hands of nuns and priests. One night at the age of nine he escapes from his dormitory, breaks into the office and discovers a letter from his mother. She has entrusted a large sum of money and a brief history of the boy's antecedents to the orphanage, asking that he receive it at twelve years. The money is all gone of course, but he keeps the letter. So the boy knows his identity. He escapes, flees to Cork and becomes a cooper's apprentice. That is Finnian Chance, your sometime lover's father."

"You are telling me that Laghles, whom I knew as Hoche, later became the grandfather of Chance?" said Kalyenka.

"That is correct."

"How is that possible?"

"A lapse in the integrity of Laghles' continuum perhaps?" The *Sarhang* put a hand to his forehead. "Somehow they share the same *apeira*, though they are discrete individuals, born of different eras.

Again I suspect the Enlil Effect. Or possibly the infection of the Skein."

"How do you mean?"

The *Sarhang* clasped hands behind his back and strode to the brink of the Riemann node, staring out into the jungle. "As I have explained, there are two profound disruptions contending in the *khutiverse*. First is the Enlil Effect. Second is the Skein simulacrum, which is replicating exponentially in the manner of a virus. Both are significantly disturbing the cosmic *khuti* flow."

"Is that disastrous?" said Kalyenka. "How concerned should I be?"

"Well," said the *Sarhang*. "Since the universe functions on applied chaos it is kind of normal, as far as strangeness goes."

"What on earth does that mean, Augustine?"

He turned to regard her gravely. "The *khutiverse*, to human thinking, is strange beyond measure. Any knowledge one may hold about it is constantly confounded, because it changes so fast you have to constantly re-appraise your understanding. In that way it is a macrocosm of the *Gёttīg*. One cannot pretend to completely assay the shape of any phenomenon on your earth, as the first principle of *khuti* dynamics means it is subject to constant evolution.

"Complete awareness is the key, openness to change. The Buddhists got it right. You have to be empty, let knowledge flow through you like water. The Hermetic tradition admonishes us to remain constantly aware because reality is ruthless, unequivocal. Those prepared for violent change may ride it out. The inflexible will be destroyed, as monarchists discovered when they ignored the revolutionary movements of Europe."

The *Sarhang* returned to his seat at the table.

"But I digress. Adopted by a kindly family of Irish Republicans, Finnian Chance grows up under English repression. He becomes an ardent revolutionary, joining the Society of United Irishmen. He

fights with Buonaparte's Irish Legion in Spain, where he is captured
by Spanish partisans and suffers horrific torture. When he returns
home he is imprisoned by British police and tortured further.

"Upon release Finnian marries Chance's mother, the daughter
of an English Protestant couple in Dublin. Incarcerated again for
his role in a bombing, Finnian dies shortly after his son, Sebastian
Lafayette is born. The boy grows up plagued by intergenerational
gene traumas, which he is bound to relive."

"Wait," said Kalyenka. "You're saying that Finnian's traumas were
transmitted into Sebastian Chance's genes, carried intact from father
to son?"

"Yes of course. This is a form of neuro-determinism which can
be measured scientifically. It is visible under a microscope, quantified
by methylation marks in the chemical cell reception. They tell the
story of successive traumas playing out in the behavioural traits of
generationally related individuals."

Kalyenka was silent a moment, absorbing this information.
Then; "Is *khuti* subject to such intergenerational distribution?"

"An excellent question. And yes, there is an element of genetic
inheritance in *khuti* proliferation. Now, Chance's English
grandparents send him to an English boarding school, thence to a
military academy. He serves in India in defence of the British East
India Company. A highly talented soldier, he is later recruited into
their secret service."

"And becomes a callous killer," said Kalyenka. "Yes, I saw this
in the theta experience. He was gravely wounded, captured and
tortured, like his father and grandfather. The poor darling."

"But he escapes and resumes his deadly work," said the *Sarhang*.

*Kalyenka gazes upon a younger Chance in the chimera lens,
gunning down rebellious sepoys in Cawnpore.*

"Subject to fits of murderous rage, young Chance self-medicates
with a regime of drug use. That continues until he has a visionary

experience on psilocybin mushrooms. Disaffected by his experiences in the Raj, raddled by drugs and psychological torture, he retires from the Army and goes into private practise as a mercenary.

"Following a psychotic breakdown in Cairo he returns to England, determined to redeem himself for his foul deeds in the name of the Crown. After two years feeding the poor in Dublin's slums he is recruited by the Pale Conduit and begins working for us in a variety of roles across the planet. Ending up in Cristaña, where he meets you, thus closing the circuit."

# 4

# Tangerine Believers

Bo-Bar and Jae-Won emerged from a polaroid joy booth clutching selfies animated with glittering memes and gifs. They made for Cafe Droptop where their headsets bought crab chips, custard cakes and caffeinated yoghurt sodas before they sat in a booth made of recycled bamboo.

"You did a great job helping our friend Choi," said Jae-Won. "Roxoq's apology in *Kraze* magazine has exonerated her in the eyes of the public."

"I'd hope my friends would do the same for me," said Bo-Bae.

Jae-Won slurped on her banana soda. "You know I would. Now we have a much bigger problem. Have you seen this?"

She blinked twice, her lens sharing a link with Bo-Bae, whose eye-feed filled with the website of the Tangerine Believers, famous for their fanatical support of the assassinated American ex-President whose skin colour inspired the name.

"These morons believe he didn't die but is in hiding, waiting to reappear and take his rightful place as King of America."

Jae-Won slid up closer in the booth. Bo-Bae glanced enviously at her friend's snake print hemp shirt, wishing she was as effortlessly stylish. Jae-Won disdained web brands, buying her clothes at pop-up recycling boutiques. Some Cinnamon Girls gossiped that she was already too old to marry, but that didn't seem to bother Jae-Won. In fact she once told Bo-Bae marriage was an archaic concept which consumed excessive resources.

"The Tangerine Believers are only the blood in the bird's feet," Jae-Won said. "They're backed by mega-rich evangelists; fanatical Christians who've monopolised the US internet under the OMNI brand. They've declared all artistic expression Satanic, except for their squeaky-clean state-sanctioned films and art. They also annexed all the digital bandwidth in America and eradicated other platforms. Now they're trying to buy out our Korean platform, Eodiena. They want a global monopoly on information. But that's not the worst of it. If they take over our internet they will put an end to K-Pop. Their vapid Christian rock will be the only legal entertainment."

Bo-Bae was nearly crying. "This can't be real. Isn't it just disinformation?"

"It's real," said Jae-Won, crunching on a crab chip. "Hard to tell in this hall of mirrors, but I've had it confirmed by a contact in my company, Jeobchog."

Bo-Bae put a hand over her mouth. "There must be laws to stop Korean platforms being eaten up by Americans?"

"There are no rules to capitalism," said Jae-Won. "Except eat or be eaten."

"But we have the world's best internet service. They have the worst. Why would we let them take over?"

"Someone will make a lot of money out of it," said Jae Won. "These people are deranged, but they're very powerful. Their peak corporations have gobbled up Korean brands, making our economy subject to the American market. They've publicly stated that our alliance depends on making OMNI our only internet platform. Since the Chinese annexed Taiwan and North Korea our government is desperate for allies."

Bo-Bae wiped her nose with a pink hankie and sniffed. "Then we have to hack their web, rally the Stans, flood the internet with hashtags and fan-cams, as you did when the Texan police tried to smash the Black Lives Matter movement."

"Yes I was sixteen then." Jae Won smiled at the memory. "We still had smartphones. The Texan police were asking rednecks to download videos of what they called illegal protest activity. Black people were still being shot and killed in American streets by police and vigilantes. We could see the #whitelivesmatter was trending so we buried their racist messaging, flooding their feeds with fan-cams. I was in 127 Squad then, though most of us were banned from Twitter. I sent twenty fan-cams pulling *shimmy shimmy* moves. The Americans have made that a difficult strategy to repeat, but there must be a way to break their algorithms."

"Hash tags and fan-cams won't be enough," Bo-Bae said. "If the Tangerine Believers suck Eodiena into their web, we won't be able to rally Cinnamon Girls."

"What about your brother the gamer?" said Jae-Won. "You said he's a psychopath, but a talented one."

"Yes, he just got out of Internet Dream Village. They're still treating his gaming addiction and anti-social behaviour. He's a black metal fanatic - a long-hair who makes fun of K-Pop, calls it K-Rot."

"Hmmm," said Jae Won. "If he has anti-social attitudes he's probably suited for this job. A normal Korean would be terrified of taking on the system."

"OK. I'll try to enlist Bitgaram," said Bo-Bae. "But he won't like it. He's a nihilist. I may have to pay him."

"You're authorised to take money from the Cinnamon Girls account. This is a very special mission. There is more at stake than even K-Pop."

Bo-Bae's straw made circles in her banana soda. "This is making me very anxious. I have my final exams this week."

"I know and it's awful for you, but timing is crucial." Jae-Won stroked hair from Bo-Bae's face and looked her in the eye. "I'm taking my vacation early to volunteer for the elections. Our Democratic Party is in serious trouble. The People Power Party are playing on people's fear of China and Koreans are voting conservative. They're scared of America withdrawing from the alliance. "

Jae-Won looked deadly serious. "If the Americans impose their internet on Korea the PPP will stay in power. They want to reassert traditional values, which means women can't work. We're supposed to stay at home and be dutiful housewives. You can forget a career like I have."

"Yuck," said Bo-Bae. "Ok, *unni,* I'll try convince Bitgaram to join us. I have to go home to study now. I'll talk to him tonight."

Jae-Won smiled. "Say hello to Bitgaram. I haven't seen him since he was a pimply teenage boy."

When Bo-Bae got home, Bitgaram was in the cramped living room of the family apartment, hunched over the table. He ignored Bo-Bae but she could see he was building something. Looking closer, she recognised a plastic diorama of a *hanok,* a traditional Korean wooden house in a rural mountain setting.

Bo-Bae stared in disbelief. She had never seen Bitgaram use his hands to do anything useful, let alone something as intricate as this. Bitgaram making a *hanok* seemed weirder than the holos he made for gaming hacks. But it was, oddly enough, consistent with his archaic image.

Bitgaram's long black hair was as usual, chronically unwashed. Bo-Bae was always hassling him to part it, but he insisted a Black Metal hairstyle was important to his image. Same as the stud in his right brow and his faded black t-shirt, depicting a group of long-maned musicians in spiky armour, holding guitars like spears; above them the legend *Dark Mirror Ov Tragedy.*

"Why are you making that diorama?" asked Bo-Bae.

Bitgaram did not look up. "It's therapy, prescribed for my hyper-personal disorders by the psyche at Internet Dream Village. A *hanok* with miniature *ondol* heated rock system and *giwa* tiled roof."

"I can see what it is, weirdo, but you've never even changed a tyre on a bicycle. Why are you making such things now?"

Bitgaram gave her a fierce look. "I can't go back to Internet Dream Village. It was horrible. This therapy soothes my addictive impulses, so I can concentrate on my failings and eventually be rehabilitated into the community. This is classic *Baesaminsu*, with a mountain in back and the river at front. I am continuing in the tradition of The First Host, Yun Jeong." He bowed, clasping his hands together.

Bo-Bae suppressed the urge to make fun of her brother. "That's adorable Bitgaram. But I have a far more important job for you. A real-world mission that would be of benefit to the community and to yourself."

Bitgaram looked suspicious. "What are you talking about?"

"I want you to use your skills to help Cinnamon Girls resist American hegemony of the internet."

"No way," he said. "I just spent three months weaning myself off computers. My treatment is organic, internet-based cognitive behavioural therapy. If I compromise it I will fail again and disappoint our parents. Not to mention being arrested."

"Seriously Bitgaram. The only organic things on you are the lice in your hair. You already owe me for the money you stole. This job would be internet-based therapy, defending Korean values against the cartoon ethics of America. I'll even pay you."

"Korean values? *Gaesori!*" he said. "Pay me for what?"

"The American OMNI want to take over Korean internet and wipe out our culture," said Bo-Bae. "You've got to help stop them."

"No way sister. Internet Dream Village cured me of internet addiction disorder and transient dysphoric moods. If I transgress again I'm facing jail time. Don't get me involved in your stupid K-Pop business. That commercial rubbish is destroying real music. Also, Sad Legend are playing in Seoul next week. No way am I going to miss that concert."

"This is bigger than your stupid black metal," said Bo-Bae. "Bigger even than K-Pop. It's about Korean culture and the survival of the world. The Americans are threatening war with China and pretending the thermohaline current is a myth. They're more concerned with crowning an Elvis impersonator their King. They've already banned black metal in America. Here will be next."

Bitgaram stared at her in disbelief. "Banned black metal? They can't do that."

"Really? Have you seen the news lately? They believe they're the reincarnation of some Old Testament kingdom and that anyone who deviates from Christian law is possessed by demons and must be executed. They hung a black metal fan in Alabama three months ago."

"I don't believe it."

"Bitgaram, I've read your diagnosis, seen your rating on the Launay-Slade Hallucinations Scale. It says you were convinced the Overwatch game was real. That was enough to nearly get you committed. But the Tangerine Believers' hallucinations are even crazier than those old Q-Anons. They believe in lizard people, that the reincarnation of George Washington is coming to save them. If they get control here Internet Dream Village will seem as quaint as that *hanok*. It will be jail and execution for people like you."

Bitgaram stared in horror. "Ok, I'll help you. For a million *Won*."

"Whatever it takes, Bitgaram. If we don't stop them it's all over. You can use my account to log in and Jae-Won will give you access to the Jeobchog server."

"What? How?"

"She works for them."

"Where are you getting the money to pay me?"

"The Cinnamon Girls have a group bank account. Jae-Won has approved this transaction."

"Cool. Do you think Jae-Won would go on a date with me?"

"Don't be gross Bitgaram. Be realistic and try and see this as your patriotic duty."

"Ok, I'll try, for a million *Won*. So what do we do?"

"We use their own platform to defeat them," said Bo-Bae. "Create algorithms that supersede OMNI's, so we can get the message out to all the Stans. There are millions of K-Pop fans across the world. We'll use the power of our numbers to inundate the web with hashtags, boycott the PPP platforms and counter-programme our own content."

Bitgaram's eyes gleamed. "You mean I construct it like a game from the bottom up?"

"Yes. We game the algorithm so these white supremacist Christian *jjikki* can't broadcast their *eongteli* on our feeds."

"Ok. I'm in."

Bo-Bae handed Bitgaram her laptop, already logged in to Jeobchog's system. His fingers moved with alarming rapidity over the keys as screen after screen relinquished its data. He looked up. "This is a complex system, but their security is laughable. I've already installed an exit with a back-up to cover my tracks."

He watched the screen carefully and tapped a series of commands. "There, I'm in the Tangerine Believers' site," he said.

"Already?"

"I told you I'm the best hacker in Korea."

"Move over," said Bo-Bae, reading the screen. "Oh, that orangutang king of theirs was truly delusional. He openly claimed to be a Christian messiah."

"Yes," said Bitgaram. "But it seems to be the way these Americans operate. Their PSYRATS are off the charts."

"What are PSYRATS?"

"Psychotic symptom rating scales," said Bitgaram. "It's how they evaluate your psychosis in Internet Dream Village. As you said, my rating was high. But these people believe stuff crazier than any video game. How do they fall for it? Their government is taking over the internet but they blame China and their people believe them? How stupid are they?"

"Very."

Shaking his head, Bitgaram peered intently into the screen. He typed a series of codes. "Ok, I think I see how to tackle this," he chuckled. "It may not even be illegal."

"Are you sure it'll work?" asked Bo-Bae, hating the tone of her voice.

"Oh yeah. If the American's network is already connected to ours, it'll work."

# 5

# My Mother's Second Cousin

Bejikereene paused for breath at the top of a moving staircase. The moment she stepped upon it the assembly had started climbing around a spiral tower, while she clung grimly to the railing. Reaching a level where the tower joined another, it stopped and Bejikereene staggered onto solid ground. Glancing down the giddy drop she moaned, "What have you got us into Olaf, you idiot?"

She could hear distant explosions and occasionally the yelling of unseen people. A family of rabbits scurried past. Bejikereene followed until she came to a juncture where four hallways met.

"Where are you Olaf?" she cried and felt movement in the pouch strapped to her side. Suddenly she had a clear premonition which direction she should take. It was as if a voice had spoken and she had a pretty good idea where that voice was coming from.

"As Tištrya bound the Pairikā Dužyāiryā with a great number of bindings, I bind thee," Bejikereene reminded the thing in the pouch, giving it a slap for good measure. She proceeded along the hallway it had chosen, noting that the profusion of flowers and vines on the walls smelled sweetly, despite alarming wisps of smoke in the air. She heard the distant braying of a klaxon and an amplified voice, metallic and distant.

"Evacuate wings two hundred through two hundred and fifty six," it said. "This Hospice is under attack. All operatives report to rallying points and adopt defensive protocols."

Bejikereene looked around in consternation. Hospice? It looked more like the palace of a mad gardener. She darted through a courtyard open to the elements. Above her loomed the icy veins of neighbouring mountains. Ahead was a doorway that led into another hall. She saw three people run into that entrance, then an explosion destroyed the wall around it. She saw soldiers at the other end of the courtyard, shouting. A rifle fired and a bullet ricocheted from the statue of a naked woman, an arms-length from Bejikereene.

She looked around in near panic. Where to now? The idol throbbed on her thigh and she spotted a doorway set into the wall, surrounded by rubble. It opened onto another moving walkway, in a passage headed downward.

"I oughta be climbing," she wailed. "This is getting me no closer to my Olaf." But a high-powered weapon roared, followed by another explosion. Bejikereene jumped onto the escalator and was whisked away down the tunnel. Lights came on overhead, extinguishing as she passed them.

Adding to her anxiety was a sound which she grudgingly accepted as actual music, echoing through the hall. She looked around in consternation but could see no musicians. At least the explosions had faded behind her. Bejikereene relaxed a little and the walkway accelerated till she was fairly flying.

Gradually it slowed down and stopped, so she was able to step more or less gracefully onto the tiles of an antechamber full of strange devices. They had wheels, or things like wheels, so she reasoned they must be vehicles of some sort. But they were all damaged, either burnt or with large chunks of them shot away. Edging around them suspiciously, she proceeded onto a ruined gateway, which looked to have been blown open.

Bejikereene heard voices ahead, speaking in an unfamiliar language. She hitched up her skirts. Cradling her blunderbuss, she sidled around a corner. In the distance she saw a figure move. A man, who looked oddly familiar.

"You!" she shouted. It was the tall bald man, who sometimes came to the inn and never spoke a word, but looked as sour as the pickled eggs he preferred. He was in the company of a short brute in uniform and a tall, googly-eyed buffoon who looked like he ought to be in a palace somewhere, reviewing soldiers. Sure enough, three soldiers clustered nearby, looking nervous. Looming behind them was something big, something that resembled a man but had wings. It looked scarily familiar, but Bejikereene could not imagine having ever seen something like that before.

The bald man turned scowling, but the short soldier unhesitatingly raised and fired a gun. Plaster exploded by Bejikereene's ear. She swung up the blunderbuss and pulled the trigger like she was gutting a rabbit. An ear-shattering roar, a thump like a mule had kicked her in the shoulder and the men vanished in a pall of black smoke.

Bejikereene ran the other way, her shoulder throbbing. She spotted a doorway and headed for it, scurrying fast as she could down a flight of stairs which mercifully remained still, like stairs should. Then it was along another corridor full of strange objects. Short of breath, sweating under her heavy clothes, she glanced back but saw no pursuit.

Turning right she was confronted by a young man in a black surcoat, pointing some kind of fancy weapon at her. She stopped dead. The fellow gazed at her open-mouthed. After a moment he said; "*Ki a fene vagy te?*"

Bejikereene had learned some Rumanian from the occasional wayfarers who stopped at the Eagle's Head, enough to know she was being disrespected.

"Don't talk to me like that young lad," she said sternly. "I'd box your ears for less. Put down that gun."

"You speak my language," said the young man, but his gun did not lower. "I apologise *bună*, but what are you doing here? This is a high security installation." He looked hopefully at her neck. "Do you have a pass?"

"A pass? Don't speak nonsense boy. I am Bejikereene Beruvoskii of the Eagle's Nest and I have had enough of strange men pointing guns at me. I am looking for my husband. Have you seen him?"

The man stared in disbelief. "But that is impossible. Madame Beruvoskii. I know you. That is, I recognise you. Forgive me, you are the last person I expected to see here. I am Boris, Luca Dascalu's son. You are my mother's second cousin by marriage. You used to dandle me on your knee at the stockyards, when my parents came to town to sell their goats."

Bejikereene could have wept. "Put down that weapon, quick smart my lad. What are you doing working for these *tougrak*? A good honest boy like you." She smiled. "Now, tell me, what is going on?"

Boris lowered his weapon and grinned, though his eyes were ringed with dirt and tears. "Yes I do work for the D'Angels, and you mustn't believe the stories about them. They are good people. But they, we, are under attack. The traitor Vehemple has led Prussian soldiers into the Hospice. They are exploding everything and have killed so many people." He wiped his eyes. "They killed my friend Mihai."

Bejikereene lowered her blunderbuss to the ground, stepped forward and patted Boris on the cheek. "Don't fret my boy. I'm sure Mihai did his best. When this is all over we will honour his grave. Now, are you speaking of that bald man? The one who shows up at our inn from time to time, never speaks a word, has a face on him that would curdle vinegar?"

"That's him. The bastard. Sorry for the language, Madame Beruvoskii."

"Never mind that Boris. I just now saw that bald bastard backaways. With some soldier who shot at me."

"Jesus, Missus, where? Never mind. Will you please wait here while I make sure this section is secure? Oh and whatever you do, don't touch that button." He pointed at a red button on the wall, surrounded by signs in five different languages. Beside it on the wall was a rack in which sat twelve sleek modern weapons of the sort Boris was carrying.

Bejikereene smiled amiably. "Never you mind my dear, and be careful with those foreigners." As soon as he was gone she took one of the weapons from the rack, replacing it with the old blunderbuss, which she did not know how to reload. "Fair trade," she sniffed, and went out the opposite way, down the tunnel.

She came to an immense space where all kinds of wheeled machinery lay idle. It looked like a place that should be filled with industry and movement, but there were no people. Her footsteps echoed ominously from the high ceiling, with its complicated system of pulleys and god knows what.

Above the far wall was a screen lit from within, displaying words and symbols moving sidelong like ants. Bejikereene eyed it warily as she crept beneath it. Beyond it she came into a long chamber with tunnels at either end, disappearing into blackness. Between them were laid iron rails, crosshatched with wooden sleepers. Bejikereene had been to Cristaña city once and seen the tracks they'd laid, for what people were calling the 'iron horse'. This looked like that, only far more modern.

As she puzzled over them an alarm howled and she heard a rattling sound, unlike explosions or weapons fire. Rather it was a continuous staccato that was becoming louder. Lights showed in one tunnel and after a spell a long carriage popped out. It was linked to another, then another and another. As the train slowed down she saw carriages full of soldiers.

"That can't be good," she muttered. Hitching up her skirts she scurried back through the entrance and under the illuminated screen as fast as her tired old legs could carry her. "You'll be making me breakfast for a month Olaf," she promised.

Wheezing, she limped the last few yards into Boris' office, hearing behind her whistles and the harsh sound of men shouting orders. Taking a deep breath, she stood on tip toes and pressed the red knob. There was a whirring noise, a klaxon sounded, then a series of cavernous noises from above. She stepped into the corridor in time to see an enormous steel door crash to the ground, sealing off the train yard entirely.

Just to be certain, she went back into the office. She raised her borrowed weapon and squinted at the mechanism. It had something like a trigger, nestled by the stock. Tilting her head back, she pointed it at the red button and pulled. The weapon barely kicked in her hand, but the noise that came out of it was impressive and the button exploded in a welter of sparks and smoke.

Satisfied, Bejikereene lowered the weapon. Spotting a silver flask on a shelf she picked it up, sat on a comfortable chair, unscrewed the lid and sniffed. "*Rakia?*" She took a sip. "Ah, *rakia*. I'll just rest me weary bones a minute."

Boris reappeared in the doorway, his face ashen. "Missus Beruvoskii," he gasped. "Excuse me, but you, you closed the gate?"

"Would you have preferred I let all those soldiers in?" she barked.

"Soldiers?" said Boris. "Where?"

"In them carriages, as came in through the tunnel."

"You went down there?"

"Of course I did."

"How many soldiers?"

"Hundreds."

"Gods above." Boris seized the communications device and pressed several buttons. He held the piece to his ear and spoke into it. "This is Boris at Station One. Can anybody hear me?" There was no response. He shook the device. "Hullo? Station Two? Cengruta?" After a moment he looked up, despairing.

"There is nobody answering. I heard explosions up ahead. What do I do?"

"Do your job boy."

Boris looked at Bejikereene. "Of course. Thank you Aunty." He went over to the switchboard and flicked two switches. "There, I've turned off all power to the train yards. Any malefactors will be in total darkness. Besides, they will never get through that gate." He went silent, chewing his lip as he stared at Bejikereene. "But if they have arrived here in a train, then they have captured the depot at Cristaña, and that means the entire Hospice is compromised. Ayah!"

"Hush, there is someone outside," Bejikereene whispered. Boris picked up his weapon and strode out into the corridor. There was the sound of a shot and he dropped to the ground. Bejikereene stared at him, expecting any moment that he would jump up and smile at her. But the poor sweet boy did not move and his blood ebbed calmly onto the floor. There was so much blood and he lay there so still. Bejikereene tried to recollect his mother's face and said a prayer for her too. But she heard harsh voices outside and looked away from the body.

"Shut it, old woman," she told herself. "No point joining the poor lad.' She peeked outside. Striding toward her were three soldiers as well as the bald man, and beside him, sweet Ahura Mazdā, that thing she'd seen before, which her old eyes couldn't properly distinguish. Of course, it was one of the flying devils that attacked the village.

"Olaf, if ever I find thee, I will wring thy neck like a chicken," Bejikereene vowed as she levelled her weapon. The flying devil, towering over the other men, was stomping rapidly towards her on metal legs that sounded like doom.

She tightened her fingers and the weapon made that rattling noise, and the devil shuddered as pieces of metal sprayed from its carapace. Behind it the soldiers exploded, innards sprayed against the walls, bodies flung violently backward. But the metal devil kept coming.

Bejikereene felt a tight knot in her gut and an overwhelming urge to run. She stood her ground and pressed the trigger again. The devil came on, but its face was dissolving and it faltered. She ran a finger along the side of the weapon and finding a button there, pressed it. There was a whooshing sound and the devil was enveloped in flames.

Through spiralling smoke Bejikereene saw the bald man and his cronies turn and flee. The devil wheeled stiffly around and followed, while Bejikereene continued to riddle its metal hide with whatever that wonderful weapon was churning out.

# 6

# Starlit Realms

Baron Codrūt Casimir Ancoulsis looked up from his desk. The clock on the wall of his room in Watson's Hotel told him night was almost done. He chuckled mirthlessly. Time. A practical concept when it came to coordinating his sleeping hours with those of other humans. An absurd irrelevance when it came to dealing with numinous beings in an infinite plane of existence.

Hermetic studies had taught him the specific irrelevance of this notion. Things changed, certainly. The biosphere of a planet evolved, devolved. Terrain shifted, was torn apart, reformed again. Humans were born, grew and died. All this activity was modulated by relentless machinations of the ever blooming Cosmos. The trick to understanding was to see it from the other side - from the *Mēnōg*.

Denizens of the sacred realm saw a series of continuums blooming in four-dimensional space, most of whose human inhabitants, blinkered by species-survival imperatives, blocked out the inconvenient realities of the natural world.

The Ancients, steeped in occult praxis, understood it implicitly. They knew the realm beyond the Veil reflected the verities of their own, but operated on an infinitely more mysterious level. It was just that they were unable to get there.

Ancoulsis had studied the occult sciences all his days. He had mastered the Enochian and Hermetic disciplines, seeking a route into the *Mēnōg* by precise, mathematical means. These too had their limitations. Few savants managed to transcend their mortal frames and enter the *Mēnōg*. The use of entheogens was thought to be essential by some metaphysical practitioners, particularly the D'Angels. But Ancoulsis, a dedicated ascetic, had found a way around that dilemma.

He blinked at his journal and yawned. The notes on his latest expedition were elaborate - a compilation of utterly surreal events. Dozens of leather-bound journals occupied a bookshelf to his left. These documented his travels across six centuries.

But though he was close to reaching his objective, the activities of Enlil remained enigmatic. Only once the god's schemes came to fruition would the Balkan League become a reality.

Meanwhile Ancoulsis must balance Enlil's dazzling manoeuvres with the situation on the *Gēttīg*. The Prussian Chancellor Bismarck's Congress of Berlin was about to divide the Balkans still further, awarding Cypress to the perfidious English, pandering to Russia and the Hapsburgs of Austria. Romania, the Serbs, Bosnians and Herzegovinians would lose more land to the cursed Hapsburgs.

Rather than allowing a united Balkans as a bulwark against the Ottoman, Bismarck wanted the Turks to retain Constantinople and keep the Russians in check. The fraudulent notion of a Bulgarian Exarchate was a sop to the Russians. Though Pan-Slavic nationalism was on the rise, it would inevitably come under the heel of the Tsarist's Holy Alliance.

Even Macedonia was to be ceded to the Turk, who should have been kicked out of Europe forever. Nor would those dregs satisfy them. Though their Empire was in decline, they would strike again if their humiliations were sufficient to goad them into war. Already their Caliph was on the march and had been invited into the Hospice of that damnable, interfering *Sarhang*.

As usual, Bismarck was playing chess with the other nations and the Balkans were his pawn.

But all of Bismarck's conniving would be countered and the Balkan League given a powerful hand in the coming wars, if and when Vania's mission was successful. Her manuscript lay open on the desk beside Ancoulsis' own. Its emotional shadow in the *Mēnōg* would become a powerful talisman - if she survived.

Ancoulsis returned his attentions to his own journal, documenting journeys along his *apeira*. It began with the period before his awakening, when he was yet an innocent lad in the fourteenth century. He enjoyed re-reading this work, written in the style of a Homeric narrative. Revising it helped reinforce his sorcerous praxis and remind him of his patriotic duties.

Having been born into a monied family in Moldavia he, Codrût Ancoulsis had the privilege of tutors in academic disciplines, in riding and the arts of war. His father Vlad Ancoulsis was a *boyar*; a wealthy landowner and man of some influence under the reign of Dragos Vodâ, the hero who stopped the Golden Horde of the Mongols.

Young Codrût had been an adept student, speaking good Latin and Greek by his eighth year. His father made him learn Turkish as well. "You will need these skills in years to come," Vlad told the boy. Since the fall of Constantinople, fear of the Turks equalled that of the Mongols and Tartars in centuries past. Vlad Ancoulsis foresaw that his son could be a vital intermediary with invading powers, should the fates fall that way.

In the intervals between fighting Mongols, Tartars and Hungarians, the *boyar* pursued business interests across the Balkans. With the survival of his beleaguered homeland foremost in his heart, Vlad fostered military ties with the Serbian King Vukašin Mrnjavčevic.

Vlad sent Codrût to study at Rakovica Monastery in Belgrade, one of three boys to be trained as courtiers. The lad rapidly surpassed all his tutors and was obliged to study independently. Vlad engaged a sergeant from the King's *vojstatik* troops to drill his son in archery, swordplay and military tactics, alongside boys from the royal family.

After graduating, a letter from an influential uncle found Codrût a post as interpreter at the court of the *Gospodin* Vuk Branković in southwestern Serbia. Codrût excelled at his work and was twice invited to dine at the *Gospodin's* table, joining his inner circle for a riotous night of rakia and *karikás ostor,* the bloody whip game.

But the ever-present Ottoman threat was realised when the host of Sultan Murad Hüdavenigaâr defeated King Vukašin at Maritsa. Marching through the mountains, Murad confronted the Moravian Serbs on Branković's territory. As vassal to Prince Lazar Hrebeljanović, *Gospodin* Branković joined his army at the field of Kosovo, determined to stop them.

An alliance of Bosnians, Albanians, Bulgarians, Greeks, Macedonians and Hungarians were sworn to fight for Prince Lazar, known as The Tall. Codrût was thrilled. He had inherited his father's dream; a reunification of the Balkan people to match the glories of the Bulgarian Empire.

On the night before the battle, the air was filled with the smell of incense and the chanting of priests. Having no stomach for prayers, Codrût stole away to his tent, where he continued reading the *Compendium of Natural Sciences,* a cosmological treatise by an unknown author. It was a parting gift from his father, who had also passed on his obsession with astrology.

The moon was entering a rare and significant phase and a peculiar phenomenon was expected the night *after* the battle. Radiating a royal purple in its fullness, the Murex Moon was an aberration that could not be explained by accepted cosmological laws. It was associated with occultic processes footnoted in the *Compendium.*

So while knights prayed and retched in anticipation of the next day's slaughter, Codrût absorbed the lore of *anima mundi* by the light of a candle until it melted away. He rose before dawn to chart the positions of the stars.

Codrût finished taking notes as the rising sun burned away morning mists. Munching an apple, he looked out over the valley where the opposing armies took position, tens of thousands of spears, shields and helmets glinting in the sun. As a valued aide to Branković, Codrût was not allowed to fight. He watched from behind the right flank, where the *Gospodin's* forces were arrayed.

Trumpets blared and heralds galloped back and forth between Prince Lazar and the *Gospodin*. Branković's mounted *gusars* formed up and charged the Turks with great vigour, forcing the left wing back upon their camp. But while Turkish archers and Prince Lazar's knights duelled in the centre, Branković inexplicably wheeled his men around and fled the field.

Without Branković, the Turks enveloped and destroyed Lazar the Tall's army, though a desperate charge by twelve Serbian knights burst through the janissaries and killed the Sultan himself.

As evening fell and the slaughter of the Serbs continued, Codrût rode southwest with Branković into Macedonia, but at dusk slipped away and headed north on his own. Intent on reaching Belgrade, he worked from the saddle all night with notebook, astrolabe and quadrant, documenting the eerie intensity of the Murex Moon. Under his scrutiny the Moon seemed to elongate, its purple colouration seething with celestial tides. Codrût shivered. It seemed to him that this cosmological oddity, occurring on the eve of an epochal defeat, presaged an ominous future for Serbia.

Indeed, Prince Lazar the Tall perished even as the Turk annihilated a significant proportion of young Balkan males. The new Sultan Bayezid, known as The Thunderbolt, had access to countless reinforcements and Codrût understood implicitly that this defeat would impose centuries of subjugation upon the proud Serbs.

Codrût made it to Belgrade, where he joined the court of Lazar the Tall's son Stefan Lazarević, who swore fealty to Sultan Bayezid. Codrût was part of a delegation arranging the terms of Stefan's vassalage and the marriage of his sister, Princess Olivera Despina to the Thunderbolt.

As an interpreter he had access to Prince Stefan's library, a rare treasure indeed. In this refuge Codrût spent entire nights poring over reproductions of the Byzantine Emperor Justinian's *Corpus Jurus Civilus*, as amended by King Dušan's *Code*. It clearly laid out a template for the integration of ethnic groups on the Balkan Peninsula. Codrût also mastered Constantine VII's *De Administrando Imperio* and even found a copy of Albertus Magnus' condemned opus, the *Speculum Astronomiae*.

Though he despised the Turk with all his being, Codrût steeled himself against the impulse to petty revenge, determining instead to ingratiate himself with the hated oppressor. Under cover of that fealty he would implant in shattered Balkan populations a dream of unification that would ultimately defeat the Turk from within.

In the Sultan's court at Novo Brdo, Codrût distinguished himself with a nuanced understanding of Turkish etiquette and law. He was paid a high compliment by the Sultan's *khoja* after successfully negotiating Prince Lazarević's tribute of ten thousand gold ducats. Codrût became an indispensable member of Stefan Lazarević's entourage and eventually favoured by the Sultan himself.

A year later he was named as *Dragoman*, Serbian ambassador to the court in Constantinople. With his fluency in Greek, Turkish, French, Italian and German, Codrût enjoyed a meteoric career, becoming a key negotiator with the satellite nations now known collectively as Rumelia. He travelled to Rome, Venice, Vienna and Paris to treat with feudal lords, Popes and Emperors. Married four times, he held the titles of Grand *Spătar*, *Grand Vizier* and member of the Princely Council.

But Codrût never forgot his rebellious father, who was boiled in oil when the Turks invaded Moldavia. He never forgot Vlad's dream of a united Balkans, and he cherished the debt owed by the Ottoman Turk. And all the while, bowing and scraping to Pasha and Emir alike, Codrût was watching and remembering. Noting the strength and dispositions of the Sultan's janissaries, the deployment of his cannon and the morale of his armies.

Though he despised his oppressors, none were more polite, more gracious and charming than he. Though famous as a host, he did not drink nor indulge in his guest's debauched pleasures. With great patience he listened to Pashas in their cups, mentally noting their weaknesses and vices, the riches of their treasuries and the virility of their politics.

Ancoulsis ate heartily and listened well. He wore a red sash over his embroidered *kaftan*, a *kalpak* upon his head, leather slippers and expensive furs, all essential to the air of careless opulence that carried such weight in the Turkish courts. He became a skilled calligrapher, decorating official letters with mythical creatures, roses and hyacinths. His house was adorned with *Iznik* tiles, carpets from Cairo and silk hangings from Bursa. It boasted an enclosed court with a domed portico and minaret out front, calculated to cultivate the esteem of his peers, the men who called him an "honourable Turk".

But in private Ancoulsis was a different man. He maintained a hardy physique with constant hunting and riding. In the company of friends he practised the banned martial art of *trântâ* and out-fenced every contemporary. His private studies consumed him and he slept at most three hours a night. He amassed a library of occult books, taking especial interest in Enochian and Hermetic epistemologies.

Sultan Bayezid the Thunderbolt died, and Ancoulsis was allowed to return home. He bought a house in Belgrade from where, as the new Sultan's envoy he toured the turbulent Balkan dominions. Ever scrupulous in his duties, he displayed every outward semblance of unimpeachable loyalty to Islam while holding covert meetings with Armenian dissidents and Greek outlaws, financing Slovene militias and Romany bandits, assaying the fighting mood of the people of the Balkans.

This was, as ever, prodigious. The Bulgarians were in a ferment. Their territories having been parcelled out to the Sultan's favourites, they were subject to cruel and capricious taxes, their sons dragged away to become janissaries, their daughters to the harems of the conquerer. Armenia was on the verge of a general uprising. The Croats, Bosnians and Serbs periodically revolted against Turkish excesses and the Macedonians were in a state of perpetual insurgency.

Rebellions were quelled with exquisite barbarism. Thousands of corpses lined the roads, impaled or crucified upside-down for the edification of slave convoys on their miserable journey to Constantinople. Ancoulsis displayed no revulsion as his carriage passed them and he joked with Pashas and Emirs over *shisha* pipes and sherbet in the evenings. He suppressed his rage under a veneer of grave devotion and the Turks trusted him completely.

But Ancoulsis was plagued by another disquiet. One evening, ninety years after he left his father's home, he stared dry-eyed at his reflection in a mirror. It seemed he had reached the age of sixty and aged no further. Though all his old friends were dead, every morning he saw the same face staring back. Previously he'd suppressed any reaction to this phenomenon, but on this evening an existential horror overwhelmed him. He bit hard down upon his lip and willed himself to stare deeper. Why?

He had heard whispers behind his back, rumours of witchcraft to explain his agelessness, but none dared speak them aloud. Now Ancoulsis wondered himself. Had his fascination with the occult enabled some contact malediction - was he an unwitting accomplice to sorcery? Or was there some natural explanation for his robust health?

He'd never been addicted to pleasures of the flesh. He had no time for the caterwauling of priests or the hollow philosophies of their one-eyed gods. He took no solace in drink or opium. His ennui was only quenched by work or by hunting, riding and fencing and at night, reading and writing.

But he became consumed with discovering the source of his perdurable existence. Having secretly purchased a manor deep in the Transylvanian mountains, he built there a library of occult grimoires and arcane tomes. He paid a small fortune for a copy of *The Mirror of Simple Souls*, a mystical treatise composed in Old French. Its discourse on the Soul's journey to union with the divine seemed to answer some of his questions, but he needed more specifics.

To that end, Ancoulsis decided his long years of servitude were over. One day he did not keep a tryst with a royal tax collector. The next, he did not reply to the enquiry of a visiting Pasha. After a month's absence the Rumelian Emir dispatched soldiers to his house. They found it empty. Ancoulsis had vanished.

He had already transferred his effects to the Transylvanian manor. Posing as a retired Cappadocian tax collector, Ancoulsis renewed an arrangement with the local Pasha, heavily bribed, who asked no questions and kept his soldiers away from that valley.

Freed of the Turk, he bent his will toward studying books and the stars, seeking clues to his dilemma. A year later, having found no conclusive answers, he decided to begin more active resistance to the Turk. To do so he needed to manufacture a new identity.

This was done easily enough. Having previously selected Veaceslav Ancoulsis, a second cousin of a noble but impoverished Wallachian family, Codrût financed a Turkish education for the lad, got him into the right military academy, then a promising career as an officer in the janissaries. He arranged a posting to an obscure Armenian fortress, where after six months Veaceslav Ancoulsis perished in a hunting accident. Fortunately Codrût Ancoulsis happened to be visiting and was able to see to it that the poor lad had an honourable burial.

Before the body could putrefy, Codrût spirited it away to a forest hut, where he had arranged the materials for a Hermetic ritual. Surrounded by powerful talismans he chanted conjurations, gleaned through careful study of *The Mirror of Souls*. Over several hours Codrût merged his consciousness with Veaceslav's corpse, ensuring it would inhabit his original *apeira*.

The next morning he rode home in the body of Veaceslav, having buried his own without ceremony or regret. Accustoming himself to his relative's longer limbs and deeper voice took practice but soon Codrût was able to ride and fence as lithely as in his previous body.

Communications were slow through the Ottoman's fractious empire and it was easy enough for Veaceslav Ancoulsis to appear in the city of Piteşti with expertly forged papers. Ancoulsis became a highly efficient quartermaster to the resident Pasha, who did not suspect that his new *çorbaci* was fomenting rebellion among local peasants, equipping them with weapons and gunpowder from the armoury while amending ledgers so skilfully that no evidence of their theft would ever be found.

This situation endured for thirty years and the power of the Turks waned considerably in Piteşti, local tribesmen conducting a terror campaign that imprisoned the occupiers within the city walls and made supply caravans few and fearful. When Veaceslav's body in turn became decrepit, Ancoulsis found a new candidate to take its place. He reappeared in Belgrade, where another relation was sacrificed for the dream of the Balkan League. Using this stratagem, Ancoulsis continued his work in ten consecutive bodies throughout the centuries after the battle of Kosovo.

With the fortune he'd amassed as *Dragoman* he travelled through the Balkans, exhorting tribal chieftains and bandits to action. He inserted himself into the Albanian revolt, but witnessed their defeat at Gjirokastër and the massacre of five thousand rebels.

Another century passed. He saw the Bosnians annihilated after their fortress at Jajce fell, then advised and armed the Croatian *Uskoci* in their endless guerrilla war. With Ancoulsis' advice the Wallachians and Moldavians defeated several Turkish armies, but always the superior numbers of the invader kept them from consolidating.

Two generations later a Hungarian army failed at the battle of Mohacs. Even Buda and Pest fell, condemning the Magyar to centuries of Ottoman tyranny. Ancoulsis was instrumental in the revolt of Mihail the Brave, whose Transylvanians defeated the Turks time and again, recapturing Ancoulsis' homeland of Moldovia. But the superior numbers of the Ottoman defeated even that great general in the end.

As the Crusades raged across Balkan lands, Ancoulsis' beloved Belgrade was destroyed and rebuilt. His people suffered underfoot as decades of warfare between East and West were resolved on their soil. He travelled to Venice, saw Crete conquered, Tinos and Aegina crumble under the onslaught of the Turk.

He hired out as adviser to a series of warlords, saw the island fortress of Rhodes enrubbled, fought with the Knights of St John that held Malta, saving the Mediterranean from Muslim domination. Finally the Holy Roman Empire allied with Russia, Venice and Hapsburg Hungary for a sustained campaign. After their victory over the Turkish navy at Lepanto, the Polish-Lithuanian compact joined this nascent Holy League. Gradually the tide was turning against the Ottoman Empire. Emperor Leopold I lifted the siege of Vienna and following triumph at Zenta, rolled back Ottoman forces in Hungary as Russian armies pummelled them in the East.

After five centuries of struggle, the power of the Turks was finally waning. But into that vacuum a new conquerer rushed. The Austrian Hapsburgs, who had long coveted the lands to their south, became the new despots of the Balkans.

Ancoulsis had anticipated this development and without hesitation bent his will towards vanquishing the new foe. Again he determined to defeat them from within. He had spies in the court of every principality, of every freshly conquered city.

He encouraged the writings of Paisus, a monk whose manifesto *Istoriya Slavyanobolgarskaya* reawakened a sense of national identity amongst Bulgarians. That bolstered resistance in neighbouring countries and Ancoulsis' movement found momentum.

But Paisus distracted Ancoulsis with the gift of an ancient book, found in his monastery centuries before. Translated from ancient cuneiform, it was titled *The Curse of Akkade*. In it Ancoulsis read of a Sumerian god; *Enlil, the roaring storm that subjugates the entire" "land, the rising deluge that cannot be confronted*

This god bequeathed a magikal idol to his worshippers, to protect them from the priests and followers of Marduk the Usurper. The idol had been passed down from the Akkadians through secretive pagan cults. It was alleged to have been possessed by Alexander of Macedonia and lost somewhere in Persia. Intuition told Ancoulsis that this idol was somehow related to his unnatural longevity.

As a dog instinctively eats a certain type of grass because it assists the passage of food through its bowels, so did Ancoulsis follow his intuition. Clues in *The Curse of Akkade* led him to another work; the *vahks* of Laleshwari, an ancient Kashmiri mystic.

Intrigued by her noetic poems, he travelled to India. The night he landed in Calcutta, Enlil spoke to him in dreams. Consulting with holy men and seers, quoting cryptic phrases that fell unbidden from his tongue, Ancoulsis discovered signs that led him unerringly to the Himalayan mountains and eventually, the idol.

The instant he found that luminous, maddening periapt he knew why his lifespan had been so unnaturally extended. Certain knowledge formed in his brain that the idol had affected his *apeira*, drawing his life span out towards some as yet unknown end. Though he did not understand the idol's motivations, he knew it had enabled his centuries of scheming for the Balkan League and that was enough.

Now his researches found new agency and Ancoulsis discovered occult grimoires which bestowed the secret of travelling along *apeira*. Armed with that knowledge he was able to traverse his life span in both directions, finding new ways to advance his cause. But his Indian sojourn was cut short. Hapsburg agents were on his trail and very nearly caught him in Bombay.

He fled with the idol to revolutionary France. Enthralled by the genius of Buonaparte, Ancoulsis fought with the Revolutionary Army, the idol assisting him to become a member of Buonaparte's staff. Later he joined the retinue of the arch-negotiator, Prince Charles Talleyrand, helping negotiate the Treaty of Luneville with Austria.

But in the blink of an eye Buonaparte's Empire was destroyed by a resurgence of the Holy League, under the command of the Generals Wellington and Blücher. In its aftermath the Spring of Nations sparked revolution all across Europe. Nationalism was the spirit of the age and in it Ancoulsis recognised his chance to free the Balkans from oppression.

He returned home, collaborating with the idol to manipulate a rebel leader known as the Karageorge and seduce the first iteration of Kalyenka, among others. For a time the Serbs had their own kingdom and even Greece gained its independence.

Though these revolutions ultimately failed, they demonstrated that human populations possessed the collective will to rise up against their oppressors. The imminent advent of a Murex Moon, seen only once since the battle of Kosovo, demonstrated that a new cosmological hinge point was at hand.

With the armies of European tyrants converging on the Balkans, Ancoulsis was poised to complete his long-laid plans. Once he had disposed of his chief rival, the English plutocrat Lord Cockwattle, he would be free to assume control of the Balkan League.

In his room in Watson's Hotel, Ancoulsis closed his journal, frowning. Sensing a disturbance in the ethers around him, he looked at the idol. It was throbbing, broadcasting an alert that told him some emissary from the starlit realms was close by.

He looked up and smiled. "Good evening Augustine," he said. "I was wondering how long it would take for you to find me."

# 7

# Bamboozled

Doctor Amordule clicked a button, switching off the gigantic screen behind her. "That concludes our presentation on the technological achievements of the D'Angels."

Below Amordule, in the Great Hall of the Exposition, various heads of state, generals and other officers of consequence glanced around uneasily. Had not the promotional literature for this Exposition declared they would be able to bid for technologies with military applications? So far they had been shown a few weeds, some useless innovations to do with feeding the poor and an equally puzzling cure for tuberculosis, a peasant affliction which helped keep their numbers in check. Why were they being bamboozled?

This farce had gone on too long. It was starting to feel like an ambush in the making. Fingering hidden weapons and tonguing for a drink, the proud soldiers of Europe wondered how they had landed in this mysterious, dim-lit hall full of women and *kaffirs*.

Amordule paused and looked at her audience. Ranged around the expanse of the Exposition Hall, the officers and aristocrats stared sullenly back at her. A few were sprawled, snoring in their chairs, but Amordule noted that in one corner several officers of different allegiances were huddled together, deep in conference. She nodded to her burly Nigerian chief of security, Abaeze Uche and he strolled over to stand behind them, forestalling any violent schemes.

Amordule cleared her throat. "Soldiers and er, aristocrats, I invite you to attend a function in our ballroom. There you may bid on some of the items we have displayed, relax and enjoy the entertainments we have prepared. Please follow our events coordinator, Alfhild."

A tall Norwegian woman opened a set of double doors at the far end of the Hall. Looking at each other for reassurance, the younger officers moved towards it, ushered on by their commanders. A Polish lancer captain and a Silesian hussar peeped inside and hurried back.

"It appears to be a formal reception room," the lancer whispered to his major, who in turn reported to an adjutant of Commander Hieronim Nekanda Trepka. The Commander strode into the chamber, amidst a bustle of primping aide-de-camps.

"Go, go," the Duchess of Sforza ordered her retinue, and they also advanced. Seeing this, the Albanians, Silesians and Serbs surged forward and soon all contingents were hurrying towards the double doors.

The foremost officers emerged into a chamber glowing with light from unseen sources. At the far end of the room was a stage where musical instruments were set. Chests puffed out, shoulders back, the officers strutted, leering at *tougrak* attendants bearing trays of food and drink.

"What is this?" demanded the Serbian brigadier Yaklovev, staring in disgust at an offering from a Japanese waitress. He had been permitted to return to the enclave, upon giving his word not to make further trouble.

"A delicacy made of fungal fillets, baked in a pastry," the waitress replied gravely.

"Ach, rubbish. I want meat! Meat, you hear?" Infuriated by the waitress's polite smile, Yaklovev stormed over to his fellow officers, who stood gazing in bewilderment at complex carvings adorning the walls and ceilings. A queer melancholy had seemed to infect them when they entered this outlandish hall.

Graven in wildly extravagant designs, stylised nudes chased each other across the walls, provoking conflicting sensations of lust and wonder in the onlookers. Yaklovev watched with dismay as the carvings seemed to come alive, melding with his own lewd thoughts, igniting unwelcome memories of sadistic sexual encounters - the only kind he knew. The officer's backslapping, whoops and catcalls tailed off into nervous laughter and brooding silence as the lurid carvings merged with half-remembered raping exploits and foul battlefield deeds.

Amordule watched from behind a protective cordon of *Securité* as the officers hunched their shoulders, staring blankly into mental torment. Was it unethical, she wondered, to expose these men unwittingly to the theta waves? Probably, she decided, but they had forced their way here with fire and steel. "They are only being exposed to themselves," she whispered to Alfhild, who put an arm comfortingly around her shoulders.

Yaklovev, the Butcher of Krakow, saw himself standing atop a mass of corpses. Piled into a great trench excavated from frozen soil, the bodies were sprawled atop one another, black blood coagulated across slack white faces. In a frenzy of exultant rage, Yaklovev studied his victims, shooting any that moved, any whose eyes fluttered, who groaned aloud or sobbed piteously in their agony.

Watching the scene through his mind's eye, Yaklovev saw even his own men observing him with disgust. These were hardened soldiers who had killed all across the Balkans, yet even they quailed at the deeds of their infamous general.

"Vermin," he screamed. "Traitors, cowards!" But across the veil they did not hear him and Yaklovev was left to fulminate to himself, trapped in this living memory.

In the next instant he saw himself as a ten-year-old boy, being raped by a priest in the sacristy of his village church. He screamed in impotent rage, feeling again the scalding pain in his intestines, the humiliating domination. More images crowded into his mind. The massacres of entire populations, the murder and rape of hundreds of women, all sanctified by churches and kings. Yaklovev fumbled blindly in his jacket, pulled out a pistol. A steady shriek rose from his throat as he saw his victims multiply in memory. The pistol came up in his shaking hand and he screamed as he shot himself in the head.

The other officers scarce seemed to notice, each engulfed in his own internal interrogation. They gibbered and howled, some rolled on the ground screaming. Two more shot themselves. Even the Duchess of Sforza and the Duke of Petrograd were afflicted, battering themselves into walls in their anguish. Two of their staffers began fighting; eye-gouging, biting, slamming each other's heads into the floor. The Polish Commander Hieronim Nekanda Trepka had already run, screaming incoherently, from the room.

Amordule looked to her chief *Securité*. Abaeze Uche, his face creased in sorrow. Uche signalled to a technician who stood by. The man stroked a fungal tendril poking out from the wall. In the wretched minds of the officers, the haunting visions ceased.

Spitting out an ear, a Polish major stared in disbelief at the carnage he had wrought on his groaning cousin. The Duchess of Sforza stood naked, having torn all her clothes off and scratched her own face to ribbons. Dazed officers hastily draped her with cloaks and ushered her to a seat where she rocked herself gently, staring into space.

The Duke of Petrograd lay dead, having stabbed himself in the heart.

The survivors adjusted their uniforms and stared bleakly around. Seven men had gone quite mad and required tranquillising by the *Securité*. They were laid onto stretchers and lugged to an infirmary. D'Angels attendants offered the survivors bandages and hot drinks. A psychologist with twelve languages spoke to those least afflicted. The officers sat on comfortable chairs, some sobbing, some clenching fists and glaring belligerently at any who came too close.

At the bandstand, a group of musicians stood patiently, arms folded over their instruments. In contrast to the uniforms of the officers, they wore loose-fitting, colourful clothes. Their hair was long, some were bearded. They watched and spoke softly amongst themselves.

A slight woman of the northern steppes sat behind a drum kit. She began teasing out a snare rhythm, embellished by the timbre of a tom drum. Beside her a tall Sudanese embraced a cello, plucking out bass notes as scaffolding for the forays of a Chilean clarinettist, the stentorian lungs of a Kenyan saxophonist, the pentatonic jabs of a guitarist from the Mississippi Delta, the drones of a cross-legged sitarist. The music began to assemble itself, gathering momentum as each trill, chord and beat evoked fresh nuances of joy and sadness, compelling the listeners to move, to sway, to dance, to sing.

The officers were transfixed. Despite themselves, some responded to the music. Minds scoured by the theta waves, they behaved with uncharacteristic fervour. As the music grew in intensity, dormant instincts were activated and the half naked men began to move in time, responding to the primal demands of their long-suppressed DNA.

The band kicked into a powerful groove, borne on the soul of Caribbean slave songs, the stoicism of Cambodian rice-farmers, the complex harmonics of throat-singing Tibetan monks. It carried the exuberant rhythms of Haitian dancers and the crazy abandon of the Casemance dancers of Senegal.

The drummer was the band's centre of gravity, her beats pushing and pulling on space-time to create a groove that tumbled with joyous abandon and snapped with mathematical precision. Her arms wove an intricate threnody, lagging between each beat with what could have been micro-seconds or an eternity, though the band never strayed from their swinging tempo.

A woman emerged from behind a velvet green curtain and came to the front of the stage. Her freshly shaved skull shone translucent through her scalp. Her brown eyes were ancient pools of melancholy and joy, face supple with emotion, lively as a river in spate. She moved with the music and the music moved within her.

A black man with six fingers on each hand laid aside his guitar and leaned into a microphone. "Introducing Julie Brown - AKA the Womb of Time," he announced, and Julie Brown snapped her head backwards and ululated a note that made the officers cry.

She began to sing. Her technique was masterful, throat, cheeks and lips finessing vibrato and timbre, compelling passions like winds in a ship's sail. She honked and howled and spat and growled. She sang in Malian, she sang in Gaelic, she sang in Catalan. She sang the *ghazals* of Hafiz the Persian and the Egyptian temple songs of Nehmes Bastet, the *sirventes* of Ermengarde of Occitania, the *vahks* of Laleshwari and a thousand other balladeers throughout all the ages of humankind.

"Dig it," she sang. "Listening is living and music is life."

The officers howled, for a wavefront of *khuti* surged within them. Their bodies moved but their eyes stared into oblivion. A Hungarian regimental band leader approached the bandstand, tearing off boots and epaulettes, imploring the musicians to let him join them. Soon he was happily playing a snare drum, improvising cadences over the Mongolian's beats. Impaled by his frantic rhythm the music spiralled into a storm. Frenzied officers tore off their remaining clothes and bayed, ignoring rank and prestige as they bounced off each other in the derangement of their dance.

But Amordule was still, attuned to something beyond hearing. The entire mountain was shaking, diminishing even the frantic power of the band. The rumble of drums masked a subsonic boom, but soon it was unmistakeable, emanating from the very floor.

Julie Brown shrieked and fell as if struck by a mighty blow. The musicians ceased playing. Dropping their instruments, they rushed to her aid.

Amordule looked to Abaeze Uche. He made a hand signal, summoning his *Securité*. Half of them assembled in an outward-facing phalanx around Julie Brown. The others rushed through a doorway that opened in the wall and disappeared into the mountain.

# 8

# Weft and Weal

Kalyenka sipped tea, staring out of the Riemann node into the prehistoric jungle beyond. It was almost pretty in its alien geometry. The sunlight had an ultraviolet quality which suffused the waters with a gossamer sheen. Ungainly winged insects strafed the surface, fighting fierce battles in competition for smaller prey. Unnerved by the mastications of a gigantic beetle feasting on an equally outsized arachnid, Kalyenka transferred her attention back to the interior.

Further along the table sat the *Sarhang*, hands folded in his lap. His eyes were closed but the lids moving - a sure indication he was engrossed in some quantum operation. Kalyenka gazed on his almost translucent olive skin, reflecting the outside light with a radiance she had observed in children and certain beautiful women. Despite his unremarkable countenance the man did exhibit an ethereal quality. She supposed he ought to, being after all an allegedly transfigured being.

They were having a break from his Tale. He had reassured her that no time at all was passing in the outer world, that her eidolon had no physical component, so her fatigue was psychosomatic, whatever that meant, but she just knew that she needed space, and silence, and the absence of the confounding images of the chimera lens. Time to think, time to process.

She felt like she had been listening to him speak for days, yet she had not slept and for all that it could have been mere hours. This Riemann node seemed a bowl of fever dreams through which she swam like a disembodied ghost.

The phenomena the *Sarhang* had shown her were puzzling enough; this mad tale of gods and demons, a conspiracy of evil men, but what was really troubling her was that it seemed she had three sets of memories. Her experiences within the Riemann node depicted her as a young woman in three distinct epochs, each in neighbouring provinces of the Balkans. What was going on there?

Ancoulsis seemed to be the common link. He figured in each of those lives. As the *Grófka* Kalyenka Žerotín, daughter of the Duke and Duchess Dežër Žerotín, natives of Cristaña, she knew Ancoulsis as the aristocrat who helped defend her against the assassin sent by the Queen of Cristaña.

The chimera lens had also awoken memories of herself as Kalyenka Musatei cā Vlach; a native of neighbouring Wallachia. This Kalyenka's father owned a salt mine at Ocnele Mari. He was an influential man with contacts all over the Balkans including Baron Ancoulsis, a political agitator of independent means. Ancoulsis had taken an especial interest in Kalyenka during his frequent visits to the household.

It also seemed she inhabited the life of a Russian countess, visiting Cristaña during the Winter Uprising. It was there that Ancoulsis introduced her to Hoche, the French agent who so uncannily resembled Chance. She slept with that delightful fellow after a ball, just before an attempted coup by Bonapartists. Or rather, that version of Kalyenka slept with him - was it really her? Something had happened afterwards, something so awful that the memory had been eclipsed.

It was all too puzzling. She turned back to her painting and took up a brush, dabbing it into a mound of white oil. The familiar smell of paint and turpentine made her relax.

She had earlier willed the canvas to grow larger again, in order to accomodate its multitude of subjects. She stepped back to examine it, finding a pleasing symmetry in the interplay of individuals and incidents.

"That is an interesting addition," said the *Sarhang*, indicating an image of Kalyenka, naked, bruised and bloodied, brandishing a double-barrelled pistol.

"Yes. I'm not sure where that came from," Kalyenka said. "It appears linked to this image of Chance." She pointed to the torso of a naked man, his face indistinct. "It's the transmissions. I can barely keep up. The process is like automatic writing. I'm barely aware of what I'm painting."

The *Sarhang* peered into the work. "Can you give me any contextual overview? I may be able to help."

"The big swirling spaces are abstracting emotional energies," Kalyenka said. "Some of it references my theta experience with Chance. You can see that the moon features heavily. There are characters in period dress who look oddly familiar. Ancoulsis has popped up in there too. How is it that he has not appeared in your tale?"

The *Sarhang* considered this a moment. "Hmmm. Ancoulsis is an enigmatic character whose concerns are more, well, localised than mine. There is synergy in our work but we are hardly allies. I see that he is beside you there at a lavish ball."

Kalyenka looked closer. Wearing an archaic gown and jewellery, she was dancing with Ancoulsis. "Yes. He attends a grand ball with each of the three women I supposedly embody. How is that possible? Am I going mad?"

"Not necessarily," said the *Sarhang*. "Can you identify each woman?"

"Of course," said Kalyenka. "One is me, Kalyenka of Cristaña, who fought the Hapsburgs, had a dalliance with the King and whose eidolon is standing before you now. The other Kalyenka lived in Wallachia about sixty years earlier. She was acquainted with a rebel leader known as the Karageorge. It seems I was also a Russian countess named Kalyenka Minskovna Javakhadze, visiting at court during the long ago Winter Uprising, when a young Frenchman named Hoche came to incite a revolt against King Neculcea, the grandfather of our current King Gustavus."

The *Sarhang* scrutinised the images. "Fascinating. The transmissions indicate that you are acting as a medium for the diffusion of numinous data. My immediate hypotheses is that the ball is an event outside of subjective time, suspended in the *Mēnōg*."

"Is this what you meant when you said I was acting as a kind of shaman?" asked Kalyenka.

"Yes, exactly. It is the predilection of artists to willingly take a descent into novelty, subjecting their subconscious to the *Mēnōg*. As a shaman does, they return to report their findings. That creates agency to make change in the world."

Kalyenka stared open-mouthed at the *Sarhang*. "Well, that puts it into perspective. I never quite understood what you were on about till now."

She looked at her painting. How many other selves would come to light if she kept exploring the phantom world of this narrative? The *Sarhang* had already hinted at other incarnations; in the theta experience she'd caught glimpses of previous selves. For that matter, how did Ancoulsis appear so agelessly in all these lives, separated by so many decades? It was all very unsettling.

"Many things are possible in an infinite universe," the *Sarhang* said abruptly, apparently apropos of nothing at all, until Kalyenka realised he'd been eavesdropping on her thoughts again.

"Well I'd like to understand some of them," she said.

"Excellent. Tell me about Kalyenka Musatei cā Vlach."

Almost instantly an answer arrived on Kalyenka's tongue. "As our surname suggests we were of the Vlachs - an ancient Balkan people. My father supplied salt to the Grand *Vožd* of Serbia, the man known as the Karageorge. Ancoulsis was the middle man in that transaction."

The *Sarhang* was pacing the floor, hands laced behind his back. He stopped and touched a hand to his forehead. "Ah, you are referring to George Petrović, the rebel leader who fought the Turks in the First Serbian Uprising, the man otherwise known as Black George."

"Black George?" said Kalyenka, startled. "That is also the name of the bandit chief who plagues the Carpathians now. But he is nothing like the Karageorge. Oh, both are big, swarthy men. But the Karageorge was handsome - and dear god - it was Ancoulsis who introduced me to him."

"Did he? That is *very* interesting."

"Yes, he insisted I meet the Karageorge when my father hosted a ball in his honour. The Karageorge could not have been more different to the bandit chief, who affects the dandified costume of a Turkish pasha. The Karageorge wore peasant clothes that belied his superb physique and warlike appearance - I had quite the passion for him. During his campaigns against the Turks it is said that he murdered his stepfather and hung his brother for raping a Serbian woman."

"Yes, I have studied his *apeira*," said the *Sarhang*. "The Karageorge, AKA George Petrović was a fearsome warrior who fought with courage and cunning against the Ottoman oppressors. I cannot follow his *apeira* after the ball at which you met him, which suggests that the idol came into his possession at this point.

"On the verge of defeating the Turks a year later, the Karageorge inexplicably fled across the Danube. At that point I can clearly see his *apeira* again, meaning he no longer has the idol in his possession. Resistance folded and the Turks returned, wreaking savage vengeance. The Karageorge was betrayed by the Hapsburgs and assassinated by Milosh Obrenovitch, a rival rebel leader."

"I also knew Obrenovitch," said Kalyenka. "I was present when he met with my father to renew the salt deal. As the new Prince of

Serbia he denigrated the memory of Karageorge and I hated him for it."

The *Sarhang* leaned on the table, waggling a forefinger against his nose. "Obrenovitch was later exiled and the Karageorge's son Alexander crowned as *Vozd*. I can see that Ancoulsis is involved in both these events, appearing as an adviser to the Karageorge and later to his son. The Turks are finally evicted, only to be replaced by invading Hapsburg armies. That brings us closer to your incarnation as Kalyenka Žerotīn."

"I wish you wouldn't talk about me as if I were some other person."

"Let's not split hairs Kalyenka. Your part in these affairs is what is important, not what your name was at the time. Now, when the Magyars rose against the Hapsburgs they were led by a renegade Slav, Lajos Kossuth."

Kalyenka sniffed. "Yes, Vania and I were intimately involved with Kossuth's insurgency."

The *Sarhang* interrupted; "Concurrently, the second Black George appears in Cristaña as a feared bandit chief."

"Do you think there is some connection between Ancoulsis and the bandit?" asked Kalyenka.

"There must be," said the *Sarhang*. "The fact that I cannot see some of Black George's *apeira* indicates that the idol is involved. Certainly it was Ancoulsis who gave the idol to Chance, so we know he had been in possession of it. I suspect he had earlier given it to the Karageorge, then stole it from him before he fled."

"Ancoulsis showed up again during the Hungarian revolt," said Kalyenka. "I was in the bath in my apartment in Buda, preparing to join the army at Székelykeresztúr when there was a knock at the door. Vania was out, so I hurriedly dressed to answer it. Ancoulsis stood there, looking not a day older than when I had last seen him in Cristaña."

*To Kalyenka's surprise Ancoulsis appears in the lens.* "I thought you said Ancoulsis was impervious to observation?"

"He has been, to me," says the *Sarhang*. "It is you who focussed the lens into this moment. Your facility with it has expanded exponentially."

"Oh." Kalyenka watches as Ancoulsis settles into an armchair opposite her younger self. He is wearing the baggy silk suit of a *boyar*, embroidered with gold thread. His face is wan but his eyes are calm and inscrutable.

*"My dear, you must return home immediately," he says.*

*"Why?" asks the younger Kalyenka.*

*"You must have read my letter? Cristaña is on the verge of revolution. There are people at court, Duke Destricuke among them, who are prepared to act but uncertain what to do. They would listen to you, a veteran of several revolutions. But agents of the Hapsburgs have financed loyalists to engineer a counter-coup. If they prevail the Austrians will take the country or worse still, it may fall to the Russians. If you return immediately you can strike first, topple the puppet king and establish an interim government. That would give us leverage to extend the Revolution into Cristaña, thus protecting the northern flank of the Balkans. This is a crucial moment in the struggle for control of Eastern Europe."*

*Kalyenka-in-the-lens sighs. "Very well."*

*"We should leave immediately," says Ancoulsis. "In twenty four days the Austrians will attempt their coup."*

*"I have to buy a horse."*

*"I have fresh mounts outside."*

*"Very well. Please, leave me alone a moment. I have to write a letter, to explain my absence to Vania."*

*"Then hurry," said Ancoulsis. "Hapsburg spies will be watching the borders. We must cross them well before the day of their intended coup."*

*As Ancoulsis rises and leaves the room, Kalyenka examines his expression through the lens.*

"He looks entirely too smug."

"He does," said the *Sarhang*. "What happened next?"

"We rode to Cristaña. I established contact with the revolutionaries at court. We planned to seize power during a grand ball in the palace. But that is where it everything goes awry. For my memories tell me I attend the ball as the Russian countess Kalyenka Minskovna Javakhadze, wearing an exquisite *robes en chemise* with a gathered bodice, a daring ensemble for that era, but something I wouldn't be seen dead wearing in this century. Yes, damn your eyes, I attend a ball in the *previous* century as a Russian Kalyenka, in full control of all her faculties, not at all concerned about revolutions, or any other me.

"Ancoulsis introduces me to Hoche at that ball. A dashing Frenchman with an inexplicable Irish accent. The news is all of Buonaparte's victories across Europe and monarchists everywhere are panicking. The atmosphere at the ball is explosive and Hoche and I have wild, passionate sex after it. Curiously enough I don't remember what happened next, but Hoche disappeared. Next thing I remember is me, the *Grófka* Kalyenka Žerotīn, returning home after the original ball, to which I wore my favourite scarlet gown."

She looked down at the same garment and stroked the material fondly.

"Our coup is foiled by Hapsburg agents. Fifty plotters are executed, but somehow I and Duke Destricuke escape suspicion. On the same day the Hungarian revolution is quashed at the battle of Székelykeresztúr. Ancoulsis warns that the Hapsburgs are seeking me by name, so I flee to my family's remote chateau. Within months both my parents die and my conniving brothers take most of their wealth, but I inherit enough to live comfortably. I change my surname to Menschievr and stay in Cristaña, quietly devoting myself to my art. Later I am introduced to the King and well, you know the rest."

The *Sarhang* pondered the image of Ancoulsis in Kalyenka's painting. "Ancoulsis certainly placed himself at the fulcrum of many decisive events. That is troubling in itself."

*The lens shows the severe face of the lawyer Lajos Kossuth, speaking in a crowded hall.*

"It should not have escaped your notice that although Kossuth was a Slav, his loyalty was to Hungary," said the *Sarhang*. "Loyalties are complex amongst Hungaro-Slavics. They owe political allegiance to the Kingdom of Hungary, yet remain culturally Slavic. But Kossuth's loyalties seemed to be entirely Magyar."

The *Sarhang* tapped his fingers on the table. "It is clear that Ancoulsis would not have supported such a man. He is devoted to the idea of a Pan-Slavic nation. Kossuth's denial of Slavic hegemony would have made Ancoulsis perceive him as a danger to the Balkan League. Which makes me think of treachery. Ancoulsis was in a position to divulge the Hungarian strategy at Székelykeresztúr to Hapsburg spies in Cristaña."

"No, surely he would not?" Kalyenka said.

"We must hope not," said the *Sarhang*. "But to be certain we will delve deeper into his *apeira*. Would you focus on memories of him, please Kalyenka?"

Kalyenka summoned recollections of Ancoulsis, her brush sculpting his eyes on canvas.

*The lens shows him wearing the simple frock coat and leggings in which she remembered him most clearly. Going deeper into her* apeira *she sees him clad in the tall* işlic *hat and embroidered sheepskin vest in which he introduced Kalyenka Musatei cā Vlach to the Karageorge. Deeper again, he sports the extravagant domino cloak and pleated boyar shirt of the* Dragoman *Codrût Ancoulsis, whose diplomatic skills allow him to straddle imperial borders during the Ottoman occupation.*

*Suddenly another Ancoulsis appears in the chimera lens. He is attired in modern shirt sleeves but looks no older. Seated at a table, he is poring over a sheaf of papers in a sumptuous hotel room. To Kalyenka's amazement and evidently that of the* Sarhang, *Ancoulsis looks up, directly into the chimera lens.*

*"Good evening Augustine. I was wondering how long it would take you to find me."*

# 9

# Mere Women

"Who was that p-peasant woman?" demanded the Kaiser. "She knew you. H-how did she defeat your supposedly invincible m-machine so easily? V-vumple, answer me at once."

The Kaiser glared at Vehemple. They were crammed with Teufel and the automaton into an elevator, whence they had decamped after being strafed by Bejikereene. Vehemple did not respond. He was examining his automaton, which had taken considerable damage and was leaking hydraulic oil. Teufel jabbed a pistol into the Dutchman's side.

"Answer the Kaiser, *dickkopf*," he said. "You are responsible for the deaths of three more of my men." Silently Vehemple turned his mud-coloured eyes on the Kaiser.

"She is the *hausfrau* from the tavern of the Eagle's Nest, the village atop the closest mountain. What she is doing here, wielding a *Securité* weapon is a riddle you may care to pursue. I have no interest in it. But the sow has damaged my *verkeerslicht*."

"I don't care who she is V-Vingle, I want to know w-what are you going to do about her, you bungling *trottel*. If we are to be b-beaten by mere w-women, how are we going to get my troops into this *höllenloch*? Teufel, why d-did you not intervene?"

"I apologise sire," Teufel grunted. "I was wounded in the fusillade and had to get you out of range. I thought only of your safety."

Peering down, the Kaiser saw that Teufel was bleeding through his uniform in three places. He cocked his head belligerently. "Nonetheless Teufel, you should have k-killed that insolent cow. Her intervention has d-distracted me, leaving my jaegers to b-blunder about directionless in this hellish maze."

Teufel did not blink. "*Ja*. I should have eliminated the threat sire. I am ashamed."

"Enough of this nonsense," said Vehemple. "Your jaeger regiments will already be in the station. Regardless of whether we are there to greet them, if they have any initiative at all they should be able to fight their way to the upper levels."

"D-do not think to lecture me on military t-tactics," sneered the Kaiser. "No one knows the m-military better than me. Return this conveyance to the level of the t-trains, s-s-s-so I can deploy my troops through it. Teufel will dispose of the *hausfrau*."

"That is impossible," said Vehemple. "This is the executive lift. It bypasses all other levels, travelling directly to the topmost level of the Hospice. It is not able to carry more than five individuals at a time. If it detects more it will not move. This is not the solution to deploy your troops."

"So, that is where you are t-taking me now Vempling? To the headquarters of this f-facility?"

"*Da*, that is correct," said the Dutchman. "We proceed to the *Sarhang's* Citadel in the topmost tier of the Hospice, where we will assume command of the facility."

The elevator stopped and its door slid open. Teufel pivoted stiffly into the corridor, carbine extended, to survey both directions. "This section is clear," he said faintly. "Dutchman. Indicate our next direction of travel."

But Vehemple had already exited the elevator and was walking east, accompanied by his battered automaton. Teufel's voice cracked as he shouted. "Vehemple! I asked you a question. While you are under my command you will obey orders."

"Your war-play is tiresome," said Vehemple over his shoulder as he strode away. "In any case, I am not under your command. If you point a gun at me again my automaton will destroy you."

Teufel looked at the automaton, which swivelled its head to stare at him through cold mechanical eyes. The Kaiser tapped Teufel on the shoulder. He made the combat signal with his right hand meaning, 'wait' and passed his left hand across his throat.

Teufel nodded, his face gaunt with pain. He limped carefully after his Kaiser as Vehemple and the automaton traversed intersecting corridors, paying no heed to the artworks adorning the walls, nor the peculiar nature of the architectonics. Hearing the distant sound of gunfire, they stopped to listen.

"Those are Dreyse needle guns and Mausers," said Teufel through gritted teeth. "Our jaegers are in the building."

The Kaiser bellowed to Vehemple. "Dutchman, h-halt. I can h-hear my troopers fighting. Why can they not j-j-join me?"

Vehemple turned from the corner of the next intersection. "The *Securité* will have formed a cordon at the level below us. This is a formidable fortress. It will be difficult for your troopers to break through. But never fear, I will arrange for a diversion when we access the office of Doctor Amordule."

"Who is this doctor of the strange name?"

"Amordule? She is in charge of the facility while the *Sarhang* is out of action."

"A woman is in charge?" sneered the Kaiser. "No wonder these *tougrak* are unable to keep us out of their fortress. Hoho, we will see to her now."

"Very well," said Vehemple. "Up these stairs. I have been waiting for my revenge upon this *ersatz* doctor. Quickly, so she does not get wind that we are coming."

Vehemple strode up the stairs, the Kaiser immediately behind him. Teufel hobbled well to their rear, using the railing to haul himself upwards, face ashen and lined with suffering. Behind him the automaton ascended with an unsteady gait, dripping black oil and generating a smell of burnt ozone.

# 10
# The Ecology of Souls

"Can you see me, Codrût?" asked the *Sarhang* calmly, though Kalyenka thought she detected a flustered note in his voice.

"No I cannot," said Ancoulsis, peering back through the chimera lens. "But I have a device to detect any scrying apparatus trained upon me. I am looking up into a flickering mote of light."

"That would be the locus of energies emerging from numinous space," said the *Sarhang*. "But it is curious that we can see you without a host for the chimera lens. That is the doing of Kalyenka, who is with me also."

"Hullo Kalyenka, what an odd way to meet again after all these years," Ancoulsis said. "Have you too become a transubstantiated being?"

Kalyenka laughed. "No. Ancoulsis, I may have aged, but not by hundreds of years. You look hardly different."

Ancoulsis said nothing, but an enigmatic smile played on his lips.

The *Sarhang* interrupted. "So, Codrût. Let us get down to it. I'm sure you are aware we have reached a crucial stage in the attack of the *Ḷimmûm*. Their Skein simulacrum has metastasised, endangering this *Gēttīg* and the cosmic balance of the *khutiverse*."

"Yes Augustine, I am aware that Cockwattle is approaching the completion of his project," said Ancoulsis. "I have taken steps to stop him. You should assist me."

The *Sarhang's* face was impassive. "Are you still set on the course of action I advised you against?"

"You know that I am. Like Kalyenka, I am descended of the Vlach people, close cousins to the Slavs. For too long we have been caught between warring powers, made subservient to their empires.

It is my mission to unite them. Only by establishing a Balkan League will we be strong enough to stand up against the Russians, the Germans, the Hapsburgs and the Turk. And only by working with the idol of Enlil am I able to ensure that this eventuates."

"You are talking about temporal human objectives," the *Sarhang* said, "yet you are using numinous methods which endanger us all. It is a reckless, shortsighted strategy, doomed to failure."

"So you keep telling me," said Ancoulsis. "But all human methods have failed. It is only through the agency of Enlil that the Balkans will be freed. That will establish a new balance of power and prevent the all-consuming continental wars which would otherwise be inevitable."

"No," said the *Sarhang*, with emotion that Kalyenka had not yet heard him employ. "It will guarantee that something worse happens. Quite apart from the cosmic reverberations, on earth you would merely be replacing one set of autocrats with another. Reprising the endless wars that have plagued humanity since Çatal Hüyük. I cannot allow this meddling."

"Which particular meddling are you referring to?" purred Ancoulsis.

"My prognostications indicate you have been intervening in Kalyenka's *apeira*, as well as that of my agent, Lieutenant Colonel Chance and the bandit chief Black George, among others."

Ancoulsis flicked a hand dismissively. "It is true that all three were identified by Enlil as pivotal points in the *khutiverse*. It seems he engineered precise malfunctions in their *apeira*, in order to advance his schedule."

"Yet it is you who enabled Enlil," the *Sarhang* insisted, "by deploying the idol tactically."

Kalyenka slapped a hand on the table. "So it *was* you, Ancoulsis. You who manipulated my *apeira*, all the while posing as my friend. You used me, you used all of us, to advance your schemes?"

Ancoulsis sniffed and reached for a cigar. "Yes Kalyenka, I assisted Enlil with his machinations, in pursuit of a greater good. But as I explained to someone recently, once you have been in contact with the idol, it is always going to have affected your *apeira*, somewhere along the scale. It is your destiny."

"That is the slave dealer's defence," said the *Sarhang*. "You of all people know that destiny is not an accident. You must bend your will towards something in order for it to happen."

Ancoulsis glared fiercely through the lens. "As you also know Augustine, Enlil is following a long-term strategy over tens of thousands of years, eclipsing the petty ambit of human lives. He is using that cosmic viewpoint to outmanoeuvre the *Ḷịmmûm*."

"Oh yes Ancoulsis. I have seen Enlil's work. And I know that meddling in *apeira* leaves a vast rupture in the *khutisphere*, which will be inevitably be filled by the Qliphoth. Is it not true that you personally intervened in the *apeira* of Kalyenka's friend, Vania? Where is she?"

Ancoulsis looked momentarily startled, but his eyes quickly hooded over. He carefully lit his cigar. "Vania is safe, for now at least. She volunteered for a mission and is even now setting about the destruction of Lord Cockwattle, chief of the *Ḷịmmûm*. I am protected by Hermetic means against the dangers of the *Mēnōg* and because of that, Vania is as secure as I can make her in this dangerous business."

He indicated the papers on his desk. "See, I have Vania's manuscript. It is the testimony of her life and that of her mother and as such it functions as a correspondence, a talisman for her soul. Through it I can protect her."

"But Vania disappeared twenty years ago," said Kalyenka. "Where is she?"

Ancoulsis blew out a plume of aromatic smoke and Kalyenka wished for another pipe. He spoke through the fumes. "Here in

Bombay, for now. But for her it has been three months only. She is under the influence of Enlil."

"You have given Vania the idol?" said the *Sarhang*, aghast.

"She has taken possession of it, in order that she might engineer an attack upon Cockwattle."

"That is a grave mistake Ancoulsis. You have endangered her soul as well. As if you had not done enough to Kalyenka and Chance."

Ancoulsis shook his head slowly. "Kalyenka's involvement is an accident of her birth, for which I am sorry. Chance is a professional who entered this scenario willingly. As a result his *apeira* is infected retrospectively. I gave him the idol at Enlil's direction, so that through him it would return to the continuum of Black George."

"So the bandit chieftain is indeed of the same *apeira* as the Karageorge?" said the *Sarhang*.

"He is," said Ancoulsis. "Black George's mother was raped by the Karageorge's brother, an act for which he was executed. Rejected by her family and quite deranged by the atrocity, the woman fled into the mountains and became a whore, eventually the madame of her own brothel. The issue of that rape, a boy, came of age in the brothel, working as a procurer and bodyguard. He was highly intelligent but psychopathic, damaged by various intergenerational traumas as well as the shocking degradations inflicted on him. He killed his mother, known as Fat Ursula, and fled to a life of banditry."

Slowly, deliberately, Ancoulsis poured a glass of water from a carafe on the table and took a sip. "Once affected by the idol the Karageorge's *apeira* was doomed to live on in Black George. Which means the bandit chief has a part to play in Enlil's long term plan. I am merely the actuator of his plan. The corollary is that it enables me to combat the Holy Alliance, which is, you must agree, a mutual goal of ours."

"I do not. Our goals are incompatible," said the *Sarhang*.

"Oh, how precious," said Ancoulsis. "But *dragă mea*, we use the same methods. I know that you have sent Chance along his *apeira,* in order to use the idol to combat the *Lịmmûm*."

"How do you know the whereabouts of Chance?" the *Sarhang* demanded.

"I planted a silver hip flask bearing my coat of arms on King Gustavus' battlefield, when he saved his nation from invasion by the Magyar. Sorcerously charged, it travelled eventually to the inn of the Eagle's Head and thence into Chance's hands. It is a talisman into which I have invested geomantic energies. Through it I have been following his movements."

"Even then, at the battle with the Magyars you betrayed me, Ancoulsis?" said Kalyenka. "When I thought you had come to help?"

"Do not be dramatic Kalyenka. I did the bidding of the idol, just as I stole it from the Karageorge, before his ultimate failure against the Ottoman Turk."

"Did you use a similar strategy on Kossuth?" asked the *Sarhang*.

"Kossuth was a fool. I had to stop him before he sent his armies further afield. If he persevered in his offensive the Russians would have had an excuse to annex Hungary, and they would not have stopped there. Serbia would have been next, then all the Balkan lands would have come under the Tsarist heel. I simply let it be known to certain parties where Kossuth's armies would be. They were seeking battle anyway, and they found it."

"So you did betray us to the Holy Alliance?" said Kalyenka. "That is why they caught us flatfooted at Székelykeresztúr? Oh, you swine Ancoulsis."

"I had no choice," snapped the baron. "It is no more than I did with the Karageorge. He had outlived his usefulness. The idol abandoned him and without it he lost his *khuti* and his nerve. It seems only I can handle the idol."

"Handle the idol?" said the *Sarhang*. "You think to control the correspondence of an entity so powerful that he caused the Great Deluge? So puissant that the other gods could not even look at him? Can you not see Ancoulsis? You have been duped. The idol has used you to transport it around this world, furthering its aims only. It does not care about your Balkan League. That will be destroyed along with everything else, once Enlil's work is done. He is concerned only with defeating Marduk and re-establishing the Earth Entity."

"Also two of your ambitions," said Ancoulsis wryly. He leaned back in his chair and stretched, blowing a languorous river of smoke at the ceiling. "I am aware of Enlil's volatility. But my Hermetic training has taught me how I might harness his powers through the idol, which does not, I might add, represent the fullness of his might, but relies upon humans to move it around the *Gēttīg*."

"You think this to be so," said the *Sarhang*. "But the idol will turn on you when it is ready. Ultimately it is *your* earthly ambition which is driving you. You are only interested in killing Cockwattle because the man owns vast tracts of land in Bulgaria and is monopolising its salt and coal reserves. Is it that you wish to be the King of this Balkan League? To join the *Ljmmûm*? Because in effect you are assisting their schemes - and ultimately their Holy Alliance will destroy your dreams of a Balkan league."

Ancoulsis looked away. "Bah. I harbour no such ambition. I prefer to stay in the background and advise others, for the ultimate good of my people."

"Then you must see the bigger picture," said the *Sarhang*. "Uniting all of humanity against Cockwattle's ilk, so that we might overcome them and re-energise the Earth Entity to face our mutual destiny. Human history is nothing. A mere hundred thousand years. If you place all your cards on an anomaly in the cosmic expanse then you are a fool. Far wiser to put your money on the long-term goal - getting humanity to the stars."

"*Rahat*," snorted Ancoulsis. "That is a fantasy for old men and priests."

"Is it? Why do you think the *Lįmmûm* are trying so hard to stop humanity from throwing off the shackles of priests, kings and tyrants? Because they know humanity is capable of reaching the *Mēnōg*, and when that happens, the *Lįmmûm* won't be boss clown any more. Because they don't have the imagination to see they could be part of something much greater."

Ancoulsis shook his head, fingers twisting his cigar. "If humans are so insignificant, why do the entities of the *Mēnōg* desire so greatly to consume our *khuti*?"

"Because to them your *khuti* is mere food, as grass is to a cow," said the *Sarhang* gently. "Because you have not yet evolved. But I know that you *can* evolve and because I have been human, I care. I don't want you to be mere fodder any more. I want you to join us out here in the *Mēnōg*. Come Ancoulsis, deliver Vania and her manuscript to me. In combination with Kalyenka's painting it will create a formidable conjunction of *khuti* to combat the Skein. It is not Enlil but the arts and emotion, these artefacts of manifest *khuti* that will save us."

Ancoulsis laughed, a short, bitter sound. "Oh Augustine, you enlightened fool. How you pontificate and wheedle. But the arts will not save you. What is important is power, here, now, on this *Gēttīg*. We small, freedom-loving states must unite against the overweening Turks, the Germans and the Austrians, against the colossus of Russia. Our evolution will come through musket and cannon, not through emotional scribblings."

The *Sarhang's* eyes hardened. "You deny the power of emotions Ancoulsis? You who profess to be a sorcerer? Yet cannons, swords and muskets do not make war. It is men whipped into a frenzy of emotion who plunge bayonets into each other's hearts. It is the music of drums and bagpipes, the artistry of patriotic flags, the rhetoric of orators that inflames mass delusions; it is these things that make war."

The *Sarhang* paced the length of the table, hands clenching and unfurling before him. He turned with hands made into fists. Kalyenka had not seen him so passionate. "Your flag-waving will only destroy your cause. Nationalism is a useful notion for fledgling communities; even the name Hungary derives from the *Onogur*, the medieval alliance of nomadic tribes. But it never ends well. Remember that the Epic of Gilgamesh was written as a warning. Has not your dabbling in the arcane arts convinced you that humankind must elevate itself above petty power struggles, if you are to evolve to the *Mēnōg*? We must unite *all* of mankind, otherwise we will be defeated by our base egos, by the *Limmûm*."

"I am not convinced we can be elevated to the *Mēnōg*," said Ancoulsis quietly. "I believe the destiny of mankind is on earth. That science is our only ally."

The *Sarhang* slapped his table. "You who have seen the glory of the *Mēnōg*? Who has used its cogency to advance your cause? Who has grasped the profundity of the ecology of souls?"

"The what? Oh, Augustine. What nonsense are you speaking now?"

The *Sarhang* growled, and Kalyenka eyed him in astonishment. He seemed to have grown in stature and she could feel a visceral power in his voice as he upbraided the Moldavian. "Do not feign ignorance, Ancoulsis. Your Hermetic training has taught you that when humans die their souls pass from the *Gētīg* into the *Mēnōg*. That they join the flow of nature moving towards its better self. That nature is about evolution; from atomic cells through biological metamorphosis to human beings, from there to a point where biology becomes no longer relevant, where we become pure *khuti*.

"The transmissions, the very architecture of nature, these are the souls of our ancestors speaking to us through the veil, the language of the dead made solid. We become what we behold. You have forgotten that this ecology of souls constitutes humanity's place in the divine cosmos."

"I have forgotten nothing," said Ancoulsis and now his voice was ragged and harsh. He relit his cigar. "I prioritise these matters in hierarchies of scientific consequence."

The *Sarhang* leaned forward, as though to pass through the chimera lens and confront Ancoulsis. "You cannot rely on science alone. That ignores emotion, art and intuition. None of these things alone constitute the path for us to tread. Only in synergy can they guide us to the *Mēnōg*."

"What does that even mean, riddler?" snapped Ancoulsis.

"Science seeks to explain arcane knowledge away as mere yearning for something that is beyond reach," said the *Sarhang,* and now he sounded angry. "But science too, is limited. It is useful for understanding mechanistic principles, but it cannot break down and explain emotion, and emotion is the primary experience of being. The universe is constantly in flux, so to depend upon science alone is laughable. You have trodden too far down that path Ancoulsis, and you do not have the navigational equipment."

Ancoulsis stared bleakly into the chimera lens. "You are a fine one to talk, Augustine D'Angel. You have refused your mortality for a place amongst the entities of the *Mēnōg*."

But the *Sarhang's* voice had taken on a strident tone that resonated in Kalyenka's heart with an intense *rasa* sensation and she looked at him in wonder, remembering that this normally mild-mannered man, or rather his eidolon, was actually a transfigured being and something close to her conception of a god.

"Yes, I have taken my place among the dead, Codrût Ancoulsis," he said. "I live through the Veil as though I died a mortal death and became ether through the power of nature. But you, Codrût Ancoulsis, you have become transfixed by locality, by schemes of dominance and power. You have forgotten the timelessness of eternity. But the veil cannot be ignored. I tell you that you cannot deal with Enlil and expect to triumph."

"Thus we come to the same impasse as before," said Ancoulsis, but his voice was faltering, and he did not seem so certain of his troth. "Though we work to similar ends we will never agree on our methods. In the meantime I cannot allow you to compromise my work. I say to you Augustine D'Angel, goodbye. Kalyenka, for your suffering I am sorry. I will look after your friend Vania as best I can. *Zdravo.*"

The chimera lens went blank. Kalyenka looked at the *Sarhang*. His face was grave. After a moment she put a hand on his shoulder. "You tried, Augustine."

One hand stroking his chin, he murmured, "He will come to the Hospice now, to seek to force his case in the tumult of invasion."

"Do you think he would do so, now that he is unmasked?"

"*Because* he is unmasked. Ancoulsis is a dangerous man, Kalyenka. He will cause more harm yet, before he is brought undone."

"How did you know that Ancoulsis was working with Vania?" asked Kalyenka. "We have not seen her in the lens."

"That was guesswork," said the *Sarhang*. "Based on his location in Bombay and the fact that we know she sailed out of Trieste on a southbound cutter, it seemed probable that she was bound for India. Excuse me Kalyenka, I must go back into the *Mēnōg* now, to see how much damage this foolish man has wrought."

He closed his eyes and his face went blank.

Kalyenka turned to her painting. She examined it for some moments before she took up a brush, whereupon she found herself adding a new dimension.

*Chance is foremost in a sea of faces, but the cascading images make it difficult to ascertain what is transpiring.*

*Architectural forms develop, hints of the trans-epochal tropes that make up the Hospice. Huge, unravelling waves of light, a horizon of emotion embroidered beneath immanent stars.*

*She paints the moon, a deeply magenta obsidian oval. Beneath it fester the frantic tribulations of humanity. She recognises the purple city of Chance's vision, even glimpses the Madre peeking from beyond those high walls. She hears a voice; "We are of the same breath, you and I."*

*Vania has entered the painting. She has become reconfigured, stern and fey. Kalyenka sees that she is associated with a sprawling, web-like lattice and thinks of her sobriquet, the Spider. The idol too has changed semblance, transforming fully into the god Enlil, rampaging through the heavens. Kalyenka shivers.*

*The transmissions are almost overwhelming now, arriving as sound and fully realised visions, an experience as intense as the theta waves in the Hospice. Kalyenka sees naked, olive-skinned people in a temple, smells strange incense, hears voices raised in song; the chanting of a choir in a heptatonic Lydian scale.*

Enlil who sits broadly on the white dais,
on the lofty dais,
who perfects the decrees of power, lordship, and princeship,
the earth-gods bow down in fear before him,
the heaven-gods humble themselves before him.

*Her fingers keep working and find resolution; shapes engulfed in fields of colour. As Kalyenka paints in the last notes of an evening sky she realises her work is almost done. A node of bright light forms in the top right hand corner. In the bottom left a knot of darkness which grows exponentially. Symmetry. The painting begins to move and make sense. There is a resolution and light is the key.*

"Wait," said the *Sarhang*. "Something strange is happening."

Startled, Kalyenka turned to him. The *Sarhang's* face was deeply troubled.

"Your painting has almost completed the circuit," he said. "It has activated the *khutiverse* onto an unstoppable trajectory. "

Kalyenka turned back to regard the canvas. "Yes, it seems nigh complete. But there is a new theme emerging which I don't understand."

"It is Ancoulsis," the *Sarhang* said. "His rupturing of the *khutiverse* has made him vulnerable. Somewhere along the line he has been ensnared by Marduk and the Qliphoth have traced us back through the Skein. We are betrayed."

He stared at the painting and Kalyenka heard him gasp.

"Wait," he said. "Your depiction of the Qliphoth is accurate, but in Marduk's silhouette I detect another reality, cloaked by the many guises he has worn. First in Sumeria he was Tutu, then Marduk, the bull-calf of Utu, then to the Hebrews he was Merodak. To the Babylonians he was falsely claimed as the son of Enki, promoted by Nebuchadnezzar I to 'King of the gods, Lord of his Lands', the title previously held by Enlil."

The *Sarhang* paused, listening, and Kalyenka fancied she felt a tremor through the Riemann node. He frowned, indicating a shadowy figure in Kalyenka's painting. "Marduk stole the fifty names of Enlil and usurped Tiamat in Babylon, just as he had done the Bearer of the Lightning. As Ashur he assumed leadership of the Assyrian cults, till their empire was destroyed by the Sea Peoples. As Assaluhi the Incanter he imagined himself out of the minds of men and was dissolved into the ethers. But I see now that this was a trick of the *Lĭmmûm*, and that they bade Marduk wait in the nether regions, till they could use him again to further their diabolical schemes."

The *Sarhang's* voice intensified, reverberating like a hammer clanging on an anvil. "With the Sephiroth held in thrall, the Qliphoth sealed off the axis of Hod and Netzach, denying humanity access to Tiphereth and the glories of the *Mēnōg*. And thus the

*Lịmmûm* triumphed over Nature. In the absence of immanent light they imposed priests and churches on humanity and had a free hand to wage interminable war, leeching off humankind and destroying the earth at their leisure."

Now Kalyenka was certain something was wrong. She felt a shift in the fabric of her work, and though the *Sarhang* kept talking, his words seemed to be coming from far away. "But Marduk waited in the shadows, and I see now he was plotting with the *Lịmmûm* over their greatest conspiracy. What that is I am still not quite able to grasp."

They both stared intently into the painting and it wavered under their gaze, colours billowing as if liquid. Part of Kalyenka's mind could not help but admire the effect. But the entire library quivered underfoot and shelves of books abruptly disappeared.

"My hiding place has been discovered," cried the *Sarhang*. "We are under attack. The Womb of Time has been destroyed. The Chthonic Gates are neutralised and the Citadel left vulnerable. Julie Brown has begun her transubstantiation. Yet if the *Lịmmûm*'s attack is successful she will not become the Cosmic Shekinah."

The Riemann node quivered and the *Sarhang* disappeared. For a moment Kalyenka was staring into an abyss of stars, animated by such dark energy that she fell back, faint. When she opened her eyes the Riemann node was empty. Beyond its curving walls was blackness. Before her the *Sarhang* re-appeared, strobing against a background of white light.

"What is happening Augustine?" cried Kalyenka.

"The Riemann node is falling apart," he whispered. "I am dissolving into data. I must go now, before I cease to exist. I will hope to reassemble myself in the *Mēnōg*."

The *Sarhang* disappeared. Kalyenka was looking into an impossible void. For a second she wished she could paint it. A disquieting sound filled her ears, a whining drone increasing in pitch.

She heard the *Sarhang's* voice above the tumult. "Do not fear. I am sending you to the Centre of the Atom."

"What does that mean?" she said.

"Safety. I have an ally in the metaphysical realm who will assist you, but you will have to travel between worlds. As a mortal you will be affected by random events, blowing you into dangerous *apeiron*. When you arrive in your corporeal body you will remember none of your experience in the Riemann node.

"But you will remember this. In the Hospice you must find Doctor Amordule and tell her she is now at the helm. That she must immediately activate the Cosmic Shekinah. Remember, Kalyenka, Doctor Amordule must activate the Cosmic Shekinah."

"What will become of you?" asked Kalyenka, but the *Sarhang* was no longer there. She was rushing, impossibly fast, down a black tunnel. She heard a roaring sound, then all was silent.

# 11

# The Lady of Damp Shadows

Events were not becoming any clearer in Proko's head. The delirium was persisting, and the *tougrak* castle was so full of bewildering things. Strange pictures full of naked people, statues that wore no hats, nor were of famous men as they ought to be, but instead were just women or nonsense shapes. Trees where none should be, animals staring at him.

Then there were the things happening in his head. It felt like an ogre was in there, banging saucepans together, expanding and shrinking his skull at will, letting all kinds of horrid lights in. It hurt, not like when Black George would clout him over the ears, or when he'd been drinking mountain moonshine and woke in the morning without fresh water and his eyes and tongue swollen to twice their normal size. It was an all-over body hurt, more specifically a brain hurt, Proko's thoughts being damaged, painfully and permanently, one at a time.

Worse, the multitude of anxieties that usually came at him singly were crowding in like church-goers on St Cyril's Day. He was unable to distinguish which of these were real and which were fantasies. Like a dream, only much, much worse, where his father, the local priest and even that bastard Chance were chasing him. Crazy landscapes kept opening up, so vivid that he was lost in them, like the time he got the flu and lay in his grimy pallet for weeks. Nightmares of rolling in grass so nauseatingly soft that he couldn't get out, try as he might.

Then everything would change. One moment he was barrelling through some city, buildings hauntingly empty but full of voices, the next he was crawling through a dank sewer, rats gnawing his ankles. It was terribly exhausting. He would start walking, hoping the hallucinations would fade away, but they stayed with him; Black George standing over him with a knife, Alžbêta whining at him for having never done an honest days work.

Which wasn't true. He had tried to be an honest worker, once. His father-in-law convinced Farmer Ulgo to let him pick olives one season. For a whole morning Proko worked at it, but all the while he was thinking about an opportunity his cousin, Petrov Morlulian had offered.

"There is a certain merchant in the next valley," Petrov confided over a jug of stolen cider one day, as they lounged under a tree in the creek below the Eagle's Nest. "It is well known he has a chest of silver hidden somewhere in his house. And he eats the finest sweetmeats for breakfast. Besides all that he is Armenian and a Jew. Everybody knows it is Christian and proper to rob Jews. They hatch eggs full of devils. It is our sacred duty to intervene in this terrible situation. What we are doing is a crusade, Proko. The Pope would have us sainted, did he know."

That was enough for Proko. He had a great deal of respect for the Pope. He had often suspected they would get along fine, did the Pontiff ever get lost in the mountains and ask Proko for directions home. He would discover that Proko was a fine fellow, full of wit and wise opinion, and would probably ask him to his palace in Rome for dinner.

"Ask me to come and live with him I expect," he said to himself.

"What?" snapped Alžbêta. "Who are you talking about?"

"The Pope," said Proko. "He'd find me a famous fellow, were we to talk, man to man."

But Alžbêta shook her head silently. Proko noted with satisfaction that she did not laugh or mock him. He had educated her not to do that, the last time. She did make him go to work next day though.

Rising before dawn was hard enough at any time, but the sour wine Proko had filched from his neighbours made it all the worse. He gave Alžbêta a lazy backhander when she shook him awake for the third time, but the urgent need to urinate drove him out of bed. When he returned from the front yard he found the door barred against him. Cursing his wife, his children and all the gods roundly, he trudged downhill through freezing blackness to Ulgo's farm, where he had agreed to pick olives.

He kept at it till midday, despite experiencing all the bad luck in the world. He'd forgotten his bottle and so he thirsted. No-one had provided any bread, so his belly roared like a brown bear. His old wound played up in the damp shadows and he could not walk without limping. The sun was too hot and the breeze when it came was too cold.

He looked at the basket of the old woman in the next row. It had three times as many olives in it as Proko's. "Help me out Mother," he said. "Give me some of yours."

"Pick your own, wife beater," she hissed, and when he made as if to strike her, produced a knife from under her shift. "Make it easy for me," she said. "Come closer with your magnificent fighting skills so I can stab you in the dick."

"Devil take this job," Proko yelped, and threw his paltry haul of olives on the ground. He ran to Petrov's dwelling, a tumbledown shack in the woods. "Come, let's visit the Armenian," he said.

And so Proko had entered the profession of thief and mercenary, which he followed through disaster and affliction ever since, abandoning his family to live in caves with Petrov, constantly bullied and humiliated by Black George and his cronies. They revolved around his head in a fever dream now, calling him names till he could not determine whether he was alive or dead and in hell. Petrov was talking to him from the gibbet, maggots crawling out of the hole the rope had torn through his throat and Proko screamed until his own throat was hoarse.

Eventually he just curled up into a ball under a tree and lay there sobbing, while the dreams rolled around in his tired brain. After a while he fell asleep and there seemed to be some peace.

He sat up and was, inexplicably, in a warm, sun-filled meadow. A Lady sat beside him, talking gently. Not like most people spoke to him, as if they were afraid he was going to pick their pocket or borrow some money. Which was a reasonable assumption, but if they left their doors or windows open and money lying around they couldn't blame him for borrowing it.

The Lady was saying things he couldn't quite grasp. She looked somehow familiar, as if she were every woman he had ever known but one in particular, one he should be very wary of. She was sort of like the witch woman he and Petrov had tried to kidnap on Black George's orders, but even more like a picture of a saint he had once seen in a church.

She was kind and patient and that made Proko want to stick her with a knife, but she stared at him with those eyes till he whimpered like a puppy and started to explain that it was everybody else's fault, mostly his father and probably Alžbêta's but the lady just looked at him.

"It's never too late to turn away from evil," she said.

"But how?" Proko whined. "I don't know how. Every time I turn around someone is stopping me from doing good."

"Perhaps you could prevent Black George from any more foul deeds," she suggested. She had such a kindly face and her eyes were such deep pools that Proko found himself wishing he could obey her, and the small part of him that wanted to rob and kill her was being slowly pushed away.

"But he'll murder me, if I raise a hand against him."

That made a lot of sense and Proko was about to repeat it when the Lady gazed at him with extra intensity.

"Do you know, Proko, that your name is derived via an impossibly convoluted continuum loop from an eminent Byzantine man of letters named Procopius, who most famously wrote a scandalous tell-all about his former employer, the Emperor Justinian and his wife the Empress Theodora?"

The Lady's voice was liquid and calm and made Proko want to sleep. But she continued. "Also that your personal *apeira* derives at least in part from this selfsame gentleman? Making you a kind of distant relation and in a way, obliquely at best, of similar endowments?"

Proko found that if he tried to look too closely at the Lady she tended to fade out and disappear. It was more convenient to close his eyes and simply let her talk. "That kind of eminence can be greatness," she said. "But greatness does not derive from eminence. You have been other things in the course of your *apeira,* Proko, lesser and greater things. But surely you must strive to elevate yourself above your present lot?"

Proko could not decipher a quarter of what the Lady was saying but it splashed around in his reptilian cortex and made a few associations, leaving him with the vague concept that he was, however tentatively, connected to something historical and perhaps even important. That it was in his blood. That he was, somehow, rooted in the world and at least implicitly of value.

"Greatness is within us all, Proko," the Lady finished. "The seeds simply need to be tended so they may flourish. Even in death there is greatness, for death is the place we all go, and if we embrace our fate and go happily with it, then greatness is enabled."

While she spoke Proko saw a pattern of evolving images unfold in his head. They came out of nothing but melded together and assumed fantastic, eloquent shapes. In those formations he recognised messages and meaning. He understood somehow that the Lady's voice was creating them, that they were language manifesting in some novel way. They spoke to part of him which didn't require explanations, but just absorbed their crazy notions as reality.

Proko dared to smile. Suddenly he understood that if he was killed in this *tougrak* place it did not matter, for he would be entering something that stretched above him, on and on into the stars, into oblivion. He realised that he was already becoming part of the whole thing, part of the trees and the mountains and the sky, part even of this weird, fabulous, haunted building and that if he could accept that and obey the Lady's wishes then he would no longer be tormented by the pain of just being Proko.

It was an astonishingly simple idea, so absurdly obvious that he laughed out loud. He wanted to hug the Lady now, to tell her he understood. But when he looked for her Proko realised he was alone. The Lady was gone, and for an instant he was struck by a pang of intense sorrow and missed her like a warm blanket on a cold night.

He looked around and saw that he was still in the house of the *tougrak*. For once though, he did not feel beset by constant terror and anxiety. He felt whole, almost happy. He slowly got to his feet and started walking. The buzzing sound was gone, and he felt that he had a mission, though he was not entirely sure what it was.

# 12

## Sweetmeat

Kalyenka emerged into agonised consciousness. She was unable to open her left eye and light smeared painfully through her right. Her head ached abominably and she felt as if her vagina had been hacked apart. She moaned aloud.

From somewhere in front she heard a throaty chuckle. "It's awake," said a thick male voice.

Kalyenka tried to sit up against stabbing pain and a warm rush in her groin. She blinked down at blood, dripping from her naked loins onto the otter skin rug. Harsh male laughter.

"Oho, my beauty. Enjoyed that did you? Want some more?"

Her throbbing head tilted, swollen eye opening. Through the blurring light she could make out two burly men sitting on her couch. One of them, heavily bearded, drinking from an upended bottle of wine. The second, bigger, bald and ugly as a turtle, grinning. "Ready to party again darling?"

"I haven't had a sweetmeat like that since we sacked Krakow," said the beard. "Haw haw."

The third man, the old one in the suit, was gone. So was Hoche for that matter. A wave of nausea and Kalyenka rolled onto her side, hands clawing the darkness. Like animals off a leash her fingers swept under the bed, raking through discarded clothes and bedsheets while she shuddered, trying not to scream. What happened?

She had been in bed with Hoche. He was saying something peculiar when these men burst through the door. She had sprung from the bed, pulling a sheet around her naked body. Glancing back she saw Hoche aloft, searching for a weapon. Then, a flash of light and he was gone - the old man along with him.

It was too strange. Perhaps she was hallucinating. Too much absinthe. She certainly felt unwell. She had evidently been raped and beaten. Her mind felt its way, cold and rational through the pain and fear. Have to deal with these two first. Put the strange things to the back of her mind. Fingers worming through discarded sheets closed on something smooth and hard. Hoche's double-barrelled pistol. Beside it a dagger, and something else.

She lay still, trying to identify what her hands had found. Nothing of hers. Must be Hoche's. Before he disappeared he had been staring down at something in his hands. A figurine, holding something aloft. A lightning bolt? Seeing its face she shuddered, recoiling from those cold entoptic eyes. Her head was spinning, points of light needling through her brain. She cried out. The world turned over and she saw a rush of images - Hoche in a variety of outfits, the latest a blue uniform, very smart, French.

Kalyenka's head spun and she retched. Then she was standing in another place, wearing unfamiliar clothes which a cursory glance found flattering. It was certainly not the livery of any royal family she knew. Was she dreaming now? In any case, why was she wearing a uniform? She was no soldier, nor a domestic.

She was inside a long hall, full of people seated in rows on plush chairs as if they were at the theatre. It was like a train she had once traveled in, only three times as wide, and a lot quieter. Despite the alien decor, like an illustration out of a German periodical, it was an oddly familiar scene. The smell was very different to that of her chambers. Strange chemical odours.

Some of the seated people, all of whom wore extraordinarily recherché outfits, were staring at her expectantly. In her hand was a tray. A silver jug filled with steaming liquid and several smaller vessels. Her sleeves were interestingly clad in an azure cuff, attached to a tight fitted sleeve. Her gaze followed that arm to her bodice, which, like the rest of her, was encased in a not unattractive livery, though the train was indecently short. Dear heavens, her knees were showing.

Then she saw Hoche (why did she think of him as 'Chance'?), sitting by a window, outside of which clouds were racing by. She stared and he was staring at her. A voice came out of her, though she had not willed it. "We are of the same breath, you and I."

The entire space seemed to shudder and drop and her stomach fluttered, but nobody else seemed to notice. Her eyes were drawn to an old man with bulging eyes, standing further along the carriage from Hoche. He had something in his hands and Hoche was leaping out of his seat, lunging at the old man. People were screaming.

But Kalyenka's mind was whirling again and she was in another vision now, walking with Hoche, or Chance, whoever he was, through a mountain valley. He wore different clothes and she was in a scarlet dress, one she was unfamiliar with but she liked the fit and the way it clustered around her thighs. Hoche was talking and though Kalyenka liked the sound of his voice she was preoccupied by the pain in her groin and her own voice asking 'why am I here now?'. In front of them strode a tall, very ugly man. "Vehemple," said her own voice. But who on earth was he?

"She's daydreaming," said an awful voice. "Can't keep her mind off it. Who do you think she fancies more, Chepo? You or me?"

She was back in her chambers in Cristaña, on her knees staring up at the rapists, conscious of her nudity, of the awful pain in her loins. She stood, slowly, painfully. In one hand she held a double-barrelled pistol, in the other the idol. The two men gawped. Chepo, the one with the bottle, took a long, slow drink. The other slowly rose, extending his hands.

"There you go darlin', put it down. We'll take care of ya, never mind."

Despite the pain in her groin she almost smiled. The man's teeth were few and disgustingly brown. She could smell his breath and she shuddered, for she remembered that stench, hot in her face after he knocked her to the ground and forced himself inside her. That reminded her of Hoche, for he had been inside her not long before, but that had been wonderful.

The shot was stunningly loud in the bedroom. She heard birds outside, cawing as they scattered. The rapist's head made an astonishing mess, splashed against the wall and all over the bed. His body fell, heavy and loose onto the carpet, drenching it in blood that mingled with her own. The other man, Chepo, dropped the bottle as Kalyenka turned the pistol towards him. Looking up at it, he grinned.

"Know how to cock that do ya darlin'?"

Chepo's ugly grin vanished as Kalyenka's thumb cocked the other barrel. A flash of her father's smile as she reloaded a shotgun. Behind him she could see a flowering slope of the highlands where he taught her to hunt, after her mother had died. Confusion; that man was not her father. She had never hunted.

But even as she stared at Chepo, finger tightening around the cold trigger, Kalyenka was distracted by another spectacle, appearing complete and entirely real in front of her.

An olive-faced man in spectacles was standing by a table, before a huge painting that pulsated with colour and strife. She clearly recognised it as one of hers. The brushstrokes and predominance of blues in the palette, these were unmistakable. But she could not place the context of the work; a profusion of people in archaic costumes, gruesome slaughter on ancient battlefields and a boil of livid smoke climbing the thighs of a mighty mountain.

"Kalyenka," the olive-faced man said. Behind him was a towering bookshelf, and his expression became urgent. "Look into the painting."

She saw there a confusion of images that gradually resolved and made a story, somewhere deep in her mind. Ancoulsis was in the middle of it all.

She remembered now. It had been Ancoulsis who spoke of the Winter Revolt, when the old king Gustavus had been toppled and his son raised to the throne. Ancoulsis who was at her father's side when the Karageorge ruled Serbia. Ancoulsis who encouraged her to fight again, in Hungary. She saw him now, talking to Vania in Buda. But who was Vania? What Winter Revolt? She had never painted in her life.

And it was Hoche, who also seemed to be Chance, whose dear face kept returning to her. She was Kalyenka, who was also these other women, just as Hoche was Chance. She felt a great yearning as she told him; "*Biz eyni nefesdeyik.*" She said it again. "We are of the same breath, you and I."

Then she was inside the Riemann node, staring at herself staring down the double barrels of a pistol at a man with desolate teeth. The idol glinted in the hand of her other self. Its entoptic eyes shimmered with knowing malice. Kalyenka-in-the-lens looked up.

On the other side of the lens Kalyenka watched herself give an exaggerated wink. She heard the voice of the man with bad teeth, but Kalyenka-in-the lens pulled the trigger. There was a roar, and the chimera lens went blank.

# 13

# The Limits of his Experience

The Caliph followed the *tougrak* soldier into a hall under the mountain. Behind came his janissaries, deprived of muskets but each harbouring a secret blade under their tunics. Strange visions assailed them, demons whispered in their heads, but they kept their eyes fixed on their Caliph and followed.

They passed through the hall, a set of double doors and into a vast chamber. At the further end stood another deputation of *tougrak*, armed with *garip* weapons. The Caliph nodded to his *Izci*, who strode forward and spoke with them. He returned with a disturbed expression.

"Sacred Lord, there is a woman here who says she must speak with you."

"A woman?"

The man looked abashed. "It is passing strange my lord. It seems that she is in a position of authority. Soldiers defer to her orders. They have very powerful weapons."

The Caliph pondered this most unusual situation. It was without precedent in his understanding. Finally he reasoned that since nothing else he had encountered on this expedition had been within the limits of his experience, precedents must be set.

"Very well. Admit this woman to my presence."

The *Izci* fidgeted. "My Lord, the woman dared express the sentiment that you should approach her."

The Caliph glared at this unfortunate fellow. It took him a moment to decide against removing the man's head. Without a word he strode towards the *tougrak*, his soldiers hurrying to keep pace.

The woman stood brazenly at the doorway. She was dark-skinned and her lack of *purdah* oddly disturbing. Behind her stood five of the *tougrak*. Without waiting to be addressed, the woman spoke;

"Good afternoon, Caliph. Welcome to the Hospice of the D'Angels. I am Doctor Amordule. I am afraid I shall have to dispense with any formalities, as this facility is currently under attack and we are on an emergency footing. You have been allowed access to this high-security enclave as the advised ally of an employee of the Hospice. I believe you have made the acquaintance of Lieutenant Colonel Chance?"

The Caliph assessed the strange armour and weaponry of the *tougrak* soldiers. Staring over the woman's head, he sniffed. "Considering the circumstances I will overlook your rash impropriety."

The woman stared at him, seemingly puzzled. The Caliph felt oddly compelled to explain himself. "In addressing my person you have failed to prostrate yourself and beg permission to speak, a crime properly punishable by death."

Doctor Amordule sighed. "Yes, that's all very well and good Caliph, but I am not one of your subjects, nor am I in any way subordinate to your person. Now my good fellow, will you kindly address the matter at hand?"

For a moment the Caliph was speechless. He had never been accosted by anyone, let alone a woman in this manner. She shamed him in front of his soldiers. But he refrained from taking her by the hair and whipping her. Instead he set his jaw and spoke in an offhand manner. "In regards to your impudent question, yes, I have also employed this individual, to assist in overcoming my enemies on the field of battle, not that it is any of your concern. Where is Lieutenant Colonel Chance?"

Apparently unaffected by the Caliph's remonstrations, the woman replied.

"Oh, you do not know either? He has gone missing. He may be preoccupied in the *Mēnōg*. For now, we are following his recommendation in requesting your assistance in a delicate matter. This facility is under attack. Many of our security forces have been killed and it seems that our defence perimeter has been disabled. The Hospice is vulnerable. At this moment we are seeking assistance. Would you, Caliph, be interested in a temporary contract as defender of this facility?"

The Caliph stared. Unused as he was to being addressed by any woman without a *burqua* or other form of traditional modesty, this oddly alluring creature was punishingly frank. Not even his generals or mullahs were this forward.

"Come now Caliph," she said. "We do not have time to dilly dally. If you assist the Hospice in this time of dire need you will of course be amply rewarded. If you prefer not to assist in this matter I will have my men escort you from the premises so we can get on with it."

This was too much. The Caliph's first instinct was to order the woman beheaded. Indeed he had begun to dramatically unsheathe his golden scimitar before he realised his hand was apparently glued to the hilt, which was stuck to both scabbard and belt. He looked around desperately but it seemed that his men too were frozen in place. That infuriatingly attractive woman was staring at him, unabashed. He forced himself to return her gaze. She had such excitingly liquid dark eyes. An excruciating moment passed.

"Assisting you would be my fondest wish," he replied grudgingly.

"Excellent," said Amordule, rolling those eyes. "Now that's settled, if you and your men will kindly follow me. A further detachment of your troops are being admitted to the facility."

Refusing to look at his soldiers, the Caliph stiffly followed Doctor Amordule and her soldiers into a large chamber, where a selection of oddly dressed musicians were packing up their instruments. In the centre of the hall a solid mass of flowered vines extended from floor to ceiling.

Behind him another door opened and more janissaries warily emerged. When they saw their Caliph they cheered. Some forgot themselves and waved daggers in the air, but the *tougrak* made no move to stop them. The Caliph raised his arms and his soldiers subsided.

"Silence my children. We have been chosen by Allah to fight the spawn of Satan, the Teutons and Templars who have ravaged our lands since time immemorial. Our new friends the *tougrak* will issue us with *garip* weapons. Do not fear. They are not in league with Shaitan."

While his men cheered, the Caliph looked in vain for his Mullah. Failing to see him among the janissaries, he realised this was quite a relief and did not pursue the matter. The *tougrak* were issuing strange weapons which his janissaries regarded with trepidation, so the Caliph took one of them up. He watched a *tougrak* instructor fire at a target on a far wall, disintegrating it. The Caliph aimed at another target, destroying it with one burst. His soldiers ululated excitedly, firing into the air.

A *tougrak* officer approached. "Kindly order your men to curtail their enthusiasm."

"*Kesmek!*" shouted the Caliph and there was silence.

"You will respect the wishes of these *tougrak*," he ordered, though he could barely restrain his jubilance. Turning to the officer he spoke in Hungarian. "Tell me, where is the good Doctor?"

"She has gone to take charge of the Hospice's defences. She will brief you further when the immediate danger is passed."

"As god wills it," said the Caliph. "Now, where am I to take my soldiers? They are eager to come to grips with the enemy, for the glory of Allah."

"If you will follow me, I will take you to the infiltration zone."

The Caliph turned to his waiting men.

"Take up the weapons of the *tougrak* and follow me."

Cheering, the janissaries surged forward. But entering the *tougrak* palace, they faltered. Some cried out in anguish, others prayed aloud. The Caliph too felt uncertain. A bewildering disquiet had emerged in his mind. He wondered if he was feverish, or whether he had been poisoned. He turned on the *tougrak* officer. "What is become of me?"

"My apologies," said the officer. "You must be feeling the effects of the theta waves. I am assured they have been dialled down, nonetheless some resonances may be disturbing. "

Indeed they were. The walls of this corridor appeared to be dilating. Some of the Caliph's soldiers were laughing, others had dropped their weapons and wept openly. The Caliph felt an overwhelming emotion - a protective love for his men. It almost unmanned his dignity. He had to restrain himself so as not to hug the nearest soldier, who was favouring him with a beatific grin.

"Soldiers," he said. "My brave, invincible guardians of Turkey, hold fast! We are in the halls of Paradise. But the enemies of Allah are near. Hold fast!"

Despite the exceedingly strange environs and an orchestra of flutes playing in his head, the Caliph pressed forward. Gradually the music and visions abated. He still felt oddly exultant, full of energy and profound optimism. A thousand thoughts jostled for his attention but above all he had the feeling that great things were coming and the bewitching Doctor Amordule was one of them.

He and the *tougrak* officer exited the hallway and found themselves outside in afternoon sunshine on a high rampart, looking down on a mountainous slope. His janissaries disgorged from the building and fanned out across the ramparts of the wall on which he stood. Before them hundreds of Teutonic soldiers, tiny with distance, were charging, firing as they came. Even as he watched he heard the whistle of an incoming shell and a section of wall in front of him exploded.

"Your enemies," said the *tougrak* officer and began firing. The Caliph turned to his men. "Soldiers of the Caliphate!" he shouted. "You are in the sight of Allah! Destroy his enemies!"

Even as he spoke scaling ladders broached the walls and jaegers were firing as they climbed. The Caliph's men straightened their *bork* hats and screamed; "No hero but Ali, no sword but *Zulfikar*! Long Live my Sultan!" They hurled themselves at the invaders.

Amidst that unholy din the Caliph felt all restraint leave him. His sword leapt out of its scabbard into his hands and he howled as he flung himself into the fray.

# 14

# Get a Room

The swirling ethers on the surface of the Murex Moon were disturbed by the arrival of a human form. Chance emerged, warily scanning a luminous, shifting landscape. A shapely ankle materialised beside him, close enough to touch. A scarlet dress appeared above the ankle. Chance stared in disbelief at Kalyenka.

She returned the gaze, gasping, then stepped forward to entwine her arms and one leg around him. They kissed and stepped back, unable to hide their delight, though Kalyenka glanced uncertainly at her bizarre new surroundings.

"This only gets stranger," said Chance.

"Don't try to keep track," she replied. "I just read about you in a history book."

"I just crawled out of bed with you," he said.

"That sounds about right," Kalyenka said. "In Cristaña, in 1797? We had terrific sex, yes?"

Chance coloured. "1797. I was not alive then. Surely these are ..." His voice tailed off and he looked at her uncertainly.

"False memories?" she asked, smiling. "Or intersectional events caused by quantum entanglement?"

Chance gaped.

"Don't worry," she said. "I copped that phrase from the *Sarhang*. I take it to mean we're entwined across several realities through time, which isn't real anyway. The good news is that we have most certainly been intimate in one of them, even if you don't remember it."

"Could it be?" he said. "Could there be, as some scientists have suggested, parallel universes existing contemporaneously with our own?"

"Something like that," yawned Kalyenka. "It seems that idol you're holding has complicated matters enormously, compressing our consciousnesses into consecutive bodies."

"So we're stuck inside a time loop, because of something that happened in the past?" asked Chance.

"Or the future, depending how you look at it. But we definitely have *very* tangled *apeira*."

Chance touched Kalyenka's face, moving closer to her. "Are we even now in our actual bodies, or inhabiting some kind of eidolon? You feel real."

"So do you, my darling."

A third party appeared in the mists, unseen by Chance and Kalyenka.

"Did youse wanna get a room?" laughed Kulan, and they disengaged, only then realising they'd been tightly clasping each other's hands.

"Kulan! Where have you been?" demanded Kalyenka.

"Lost in the *Tjukurrpa*," Kulan said. "Not a bad place to be. Who's the boss for this joint?"

"I am," said a sepulchral voice.

A figure stood before them. Vaguely humanoid, it was composed entirely of shadows, which in the eerie light of the were-moon implied more than they showed. Chance found that looking straight into its nebulous countenance produced a reaction in his mind, something like the hallucinations provoked by the idol of Enlil, only of an alien order, divorced entirely from any notions of human provenance. He shivered.

"Allow me to introduce myself," it said in a voice that sounded like the leathery skin of a long-dead corpse being penetrated by a grave robber's shovel. "I am Aiwass, an entity of this plane. No need to be alarmed," it insisted, as Chance raised the idol. "I am not here to attack you. I am here to parley."

"Where are we and sorry, but what are you?" asked Kalyenka.

"I am also known as Ra Hoor Khuit, the Centre of the Atom, but here in the moon realm I am Khonsu," it hissed. "However at this stage names are immaterial. You are in my domain and I am within my rights to annihilate you, so kindly keep quiet and listen."

"This looks nothing like the moon," said Kalyenka, and the shadows fluttered in agitation.

"This space technically inhabits a quantum phase of the satellite which circles your planet," Aiwass said. "It is intimately connected with the destiny of your Doctor Augustine D'Angel, who propelled you hither just now. Your lover will tell you all about it, provided you survive."

"Why do you not take proper form?" said Chance. "Your current manifestation is a little unnerving."

"There is no point in manifesting my true self, it would only confuse you," snapped Aiwass. "Nor will I take the default position of presenting as some demon out of your storybooks. That would be mere theatrics."

"You a Sephiroth?" asked Kulan.

"Yes," Aiwass said. "I am known to Hermetic practitioners as the emanation of the Neteru on this Murex Moon. But who I am is largely irrelevant. If these two can satisfy themselves that I am a denizen of this plane who wishes to assist in their endeavours, we will be able to get on with it."

"Stand down, Chance," said Kulan gently. "This fella's no feather foot man."

"Why do you wish to assist us?" insisted Chance. "The last creature I encountered here was not so hospitable."

"Do please lower that idol," said Aiwass. "It irritates me. It is no use to you anyway. Enlil has no real power here on my Moon. As to that fraudulent wraith you met earlier - it was a creature of the Qliphoth, not a genuine resident of my plane."

"Can you give me some surety?" asked Chance. "Before I lower the idol I'd like to be certain you're not bilking us."

Aiwass billowed and bulked huge before them. Shadows flickered angrily across his visage. "Why do I wish to parley? We have a mutual goal, it would seem - to rid ourselves of a common enemy. I am referring of course to an *egregore* of evil from your plane. You have been calling them by an Akkadian name - the *Lĭmmûm*, which we have also adopted. We have been dealing with them for thousands of your years."

"These people are your enemies?" asked Chance. "I assumed you were in league with them."

"Not in league, but in thrall. This will take some explaining. Why don't we repair somewhere you might be more comfortable."

Suddenly they were in a sumptuous chamber, lined with unfathomably complex artefacts whose organic moving parts rolled, shifted and sighed. Chance and Kalyenka found themselves nestled on a kind of chaise lounge that might have been made from the carefully preserved hide of some mythological beast. Their nostrils twitched at a pungent, alien scent, pervasive but not unpleasant.

Kulan arranged himself on a fabulously carven armchair, looking around with approval at the walls and fittings, richly fabricated of the same lambent material. "That looks like pure *Xerion*," he muttered.

Aiwass sat before them on a modest throne, now manifesting as an aquiline figure in black robes, face hidden behind a golden mask. When he spoke the voice was rich in timbre, deep as an abyss in the ocean.

"Is that better? I can have refreshments brought in if you require them. No? Very well. Let us not indulge in polite conversation. There are pressing matters to attend to. I will first explain the threats posed by your *Lĭmmûm*. They came to our attention during your Bronze Age. At great expense in *khuti*, expressed through the blood of animals and human sacrifices, Ea Nasir, the High Priest of Gilgamesh created an *egregore* to negotiate with denizens of this realm such as Enlil, Marduk and myself. He promised us the *khuti* worship of human devotees in return for our assistance on the earthly plane.

"Enlil refused him. He had already carved out a role on Earth, appointing himself nature guardian, directly opposed to the *Limmûm*. His war with them began at this time. Like Enlil, I was suspicious of the *Limmûm* from the start. They are mountebanks, confidence tricksters. Their hubris is astonishing, even for humans."

"Why then did you choose to assist them?" asked Chance.

"Marduk convinced me. Ea Nasir and his descendants used standard theurgical practises, rituals based on Solomonic *magik*. Their *egregore* approached us by the requisite channels, satiated our *khuti* requirements. They had the talismans that would protect them, knew the correct correspondences to entice us into trading power for power. It is how these things are done. We agreed to help them and made a contract."

Aiwass sighed. "Yet they appalled me, as most humans do. You are a wholly disagreeable species; fractious, greedy and bullying. Given a perfectly evolved world, you have managed to destroy many of its natural functions and seriously degrade its biological integrity over the course of a few thousand generations. Your worst traits are exacerbated by the *Limmûm*, who exploit your faults in order to dominate you."

"Nonetheless Marduk insisted that we needed the *khuti*, so myself and others enlisted as mercenaries. We appeared as men in battle - albeit men with extraordinary powers - later to be immortalised as the gods and demons of various mythologies. We won battles for the *Limmûm*, established empires, notably that of Gilgamesh."

*Aiwass showed a vision, much like the* Sarhang's *chimera lens, in which, to Kalyenka's chagrin, gigantic warriors in glittering armour slaughtered ranks of mortal soldiers.*

"So you are a friend of the *Lįmmûm* after all?" said Kalyenka.

"Do not interrupt," said Aiwass in a chilling tone. "No. I am of the Sephiroth, and we are entities far removed from your mortal concerns. But there is more. Marduk made a secret deal with the *Lįmmûm*, betraying Enlil, whom he banished from the Earth. But the cunning Enlil wrought a powerful idol in his image and hid it. That gage has endured as the bane of the *Lįmmûm*, creating havoc with their plans."

"Yes we know all about this idol," said Kalyenka. "It has been keeping us most entertained. How long has it been causing trouble on earth?"

"Do not ask me to describe your artificial measurements of *khuti*," snapped Aiwass. "This was a moment ago by my reckoning. It is hard to place events within your system of time - to me your past is synonymous with your future. But I am verging on forbidden territory here. I am not supposed to discuss matters of time and space with humans."

Aiwass extended a golden gauntlet in Chance's direction. "Due in no small part to the idol in your hand, I am making an exception in this case. There is more at stake than giving you clever monkeys a glimpse of the fabric of the universe."

"For Ea Nasir had tricked us also. In the course of our work for the *Lįmmûm* we Sephiroth became addicted to human *khuti*. We found that we could only travel between the planes when the *Lįmmûm* doled out that precious resource. To prevent us from establishing private lines of *khuti* supply with humans, Ea Nasir had scholars rewrite their texts. We became demonised, falsely named as the Qliphoth - The Hinderers, the Smiters, the Painful Movers, the Ravens of Dispersion and even Hod Samael, the Poison of God. This convinced the ignorant that any spirits of the metaphysical realm were their enemy, though it was the *Lįmmûm* who preyed on their children, who kept them in servitude and eternal war."

"Marduk's betrayal established him as chief lieutenant of the *Lịmmûm*. Thus he was able to survive successive empires of men, transfiguring as different gods, first Tutu, then Marduk, later as Ashur of the Assyrians. By your reckoning this was several centuries before the birth of Jesus Christ, a megalomaniac who set himself above all other spirits. Now your *Sarhang* tells me something else about that entity, also about Mohammed, his greatest rival. Something quite profound. The *Sarhang* says he discovered it within your painting."

"You are in contact with the *Sarhang*?" said Kalyenka. "He is alive then?"

Aiwass' eyes sparked like an exploding sun. "Enough to tell me that your painting has revealed Marduk's secret."

"It has?" Kalyenka glanced uneasily at Chance. "But I don't know the secret myself. How could I possibly have painted it?"

*Aiwass invokes a vision of the painting. He focusses on Kalyenka's depiction of the war with the* Lịmmûm *as an enormous game of chess. Upholding the board is Marduk, a many-legged monster with two heads, partially obscured by smoke and flames.*

"The *Sarhang* says the clues lie in the images you invoke. With the power of your *khuti* they resonate in the *Mēnōg*, magnifying reality so they project the true nature of Marduk."

"And that is?"

"Look for yourself."

Kalyenka and Chance examined her work more closely. The smoke shifted and the two heads were revealed to be of dark skinned, bearded men, each exhibiting a blank-eyed stare of Messianic fervour.

"Jesus Christ?" said Kalyenka.

"And the Prophet Mohammed?" said Chance.

"Precisely," said Aiwass. "Marduk and the *Lịmmûm* desired greater control over humanity, that they might elevate themselves into the ranks of the Sephiroth. So Marduk subsumed these two entities and used the *khuti* of their worshippers to increase his powers in *Mēnōg* and *Gēttīg*."

"He what?" said Kalyenka. "Marduk is Jesus Christ and Muhammad? The same creature? But that's impossible, surely. It's not going to be a popular opinion on Earth."

"Nonetheless it is true," said Aiwass. "All the *khuti* of Islamic and Christian worshippers was transferred directly to Marduk. We Sephiroth should have rebelled then, but we had become addicts, dependant on human *khuti*. We were entrapped and forced to assist them. That is how they so completely ensnared humanity into endless war and slavery. Only the far-seeing Enlil was able to subvert their plan."

"Enlil is on our side then?" said Kalyenka. "I'm confused."

"Enlil is on nobody's side," said Aiwass. "Let me explain, impudent human. Upon our betrayal I scried deeper into the *Ljmmûm's* conspiracies. I learned that after they subdue the earth they planned to assault the *Mēnōg*, unable to imagine that this will destroy them too. Finally awake to their diabolical intent, I fled home to my Moon and weaned myself from their *khuti*. They have not been able to assail me since.

"But Marduk had his Qliphoth do the dirty work for the *Ljmmûm*, contriving eternal wars and division on Earth. They created the Black Plague and other afflictions, whereby they drove the peoples of Europe and the East into the cults of Christ and Mohammed, or else into scientific rationalities which abrogate the numinous power of nature."

*A ghastly vision materialises: a sickly cloud engulfing all of Creation. Kalyenka recognises it as the last thing she painted.*

"The *Ljmmûm's* war on nature has found its ultimate expression in this Skein," said Aiwass. "It is the greatest threat to the cosmos, enabling the *Ljmmûm* to infect even the *Mēnōg*. But before they can deploy it properly, they must first introduce it into the *Sarhang's* Hospice."

"Is that possible?" said Kalyenka nervously.

"They have already tried once. I detected a Skein wormhole opening into the Hospice, but shut it off before they were able to enter."

Kalyenka lowered her eyes. The golden mask seemed to be staring into her very soul. "So the *Sarhang's* vision was true," she whispered.

"Yes," said Aiwass, and before Kalyenka blossomed a vision of Earth's future.

*Obese gluttons, blinkered by luxurious technologies, clamour for novel sensations. Their machines process nature into placebos, empty surrogates for* khuti. *Festering societies, sedated with cant, clowns and trinkets tear the earth apart for wealth that does not make them happy, but only leaves them wanting more.*

Kalyenka shuddered. "Why would such people allow the earth to perish under their very eyes?"

*Aiwass conducts a dark symphony; hallucinations of humanity in all its debasement. Unleashing poisons and fumes to annihilate the natural world, even as they beguile themselves with pointless amusements.*

"They are lulled into passivity, indulging in the Skein's simulacra, detached from the reality their bodies inhabit. Under its enchantment they fail to fulfil the quantum pact. Their lives are insulated against the suffering of others. Their understanding of reality has been dulled, the species immersed in a fantasy of its own superiority over nature. Their politics become a lunacy unparalleled, an organised conspiracy for the purposes of maintaining power, with no fidelity to the ideals to which they pay lip service. The Skein only amplifies that madness."

*A corpulent vulgarian appears in the vision, babbling before a rabble of sycophants. Kalyenka knows the man from her painting and sees in him a vicious and ignoble spirit.*

"The *Ḷimmûm* play on this weakness by selecting an incompetent criminal as their leader. Confused by the Skein, gullible humans exalt this mountebank; a soulless, loudmouthed gobshite, if I may use Chance's terminology. He tells improbable lies with such barefaced effrontery that these fools believe anything he says. He exalts a warped construal of Christianity, pitting it against Islam as per the plans of Neocoles and Chederlaomer, as per the blasphemy of Marduk. Thus he grants the *Ḷimmûm* everything they desire and launches their final offensive on the Cosmos. That is the *Ḷimmûm's* plan. Here is how you can defeat it."

Aiwass raised his gilded arm and pointed at Chance. "You must travel along your *apeira* into what you think of as your future, to ensure that the *Ḷimmûm's* plans do not come to fruition."

"How am I to do that?" said Chance. "I don't have any control over my movement through this *Mēnôg*."

"I will send you there," said the wraith.

"And what am I to do when I arrive?" asked Chance.

*Aiwass' vision shows the Tree of Life, just as did the* Sarhang's *chimera lens. Kalyenka recognises that close to Earth, along the axis of Hod and Neztasch is the Qliphoth's obstacle, blocking the* khuti *flow. Chance sees it too, and Kulan nods thoughtfully.*

"Allow me to continue," said Aiwass. "The Qliphoth's blockade has dammed up the *khuti* flow, creating a massive distortion of space-time. Deprived of *khuti*, humanity's very souls begin to break down, enabling the Skein to flourish. The only bridge across that dam is the Cosmic Shekinah, but it cannot be established until this stranglehold is broken. Otherwise the *Ḷimmûm* will hold humanity in thrall, just as they did me and my fellow Sephiroth. To prevent that this blockade must be destroyed."

"I am confused," said Chance. "If they have dammed up the future is that not the end? How can we change the future once they have created it?"

Aiwass sighed. "These humans are very slow. Perhaps you can explain Kulan?"

Kulan chuckled. "No worries Uncle. It's a funny old cosmos, Chance. Your future isn't some fixed, immutable destination. It's the sum of the conscious actions of every human, a shifting point on the four-dimensional *Tuat* map."

He pointed to the idol. "So our deeds in any sphere affect the Cosmos in a four-dimensional wave. In that spirit, if an iteration of Enlil can be physically placed on the Qliphoth's blockade and triggered through the *khutiverse* by an act of Hermetic sorcery, it'll bugger up that *Lịmmûm* mob all down the line."

"I see," said Chance. "Assuming I could get to this blockade, how exactly would the idol perform this miracle?"

"The idol's filled with the force of the god," said Kulan. "Its microcosmic structure is incredibly dense, exerting great mass in the *khutiverse*. Properly triggered it's got the juice to dislodge their blockade, restore the *khuti* flow. But it's gotta be done quick-smart, else the Skein will infect the Hospice."

"Righto," said Chance. "I'm up for it. Will the operation destroy the Skein?"

"No, but it'll jigger the *Lịmmûm*'s plans. Give the *Sarhang* an opportunity to regroup, till he can counter-attack. Most important, it'll allow the Cosmic Shekinah to manifest."

"I assume you're aware the *Lịmmûm* have found the *Sarhang*?" interrupted Kalyenka. "He's had to recalibrate, or something."

"That is why he sent you here," said Aiwass. "It was the correct thing to do. But all is not lost. The *Lịmmûm* have overlooked me in their hubris. As this D'Angel Moon reaches its zenith my strength is replenished. I will assist you to destroy their Skein and oust them from the *Mēnōg*. Now we each have an appointed role in this struggle."

"We do?" said Kalyenka. "What exactly is that?"

"That will become clear as you embark upon your *apeira* once more. Firstly, you must enter the portals yonder."

Kulan, Chance and Kalyenka looked to the far end of the chamber, where the gaping mouths of three tunnels had emerged. They vibrated, howling with powerful energies, the gyres of cosmic engines.

"Do not fear the void," said Aiwass. "Chance, you will be sent to the *Ḷịmmûm* blockade. Kalyenka, you must return to the Hospice, to activate the elemental forces within your painting."

"Elemental forces?"

"Of course," said Aiwass. "They shine through the void like a beacon. Your work has become the focal point of the Hospice defences."

"Oh."

"Kulan, will you linger?" said Aiwass. "We have other matters to discuss."

"*Yuwah.*"

"I won't shake your, er hand," said Chance. "But sure I thank you, Aiwass Khonsu, great Sephiroth."

The spirit nodded, and his eyes flared violet.

Kalyenka embraced Kulan. "Farewell again, my friend."

Kulan grinned. "You'll be right sis. Go hard."

She nodded to Aiwass. "Thank you, er, Aiwass of the Sephiroth. I hope we are worthy of your trust."

The spirit nodded, and his eyes flared violet.

Kalyenka turned to Chance. "*Biz eyni nefesdeyik,*" she said. "We are of the same breath, you and I."

Chance seized her, and they kissed as if this were their last. Then they turned and walked hand in hand to the far end of the chamber, parting with a lingering glance. They entered their respective voids and were swallowed up in the roaring darkness.

# 15

# Dimity Pocket

Bejikereene pursued the bald man and his entourage along the hallway till they disappeared through a sliding metallic door. She had seen the bald man touch a panel beside the door before it opened, so tentatively pushed a red button, expecting him to jump out and attack her. Nothing happened. She touched a blue button but when the door suddenly opened it took her by surprise.

"Mazdā!" she shrieked, grabbing for her weapon, but had the Prussians been there they would have had the drop on her. Bejikereene remembered weapons drill in the forest, when she was ambushed by her father one spring morning. He tapped her nose sombrely. *, Your enemy will not wait for you to be ready* " sufletel. *You will be dead.*"

Bejikereene scowled. She gazed suspiciously through the open door, but the steel-walled chamber remained empty.

"More *tougrak* deviltry," she muttered, and whispered another binding spell. Stepping inside she saw a bewildering array of buttons on the wall. She pushed them at random until a bell chimed, the door slid closed and she felt the chamber move.

"May Ahura Mazdā protect me," she muttered, bracing herself against the wall as her stomach rolled over.

After a few moments the accursed room stopped moving and the door opened on a different corridor. Bejikereene stepped warily onto a grassed floor with tendrils of unidentifiable plants growing up through it. An owl stared at her from a moss-filled nook on the opposite wall. That at least was a good omen.

There was no sign of the ugly bald man or his cronies. Bejikereene turned right and moved cautiously towards an intersection of corridors. Around the corner she heard a man speak plaintively in Bulgarian. "But I have not had any breakfast."

"Forget breakfast, Timotei," said a woman's voice. "We must go on patrol. Before the radio stopped working I was told there are Prussians at large in this section of the compound."

"I thought they had been confined to the lower floors?"

"There has been a confirmed sighting of Vehemple on this level. In company with two suspected Prussians and a probable weaponised automaton."

"*Rahat*," said Timotei. "But think, Crenguta. How do we know where they are if our communications are broken? We had better stay put and build up our strength with some *strandzhanka* and coffee."

"You would do better going on patrol Timotei," said Bejikereene, stepping around the corner, weapon slung over her shoulder, empty hands outstretched before her. "There are Prussians everywhere."

A chubby young man and a taller woman in the same body armour spun around, levelling weapons, faces white with shock. They were standing beside a table in a room full of maps and charts. After a moment the young woman Timotei had called Crenguta said, "Who in *ebasi* are you?"

"An enemy of the bald man - what did you call him, Vemple?"

"Vehemple. The Dutchman. Piece of *câcat*." Crenguta spat. "But wait, how did you get here? How did you come by that weapon?"

"Never mind that, child. I am on your side, I think. I am looking for my husband Olaf. I will be no trouble. But you need to get more people. Those Prussians have shot Boris down in your place of the trains. There are hundreds more of them stuck in the tunnels, trying to get out."

"Boris? Dead?" Crenguta said, her weapon still pointed at Bejikereene. "How do I know you did not kill him?"

"We have no time for this, Crenguta," said Bejikereene. "I did not kill Boris. I know his mother. Do I look like a villain?"

"You look like my grandmother. Tell me of this train full of Prussians. How did you escape them?"

"Do not be cheeky. I shot the buttons and the door closed. They are trapped in the place of the trains."

The young woman stared open-mouthed at Bejikereene. "You trapped the Prussians?"

"Yes, daughter. Let us have enough of this nonsense. Let us instead find your Vehemple. And Timotei, when this is over I will cook you dumplings."

Timotei smiled, but the young woman still did not lower her weapon. "I'm sorry *babushka*, but I cannot allow you to roam freely around the Hospice and Vehemple's laboratory is especially off limits. You will have to surrender that weapon for a start."

Bejikereene stared at Crenguta. Loathe as she was to start a dust-up, she was damned if she was going to hand over her gun. She felt the idol throb against her hip and began a fresh binding spell but was dazzled by a blinding light. She blinked and saw that Timotei and Crenguta had lowered their weapons. They were staring, transfixed into the light, which Bejikereene realised was blazing from the idol's pouch at her hip. She felt the urgent need to say something.

"Have you a key to the place of Vehemple, Crenguta?" she asked. Crenguta took a device from her belt and gave it to her without a word, face blank and incurious. They were like no keys Bejikereene had ever seen, but she accepted them and smiled. "You had better get down to the station and see to these Prussians," she said and Timotei and Crenguta strode silently from the room, in the direction Bejikereene had come from.

"Sorcery," said Bejikereene in disgust, but had to admit that Enlil had so far led her right. She took off in the other direction, following the clear will of the idol. Traversing a long hallway she passed a series of rooms and courtyards, high windows looking out onto the mountains. In the distance she heard shouting and the crash of weapons. Raising her own gun she looked warily for a target but none presented themselves, so continued till she came to a steel door.

There were no buttons this time, not any other apparent method of opening this door. Bejikereene remembered the keys Crenguta surrendered and took them from her dimity pocket. There was no visible keyhole, but she touched them to a panel by the door and it slid obligingly aside.

The air reeked of ozone and smoke. Through acrid fog Bejikereene could see an array of mysterious apparatus and steel topped benches, like the kitchen of a *tougrak* maniac. "Oh no you don't," she muttered, for the idol was stirring restlessly at her hip.

Finger on the trigger of her weapon, she stepped into the room. Sidling past the benches, she gazed suspiciously into a succession of high glass-fronted cabinets, seeing only strangely shaped glass and devices within. In the centre of the room was a double-glazed glass chamber with a huge machine inside. Through its refraction she could dimly see a large body, sprawled on the floor.

Her heart leapt, for she recognised the jerkin she'd knitted. Keeping the weapon trained at eye level she rounded the glass and saw, lying on the ground as if dead, her great lunk of a husband. Not far from him was the broken body of a woman, strewn against a blood spattered wall. Bejikereene tore her gaze from that awful thing.

"Olaf!" she whispered and scurried to kneel at his side. His face was covered in blood and a broken tooth was stuck to his lip. His nose, already smashed in a thousand tavern brawls, was bent all out of shape. She put a hand on his chest and felt a faint heartbeat. He was barely breathing.

"Praise be to Ahura Mazdā," she said. Pulling the haversack from her back, Bejikereene knelt and rummaged, extracting a jar of smelling salts. Wiping away blood with a cloth, she applied the lip of the jar to Olaf's hairy nostrils. His chest heaved and he shuddered.

His eyes opened and fresh blood gushed into his stiff and filthy beard.

"Wake up, you big baby," Bejikereene commanded and slapped him on the cheek. He coughed and stared blearily up at her.

"Here, drink this," she commanded gruffly. She put the flask of rakia to his lips. Olaf gulped involuntarily and his eyes opened wide. Spluttering, he sat up. "Alright, alright," he moaned. "You are killing me with your nurse-maiding."

He looked around in alarm, his gaze taking in the body of the woman, then back to Bejikereene. "Rilka," he said and shook his head, groaning. He put his arms around Bejikereene and buried his face in her neck while she gently rocked him. After a while Olaf pulled away and looked at her. "How did you find me, woman?"

"How did I find you? Ungrateful oaf. Thank you for rescuing me, wife, should ha' bin your first words, but 'how did you find me' is all I get?"

"You are right, my love," wheezed Olaf. "And I'm grateful. That *tougrak* thing near to kilt me with its bare fists. It must have kilt Rilka. Poor lass. I took a piece out o' it though. It was going to kill me, no mistake, but of a sudden it stopped beating me and disappeared. I must ha' swooned, for next thing I know it's you beating me up."

"Ne'er mind that," said Bejikereene. "You can boast about your fighting skills later. Now it's time to get us out of here. This place is all going to hell and we got to get home. There are foreign sojers messing up our village."

"But we can't leave yet," said Olaf, lifting himself up on one elbow. "Mister Chance give me two jobs and neither of 'em is done. I'm to find the witch-lady yet, the one from down mountain."

"Witch lady?" whispered Bejikereene. "Find the witch lady is it?" Her voice rose steadily. "When your own wife is standing in front of you, who you left up on the mountain with thieves and rapists. No sooner have you come down to the house of the *tougrak* with the wife beater, no sooner have I rescued you from their devils than you want to go find the witch lady. I should have listened to my mother when she ..."

"Be calm woman," said Olaf. "There's more at stake here than us or your mother. I'm given to understand that the witch lady is tied up in all this, that saving her hide is gonna count for five of me."

"Calm be buggered!" snapped Bejikereene. "The time for calm was weeks ago, before your foreigner came in and stirred up the hornet's nest. Very well. The sooner we find your precious witch lady then, the sooner we can get gone outta this accursed place. Lead on, great warrior!"

"Wait," cried Olaf, for Bejikereene was dragging him to his feet and he hurt all over. "Wait, before you go bossing me about, tell me how you came to find me, in all this huge and strange castle?"

"Well, if you'd believe it, I was told which way to go by this." Bejikereene extracted the idol from her dimity pocket. Olaf's astonished gaze flitted from her to the idol and back again. "How in Christ's holy blood did you come by that thing?"

"I took it out from under our bed," she said fiercely. "And if I'd a known you kept such a thing under where I slept I'd a boxed your ears for it."

Olaf stared at her, mystified. "But I took it, when I went down mountain with that eegit Proko."

"Don't talk nonsense Olaf. The *tougrak* has addled your brain."

"No, wife, I took it. Gave it back to Chance, the foreign gentleman, just ere he sent me to find this place and blow it up. I know I did woman, so stop shakin' your head. You must have gotten hold of a fake somehow."

Bejikereene snorted. "This thing ain't no fake Olaf. If you'da seen what it could do you wouldn't talk such rubbish."

"What d'ye mean? What does it do?"

Bejikereene looked nervously at Olaf. "Well, it talks to me, for starters."

"Now who's addled?" said Olaf. "No, I confess it, there were voices coming from the statue I held too. But I did me best to ignore 'em. Mind you this whole place, this Hospice as they call it, is mighty queer enough. Talkin' statues ain't nothin' to worry about. But really? How does it talk to you?"

"Well," said Bejikereene. "You know how my ma and da had certain beliefs ..."

"I know they was pagans, and taught you some of their pagan ways." Olaf looked at her suspiciously. "Has you been dabbling in their old magic books or somethin'?"

"Never mind. Just follow me."

"Wait, where are those explosives?"

"What's that underneath you, you lunk of a man?"

"That's a relief. I thought for a moment that mannikin had stole it. Lord knows what it could do with this stuff. Well, I've to do what Mister Chance asked."

"What's that now, ye babbling' fool?"

"Blow this place up."

# 16

# No Paradise

When Chance and Kalyenka vanished back into the *khutiverse*, Aiwass took off his golden mask. Kulan, whose visual capacity remained intact, gazed calmly into a seething vortex, the visage of Aiwass receding into infinity. "I have some information you will be glad of," the Sephiroth spirit said. "I am happy to exchange it in return for some of your data."

"You not gonna humbug me are ya?" said Kulan.

"I have no interest in deceiving you - for the present, anyway. I merely wish to familiarise myself with your *Tjukurrpa* logic and how you plan to proceed. It may be vital information in the battle to come."

"I reckon you woulda turned purple and disappeared if you was lyin'," said Kulan.

"Whatever that means," said Aiwass. "Now, I know you are familiar with traversing the *Mēnōg*. The techniques of your Cleverman training are known to us. Also that you have tried once to destroy the Skein."

"Yeah, I seen that thing," said Kulan. "It resisted Zhāng Sān's quantum missile. Well, the Qliphoth did. Without them the *Lĭmmûm* could never get their Skein into the *Mēnōg*. They hollow men, got no emotion, no spirit in them. My people call 'em *Mamu* - energy vampires. But they powerful, and their Skein is growing."

"Tell me of your mission," said the wight.

"When I was hit by the Qliphoth my entire being fragmented. I was nearly lost. That Skein couldn't hold me though. My spirit broke free into the *Mēnōg*. Slowly, slowly my consciousness reassembled itself."

"Interesting," said the wight. "This Skein seems to lack depth or infrangibility."

"Like its creators," said Kulan. "I retraced my route through familiar constellations back into the *Tjukurrpa*. Found my old Clever-man. He told me I should go deep into *Tjukurrpa*, find the rock and roll. Sometimes I can't understand his story - he talks in riddles. But once I landed back in Tjutatjitji I worked it out pretty quick."

*Kulan summonsed a vision of the Spirit Lights band leaning into their instruments, wielding wild rock and roll grooves. The watching* Anangu *brandished artefacts that glittered with the deadly menace of the Skein.*

"They got different *Tjukurrpa* in there! *Yuwah*! Rock and roll! Deadly. People addicted to' little machines that operate the Skein. Even out in the desert the virus is spreading. But I used the power of my countryman's rock and roll. It's music y'know, but loud. Got that into one of the little machines, drove that music *into* the Skein. Power of the desert, channelled by rock and roll. You know the rest."

"Indubitably," said Aiwass. "The *Limmûm* have not yet detected your stratagem, but it is doing enormous damage to their Skein. Otherwise they would have already overwhelmed the Hospice."

Kulan made a face. "They've always overlooked our *Tjukurrpa*, just as they overlook my *Anangu*. *Tjukurrpa* connects directly to the Earth Entity. Rainbow Serpent, *Yuwah*! Every rock, every mountain, every river, every tree rooted in that entity. *Limmûm* don't know how to deal with that mob."

"I will never understand you humans," said Aiwass. "You disdain the glories of a planet imbued with all the best qualities of the *khutiverse*."

"Steady on," said Kulan. "Don't go confusing those *Limmûm* with my people. They a different species. Their *khuti's* degenerated so much it no longer functions properly. *Ka* can't synch with *Ba*, too much *khaibet*, all that business.

"Fear of divine retribution and the idea of a reward once they die. Keeps 'em worried about their behaviour, starts 'em up praying to gods they invent in their heads, ignoring the Creation god that's right in front of 'em.

*In Kulan's vision priests and politicians pray, celebrating their vast wealth in a church whose dimensions mock the poverty of its audience, watching through simulacrums of the chimera lens.*

"They mistake Yesod for Tiphereth, giving them a false idea of the *Mēnōg*. Lose the streaming power of the divine and the *khuti* cycle stops. Thus isolated, their social identities become paramount and they no longer honour the quantum pact.

"Only in my country where *Anangu* live in the immanent light of the Rainbow Serpent is *Tjukurrpa* preserved. Our culture knows there's no paradise in the after-life. It's in the present, in the natural world. Respect for that concept is our Law. But because we black, because we on the other side of the world, they overlook the power of *Tjukurrpa*."

As Kulan spoke, he cocked his shoulders and his hands moved, making shapes that became apparitions glistening in the *Xerion* chamber. The story came alive, a vision cascading through epochs.

*Red-coated soldiers firing at bands of elusive tribesmen, naked but for ochre markings and long spears that rained down faster than any musket could shoot.*

"They declared our country *terra nullius*, belong to no one. Come in with cannon and muskets against our spears. We fought hard but they used disease and poison to wipe out our peoples. Our great warriors, Pumulwuy, Jandamarra, Bussamarai, Calyute, Dandalli, Eumarrah, Kickerterpollah, Multuggerah, Musquito, Tarerenorer, Truganinni, all their names erased by *Limmûm* who declared there were no frontier wars, no massacres of innocents."

Anangu *women, children and old people herded through bushland by white men on horseback with whips and rifles. Screaming, desperate, holding onto their terrified children, the* Anangu *are driven onto an escarpment and plummet screaming over the edge, onto the rocks below.*

"When only a few scattered tribes were left they rewrote history, said we had no agriculture, no land management - though their explorers witnessed agriculture, towns and dwellings. Took our children from us, destroyed the family connections that bind our culture. Handed them over to Christian priests and orphanages where they were raped, beaten, put to slave labour."

Now Kulan was circling, making spears of his arms.

*His vision shows a land laid waste, trees annihilated, domains divided into vast mathematical allotments. Cities arise and grow, sprouting road networks that worm ever deeper into the land. Rivers fester, dry up. The land burns. The vision follows one road into immeasurable desert where vehicles cluster, soldiers and scientists peering through devices at a point from whence a mighty roaring arises, an eclipsing flare and a pillar of fire and smoke rears over the land.*

"*Maralinga*! That *Lịmmûm* invasion obliterated the quantum pact. Dismantled the fish traps, cut down the forests, poisoned the rivers. Erased our oral history, the songlines that map stories and create the cosmos of our being. Because of that onslaught the Rainbow Serpent has gone deep. It'll take more than the Cosmic Shekinah to wake and restore her to full power."

In response to Kulan's story Aiwass was changing shape, growing, becoming incandescent. His voice became a cipher, music condensed into word.

"I can confirm for you that the colonial Governor Lachlan Macquarie was a Qliphoth - its real name is Shemhamphorash."

*Kulan sees a giant arachnid with three heads; that of a bullfrog on the left and a tomcat frowning on the right. On its central head is the countenance of a dispossessed Duke. But it casts a glamour over the*

*English invaders, so they perceive it as an army officer in a powdered wig.*

"It was hired by the English to wipe your people out. But it failed, and their survival is testament to your deep-rooted power. There is more. Shemhamphorash scried across the continent to locate the *Tjuringa* stones."

"*Tjuringa?*" said Kulan. "Our sacred talismans, corresponding to entities under venerated waterholes and mountains. They went missing during the *Ljmmûm* invasion."

"So I believe," said Aiwass. "After locating several *Tjuringa*, Shemhamphorash travelled to the centre of the continent. Disguised itself as a Clever-man and tricked another into showing where the most sacred stone was buried."

"Serpent *Tjuringa?*" said Kulan, aghast. "That's the key to awakening the Rainbow Serpent."

"Yes," said Aiwass. "Shemhamphorash stole it and sailed away, presented it to the *Ljmmûm* in England."

Kulan grimaced. One foot stamped and his dance was stilled. "Gammon. That's why they were able to defeat us. Without it we will not be able to awaken the Serpent."

"Never doubt Kulan," said Aiwass. "Now I can deliver my tidings."

The Sephiroth floated across his *Xerion* chamber. It lost all dimension, becoming depthless amaranthine. "While still in the *Ljmmûm's* employ I visited their domain and retrieved the *Tjuringa*. Now I have it here."

Kulan too was levitating, surrounded by waves of light. "You got that Serpent *Tjuringa*? Deadly. Show me."

Aiwass made a gesture and a monolith appeared, hovering between them. Made of primordial stone, it was cylindrical, tapered at both ends. Into it were carved patterns and shapes suggestive of organic processes, at its thinner extremity was sculpted a serpent.

Kulan clapped his hands together slowly. His bracelets jingled, even in this rarefied atmosphere. "*Yuwah*," he breathed. "*Tjukurrpa katutja ngarantja.*"

Aiwass' luminous eyes focussed. "That is the correct *Tjuringa*?"

"*Yuwah.*"

"You are equipped then."

Kulan nodded slowly. "Now I must go deep, to ensure that the Serpent hears the call and answers."

"Happy hunting," said Aiwass.

"*Yuwah.*"

As the spirit watched Kulan began performing a ritual dance, feet stamping down from bent knees. He chanted as he moved and a gyre of energy formed around him. Aiwass's golden chamber disappeared and Kulan left the vapours of his magenta moon.

He sang out loud, enacting processes of quantum mechanics on his energetic being. He reentered his *Tjukurrpa,* dancing in a whirling cosmos, surrounded by exultant spirits.

Now Kulan stood before a campfire in a desert landscape, under stars drizzling through luminous sky. The *Tjuringa* was there, lower half embedded in the soil, upper half standing tall, the serpent glinting in starlight. An old woman sat across the campfire, weaving a basket with plaits of bark and plant fibre.

"Hello Aunty," he said and the woman nodded, not looking up from her work. Out the corner of his eyes Kulan could see various entities watching. He recognised ancestors with his mother's face, remembered from long ago.

Eventually the old woman looked up from under bushy eyebrows. "You sure been gettin' around, Kulan Pulnyuu. You one flash mob smartypants."

"Learnin', Aunty," Kulan said. "Learnin' proper way. But those feather-foot men out of control now see? Reckon they big mob enough to take on all the planet and the *Tjukurrpa* too."

"Gammon," she said. "No hope." She cocked an eye at the *Tjuringa*.

"You found my old stone eh? Good job. That feather-foot man come here thievin', bugger it up for everybody, now the shoe on the other foot, eh? Well, suppose I better do somethin' about this mob. Can't have 'em stuffin' everythin' up for everyone else. They done enough trouble already y'know?"

"*Yuwah*," said Kulan. "*Palya, palya.*"

The old woman stood up on creaky legs and put her weaving down on a nearby log. She raised her eyes and began chanting in a language too ancient for even Kulan to recognise. Her voice took on a high keening note and light streamed from her eyes. She raised her arms and sang and in her place was a pillar of fire with the sinuosity of a snake that roared upwards into the constellations. The stars turned blue and vanished.

"*Yuwah*," said Kulan. "*Palya, palya.*"

# 17

# Juche

*"Mabsosa!"* shrieked Bo-Bae. *"Geumanhae I saekkideul-a!"*

She'd just seen a red-jacketed youth run ahead of hundreds of others and push over an elderly man, in the grounds of her high school.

The campus at Kyungbock High was commonly used as a polling place for presidential elections, but it had never before seen such a tumultuous event. Bo-Bae watched with horror as two seething mobs faced off in the concourse, separated by police wearing body armour, wielding shields and long black truncheons.

Red-jacketed People Power Party supporters, mostly young men, were clashing with older Democratic Party people, who'd been forced out of the polling area. Ten people had been dispatched to Hae Jeong Hospital after sustaining injuries from the melee. Ambulances sat waiting outside the school grounds.

A police guard was posted on the long line to the polling station. Reporters from *Hankyoreh* and the three *Chojoongdong* right-wing newspapers were speaking urgently to camera. Photographers were snapping voters, most of whom cowered away or covered their faces with umbrellas.

The school had only recently become a mixed gender campus and that decision was controversial enough, network reporters embarrassing parents who came to collect female students after classes. Their attempts to avoid interviews had been lampooned by conservative veebloggers and one young girl committed suicide after being singled out by Lee-yong-jion, the most notorious of these firebrands.

But the national election made the school a focal point for hostilities, inflamed by extremists who'd infiltrated the school board and openly vilified DP members. Bo-Bae's parents were among them. Her father had been outed by Lee-yong-jion and punched in the face that day.

Bo-Bae was not old enough to vote, so she stood with her friends from Cinnamon Girls behind the boxwood hedge the police were using as a cordon. She watched fearfully as PPP thugs surrounded the blue banners of the DP. Brandishing a megaphone, a tall, heavily acned teenager in an outsized suit was braying hateful slogans; "When *kkondae* tell you be good, watch out for a dragon in the trees."

*KKondae,* what Westerners called a 'boomer', was what Lee-yong-jion called Bo-Bae's father on his veeblog rant. Bo-Bae thought it better described conservative men who voted PPP.

Her mother and father were active in the Candlelit Revolution of the early 2000's, which impeached a corrupt President. But their values were regarded as obsolete by a PPP generation obsessed with plastic surgery, gaming, urban slang and hairstyles.

They'd formed militia gangs, sworn to terrorise DP supporters and enforce an upbeat brand of xenophobia. The police seemed powerless or unwilling to prevent them from forcing older people out of the school grounds altogether.

"Are your parents in there?" Bo-Bae asked Iseul, her tall, geeky friend whose braces made her lisp. "No, they went home after voting," said Iseul, eyes downcast. "Your father was very brave," she said. "But I think you will have troubles at school now."

"Yes," Bo-Bae agreed. "I'm afraid I will lose grades. My head teacher is a totally pilled PPP *seondongja.*"

She looked around for Bitgaram. Having turned eighteen that month, her brother had voted earlier, but she could not see him now. He must have scurried off. Not surprising. He was a target for the senior boys with his long hair, nose piercing and black metal regalia.

Though he'd been expelled from school for fighting he didn't regard it as shameful, but wore it as a badge of honour in metalhead circles.

"I have to go now Iseul," Bo-Bae said. "My father didn't want me to witness these awful scenes."

Iseul bowed. "I'm going too. As soon as I finish my maths assignment I'll send Cinnamon Girls' hashtags."

"Thank you. It's important we pressure the government not to suppress free speech platforms."

Bo-Bae rode her bicycle home through the busy streets of Jongno-gu. PPP supporters seemed to be everywhere, chanting their awful slogan, "*Myulgong!*" or "Crush Communism!" Her father told her this phrase came from the Korean War but was revived by the current President as a pejorative against anyone with left-leaning tendencies.

As Bo-Bae turned off the main road in Muak-dong to pedal uphill to the family's apartment block, she heard a voice shout "*Myulgong!*". Coming towards her was a gang of teenage boys in suits with red ties. They surrounded her, jeering. One of them grabbed her handlebars and she instinctively poked him in the eye with her index finger. He shrieked and fell. In the confusion Bo-Bae screamed "*Juche!*" and pushed the bike forward, the front tyre running over someone's foot. Then she was past them and pedalling hard. "Communist bitch!" one of them shouted and a stone bounced off the back of her head.

Bo-Bae pedalled furiously till she got home. Holding back tears, she locked her bike in the basement and took the elevator up to the third floor. Finally safe in her bedroom, she lay on the bed and cried, shaking, for ten minutes.

When she'd recovered somewhat, the first thing she did was open her eyetop and log into the Cinnamon Girls' Honk account. Some PPP troll had repeatedly honked '*Myulgong*' on their home page. Inspired by her involuntary use of the term '*Juche*', Bo-Bae decided a fitting response would be to honk it. Originally a Japanese word for a divine entity attached to a particular environment, South Korean leftists adopted *'Juche'* ironically as a reference to conservatives' love of their US allies.

She eye-typed the single word, *'Juche'*.

Blowing her nose on a vintage Pororo the Little Penguin handkerchief, she closed Honk and opened an OhmyNews stream to watch their election report. To her surprise she saw Jae-Won speaking to camera. Bo-Bae knew her friend posted stories to the network as a citizen reporter, but it seemed weird listening to her familiar voice broadcasting to millions.

"Since the Tangerine Believers disrupted the last US election with new voter suppression laws, an election which their Republican Party controversially won, it's become the model for autocratic governments. The PPP won the last election under highly controversial circumstances. Voter intimidation and suspect handling of optical scanner machines placed their win under a cloud of suspicion, which was in no way allayed by the conviction of two National Assembly members on fraud charges over an illegal land development in Bukhansan National Park."

Bo-Bae thought Jae-Won looked very sophisticated on camera. Her friend refused to have the plastic surgery that most other reporters and many Cinnamon Girls regarded as necessary to get on in life. Nor was she afraid to be politically outspoken, though in these conservative times that was a risky business. It was that disregard for convention which had driven Jae-Won to a successful career and inspired Bo-Bae to follow her. Now she was set on an activist's path, reasoning there was no point in working towards a career if the political mindset of the country meant she was doomed to fail.

She couldn't claim Cinnamon Girls had singlehandedly stopped the American OMNI platform from taking over Korea's internet, but they'd started a media scrum which snowballed into a storm of outrage. Right wing newspapers certainly blamed the K-Pop Stans for the failed coup. The government had not dared interfere before the election but if they were returned to power, snuffing out Korean internet in favour of the American brand would probably be their first action.

Bo-Bae felt a twinge of jealousy that Jae-Won remained so calm as she looked into camera and spoke over the shouting on the high school concourse.

"This is the first time the PPP have been in charge of an election after the imposition of their new laws, which are widely seen as voter suppression." Jae Won stepped back, panning her retinal camera over seething PPP supporters. "Their new optical scanners were manufactured by a company owned by the incumbent finance minister. The party is heavily influenced by factions from the Christian Right which owe direct allegiance to the American Republican Party."

"The PPP vowed to curtail the political effectiveness of K-pop Stans. These fan groups have received criticism for influencing elections, though most of their members are not old enough to vote."

Jae-Won showed helmeted police advancing on DP protesters. "Riot Police from Seoul's Special Operations Unit 868 have been called in to quell the violence at the Kyongbuck High School polling station. Their chief, Superintendent Gwan says the policemen are trained in anti-terrorism tactics."

The screen focused on a policeman's face, framed by gold epaulettes and large sunglasses. "We are responding to acts of terrorism from Democratic Party supporters," he said.

Jae-Won's eye-cam targeted a red-shirted youth screaming obscenities. "But I have been here all day," she said. "I haven't observed any aggression from the people wearing blue."

The policeman looked stern; "Twenty people have been hospitalised following the aggression of hostile elements. We have been forced to arrest five people."

"All the people hospitalised have been DP supporters," Jae-Won retorted, but the policeman put his hand up and the shot switched back to Jae-Won's face.

"We have to ask; who are the terrorists?" she said. "The supporters of the PPP have been belligerent in word and deed at Kyonbuck. Veeblog commentator Lee-yong-jion recorded an episode encouraging PPP supporters to chant aggressive slogans and burn an effigy of the DP candidate."

Bo-Bae closed her feed. Hearing her mother and father described as terrorists made her feel sick. It had been an awful day and she wished it would end. But she had a lot of study to do and a revision class that evening. The national college entrance exam was very soon and she had both school and night academy assignments to finish, before it came time to apply for university or an internship.

She heard the front door open and close. It must be Bitgaram coming home. Bo-Bae had changed into her favourite Japanese kimono, but put on a Doosan Bears cap to go out into the hall. Bitgaram was leaning inside the open fridge door. He stood up as Bo-Bae entered the kitchen and she could see he was concealing something in his jacket.

Bitgaram flicked back his hair as if he were at a black metal concert. She knew by his expression he was in a good mood.

"What's that in your jacket?" she asked. A sly grin came over Bitgaram's face and his free hand waved a pickled cucumber, dripping juice onto the kitchen floor. He took a bite. "Just a sick bit of tech I picked up in Yongsan Market."

"Show me."

Bitgaram devoured the last of the pickle, shutting the fridge door. He pulled out a black oblong wrapped in plastic, which Bo-Bae recognised as a computer motherboard with conspicuously large power stages. Her eyes widened. "Is that a Tsunami Z-9000?"

Bitgaram smiled. He had changed over the last months. He still wore his death metal gear and nose ring but had become less sullen and self-absorbed. After he'd reprogrammed the IT systems of Bo-Bae's employer Jeobchog, Cinnamon Girls were able to bombard social media with hashtags. They exonerated their favourite singer Choi of the nasty deeds claimed by her former boyfriend, Roxoq, who publicly apologised. After that, Jeobchogs techs traced the hacking back to Bitgaram. But instead of getting the police involved, they'd offered him a job.

He was back into gaming now, but from an entirely different perspective. His new job was designing games and player testing. Bitgaram was making lots of money and hinted he was working on a new gaming platform that could be used for other, more political purposes.

Even stranger, Bitgaram and Jae-Won had developed a special friendship. Bitgaram's responsibilities and romantic interest in Jae-Won seemed to spark a new kind of ambition. Rather than obsessive gaming and gambling he was using any time off to pursue his new hobby - taking down the PPP.

"Better," Bitgaram grinned. "It's a modded Z-10,000. You can't get these off the shelf. It's a special build done by a friend of a friend."

He'd joined Let's Go!, an environmental lobby group opposed to the devastating development policies of the PPP. Instead of a poster for *Dark Mirror Ov Tragedy* on his bedroom door there was one featuring dolphins and whales swimming by a coral reef.

As if that wasn't strange enough he was even listening to TUFF AF, a fringe K-hip-hop group, whose political raps got them banned from mainstream veeblogs. Bo-Bae had reluctantly accepted the new dynamic between Jae-Won and her brother and if it meant Bitgaram developed a social conscience, she could put up with that.

"An analog motherboard? Pretty old-school," said Bo-Bae. "Why don't you just use the cloud?"

"The Americans *own* the cloud," sneered Bitgaram. "Nothing is safe from their techs if you can't keep it in your pocket."

"Oh."

"Yeah," he said. "I know 'cos I've hacked the PPP in the cloud and found anomalies in their voter scanning system. They *are* cheating, just like we thought. We've sent the evidence to the National Election Commission but the *Chojoongdong* are pressuring them not to release anything. As soon as your exams are finished you should mobilise Cinnamon Girls again."

Bo-Bae slapped the fridge in frustration. "But hashtags and fan-cams won't stop them this time. If the PPP win office again, that's bad enough. If they get a majority in the National Assembly it'll be disastrous for social justice, for equality, for the arts. Their speech discrimination laws will make it illegal for Stans to exert any influence on social media. They'll bring us under the thumb of the Tangerine Believers and cancel our internet. There's only one way to stop them. Total war."

Bitgaram's eyes gleamed. He tapped the motherboard.

"Total war is exactly what I got this for. I've designed an entirely new system with the functionality of a game. Jeobchog's server gives me the bandwidth and processing power to hack the American internet and run my game in it. Now you Cinnamon Girls can hit them with hashtags or whatever. If you get the other Stans to pile in we'll have the metaversal force to influence public opinion against the Tangerine Believers and the PPP and force them to overturn this new law. We may be able to win the election after all."

"But don't they have complex security?" said Bo-Bae. "How did you hack their system so quickly?"

Bitgaram rolled his eyes. "Gaming skills, duh. Their algorithms are based on the conspiracy theories of the Tangerine Believers. This makes them predictable. There's no art or imagination and their understanding of situation dynamics is based on Hollywood action movies. Easy meat."

Two nights later Bitgaram knocked on Bo-Bae's door while she was studying for a maths exam. He came in and sat on the floor, crossing his legs awkwardly in the narrow room.

"What do you want Bitgaram? I've got lots of study to do."

Her brother was silent, scowling down at the floor.

"Bitgaram! What is it? Are you gambling again?"

He looked up through his freshly washed fringe. "No! No, it's not that. There's something strange going on."

"What?"

"I can't explain it. I think some weird virus has invaded my hack. The gaming space I tied in with the Tangerine Believers website has been populated by a bizarre graphic landscape. It's like some surreal painting, but coded so powerfully I can't delete it."

Bo-Bae closed her laptop. She needed a break anyway. "What's it doing? Will it boot you out of the programme?"

"No. That's the thing. It actually seems to be helping me. Autonomous characters from the painting have inserted themselves into the game. At first I thought I thought they must be PPP bots, but they're actually replacing the Tangerine Believers' algorithms with their own weird strategies."

Bo-Bae shivered. "I'm not sure what you're talking about, but it sounds scary."

"That's not all. I'm getting these transmissions as I design the game. At first I thought it was my own imagination but lately I'm not so sure. I keep hearing voices, sometimes singing crazy songs. Mostly it's one man, making suggestions as to how I can streamline my coding. The weird thing is he's always right. Either I've regressed along the Hallucination Scale or the system's been hacked by some very clever, very weird gamers and they're fucking with me."

Bo-Bae clapped her hands. "That's fantastic news Bitgaram. I think. Maybe this guy is an activist who's on our side."

"What if it's the cops, stringing me along?"

"Then they've already got you. May as well play along and see where it leads."

"I guess. If I go to jail can you tell Jae-Wong I love her?"

"Gross."

By next morning Bo-Bae had forgotten all about Bitgaram's foreboding. She had a tough exam and afterwards was too drained even to get online and post for Cinnamon Girls. That night Bitgaram knocked on her door again.

His face was alight. "I've been contacted by that man again. He requested access to the server, allowing for new players to enter the gaming space. These are characters I haven't seen before. They're like historical figures from Europe or some place. But I've given them access and now your Cinnamon Girl hashtags are having an impact on election polls. In return the man asked me to assist him with another piece of coding."

Bitgaram looked at Bo-Bae. He seemed oddly exhilarated.

"Are you sure you're not gambling?" she said.

"Yes! *Kkeo jyeo!* I told you what's happening. It's weird, but it seems cool."

"Then I think you should go with it. Have you told Jae-Won?"

"Yeah, she said the same thing."

"Then you know what to do."

Before she left for night school Bo-Bae opened Honk. She was astonished to see her '*Juche*' honk had generated eight hundred and fifty-three thousand likes.

# 18

# Mansplaining

Chance stood in a bleak, barren landscape. Frenzied flies assailed him, seeking entry to mouth, nostrils and eyes. The sky roiled with ragged clouds of dust, whipped by a merciless wind, tormented by an unblinking sun. No bird graced the heavens and he wished for his cabbage tree hat, lost somewhere in the Hospice.

"Hotter than the plains of Sri Ganganagar," he muttered.

Shading his eyes with one hand, he peered at a vastness unrelieved by trees or natural features. It appeared to have been levelled by some giant hand, or perhaps an explosion. But the roar of mighty engines shuddered the air and he realised that to his right was an echoing abyss. Indeed, he now recognised he was standing before a crater stretching to the distant horizon. Below him, within the radius of that chasm, machines made tiny by distance scraped and clawed at the black rock, that shimmered and broiled as if melting in the infernal heat.

"Sure it's a coal mine," he thought. "An open-cut mine on a scale undreamt of. This must be some far advanced future. Those machines are gigantic. The engines burn some volatile liquid, to judge by the fumes."

Some twenty yards away, on the lip of the crater, a gantry towered overhead. Chance turned towards it. But from the other direction two men were approaching on foot. They wore lurid vests labelled *Security*. "Another one of them fucken ferals," drawled one as they came closer. "How'd you get in here, dickhead?"

"Looks like he's escaped from the nuthouse," said the other. "Hang on, they all do." Both guffawed and looked at Chance as though they might decide to fight him.

Chance ignored them. Striding to the gantry, he seized the scalding rung of a ladder and climbed rapidly, wincing at the pain in his shoulder. Curiously, he felt free of cravings, though he hadn't had a shot in several hours. Perhaps it's all this four-dimensional travel, he mused.

Ignoring abuse from the buffoons, he clambered to the top of the structure. Someone was there before him.

On a platform bristling with machinery sat a young woman, manacled to it by a U-shaped metal device encompassing her wrists. She wore loose-fitting clothes, combat boots and a ring through her nose. Chance remembered this as an adornment favoured by Tamil women of the Indian sub-continent.

"Pardon me, but that *mookkuthi* is in your left nostril - don't Tamils prefer the right?" he said, wiping sweat from his eyes.

"What?" the woman said. "Are you mansplaining my nose-ring? Jesus, boomer, get over it."

"Are you an advocate of Ayurvedic medicine?" he asked.

"What? No."

"A Hindi then?"

"No, I believe in Gaia, spirit of the Earth."

Chance frowned. "But is the nose ring not a devotional adornment in honour of Parvati? Are you married?"

The woman waved away flies. "No, I'm not married. What about you? Are you a plainclothes cop in fancy dress?"

"Fancy dress?" he asked, bemused. He looked down at his fatigues, quite drenched in sweat now. "Yes, I see. That is, no, I am merely a soldier on the most extraordinary mission of my career. Forgive me. I am Lieutenant Colonel Sebastian Lafayette Chance, retired. And yourself? Sure now, your clothes match the robes of Bengali nobility with Slavic peasant costume. But you have the fair skin and features of the European bourgeoisie. Most intriguing. Who, may I ask, are you?"

"Ok, Sebastian Lafayette Chance," said the woman. "I'm a citizen protestor, engaged in non-violent direct action against the Mahari mine, which scientific consensus has proven to be a direct threat to the Great Artesian Basin and a major contributor to climate change. And I'm not telling you my name."

"Away with ye. You're a 'protester'?" asked Chance, unbuttoning his collar. "Do you protest as a profession or a religious devotion? Or do you mean you are of the Protestant faith?"

"Christ," said the woman. "I'm protesting the construction of this planet-destroying coal mine. This is a non-violent direct action to stop work destructive to native flora and fauna, a threat to the Artesian Basin and a major contributor to climate change."

"I suppose you could call me a protestor too then," said Chance. He wiped the back of his neck with a kerchief. "I've come here to enact my own little action, though I don't know that it will be 'non-violent.'"

The woman eyed him dubiously. "What are you gonna do?"

"I'm not actually certain," Chance grinned. "That is, I have a rather powerful item on my person, which I'm not entirely sure what to do with. I'm hoping that friends of mine in another, er, location are going to be able to assist me to ... well I'm not exactly sure what they are going to do either, but I'm hoping it will be spectacular. I'm sure you must be thinking I'm quite insane."

The woman looked at Chance as though she were certain of it. "What is this object?" she asked carefully. "Some kind of wifi operated drone? A bomb?"

"I must confess I don't understand your parlance," said Chance. "But I assure you it is not a bomb. It is an object, or rather a phenomenon quite outside your experience, just as this future is quite outside mine. Please, can you tell me, where exactly are we?"

"You kidding me?" she said. "You don't know where you are? Have you just teleported down from outer space?"

"Something like that, yes."

The woman gestured with her free hand at the furnace shimmering before them. "Lolz. Well Mister Chance, like me you're an illegal trespasser in the Galilee Basin in Queensland, Australia in August, 2025, on the site of the world's largest planet-destroying coal mine. The carbon output of this mine alone is enough to blow out Australia's carbon budget and pump enough $CO_2$ into the atmosphere to massively accelerate climate breakdown."

"I see. That makes a lot of sense. So this is the work of the *Ḻimmûm*?"

"The *Ḻimmûm*? Sorry, I don't know who they are. No, it's Mahari, Embalmer and Grindsoul, abetted by the Coalition Government, as corrupt a bunch of scumbags as you'll ever see outside prison."

"I see. And this thing you are chained to is the epicentre of the mine? The heart of their operation?"

"Fuck a duck," snorted the woman. "Yes. This machine is essential to their mine, Professor Smartpants. But they won't be able to work today following legal protocols, 'cos I've got it locked down. I've been here since three am, when I snuck past their security. Sooty and Scotty and Rilka got busted but the cops missed me. I called them ten minutes ago to tell them I was here. They'll be out soon to cut me off and take me to jail."

Chance nodded. He was unused to profanity from young women but supposed he should not judge the mores of future folk. "Very good," he said. "This seems the very place to deploy the idol. Perhaps we should move further away. I'm not entirely sure what is going to happen, whether it will be safe to be around when Enlil, the, er, Bearer of the Lightning makes his appearance."

"Who's Enlil?" the woman demanded. "We only need one bunny up here and I'm not locking off. Are you sure you're not just a cosplaying cop trying to trick me out of this?"

"Quite sure," said Chance. "I am, however, about to activate a potentially harmful device and I'd hate for you to be hurt by it."

"So it *is* a bomb? Jesus, are you a terrorist? An incel or something?"

"Terrorist? No, I'm a soldier. Well, I used to be. Currently on mission for the *Idi Nadi*, otherwise known as the Pale Conduit."

Blinking sweat from her eyes, the woman peered warily at Chance. "Yeah, whatevs. I think you've forgotten to take your meds mate. Anyway, I'm not unlocking, not till the media get here, though I doubt those security pricks will let them in."

"Very well, then," said Chance. "We'll have to take our chances and see what transpires."

Chance took the idol of Enlil from his pocket. Looking around for inspiration, he placed it carefully on a steel ledge.

The woman's eyes widened. "What the fuck is that? Have you just robbed your nana's jewellery box? You on the run or something? Should I be scared?"

"I don't mean to alarm you my dear," said Chance. "I mean you no harm whatsoever. This is a very ancient artefact, even more ancient now if we are in the year 2025. It is an idol believed to correspond to Enlil, an ancient Sumerian god, who will, I believe, shortly be making an appearance."

"Oh Jesus, you are nuts," said the woman. She mopped sweat from her brow with a rainbow hued cravat. "Look mate, just stay where you are will ya? You're making me nervous. And don't call me your fucking dear."

"My apologies," said Chance. "It was rather presumptuous of me. But I'm afraid I have no choice but to carry out my mission. I do sincerely hope that no harm comes to you from my actions and I do implore you to vacate the area."

"No way mate. So, what now? You're just gonna sit it there? Is that thing gonna blow up or something?"

"I'm afraid I don't know the answer to that," said Chance. "I'm trusting that my friends will activate the latent powers inside the idol."

The woman shook her head. "Well FYI, here come the cops, so you're gonna find out one way or the other pretty soon."

Chance looked down on the mine site. Still some distance off across the plain, three vehicles were approaching, blue lights flashing on their roofs. Chance stared.

"More self-propelled vehicles? Internal combustion engines I presume? Extraordinary."

They watched, sparring flies, as the vehicles approached and stopped at the foot of the gantry. Two burly men in blue uniforms exited and conferred with the security buffoons. The policemen approached the ladder, stern expressions on their florid, well-fed faces. One spoke into a small handheld device, then slowly clambered upwards. They reached the platform and stopped, red-faced and breathing heavily, to survey Chance and the woman.

"Ah, Bebop, it's you again," said the first policeman. "And who's your friend? Bit overdressed for this weather aren't ya mate?"

"Morning officer," said Bebop. "This guy is not with me. I'm not sure who, or what he thinks he is. I'm a peaceful activist protesting the construction of this mine, which will amplify Australia's carbon footprint and contribute to cataclysmic climate change, as identified by the ICCC."

"Yes, thank you Bebop, we've heard all the speeches. Now, who are you mate, and what are you doing here?"

"Good morrow officer," said Chance cheerfully. "Yes it is rather warm, ain't it? I am Lieutenant Colonel Sebastian Lafayette Chance, late of her majesty's armed forces, on assignment for the organisation known as the Pale Conduit. I'm after asking your indulgence while I perform some arcane business concerning this ancient Sumerian idol."

The policeman blinked when he noticed the idol. He glowered with furrowed brow before carefully readjusting his rather large belt with its payload of weapons, radios and other paraphernalia.

"What have you got there Mister, er, Chance?" he said. "Looks like it's been flogged from a museum or somethin'."

"It's rather more exotic than that officer," said Chance. "In fact it's an incredibly powerful object of numinous *khuti*, made, if you'll believe it, of concentrated *Xerion*, otherwise known as the Philosopher's Stone."

The policemen exchanged glances. "Tripper," said the fatter of the two. "Vietnam vet I reckon."

"Ok," said the other. "Mister Chance, I'm Senior Sergeant Ray Ratter of the Queensland Police. This is Constable James Dullard. I have to inform you that under the laws relating to this facility I am arresting you for trespass. I will also have to ask you about the ownership of that item. You don't look like the kind of person who should be carrying such a thing on your person, quite frankly."

"You're profiling this man based on his clothing?" said Bebop. "I'm taking notes Sergeant."

"Thank you Bebop. Now, Mister Chance. Irish are you? You're trespassing on private property in an inclosed area. Are you able to show me some identification?"

"As Fenian as MacCool himself," said Chance. "I have my demobilisation papers and an authentication from King Gustavus of Cristaña, if they are of any use to you?"

The policemen glanced at each other. "Where have you escaped from?" said Willis.

"Most recently a demon of the Qliphoth and the tender attentions of the *Ljmmûm*," Chance replied.

"Ok smartarse," said Willis. "We can inspect those papers later. I have to inform you now that you're under arrest and will be taken to the police station for formal charges and identification. Will you leave this place now or do we have to remove you?"

"I'm afraid I can't let you remove me until this idol has done its work," said Chance.

"OK," sighed Ratter, advancing along the platform with Dullard close behind. Chance waited till they were almost upon him before dipping one shoulder and waving his hands. The policemen found themselves facing the other direction. They snatched at empty pistol, taser and pepper spray holsters. Bebop backed away, as far as her manacle would let her.

"I do beg your pardon," said Chance. He chuckled ruefully. "That's a trick I learnt in India. Very effective. Usually results in one or two deaths. Fortunately you are both very slow. Do they actually train you in enforcement in this modern police force? Now, stay where you are, gentlemen, if you will. I'd hate to have my caution go unrewarded."

The policemen looked at one another. They seemed uncertain what to do.

Chance carefully placed their guns, tasers and pepper spray devices on the steel floor. "Officers, I have no desire to hurt or impede you in your duties, but I must insist I be allowed to discharge the duty I travelled here to perform. I ask you to walk away, climb back down the ladder and sit in your vehicle while I wait for this idol to do whatever it is going to do."

Senior Sergeant Ratter collected himself. "You're gonna be in a lot of trouble, Mister Chance. You'd better surrender yourself immediately."

But Chance was staring at the idol, which had begun to glow. He heard the voice of Menahem Ziyuni in his ear. "Chance, are you in position?"

"Yes, I believe so."

"Prepare yourself. You are imminently to be honoured by the presence of the divine entity Enlil, Bearer of the Lightning."

Bebop and the policemen were shocked to see the very air around them shiver and refract with veins of golden light. There was a blizzard of noise in which strange voices could be heard. Then a deeper voice emerged.

*Hero, majestic, battering like a storm and roaring against the rebel lands!*

*I command the storm which flattens the hostile land.*

*I devastate its evil like a vessel with seven spouts!*

The idol flared a deep indigo and for a timeless moment Chance, the police and Bebop were in a different world. A sky the shade of violet roiled above them and against it formed the chest and shoulders of a mighty thunderstorm. It transformed into a soaring winged figure, shoulders vast against the firmament.

"*!I am Enlil, Bearer of the Lightning*" it bellowed in an exotic language they all somehow understood.

There was a flash, a series of incomprehensible noises and other events that were of neither sight, sound nor touch but everyone present felt to the bone. Then nothing.

Hot winds howled across the mine. The police and Bebop stared at Chance.

"What the fuck?" Bebop said.

"You saw it too?" Chance asked. She nodded silently. The air still reeked of diesel fumes, but she felt that something in it was different. She looked at this strange man and wondered.

Chance raised his hands in the air. "Pardon me, gentlemen. It appears I've accomplished what I set out to do, I think. Go easy on me, I have a shoulder wound."

The policemen looked at each other in silence. Each tried and failed to speak. Then they blinked, adjusted their belts, coughed nonchalantly and picked up their weapons, before hurling themselves at Chance and beating him down. Securing his wrists in handcuffs, they hauled him to his feet.

"Where's the statue gone?" Willis demanded. "What the fuck did you just do to us?"

"It appears to have vanished," said Chance. "Most likely it reacted with the energetic blockade of the Qliphoth when Enlil, god of the Sumerians unleashed his lightning. I hope it has had the desired effect."

"Okay smartarse," growled Dullard. "You can use that line on the judge in Townsville. She's had a gutful of you feral mob. New protest laws are about to come into effect and you're in for a world of hurt. You'll have to wait a little bit, Bebop," he said. "We'll come back and cut you off when we've dealt with this nut job."

His wounded shoulder wedged painfully behind him, Chance managed to wink at Bebop before he was frogmarched down the ladder and manhandled with some violence into the back of the larger vehicle.

Sergeant Ratter slammed the door. Chance sat on a hot steel bench, ignoring the pain in his shoulder as he examined the internal fabrication of the vehicle, then peered out narrow windows at various items of machinery lumbering around.

Twenty minutes later the doors opened again. Ratter held something in his hand, pointed at Chance. "Righto, nut job," he said, and his hand was shaking. "Try any of your kung fu again and you'll have 50,00 volts to argue with. My fellow officers have gone off to arrest some feral at the other end of the mine, so you two are gonna have to share a ride. Don't worry Bebop, I'll lock his arms to the bars so he can't move."

Thus restrained, Chance smiled as Bebop climbed inside the vehicle. She sat silently a few minutes while the vehicle roared into life and moved off. She glanced nervously at Chance.

"What did I see up there, what did I hear?" she asked. "What the actual fuck happened? There was a guy with crazy eyes, flying in some kind of crazy costume, with what looked like a light sabre in his hands. What are you? A special effects wizard or something?"

Grimacing, Chance leaned against the wall of the jolting vehicle. Blood was flowing down his arm.

"Jesus," said Bebop. "Are you ok? Did those coppers do that? You need first aid right away."

"I'll be alright, Bebop," said Chance. He closed his eyes and passed out.

After a period of hallucinatory blackness he was woken by Bebop. "We're here," she said, staring at his bloodstained shirt. "You need a doctor."

"No doubt," whispered Chance.

Bebop winced in sympathy, but her eyes hardened when she heard the car doors closing. "Now listen to me, Sebastian or whatever your name is. Don't give the cops any more of that Sumerian god business. I dunno what we've just been through but they're not going to like it if you keep raving like a lunatic. I've got a serious message to deliver and quite frankly your crazy story is detracting from it."

But Sergeant Ratter wrenched open the door and roughly unlocked Chance's restraints. Pulled bodily from the vehicle, he was handcuffed again and dragged into a bare room, lit overhead by bars of excruciating fluorescence. "Strip," said Dullard, whereupon Chance was relieved of his clothing and given flimsy fabrics to put on.

"My shoulder could do with some attention, if you plan on detaining me for long," Chance said quietly.

"Shutup cunt," snapped Dullard. "You'll get plenty of attention when you're booked in, don't worry." He pushed Chance ungently into another room, where more policemen frowned at him. Behind a desk sat Sergeant Ratter, glaring.

"Ok comedian, now's your time to shine." he said. "Give me your full name, date of birth and place of residence."

"Sebastian Daniel Lafayette Chance, born 17 April 1816, late of 134 Northumberland Road, Dublin. Currently on extended leave from her Majesty's armed forces."

He reeled backward from a blow to his head. Ratter withdrew his arm across the desk. "Refused to give correct details," he said aloud, as he wrote on a ledger. Chance stared at him. "There was a time when I would have rewarded that blow with one of my own," he said. "Fortunately I am possessed of a more mature outlook these days."

He rubbed his head ruefully and it took Ratter a moment to register the unsecured handcuff dangling from Chance's other wrist.

"How the fuck did you ...? Right, get over against that wall." Ratter drew a revolver and pointed it at Chance, who obligingly backed up. The other policemen threw themselves at Chance and he was borne to the ground under their weight. Minutes later, beaten bloody, he was dragged to his feet. He squinted through swollen eyes at Ratter, still pointing the gun.

Ratter's pistol hand shook. "I dunno what happened out there mate, or what you did to us, but right now you're in a world of hurt. Very serious charges. Assault police, resist arrest, trespassing. How much time have you got? I'm writing you up as a violent offender, caught attempting to escape police custody. Walk ahead of me."

His shoulder and head aching, Chance was marched at gunpoint into a cell whose door slid closed automatically. He sat a while, listening to the hum of electricity and staring at scuffed white walls. Gradually he fell asleep.

# 19

# An Unfamiliar Wing of the Hospice

Kalyenka found herself wandering through an unfamiliar wing of the Hospice. She had a vague idea she should be looking for someone. Doctor Amordule? That was it. She must find Amordule.

From what seemed a long way away she heard gunfire but otherwise the place was ominously silent. Usually these galleries were bustling with people and animals, resounding with music and the low hum of organic machinery. Now they were still - only the familiar vista of layered gardens and trees, lawns, cafes and workshops remained. She could smell something burning.

Kalyenka marched warily onwards, passing through several halls, descending two sets of stairs, gazing about till her eyes lighted on a familiar, gaily painted architrave. Beyond it she recognised a massive oak tree that grew through several floors of the building, entwined around pillars and balconies, making a natural ramp and stairwell that joined several stories together. Ah, now she knew where she was; two levels up from a cafe she recognised, where she once played chess with Amordule.

She walked out onto a ramp engineered along a long branch and crossed to another landing. As she looked down on the interior of the levels below, more details emerged in her memory - of course, she was on an urgent mission to give a message to Amordule. The Indian woman was now formally in charge of the Hospice and she was supposed to do something important. But quite what, and who gave Kalyenka the errand she could not recall.

A koala bear, quite terrified, lumbered past and glancing down at it she noted that the tear in the hem of her scarlet dress, which had mysteriously repaired itself in the Riemann node, was now glaringly apparent again. Riemann node? What the hell was that?

She heard more gunfire, closer now. The Hospice's attackers must have breached the security cordons. They sounded dangerously close. Hurry! she told herself.

Down another corridor, up a stairway and along an escalator, she thumped on the door to Amordule's office. There was no reply. She pressed the intercom and heard an echoing chime on the other side of the door.

"Amordule!" she shouted. "This is urgent. You must respond!"

Silence from within. Kalyenka heard the dull crump of an explosion and the crack of rifle shots. She hammered on the unyielding door, shrieking in frustration.

A noise behind her. Kalyenka spun around. Vehemple stood there. She screamed. The Dutchman slapped her hard and as she fell, enveloped her neck and chest with one brawny arm, hoisting her to his shoulder. She screamed again but Vehemple, pressing a device with his free hand, strode through Amordule's door even as it opened, dipping his shoulder to crack Kalyenka's head into the architrave.

A soldier appeared behind him, a short man with cruel, blazing eyes. His gaze took in Kalyenka. "Who is this?" he demanded.

"My former assistant," said Vehemple. "A traitor, who conspired against me."

"Shoot her immediately," said the soldier.

"She may be of some use yet." Vehemple dropped Kalyenka to the floor and strode into Amordule's office. Dazedly, Kalyenka watched him tearing drawers open, extracting and scanning documents before throwing them aside.

"What do you look for?" asked the soldier.

Vehemple did not look up. "Plans, blueprints, documents on the organic macro-calculators."

"You think to find them here?" sneered the soldier. "Such precious things must be kept secure in a vault somewhere."

"This entire building is a vault," said Vehemple. "We have already cracked it wide open. Ach, the documents are not here." He shook his head. "It is of no importance. They must be in the *Sarhang's* Citadel. I am going there anyway."

"What are the plans for?" sniffed Teufel suspiciously.

"A weapon that will enable me to transcend this physical world."

Teufel snorted. "Weapons, jah. Give me weapons. You can keep your transcensions."

"What w-weapons do you refer to?" asked the Kaiser, striding into the room. "I have m-many choice weapons. I have a knife collection that is the envy of the civilised w-world." He stared at Kalyenka. "Who is the w-woman? Why has she not been killed? Is this lousy place f-f-full of troublesome females?"

Vehemple regarded him without expression. "She is of no consequence. I am referring to weapons of the intellect, to be used in scientific research."

"Bah," snorted the Kaiser. "You will p-procure me actual weapons, such as the nuclear device, as p-per our agreement, or I will h-have Teufel execute you."

"I have fulfilled my end of the bargain," said Vehemple. "In any case, I am leaving you now. You will want the armoury and the munitions laboratory. They are down one floor and to the north."

"Where are you g-going?"

"To my laboratory. I intend to take my share of the prize."

"Your share of what?" snapped the Kaiser. "This Hospice is m-mine now, by right of conquest."

"My share of the spoils," said Vehemple. "We agreed I was to take several items of my choice when we plundered the Hospice."

"You have n-not yet handed me the key to the Hospice," said the Kaiser. "Nor have you g- given me access to the armouries."

"You are here. It is within your power. Take what you need. Burn the rest. Blow it up for all I care."

"Take me to the armoury, n-now," demanded the Kaiser.

"That I cannot do," said Vehemple. "Until I have access to my computer mainframe. Then you will dominate the entire building."

The Kaiser stared sullenly at Vehemple. "Teufel," he said.

"My Lord?"

"Take the w-woman outside and shoot her."

Teufel stared a moment, then grabbing Kalyenka by the elbow he dragged her upright and out of the room.

Kalyenka struggled in the soldier's iron grip, till he punched her hard in the stomach. Winded, she drooped as he dragged her along. She felt wetness on her arm and looking down, saw that the soldier's jerkin was slick with blood. He stopped suddenly, as a figure appeared ahead of them in the corridor. A rather short, unimposing man in a lab coat. Teufel dropped Kalyenka and pulled out his pistol.

He fired. The man did not flinch. Teufel fired again. The bullet should have ripped the man asunder, but he stood there, apparently unharmed.

"*Fick dich!*" snarled the Prussian. "Die, poltergeist!"

"Kindly desist," said the man, most mildly.

Teufel fired again, several rapid shots in succession.

The Kaiser and Vehemple appeared in the corridor. "You!" shouted Vehemple.

"I would prefer not to indulge in these crude games, but time is pressing," the man said. He disappeared in a flash of light. Kalyenka found herself standing, freed of the soldier's grip. She looked down. He lay unconscious on the ground. Numb and bewildered, she looked behind. Vehemple and the other tall man were also lying prone, as though poleaxed.

The short, spectacled man in the lab coat reappeared, beckoning to Kalyenka. "Quickly child," he said. "Follow down this corridor. Do not be alarmed by anything you see."

Wincing in pain, Kalyenka complied. One hand holding her throbbing head, she followed the man, though he faded almost into invisibility before surging back into quite dazzling clarity. She blinked and rubbed her eyes, uncertain what she was seeing. They proceeded down a long hallway, up some broad stairs.

The man disappeared again. Kalyenka stumbled on, afraid Vehemple would awaken and come after her. Rounding a corner, she saw before her a seething violet mist, wreathing the high wall of a building that seemed quite separate from the Hospice. The short man in the lab coat materialised in front of the mist, motioning her towards a great door beyond it. The door opened, seemingly of its own volition. He disappeared again. There was no sign of him in the chamber within.

Glancing behind, Kalyenka saw no pursuit. She looked uncertainly into that damson haze, sensing a potent metaphysical power but no threat to her. Just on the edge of hearing, the threnodies of some arcane symphony welled out from it. Snatches of voices, suggesting recondite emotions and spells of puissant wisdom. Suddenly resolved, she passed through the mist and the doorway. The door closed and all sound from outside was sealed off.

She was alone in an office, facing a chair and table, a steel framed mirror on the table. On the wall hung an enormous painting. Kalyenka found herself staring into it.

There were all kinds of surreal activities going on amongst the hundreds of characters and strange objects represented in this lurid and multi-storeyed panorama. It was almost Boschian in its mood and detail but Kalyenka knew that she had painted it, though she could not remember doing so.

In one corner she saw herself, naked, bloodied and bruised. Depicted at a much younger age, she held a gun extended and Kalyenka knew then that a wild and opaque memory was reeling in from a long way away. She blinked and swallowed. Shooting two men in her chambers in Cristaña in another lifetime became vivid in her mind and with overwhelming clarity she remembered the Riemann node and the *Sarhang's* tale and she had to sit down, for she knew why she was there.

"But how does my painting come to be here, when I painted it in the Riemann node on an imaginary canvas?"

The *Sarhang's* voice answered, measured and calm as ever, though Kalyenka could not see him. "I arranged the materials in this room. They were animated by your energetic mind and reproduced here, even as your eidolon worked in the Riemann node."

"Of course you did," she replied, staring at the mirror on the table, which was where the voice seemed to be coming from. But it was not a mirror. It had a screen that shone like the surface of a very calm sea, an object very much like that she'd activated in Vehemple's laboratory, according to his instructions. As she stared the *Sarhang's* face appeared in it and Kalyenka said to herself, "I am going mad."

"Do not be alarmed," the face in the screen said, and chuckled. "That is to say, please *try* not to be alarmed. I am projecting my image from a vector in the *Mēnōg*, whence I fled after the Riemann node was destroyed. You have done very well to return. Now that you are here we can enact the second phase of my plan."

"I didn't do anything," said Kalyenka. "I just appeared here."

"Yes, but first you made some unavoidable detours, via an episode in Cristaña, followed by a rendezvous with Kulan, Chance and Aiwass."

"Oh god," said Kalyenka remembering the wraith Aiwass. Tears filled her eyes. "When is this going to stop Augustine? Why won't this painting let me alone?"

"Yes," said the *Sarhang*. "The painting is the key. It resonates in the *Mēnōg*, creating a wavefront of *khuti* that makes light of *apeira* and the *Tuat* and becomes as compelling in this *Gētīg*."

"I still don't know what the hell you're on about," said Kalyenka. "But I'm guessing this is not over yet? I mean I understand now that Chance and I have shared continuums compressed across three lifespans, entangled by the influence of the idol of Enlil."

"Correct. Your painting conveys the arc of your journey through the *khutiverse*. Now we must complete that narrative."

Kalyenka regarded the work, and her gaze was drawn to the two-headed, multi-legged beast responsible for much of the woes of humanity. "Aiwass told me about Marduk, how he's become both Jesus and Mohammed in one monstrous body. Surely that's not true?"

"Oh yes, your rendering of Marduk gave the game away. After the Qliphoth found me and destroyed my Riemann node I escaped into the *Mēnōg*, avoiding their attentions. I reassembled your painting from my excellent memory and studied it in great detail, discovering that you have inadvertently revealed the true nature of this unholy beast. I passed that information on to Aiwass and that, it seems, was enough to convince the Sephiroth to join us in our quarrel with the *Ljmmûm*."

"Amazing enough," said Kalyenka. "But please, what has become of Chance? And for that matter where is Adhira Amordule in all this mess?"

"The good Doctor has launched our Exposition," he replied, and his face creased. "She was engaged with some of the most vicious gangsters in Europe and is now leading the defence of the Hospice. I trust she is safe. Our security troopers, hired for their moral fortitude as well as their elite fighting abilities, are sworn to protect her."

Kalyenka smiled. "And Chance?"

"Well, as evidenced by my ability to project myself back into the Hospice, it seems your lover may well have succeeded in his mission, destroying the Qliphoth blockade of Tiphereth. Indeed the Chthonic Gates, removed by the destruction of the Womb of Time, have been restored. It may well be that the Cosmic Shekinah can be now deployed."

"Wait, go back," said Kalyenka. "Have we won then? Have we beaten the *Ḷimmûm?*"

"Not yet my dear. The Skein is metastasising rapidly and threatens the very existence of this Hospice. We are besieged by enemies both corporeal and metaphysical."

Kalyenka nodded reluctantly. "Very well Augustine," she said, composing her bruised face into a smile. "What would you have me do?"

"Excellent," the *Sarhang* in the screen said. "We have much to achieve and little subjective time in which to do it. We have a process to enact, then I will require you to hold the fort here while I descend again into the Skein to assist Kulan and Zhāng Sān."

"Tell me," said Kalyenka. "Vehemple and those other men outside, are they dead?"

"No," the *Sarhang* said. "Merely stunned. They may even be conscious again by now. But do not fear. They cannot get into this Citadel. It is sealed off by the Chthonic Veil and impervious to their armaments."

"I've heard that before. And one more thing," she pleaded. "Where exactly is Chance? Is he safe?"

"I do not know. I am unable to scry into his *apeira,* owing to the interference of Enlil. I do not even know whether he survived his mission, I'm afraid."

"Very good," said Kalyenka. "I have the greatest faith in our friend Chance. If anyone can survive gods and demons in a future world, it's him. Now, please direct me as to how I can help."

"I was coming to that," said the *Sarhang*. He pointed to the painting, where a group of beautiful young Asian men and women in outlandish costumes sang and danced to some uncanny choreography.

"It seems that a new element has entered our drama. We've been joined by unlikely allies from an *apeira* in the Earth's future. Millions of adherents of a Korean-based popular music form known as K-Pop have manifested *egregores* in the Skein, so large and powerful that I could not but take notice of them. These *egregores,* which call themselves 'Stans' have mustered considerable Force and Form and dealt the *Ljmmûm* such serious reversals that they are reverberating into our *apeiron*. Their unexpected intervention has given us a new source of *khuti* with which to combat the *Ljmmûm*."

Kalyenka looked about for refreshments. If she were in for more wild tales she felt the need of a drink but in this part of the Hospice it seemed that the *Sarhang* could not anticipate or provide for her needs with mere good intention. He continued talking in apparent ignorance of her thirst.

"These 'Stans' use an *egregore* technique called 'hashtags', blocking the *Ljmmûm* from controlling certain Skein functions. It seems that strategy was countered by *Ljmmûm* exigencies, but in light of that successful stratagem I have been in contact with one young man from the era.

"This young man, whose name is Bitgaram has assembled his particular Stan's data, or rather his sister and girlfriend's Stan's data - they are called Cinnamon Girls, into the topology of a computer game, which young people of that era have become adept at manipulating. Bitgaram is something of an expert at devising these computer games and inserting them into the quasi-reality of the Skein.

"I divined that the *Ljmmûm* are equally as dangerous in his *apeira* and demonstrated this to him with a chimeras lens-view of a public execution in the United States. The victim; an aficionado of the same type of music as Bitgaram. Quite shocked, the poor lad agreed to help. Between us we have devised a new stratagem to trick the *Ḷịmmûm*, using the particular topologies available in this medium."

"That sounds very complicated," said Kalyenka.

"Indeed it is. The primary weapons of the *Ḷịmmûm* in this epoch are algorithms, designed to control the flow of data and the way human minds work. The great flaw in this system is that algorithms cannot deal with emotions. They are designed to find patterns in data, but emotions are far too complex for even their most advanced computers to fathom. I have channelled emotion-based Hermetic magik into these algorithms, essentially overloading them, which has allowed us to insert our own rules of engagement.

"It seems this grand battle is to be fought by proxies, the terrain on which we fight to be controlled by this young man. He has channelled the *Ḷịmmûm* into role-playing these games, using characterisations evinced by their emotionally immature egos. Thus they present themselves as stylised heroes, mythical creatures and warriors of great stature."

"How extraordinary," said Kalyenka.

"Yes it is. In all my long life I never envisaged such a thing."

"And?"

The *Sarhang's* eyebrows raised.

Kalyenka stamped her foot. "What do you want me to do about it?"

"Oh. I have inserted your painting into the misc-en-scene of this game. In fact it has become the contextual background and narrative driver of the entire scenario, essentially controlling its natural laws. So in that regard, I'd like you to keep painting. If I may use the expression, to paint the *Ḷịmmûm* into a corner."

# 20

# Egress to the Stars

Teufel woke with a blinding headache. Ignoring the pain from his various wounds, he climbed slowly to his feet.

"Vehemple, what has transpired?"

Vehemple levered himself up to tower over Teufel. Blinking vaguely, he regarded the Prussian. "It seems we were knocked unconscious by an electronic beam of great power. The *Sarhang* would have done better to have disposed of us permanently, but his code of non-violence does not allow him to kill. *Stomme dwass.*"

"That was the *S-Sarhang?*" said the Kaiser, as Teufel assisted him to his feet. "The l-leader of the *tougrak?*"

"At least a projection of him." Vehemple's disquieting face loured further. "We cannot breach his Citadel now. The Chthonic Gates have been restored. They should have been annihilated along with the Womb of Time. It defies logic."

The Kaiser placed himself deliberately in front of Vehemple. "What has become of your p-plan V-vumple? Do you have one? Or you are just blundering from one d-disaster to another?"

Unused to facing someone of equal height at such close quarters, Vehemple's hands twitched, but he did not blink. "I am overcoming obstacles as they appear. In any case your troopers are drawing closer and we must assist them. We go now to my laboratory. Once I have accessed my newest offensive equipment, the Hospice will be ours."

"V-very well," said the Kaiser. "But Teufel will be w-watching you closely."

Teufel was indeed attentive, but his eyes were drawn with pain. The Kaiser did not notice. He had already set off after Vehemple and his automaton. After traversing several more deserted districts, Vehemple opened a concealed entrance set into a wall. They passed through and came to a premises whose central steel door was hanging, twisted and bent from its frame. Beyond it could be seen a smouldering ruin. Vehemple stared, aghast.

"What am I l-looking at Vurkle?" demanded the Kaiser.

But Vehemple did not answer. He wandered into the chamber, gaping in horror. "My centrifuge is destroyed. So much is lost. This is unthinkable."

Teufel limped inside. He leaned against a blackened wall and slid down it, leaving a streak of blood. The Kaiser stared at him, mouth working. "Teufel! On your f-feet man. This futile Dutchman has failed me again. It is t-time for a reckoning."

But Teufel's eyes were closed. He looked to be unconscious. The Kaiser looked from him to Vehemple. He leaned over and extracted Teufel's pistol from its holster. "Vidle! Your p-plans have come to n-nothing. Worthless commoner. I have placed my trust in a f-failure. Take me to my troops now."

Absorbed in examining the ruins of his laboratory, Vehemple did not seem to hear. The Kaiser shook his general by the collar. "Teufel! Am I to be abandoned by my own m-men as well as this shiftless D-dutchman?"

But Teufel was unresponsive. The Kaiser waved the pistol. "Dutchman! Fetch m-medication and get Teufel on his f-feet. *Raus!*"

Ignoring the Kaiser, the Dutchman wandered to the far end of the laboratory, where he examined what was left of his equipment. The Kaiser raised Teufel's pistol and fired into the wall near Vehemple. But even as he cocked it for a second shot, he was knocked off his feet by the automaton. Grinding metal and gears, it was raising a steel boot, poised to smash his skull when Vehemple shouted. "*Annuler bestelling!*"

The automaton froze, its boot suspended inches over the Kaiser's face.

"I warned you not to threaten me, Prussian," said Vehemple, his face phlegmatic as ever. "The *verkeerslicht* will not tolerate violence towards me."

The Kaiser was speechless. He had never before had violence administered to his person. A strangled noise issued from his throat as he stared up at the automaton.

"On your feet, Herr Kaiser," said Vehemple. "I have discovered an undamaged cupboard whose contents will assist your General. *Verkeerslicht, ophouden!*"

The Kaiser rose, warily eyeing the automaton as the Dutchman took from the cupboard a bottle and syringe. Vehemple rolled up the sleeve on Teufel's right arm and stabbed him in the bicep, pushing the plunger down on a clear liquid. He discarded the needle and stood, crossing over to examine his *verkeerslicht*. It stood immobile now, its damaged torso smoking, viscous fluids leaking onto the blackened floor. Vehemple frowned and stepped past it to face a featureless section of the wall.

"At least the saboteurs have not discovered my restricted laboratory. I must attend an urgent errand. I will return in approximately ten minutes." He touched a section of wall and it slid aside.

"*Nein,*" said the Kaiser. "Teufel will assist, to ensure you do not p-plot any devilment."

The general had swiftly regained consciousness under Vehemple's stimulant. Rising, he resumed his customary snarl.

"Very well," said Vehemple. "If you think your good general can overcome my *verkeerslicht,* you are welcome to try."

The Kaiser glared. "Ventle, you are t-testing my p-patience. You have f-five minutes, after which I will ..."

"You will what?" said Vehemple. But the Kaiser looked at the automaton and had no answer. He turned instead to Teufel, who stood shakily beside him. The stain on his jacket had demonstrably grown, encircling the circumference of the wounds. His face was pale, but he scowled with grim determination.

Vehemple disappeared. His *verkeerslicht* stationed itself outside the effacing door.

"K-keep watch on that thing," said the Kaiser, who retained Teufel's pistol. He limped away, rubbing his head. Whey-faced, the General extracted another pistol from his jacket and took up station metres from the automaton.

Inside the chamber, Vehemple switched on lights revealing banks of terminals bedecked with vacuum tubes and tape consoles. He crossed to the opposite side of the room, depressed a switch and a panel slid aside. Inside, the onset of fluorescent lights illuminated an enormous figure on a platform.

There, rigid against the wall stood a gigantic *verkeerslicht,* on the order of the flying automatons, wingless but ten times their size. Bedecked in armour and bristling with weaponry, it was immobile, crystalline eyes staring straight ahead. The Dutchman's face was impassive.

"My masterpiece," he murmured, as if discussing a cancer.

He flicked a switch on the control panel beside it and a whining noise arose. Tubes, connected by cables to the *groot verkeerslicht,* began to glow. Lights rippled along its limbs and crystalline eyes smouldered red.

Vehemple looked at his fob-watch. Half an hour till it would be operational. He pressed another button on the wall and a second panel opened. Behind it, arrayed on a steel framework was the mobile exoskeleton he had worn demonstrating the flying *verkeerslicht* to Chance and Kalyenka. Activating it, he armed the cannon on its arms. Assured that all was in readiness, he exited the chamber.

The Kaiser grinned, aiming a pistol at his face. Behind swayed Teufel, face pale and eyes nearly closed. The Dutchman stared expressionlessly. "*Verkeerslicht!*" he said.

Nothing happened. He glanced at the automaton. Its head was slumped and it reeked of burning oil. The peasant woman's shooting had evidently damaged core systems.

"Another of your inventions p-proves inadequate," crowed the Kaiser. "Now, t-take me to your supposed portal to the s-stars."

Vehemple's face betrayed no emotion. "Follow," he said, re-opening the concealed door. The Kaiser beheld the banks of machinery, in their centre a monitor screen. Behind him Teufel sagged to the floor and passed out again. The Dutchman pointed. "My mainframe," he said.

The Kaiser sneered. "This is your m-method of egress to the stars? This contraption of metal and g-glass? It looks like something my s-secretary would use."

Vehemple's face was impassive. "Nonetheless it is the portal to the Skein. The purpose for which you sought the pagan idol."

The Kaiser sat on the stool before the screen. "Demonstrate its p-purpose."

"Are you ready to transform your consciousness into the Skein?" said Vehemple. "Your corporeal form may suffer some physical consequences."

"You f-forget who you speak to, Vulunkle. I am the ..."

"Yes, yes, yes, you are the heir to the blood of Charlemagne," said Vehemple. "But you stand before the portal to a cosmic dimension that will make your lineage seem a procession of ants. It is the realisation of scientific supremacy, a gateway into the algorithmic agency of a perfect data future."

The Kaiser's face suffused with rage. He pointed his pistol at Vehemple. "Your impudence has c-come to an end, Dutchman. You have lied and l-led me into folly, b-but it is over now. "

Vehemple was silent. He stared into the Kaiser's pistol as though it were a complicated puzzle he was determined to solve. After a moment he displayed a phenomenon that had been viewed by few people on the planet. He smiled. Such a sight was horrific enough to deter the hardiest warrior, but the Kaiser, inured to manifold horrors within this accursed mansion, scarcely blanched.

"My Lord," said Vehemple. "Before you lies the instrument of your elevation to ineffable power. I will demonstrate it to you directly. But firstly you must imbibe a medicine that will prepare your body for the process."

"Demonstrate to me how it w-works or I will shoot you," said the Kaiser. Taking out a pocket-clock, he set its timer. "When three minutes expire y-y-you will receive a Walther nine millimetre bullet to the f-forehead, unless I am satisfied you have p-provided me with the materials promised."

Vehemple opened a cupboard and retrieved a bottle, labelled in what an ethnolinguist would have recognised as Sanskrit. He gave it into the Kaiser's outstretched hand.

"*Vas ist*?" demanded the Kaiser.

"An embrocation to facilitate the procedure. Based on the *soma* of the ancients, a recipe I improved upon to create a mental prophylactic that supercharges the brain and overrides human frailties. Thus the algorithms of the universe are laid bare. Wait! A drop is all that is required."

"Ha!" scoffed the Kaiser. "If it is t-truly all of that, it is w-wasted on a Dutchman. Clearly it should be used by a being whose b-bloodlines run to the heroic figures of the Golden Teutonic age. P-pour me a glass of this embrocation."

"You would not know what to do with so much," Vehemple said flatly. "In your hands it would be dangerous. In your head, fatal."

But the Kaiser had unstoppered the bottle. "I am of the b-blood of Frederick the Great! I think I would know what to do with anything of such p-power."

He peered dubiously at the contents, a blue, viscous liquid, then raised it and drank deeply. He made a face. "Ach, it is vile," he said, spitting onto the floor. He regarded the puddle dubiously. "What is this p-poison?" he demanded. "Dutchman, you have tricked me."

"It is medicine," sneered Vehemple. "It will not poison you, though you may wish you had not drunk so deep."

The Kaiser regarded him balefully. He held the bottle gingerly, mouth working in distaste, then dropped it to the floor, where it smashed in half.

"What happens n-now?" demanded the Kaiser.

"You have been given the keys to the kingdom," said Vehemple. "It is for you to see if you can open the door, or if it explodes in your face."

"Enough of your n-nonsense," the Kaiser said, raising his gun. "I am w-waiting."

Vehemple regarded the Kaiser without expression. "It will be a little while before it takes effect. You must be patient. Meanwhile I will prepare the instruments for your voyage." A flicker of evil joy had lit in his dead eyes. He turned towards another bank of instruments, but the Kaiser rose from his seat.

"You are going n-nowhere," the Kaiser snapped. "Begin the p-process."

Vehemple glanced downward. The Kaiser's pistol was jammed into his ribs. He shrugged and turned his attention to the console before him, flicking switches and reading dials. Some time passed. The Kaiser amused himself by whetting his favourite poniard on the edge of Vehemple's desk. When he saw that the action was annoying the Dutchman he pursued it with vigour. But soon he ceased, staring off into the middle distance. His face took on a wholly different expression and he began to giggle.

Glancing at the Kaiser, Vehemple observed these transformations with barely concealed relish. He had activated lights across the entire console. The Kaiser stared at the central screen, where a band of light was twisting, seeming to fold in upon itself and open up larger than before. As he watched it resolved into a tight circle that revolved, spinning faster and faster.

Now the Kaiser's face became suffused with anger. Dropping the pistol absently onto the floor he began manipulating dials. The screen image became fuzzy and Vehemple, snarling, turned. "What are you doing man? You will disturb the coding."

"Move away from the maksheen, Vurdle," said the Kaiser. "I will take over now."

"Don't be foolish," growled Vehemple, noting that the Kaiser was no longer speaking with his customary stutter. "You would not know what to do, you ignorant inbred."

But the Kaiser's attention had been snagged by the flickering lights of a smaller screen to his left. He punched buttons on the console beneath it, eyes wide and luminous. Judging he could do little harm there, Vehemple continued flicking switches on the main board.

Awoken by the altercation, behind them Teufel staggered to his feet. He reeled towards the Dutchman, aiming another pistol at his head. Distracted by Teufel's reflection, Vehemple wheeled around with startling speed and knocked the weapon from his hands. Jumping to his feet, he punched the General to the ground and bent to retrieve his gun.

He pointed the pistol at the Kaiser, who stared in disbelief.

"Lower that weapon, peasant," he roared, his face a mask of fury. "I am on the verge of embracing my destiny, and you, a mere technician, think to deny me? Lower that weapon immediately! Teufel! Dispose of this rubbish!"

But Teufel lay senseless on the floor. The Kaiser's eyes launched into individual orbits as the *soma* wrought its magic within his skull. He stood up, hands raised as if in absolution, but his face dissolved into surprise and pain, for Vehemple fired the gun, and the Kaiser dropped to the ground beside his General.

"Yes, best served cold," whispered the Dutchman. He turned back to the console and resumed booting up the *groot verkeerslicht's* mainframe. He did not notice the scrutiny of a pair of eyes, watching in silence from the doorway.

# 21

# A Shambles

Black George dumped the body of his latest victim, a small Asian woman, on a conveyer belt that ran into the maw of a rubbish compacting machine.

The woman had surprised him while he was ransacking a library, seeking valuables amongst the books. "Get out you brute," she shouted, and hit him with a shovel. She was a pretty thing, and had he time Black George would have entertained her properly. But he was impatient to attach himself to the Kaiser, so he strangled her, disposing of the body in the depot next door.

Not that there was any danger of being apprehended. Everywhere the Hospice *Securité* were in retreat. The place was a shambles, filled with parties of roving Prussian soldiers exploding things and firing giddily at random. Black George surmised they were maddened by the peculiar ambience of this hellhole. It seemed to infect interlopers with a distracting psychosis which he was not immune to either.

Indeed, the deeper Black George progressed into the building, the more he suffered from confusing hallucinations. They'd been afflicting him since he entered, but such was the state of his ravaged psyche that he'd almost welcomed them as a respite from the hatred which usually consumed his thoughts.

Now they had taken the measure of his neuroses and found the cracks in it. They'd penetrated deep, dredging up unwanted memories. Foremost among these was a set of recollections he was certain didn't belong to him, but which were making him distinctly uncomfortable.

Curiously enough these 'memories' depicted him as a somewhat more impressive iteration of himself; a taller, straighter individual known as the Karageorge, a fearless warrior who'd perished more than fifty years earlier. Though capable of reckless anger and savage violence, the man had principles and an idiosyncratic moral code irretrievably tangled in tribal Serbian patriotism.

He was in revolt against the Ottoman occupiers, personally leading fierce warriors into battle. In this iteration he was troubled by conflicting loyalties, having been obliged to execute his brother for raping a Serbian woman. Such ethics were anathema to Black George, but so insistent were these memories that he had trouble separating them from his own.

The face of the executed brother haunted Black George, for it more closely resembled his own than did the Karageorge himself. Indeed the raped woman, whom he, Black George, or rather the Karageorge had rescued, was, with the addition of a hundred pounds or so, the image of Fat Ursula, the depraved bawd of Uvass and allegedly Black George's mother. It was all too weird, a fever dream whose principals were so entwined as to be indistinguishable.

Intermingled with those memories was the image of the golden statue, that infernal piece of bijoux he'd taken from Proko and surrendered to the mad Dutchman on the Kaiser's orders. Black George knew it had an awful, eldritch power but he was uncertain what to do with it.

His memories as the Karageorge implied a deep fear of the idol. In particular he associated it with an evening before a crucial battle against the Ottoman janissaries, during which the idol was stolen from him and he lost heart and fled. Entangled in that memory was an ascetic scholar who had been advising him, a man by the name of Ancoulsis.

Black George could not see why these petty details seemed to matter, but they clearly did. They illustrated that this idol was far more important than he had surmised, that it was in fact of such paramount importance that, did Black George wish to realise his dreams of conquest, he had better bloody well see to it that the idol was in the right hands.

Above all the message he took from it was that the Kaiser was the man who could best put such a thing to use, being as how he had command of so many men, with so many weapons. Ach, give Black George that army and he would show the world a slaughter unseen since the Mongolians ran amok through Christian lands.

Resigned to pledging allegiance to this Kaiser, at least till it was no longer convenient, Black George kept looking. He ought to be where the bloodshed was thickest.

"Then we'll see some action, my boy," Black George told himself. "That Kaiser is a shrewd dog, and he'll need someone to keep order in these parts. Who better than yours truly? Black George knows every nook and cranny in these mountains, and he's killed the heads of most of the families in it."

Black George was damned if he could find the man though, in this accursed place. It was a maze of interconnecting corridors, patios and halls full of intriguing valuables. There were damned statues everywhere and artwork; queer paintings and installations. Black George had stolen enough in his time to know quality when he saw it, but he figured there was no point encumbering himself with loot at this stage. There would be plenty of time to pillage at his leisure, once he'd ingratiated himself with the Kaiser's conquering army.

Meanwhile Black George was finding it hard to distinguish between his current reality and the blizzard of blood-soaked images coursing through his head. By now the phantasms were excruciating.

The recurrent scenes of slaughter and mutilated victims multiplied and became ever more gruesome. Lengthening his stride as if to outrun them, Black George fired his gun at a weasel poking its head above a balustrade, then shot the wall beyond it, though the phantoms populating that space had vanished.

Black George shook his head and laughed out loud. "Madness?" he whispered to himself. "How could I be madder than I already am?" At that thought he laughed louder and fired shots at random as he strolled deeper into the complex.

But as he traversed yet another silent corridor, Black George espied a trail of blood, paralleled by intermittent drops of oil. He followed them up a broad staircase until he heard in the distance a curious, rhythmic clanging. Cautiously he followed, until he saw von Teufel turn a corner ahead. Black George crept closer and saw a bloodied footprint left by the general.

He peered around the corner. Sure enough, the Prussian's side was black with blood and he was moving slowly. That looked like a mortal wound. The man would not survive the day. Ho ho. What if Black George were to take von Teufel's place and save the Kaiser's hide? Even an aristocratic numb-nuts like the Kaiser would be bound to see the value in such a character.

Teufel vanished again and Black George hurried to keep up. He stopped abruptly. Just ahead were Teufel, the Kaiser and that tall bastard Dutchman. But in front of the Kaiser was a metallic monster, gigantic wings tucked over its broad shoulders. The clanging sound was the vibration of its steel-shod boots.

Black George stared, wondering just how mad he'd become. He rubbed his eyes and stared again. By Satan, as far as anything in this hellish place was real, it was that thing. A metal man, with wings no less. It was clearly damaged and leaking oil. Still, with a machine like that it was no wonder they'd gotten inside this place. That mad Dutchman must have built it. Black George reconsidered his opinion of the scientist. Perhaps he was the fellow to ally with after all.

Black George was pondering that proposition when he heard another sound from behind. He turned and saw Proko eyeballing him. Something about that rang oddly, but Black George had his gun out and was too busy scoping the ground behind the villain to properly consider it. Satisfied there were no *tougrak* lurking about, Black George bore down on the wife beater, who had not moved or spoken.

Proko stared at Black George with oddly indifferent eyes. No longer cringing and subservient, he stood his ground as the bandit chief approached. When Black George clobbered and stood over him, the wife beater did not so much as whimper.

"What are you about, boy?" Black George snarled. "Sneaking up on Black George. I've gutted men for less."

There was no response. Drool and blood oozed from Proko's mouth. Black George grabbed him roughly by the shoulder and shook him. "Answer, poltroon! I'll gut ye, sure as death I will, but I'll hear ye cry one more time first."

"I got nothin' to say, Black George," came a small voice. "Kill me if ye must."

Black George squinted at the wife-beater. "What the fuck, Proko?" One paw grabbed a handful of hair and twisted Proko's head around. He turned it the other way, as if something might fall out of the fool's ears and return him to normal. "Stand up man! You are wounded? Dying?" He examined the thief. "Nothin' wrong with ya," he roared, and slapped him hard in the face. Proko fell to his knees.

Black George eyed him narrowly. "What's become of you, ye useless piece of shit?"

Proko dared look him in the eye. "I've had a bit of a shock Black George."

"I'll give ye a shock. I'll, I'll ... what will I do?" Black George chuckled. "Not much good to me as a hostage." Stropping his knife, he considered Proko's neck. "No, we're in uncharted waters here. Might need this thing yet."

He chuckled. "Well, you're no fun any more Proko, but you might still be of some use. On yer feet *glupan*."

The wife beater got himself shakily upright. His right eye was twitching but otherwise he looked less like the Proko who Black George had come to know and more like a Proko who Black George didn't want to know. But it seemed there'd be no joy in killing him, so he shoved him ahead. "Lead on, maggot," he said. "This ain't over yet."

Proko set off boldly enough, failing to whine or lag as might usually be expected. Black George watched him carefully. They followed the trail of blood and oil till it stopped at a blank wall. Black George puzzled over that till he saw a long vertical crack and realised he was staring at a concealed door.

He pushed it open and crept through a corridor to another entrance. Passing through it he saw a chamber full of burnt and twisted wreckage. The automaton was slumped against the wall, bullet holes scoring its dented torso. Black George whistled ruefully but stopped, hearing voices raised in anger. Peering around the frame of a third door he espied the Kaiser upbraiding Vehemple, a pistol in his hand. Teufel lay as though dead behind them.

Black George had about made up his mind to intervene when he heard the scorn in Vehemple's voice. "Hold hard maggot," Black George whispered. "This Kaiser fellow might not be the goods after all."

They watched as Vehemple handed the Kaiser a jar of blue liquid, which he drank. The Dutchman busied himself with mysterious dials and levers, while the Kaiser's jaw became slack and his eyes vague and wandering. Soon he was shouting incoherently at Vehemple again and Black George listened with delight as the altercation escalated, till Teufel roused himself and tried to attack the Dutchman. Black George nodded approvingly as Vehemple tackled the wounded general, kicked him down and shot the Kaiser dead. Then the Dutchman returned his attentions to the banks of blinking machinery.

Black George considered his next move, right hand absently wrenching Proko's hair back, but the wife-beater hardly noticed. Hs eyes were fixed on the Kaiser's pistol, forgotten on the floor and next to it, a wisp of shadow that must be the *tougrak's* invisibility jacket.

# 22

# Gone

Chance woke with a start. He looked up and groaned softly. A policeman was rattling his truncheon against the bars. Seeing Chance was awake he grinned and moved on.

Chance cursed. His shoulder wound and the beating he'd taken ached infernally. Police had kept him awake most of the night, banging on the cell door every time he nodded off. But in the pre-dawn hours they'd been kept busy processing a fresh batch of protestors. He'd finally been able to sleep.

His sleep was deranged by urgent, agitated dreams. They cycled incessantly; an unresolved series of events involving the blonde woman he'd seen in his theta experience, appearing alongside Kalyenka, Ancoulsis and that cursed idol. Curiously, Kalyenka kept staring into his face, repeating the mantra; "We are of the same breath, you and I."

He dozed off again, a brief tumble of reveries before he was shaken roughly and a policeman loomed over him. "You've been bailed mate. Someone out there likes you, which is lucky, 'cos the arresting officers don't. Get dressed and follow me."

Chance forced himself to rise. Stiff and sore, he discarded the prison rags, eased into his fatigues and followed the policeman to a desk under fluorescent light. "Stand there," the officer said. "You're facing heavy charges mate. I'm obliged to tell you that your bail conditions are strict. Read and sign."

Chance read. He was ordered not to engage in any illegal activity, nor to return to either the mine site or the protester's camp, wherever that was. He signed the form with a flourish, winked at the policeman and limped out through the front doors of a building whose modernity would have almost made him interested, if he were not in so much pain.

He felt something in his pocket and took it out. It was the flask Olaf had given him, what seemed weeks ago, though it was only, what, three days? He took a swig of the spirit, shuddering with pleasure as it swelled in his gut. He eyed the flask more closely. It bore an embossed coat of arms featuring two hawks atop a snarling boar, whose Latin inscription; *Fortuna et gloria* triggered a vague memory.

Chance traced that memory to an afternoon in Cristaña, the day he met Baron Codrūt Casimir Ancoulsis, who had given him the idol. The same heraldry in embroidered miniature adorned the Baron's surcoat.

That was an intriguing coincidence and one that warranted further investigation. If two events existed coevally there was usually some design behind them, no matter how trivial. Going on the stakes in this game, such a hazard was undeniable. Chance drank off the rest of the spirit and placed the flask on the floor, just inside the exit from the police station.

He emerged blinking into a stifling hot morning. The moist air was redolent of cane-smoke with an edge of ocean. To his delight Bebop stood on the footpath, along with several other young men and women clustered around a small box on the ground, which was emitting booming noises and the strains of what Chance reluctantly identified as music. When Bebop saw him she shrieked, ran over and threw her arms around him.

"Chance, you fucking weirdo. I don't know what you did out there, but something crazy has happened."

Chance smiled wearily. "Do tell, Bebop."

"All the investors have pulled out of the Galilee Basin and the government has been forced to put a halt to its mining licenses. It took 5,000 arrests to do it. You're number 5001. Unbelievable, but true. There's other news too. The American President has been impeached. Again. He was busted in an orgy with other members of his Cabinet. He's called out the National Guard. The US is on the brink of civil war. The Republicans are backing him despite church leaders being involved in the orgy. It's rumoured there was paedophilia involved."

A high pitched tinkling noise was emitted from Bebop's person. She reached into a cloth bag. Retrieving a glowing oblong device, she put it to her ear.

"Yes?"

Chance could hear a voice, muffled by Bebop's ear. "You're fucking kidding me," she said into the device. "No fucking way. Oh. My. God."

She spoke in more arcane patois, then began dancing a jig, crying and laughing at the same time. Her shrieks turned into a guffaw, then a gurgling of such exultant glee that Chance found himself grinning. She lowered the device and beamed at Chance.

"The UN has intervened," she said. "They've put a blanket ban on all coal mining and threatened the government with trading sanctions. The media are all saying that coal mining licenses are going to be canceled and the miners have been ordered to pay for environmental reparations."

"Well that is remarkable," said Chance.

"But don't you understand?" said Bebop. "That means we stand at least a chance of slowing down global warming. Without the emissions from those mines our carbon budget is a little more manageable, despite the best efforts of our government to blow it wide open."

"Oh trust me, I'm glad," said Chance. "I'm just a little muzzy from lack of sleep."

"You poor bastard. Here, have some coffee. I've got a croissant too."

"Well that is delicious."

Bebop poured from her thermos and gave Chance a second cup. "Now tell me, you fucken unit. Where did you come from? No-one in camp knows who you are or how you got out to the mine site. What was that thing I saw? Did you spike my water with acid or something? I thought I saw a gigantic winged man stab a bolt of lightning into the pit. There was an explosion and all kinds of crazy psychedelic shit happening."

"I am a mere soldier, not an interpreter of cosmic events," said Chance. "But I believe what you saw is no more bizarre than the fact that yesterday I was in the Eastern European nation of Cristaña in the year 1867."

Bebop stared. "Yeah, right. Well, frankly, whatever. I'm not here to question your reality. Some spooky shit happened out there and who knows what the Mother has called on to defend herself. Maybe even a crazy soldier from two centuries ago. Who cares. You be who you wanna be. Do you want a ride anywhere? We're going back out to the camp if you need somewhere to stay?"

"I believe my bail conditions preclude me from going to your camp," said Chance. "But I'd be delighted to see it, circumstances permitting."

"What circumstances? You got somewhere else you gotta be?"

Chance shrugged. "Well yes, but that matter is out of my hands. Please, take me to camp."

"Sweet. Follow me. Sooty is waiting to drive us back."

Chance limped to a four-wheeled metallic conveyance and stood beside it, peering inside the windows. An unshaven fellow in a battered hat sat behind a smaller wheel in the front seat, eyeing him curiously. Bebop opened the front passenger door and sat inside. After a moment, realising Chance was still standing by the rear door, she looked back.

"Are you serious? Open the door and get in the car."

Chance touched the door. "Please explain the mechanism. I am unfamiliar with this conveyance."

Bebop opened the door from inside. Sooty, Scotty and Rilka looked from him to Bebop, who returned a thin smile. Chance sat in the back, staring in fascination at the interior of the vehicle. Listening to the engine, he tapped Bebop on the shoulder.

"Pardon me Bebop. What form of engine is powering this vehicle?"

"Jesus, are you kidding me? You're gonna play this 'two centuries ago' trip out to the bitter end, aren't you. Ok, it's a petrol motor. An internal combustion engine if you will."

"Petroleum?" asked Chance, undaunted. "Of course. The vapours explode in a combustion chamber to produce energy. Fascinating. I would dearly love to see the engine at work. Sooty my friend, would you indulge an old man and stop the vehicle so I can examine the mechanism? I would dearly love to take such knowledge back to my own world, assuming that transpires."

"Yeah, sure digger," said Sooty. "But not now. Kinda in enemy territory here."

Indeed a large vehicle had pulled in behind and two men in big hats were yelling at them. As Sooty drove away Chance stared through the car window at oddly shaped, angular buildings and straight roads, bereft of horses or manure. More vehicles of various colours and sizes passed them, prompting Chance to crane his neck through the back window, marvelling at their construction and speed. When loud, alien music began playing through the door he gaped in open astonishment. Soon they had left the town and were cruising through low hills, headed west.

Bebop tried to ignore Chance's evident amazement at everything, but kept stealing glances in the rear vision mirror. Sooty just chuckled and kept driving.

After half an hour, he caught Bebop's attention and angled eyebrows to the back seat. Bebop glanced around. Chance appeared to be involved in a conversation with himself.

"I told you he was odd," she murmured. "Jesus, you should have seen the ninja skills he dealt those cops though. I mean I know we're s'posed to be NVDA, but that was something else."

But the next time she turned her head to look at Chance, he was gone.

# 23

# Gutta Percha

The hour must be late, Vania thought, for a full, purpling and oddly ovoid moon was peering through the high window of the bungalow's sitting room. Outside everything was quiet except for the faint rumbling of a steam generator, buried in a bunker at the back of the main house. For a moment she lay still, wondering why she had woken. Then she remembered.

In the afternoon she had decided to strike. All week she'd observed Cockwattle's staff preparing for some event. Guards were doubled at the main gates and more patrolled the grounds. A succession of heavy laden pantechnicons were admitted. Uniformed porters unloaded a multitude of wooden crates, each carried inside the main house by six men.

Through her spyglass Vania identified two marques emblazoned under the East India Company's imprimatur on the crates; the British India Submarine Telegraph Company and British Cable and Wire.

Both were listed in company brochures she'd found alongside a Bible and a pornographic magazine in the parlour of her bungalow. In the unlocked bureau also remained a prospectus of the East India Company's international holdings; British India Submarine Telegraph Company and British Cable and Wire among them.

Vania had read about the company in *The Times*. Manufacturers of the latest communications technologies, they famously laid undersea telegraph cables across the English Channel and more recently from London to Bombay. These employed thermoplastic insulated cable made of *gutta-percha*, made from a tree of the same name, also used in the manufacture of medical and scientific equipment. The prospectus described it as 'a rubber-like elastomer which is biologically inert, resilient and non-conductive of electricity'.

Most of the pantechnicons were offloading only *gutta-percha* cables. This concurred with Ancoulsis' reckoning of a major communications installation. Indeed, Cockwattle had confirmed it.

Over dinner two evenings earlier the magnate crowed at length about his global empire. His pudgy face was mantled crimson, shining with sweat, prominent blues eyes stained with excess. He talked incessantly as he washed slices of beef down with claret. His voice was reedy, layered with aristocratic affectation.

"I shall be busy this week, my Italian butterfly. I regret that I may not be able to spend any time with you."

"Oh?" pouted Vania, hating herself for it. "Don't sell *me* a dog Cockwattle. Who could be more entertaining than I?"

"No-one dear Vania," said Cockwattle. "You are absolutely bricky. No, I am approaching the culmination of long-laid plans for a takeover of certain international holdings. The undertaking will involve considerable hardware and logistics. I am constructing a fantastic transmissions machine on these very premises, a contraption such as you might find in the pages of one of those writers, oh, you know what I mean, Edgar Allen Poe, that kind of nonsense. But this, my treasure, this is real. A manifestation of unique modern technologies, to be used in a rather, er, novel manner."

"Pray, don't talk in mysteries Cockwattle," purred Vania. "What is its purpose?"

Cockwattle glowed like a beacon. "Can't say, my boo, can't say. Suffice to say it involves rather extraordinary concepts which make a mockery of er, contemporary notions of space and time, haw haw. Concepts which my boffins have been developing over some years and for which, begad, they have devised a machine which will enable me to personally conclude a rather large, and shall we say, outlandish project."

Cockwattle preened, passing one greasy hand over his thinning hair. "Hearken to me, Vania de Mezzanotte, you exquisite beauty. When this little project is over, your Cockwattle will own most of the planet we stand on. Yes yes, titter if you must. I already have most of it, but after this, well, let's just say that the whole shooting match is my guerdon."

Vania pretended to sulk, reducing Cockwattle to wheedling noises and reckless promises.

"I am truly sorry my poppet, but during this rather delicate operation you must of necessity be excluded from the house. I will be preoccupied for a full night but afterwards, I expect I shall become the richest and most powerful man on the planet. And then, we shall see about that yacht I promised you."

"How splendid, but I shall probably be indisposed," said Vania haughtily, rising from the table and leaving the room, knowing just how tantalising Cockwattle would find that dismissal. His entreaties pursued her, followed by glass smashing and a torrent of abuse levelled at his bodyguards. But Vania returned to her bungalow and had not visited him since.

On Tuesday a team of technicians arrived in an East India Company omnibus. They had gone inside the manse and construction noises issued forth since, till noon today, when they abruptly left, driven away in the same vehicle. That afternoon the groundsmen locked up the big cats, saving Vania the trouble of having to tranquillise them. By two the staff had mostly vacated the premises. Watching through the windows Vania counted five housekeepers leave. By her calculations only the butler and three bodyguards remained inside the mansion.

Now, lying in bed on the eve of her attack she was reminded of something she'd read in the East India Company's prospectus.

"This year the company will complete the construction of an Anglo-Mediterranean cable. The instantaneous communications so afforded will be invaluable in managing native elements, in order to establish a profitable hegemony with control over communications and markets in fractious Eastern European territories."

Cockwattle's boasting seemed to confirm both this declaration and the *gutta-percha* installation Ancoulsis had described. There'd been sufficient components delivered to conform to the electromagnetic qualities of his precious idol.

As to Ancoulsis' other prognostications, when Vania accepted the invitation to stay at his manor a week before, Cockwattle had unquestioningly showed her to the bungalow, two decades after they'd first met. Nor had he attempted to press his ardour. On the two occasions when she felt certain he was going to force himself upon her he'd suddenly lost interest, looked around vacantly and wandered away. On both occasions Vania felt an emanation of hostility coming from the idol, despite the 'apotropaic' pouch that supposedly contained its radiations. She felt oddly safe with that sinister periapt, no matter how menacing its visions.

Enough deliberating, she decided, and threw aside the sheets. Rising naked, she drank cold tea from a stand beside the bed. She dressed swiftly, taking care to adjust the holsters for her pistol and poniard against the silk chemise she wore under her fatigues. In addition she had strapped a leather bandolero from her left shoulder to her hip. Into it she secured the apotropaic pouch that contained the idol.

Preparations complete, she unlocked and opened the door to her bungalow and peered cautiously outside. The compound was in darkness. There were no guards to be seen and she made her way through the trees without any alarms sounding. As she passed the perimeter of the first rose garden she heard voices and ducked behind a culvert.

Two English guards had paused to gossip, so Vania sank behind an aromatic rose bush. The men were reminiscing about their antics in a brothel the night before. Rather than listen she reviewed her last conversation with Ancoulsis, on the morning she left to visit Cockwattle in his Bombay manse.

After lovemaking once more they had bathed and taken a walk through the city. Ancoulsis enlarged on his plans as they strolled along the seafront, past the Portuguese gate and the wharves by the dull, leaden waters of the Arabian Sea. Despite the stench of open sewers and the omnipresent rats, the refuse heaps and old rotting piers, Vania felt intensely alive, now that she had a deadly mission to attend. She hummed a Genoese folk tune as they strolled past the old Portuguese stone forts and Colaba market.

The beggars seemed to know Ancoulsis well and gave him a wide berth as he strode along, talking, always talking. "Cockwattle's business interests in Bombay are varied but his hegemonies exclude all indigenous trade. He has a monopoly over the silk markets, controls the flow of muslin, chintz, onyx, rice, cotton and tobacco to Europe. His holdings include the coconut groves on all surrounding islands, whose natives are forbidden from their traditional trades in coir and thatched palms. They are forced into indentured labour, working on subsistence wages in appalling conditions."

"He's bought himself a peerage and seats in Parliament with the loot plundered from former rulers, with taxes levied on farmers who owned this land for generations, diamonds stolen from Madras and Bengal, with the manipulation of currency which bankrupted India."

They turned onto the Hornby Vellard, where naked men were being herded in chains by British soldiers. "Yes," said Ancoulsis. "The slave trade is alive and well in India, despite the hand-wringing prohibitionists in England, who never take the long journey to see whether their laws are enforced in the further reaches of the Empire. Cockwattle's immense wealth still derives from slavery, as does that of all the English aristocracy. This is the dread secret that the rest of the world does not wish to enquire too deeply into, lest it disturb their genteel minds."

He stopped and took Vania by both hands. His deep-set eyes stared intently into hers. "It is within our power to dismantle Cockwattle's operation, Vania. I know that his plans are almost complete. He is coordinating his coup with military manoeuvres across the Balkans. If we strike at the right moment we can bring them all undone. You should wait until his preparations are finalised, then make your attack when he is engaged in the transformative act."

"Transformative act?" mused Vania. "What would that look like?"

Ancoulsis smiled his wry smile. "That I do not know, but I am sure you will know it when you see it, unless you are quite used to paranormal events."

"I do not even believe in this paranormal you speak of," she said. "I know that your idol produces some very strange effects, but I am certain these are explainable by science. As to the twenty years that have passed, I can only imagine I have been in a coma or something and just awoken. There must be some explanation. Perhaps your fantastical tales played upon my mind, dazed and sick after that long hellish voyage. That and your extraordinary sexual abilities. Where did you learn that exquisite trick, that special fillip?"

"A gentleman does not betray his sources," said Ancoulsis sombrely. "But do not make light of this situation. And do not ever underestimate the idol. If you must, disregard its otherworldly emanations and look upon it as a hazardous artefact alone, due to the radioactive elements within its construction."

"Very well," said Vania. "If it will make you stop talking about it, I will take your bauble with me, and when I strike, if some kind of opportunity presents itself I promise I shall employ it."

They stopped to regard two street pedlars arguing over a stretch of pavement. Interrupting their bickering, Ancoulsis ordered chai from one and a muslin scarf from another. Draping the scarf over Vania's neck, he led her to a stone wall where they sat above the murmuring ocean.

"Vania, I will not cozen you," Ancoulsis said. "This is a dangerous escapade. To be blunt, you may not survive it. I would not ask you to risk your life, but we are running out of subjective time. I have twice tried and failed to gain access to Cockwattle's inner circle. I have burgled his house and nearly been caught in the act. I had to kill a tiger to escape."

"Then why do you think I shall succeed where you have failed?" demanded Vania.

"For the reasons stated earlier. Cockwattle will not suspect you, Vania de Mezzanotte. Because you established yourself in his good graces, because Enlil has arranged matters so artfully. Our plan *must* work, for otherwise Cockwattle's empire will be immeasurably expanded and there will be no way of establishing the Balkan League. And that is something we cannot contemplate."

In Cockwattle's benighted garden, the guards had moved on. Vania dismissed her reverie, steeled herself and darted across the secondary gardens, past nasturtiums, landscaped walkways and *gourami* ponds until she leaned against the wall of the mansion. She followed it around to the rear of the building and a privy entrance she knew was always unlocked.

As she climbed the embrasure she heard a noise. Turning, she saw a Sikh guard approaching at a run. He had seen her and was raising a whistle to his lips. Her poniard whipped through the air, embedding itself in his neck.

*That was a skill she had learned as a child from Ugolin, her father's highest ranking soldier. He had loved to indulge her, stole cakes from the kitchen for her, called her Principessa and taught her how to handle* knife and gun. The child Vania took readily to this instruction, encouraged by her mother, who believed women should be able to kill if necessity required it.

Ugolin too, believed in such womanly arts. "Your father will not always be able to protect you," he told her, his brutally cropped head showing scars across the scalp, the cheek and one long one from ear to jaw. "And Ugolin will one day be dead. So learn how to deal with your enemies swiftly, and you will perhaps be safer than otherwise."

Always he impressed upon her the necessity of intention. "Once you are in a fight you do not hesitate. Use your every weapon, swiftly and without hesitation, to finish it."

With Vania's knife in his neck the Sihk dropped instantly, but his death was slow, arms thrashing as blood jetted from his neck. A horrid gurgling arose. His back arched and his feet scrabbled on the tiles, till he shuddered and lay still. Vania extracted the knife from the man's neck and wiped it on his jerkin.

The garden was silent now. Vania crept to the privy door and opened it. Inside the house, she darted along the corridor, past a scullery and several closed doors till she stood in a sitting room which she knew to be adjacent to the main kitchen. It was silent, but at the edge of hearing she detected a throbbing sound. It seemed to be coming from the ballroom at the centre of the house. Indeed, from her bungalow she had observed cables leading inside, through the high window above the central front doors. Now she ran softly along a corridor in that direction.

The door to the ballroom was unlocked. Inside she could just make out a length of cable snaking through its doors. She entered the darkened room cautiously. A low humming noise arose from machinery assembled on the sprung ballroom floor.

As Vania's eyes adjusted to the dim light she saw it led to a web of *gutta-percha* hawsers and flex, woven through the ballroom in an oddly symmetrical matrix. At its epicentre, in a harness suspended ten feet above the ground was a naked man. To her astonishment Vania realised this was Cockwattle. Spreadeagled, with electrodes attached to his head, outstretched hands and feet, he hung with his belly dangling. His eyes were closed and he might have been dead, apart from the dreadful snoring.

# 24

# Groot Verkeerslicht

Alone in his laboratory, Vehemple surveyed the computer mainframe. In the midst of gears, wheels and cabling was a mirrored screen, the prototype of his Skein portal. In its reflection his face betrayed no emotion, countenance bleak as he checked the components one by one to ensure all were functioning correctly.

When he was satisfied all was in readiness, he switched on the portal. It swam with inchoate light, gradually resolving into a silhouette through which Lord Cockwattle's bloated face appeared. He looked bleary-eyed, as though he had just awoken.

"At last Vehemple. Took your fucking time. Are you ready to begin?"

Vehemple nodded absently, focused on wavering readout dials. Cockwattle reddened. "Pay attention you Dutch blockhead. Have you taken control of the *Sarhang's* hovel? Have you managed to overcome the obstacles that seem to dog you?"

Vehemple unplugged a valve. "I have seized control of the Hospice. The last of the D'Angel's resistance is about to be crushed by Prussian soldiers." Replacing the valve, he switched a capacitor on. "It is time for the final assault on the *Sarhang's* Citadel."

Cockwattle's eyes bulged. "So you have not yet triumphed? I will brook no more delays. Do not tell me there are further impediments to my plan?"

"You said you wished to be in for the kill," Vehemple said. "I have prepared the way and now is the time for you to claim the prize. There will be no malfunctions."

"And the *Sarhang*?"

"Either trapped in hyper-space or imprisoned within the Citadel, he is unable to personally intervene in the attack or prevent the full development of the Skein."

"Is that so? Well I hope you are adequately prepared Vehemple. We have been trying for many long years to kill this degenerate. Where is my ally, the Kaiser?"

Vehemple shrugged irritably. "See what I have prepared for you, to finish this task."

Vehemple backed away from the screen, allowing Cockwattle to see through the monitor to the gigantic automaton, his *groot verkeerslicht* erect on the wall behind him. Cockwattle's eyes gleamed as he took in the immensity of that machine, its barrel chest and thrusting weaponry. "You have the capability to download me into that?"

"As I said, all is in readiness."

"Hurry then Vehemple, lest something else interfere."

Vehemple moved along the console, flicking switches in a measured sequence. A pervading smell of ozone filled the room. The giant automaton began to hum and flicker with lights. Cockwattle stared, licking his lips.

"Brace yourself," said Vehemple. "The process is about to begin."

On the screen Cockwattle's face stiffened. He grimaced. Sweat oozed from his pursy cheeks. His eyes closed and his face went slack. Drool dripped from pale lips as his head lolled in a rubber harness.

Minutes passed as the mainframe emitted a cycling howl. Vehemple looked to his *groot verkeerslicht*. The automaton's square, chitinous eyes blinked repeatedly, then blazed with incandescent light. A mighty arm moved. A boot as long as Vehemple's legs lifted, then stomped down on the platform with an almighty crash.

Cockwattle's voice rang, metallic and grating from the machine. "Is it real? Did I just do that? Ha ha! It is so."

The machine took a step forward. Cockwattle's maniacal laughter rang as it rotated an arm. The enormous legs shifted and it took another tentative step forward. The gigantic robot flexed its limbs, one arm crashing into the wall with a shower of sparks.

"Be careful!" shouted Vehemple. "Do not endanger my equipment with your exuberance."

Heedless of the Dutchman, the automaton raised its forearm and fired a blast from an inbuilt cannon into the opposite wall. Exploding metal sprayed across the laboratory. An alarm sounded as blue flames jetted forth and acrid smoke billowed. Automatic extinguishers doused the outbreak with iridescent green foam.

"*Verdomte idioot!*" Vehemple screeched. "Desist from your foolishness. You are destroying my precious mainframe."

"Ha ha!" bellowed the automaton. "Send me the bill Dutchman. I am huge, a monster. Oh, point me to mine enemies!"

The Dutchman hastened to a panel set in the wall. Pressing buttons opened a huge set of concealed doors and Cockwattle advanced the machine toward them. Vehemple backed away as the automaton's head swivelled about, regarding him with unblinking eyes.

"This way," Vehemple shouted, walking carefully around the automaton. "Follow me and be careful! If you damage more machinery you will malfunction the *groot verkeerslicht*."

The grinding of gyros and servos resounded as Cockwattle manipulated the machine into a clumsy turn. Its leg clipped a bank of monitors, sparks arcing across the chamber. Gritting his teeth, Vehemple led the machine to the opening door of a huge elevator. "See, Lord Cockwattle. Mount yourself into this cage."

"Where are you taking me Dutchman?"

"To the Citadel of the *Sarhang*, to destroy the *Securité* and complete the conquest of the Hospice."

"Excellent," shouted Cockwattle as he manoeuvred the *groot verkeerslicht* into the cell. "Wait. Where are you going?"

"I will follow you directly," barked Vehemple. "The elevator is programmed to take you down to the *agora*, where you will encounter the survivors of the *Securité*. Once you have vanquished them I shall join you for the final onslaught."

"Very well, but do not be late for the party, Dutchman."

The doors clanged shut and the elevator descended as Vehemple strode back into his laboratory. Pressing a sequence of numbers on a panel opened the aumbry where sat his mechanised exoskeleton. Vehemple climbed up a stepladder and clipped himself into its harness. It powered up as he flexed the hydraulic arms and legs, elevated and panned the hand-cranked automatic cannon.

Satisfied all were functioning properly he walked the exoskeleton through the lab, narrowly avoiding the sprawled bodies of Teufel and the Kaiser. Then he set off at pace, the machine's metallic boots ringing on the floor. He entered an elevator and vanished.

When he was gone Black George and Proko emerged from hiding.

"Hooowee," cooed the bandit chief. "Did you see it? Legs the size of tree trunks. Arms made of cannons. With that thing I could carve out an empire. I must make friends with this ugly Dutchman. That golem of his will destroy anything the Turks or the Russkis have, eh, Proko."

"Yes, Black George," said Proko.

# 25

# One Way Traffic

Black George and Proko had watched in astonishment as Cockwattle's image was summoned into the mirrored screen. They heard his voice issuing, vastly amplified, from the gigantic machine against the far wall. Then the titan stood forth, ten times as tall as Black George, arms thick with steel and weaponry. Atop its glinting torso swivelled a head like a cannon turret and its eyes glittered with malignant power.

"Send me the bill Dutchman," it roared. "I am huge, a monster. Oh, point me to mine enemies!"

The Dutchman was waving his arms and shouting, but could not be heard over the racket of the engines. Smoke and explosions filled the room and Black George clutched himself with glee. Directed by Vehemple, the *groot verkeerslicht* manoeuvred itself inside a steel elevator chamber. The Dutchman pressed a sequence of buttons and the doors closed upon that colossus. The chamber descended out of sight. Vehemple strode to the opposite wall, opened another door and disappeared within.

Black George waited, listening a moment, then cuffed Proko over the head. "Go to that door and listen. Hiss if you hear the baldie returning."

He scurried over to the bodies of the Prussians. "Hoho my pretties," whispered Black George. "You'll have a few goodies on you, or I'm a gypsy after all."

He turned over von Teufel first, pocketing a tin of cheroots and wallet full of money. There was little else to interest him and he turned his attentions to the Kaiser. Black George's eyes glowed when he felt a poniard in the man's belt. It turned out to be a gold-plated piece, exquisitely made. He garnished three expensive-looking rings from the royal hands, a necklet with an engraved gold chassis, sapphire encrusted cufflinks and a sheaf of papers from the inner waistcoat pocket. But as he searched the royal crotch his hands closed on something familiar. He squinted suspiciously, then his eyebrows knotted as he hauled it out and confirmed his first inkling. The idol!

"Come back to haunt me have ya?" he growled. But the idol glared deep into his soul and Black George felt his heart spasm. He heard a crash from the room beyond and Proko dived under the console. Black George was of half a mind to stand up and greet the Dutchman, but something warned him against it and he too ducked into hiding.

About to put a hand over Proko's mouth in case the fool squeaked, Black George cut his hand on something. He looked down and saw the broken bottle discarded by the Kaiser. There was still a decent draught left in its bottom half. He eyed it dubiously, raised it to his lips and swigged the remaining liquid. Making a bitter face, he put the bottle down, smacking his lips distastefully. Then he looked up to see what entertainment the Dutchman would provide.

That ugly bastard was encased in a mechanical exoskeleton. Gyros around his limbs revolved and gears chased each other as he strode through the room, limbs moving with clockwork precision. He pressed buttons on the elevator cage, entered it and disappeared.

Black George shook his head in admiration. "I must make friends with this ugly Dutchman. That is a handy suit he's wearing, and that golem of his will destroy anything the Turks or the Russkis have, eh, Proko."

Proko did not answer. Black George clouted him and stood up. He staggered, suddenly dizzy. The room had turned a livid purple. Strange music welled in his ears and he heard a low peal of laughter from the idol. He shook his head. Things were, if possible, getting stranger.

Proko emerged from under the console, head bowed, but Black George was too weirded out to even mock him. He tried to speak but that seemed entirely too adventurous a proposition so instead he followed after Vehemple, taking exaggerated strides to deal with the sudden levitation of his spine.

Whatever he had drunk was sparking a new kind of strangeness, but the idol was directing him clearly. Black George tried to start a conversation with it but all the crazy noises seemed to be one-way traffic. It directed him unerringly to one of those elevators. Black George stepped inside, automatically pressing one of about twenty buttons. When the door closed he remembered Proko, but funnily enough the wife beater was beside him as the machine swiftly descended.

# 26

# Your Spears are Carried off by the Wind

Bejikereene and Olaf had been hearing gunfire since they began navigating the Hospice. But it was becoming louder and more intense.

"How do you know where you're going?" Olaf asked, but Bejikereene said nothing. The idol had guided her unerringly thus far. She merely responded to its impulses now, following endless turns through this labyrinth. Olaf limped after Bejikereene, wary of the weapon in her hands. He had left his behind, cracked and broken after he used it as a club on the metal monster that killed poor Rilka.

After the demolition of the laboratory he'd laid her body in a garden with an awkward prayer. "Poor lass," he said. "They'll come for ye, give ye proper burial, once this is over."

Bejikereene kissed his forehead. "Come now Olaf," she said. "The idol is impatient."

They came now onto a landing, where amongst burnt and bullet-riddled tables were the bodies of three Prussians and further along, those of swarthy soldiers with extravagant moustaches, wearing blue pantaloons. "Turks" said Olaf. "Dreaming of their precious Rumelia again, I suppose."

"It weren't Turks shooting at me, afore," said Bejikereene through compressed lips. "More like Germans, or French or some such. Soldiers is soldiers Olaf, and none of 'em are to the good."

They followed the destruction and death down a set of broad stairs to a lower floor, where Olaf recognised the peculiar arrangement of trees grown into a canopied banquet table, with sumptuous seating and plump moss for cushions. "This is where Mister Chance was talking to the African lady, when he sent me to look for the witch, Kalyenka Menschievr."

"So you *do* know your way around?" said Bejikereene archly. "Which way is out then?"

"I come in from above, chasing that bald bastard, pardon the language. Wouldn't have a clue where we're going now."

"Down, and out," snapped Bejikereene. "And the less talk the better. I need to concentrate on what this thing is telling me."

"What's it sayin'?" demanded Olaf, but Bejikereene hushed him with a flattened hand. She pointed her weapon at a hallway ahead. A broad ramp led downwards from there and the din of weaponry grew louder. The shouting and screams of men resounded and an explosion rocked the air. The smell of burning was pervasive.

Bejikereene inched forward, looking down the ramp onto soldiers cowering behind makeshift barricades, firing into the enormous unroofed chamber beyond. Olaf peered through the smoke. "Them's the Prussians," he said. "And look, more coming."

A platoon of Prussian soldiers had detached themselves from cover. Urged on by a Leutnant shouting "*Für König und Vaterland!*" they charged over the barricades and into the *agora*. A tearing sound erupted and half dropped dead on the ground, but undeterred, more emerged from beneath the ramp, running.

"We should git," said Olaf, but Bejikereene stepped forward.

"What are ye about woman?" he demanded. Bejikereene snorted. "I don't know, but *it's* telling me this is the only way out. We've got to get through this lot. Follow me hard man, and stop your whining."

"Jehosophat and all the saints preserve us," muttered Olaf, picking up a gun from the body of a dead *Securité*. "I reckernise that uniform," he said. "They're the *tougrak* alright, and believe it or not the *tougrak* are the good soldiers in this fight."

But Bejikereene was already well down the ramp and did not hear. "This too I reckon," Olaf said, gingerly untangling torso armour from the dead man. Strapping it to his broad chest, he hurried after her.

They were in a vast semi-circular concourse, with the galleries of higher levels climbing above into the limitless space of the mountainside. Before them the twisted wreckage of machines and furniture littered the *agora*, alongside hundreds of bodies and the reek of sulphur and blood. In the distance Olaf could see armoured barricades and beyond them, a towering wall of purple mist.

He gaped up at the encircling galleries, many of them afire now, and in the scope and grandeur of their construction he was for the first time truly aware of the awesome scale of this Hospice. Lowering his gaze, he took in the fortifications defying the charges of the Prussians, and concluded that Chance's friends the D'Angels must be holding out there.

Picking their way through bodies and wreckage, Bejikereene and Olaf beheld jaegers, slaughtered by bullet or shrapnel, dying in exaggerated attitudes. But shots from within the *agora* defences were becoming sporadic.

He put a hand on Bejikereene's shoulder. "That's far enough Beeney."

"It wants us to go in there," she said.

"We've done our bit and damn the statue."

"Not yet Olaf. Not yet."

But even as she spoke Bejikereene sensed the idol stirring in its pouch on her hip. "Oh no you don't," she shouted, but a blinding light blazed and she shrieked and fell over backwards.

Sprawled on the ground, she cried out; "*Your horses cannot stir from their places, they are not able to draw the chariot, your spears are carried off by the wind!*"

But this time it seemed to have no effect and a nimbus of purple light was unspooling from the pouch at her hip. Olaf took her by the arm. "Come, on your feet wife," he shouted, but even as he lifted her the light expanded relentlessly, filling the air around them.

Blinking into that glare Olaf saw a manlike being coalescing, growing in stature till it stood thrice as tall as he. Horned and winged, it looked nothing like the flying mannikins of the *tougrak*, nothing like anything Olaf had ever seen before. Its entoptic eyes glittered with unholy jubilation as it tilted its head back and uttered a fey cry that echoed in multiple octaves and shivered the very air.

*"I am Enlil, storm of majestic splendour, who pillages the Mountains all alone; deluge, indefatigable serpent! Lord whose powerful arm is fit to bear the mace, reaping like barley the necks of the insubordinate!*

*"Hero whose awesomeness covers the Mountains like a south storm; who makes the good tiara, the rainbow, flash like lightning; grandly begotten by him who wears the princely beard; dragon who turns on himself, strength of a lion snarling at a snake, roaring hurricane; great battle-net flung over the foe!*

*"Antelope of Heaven, trampling the Mountains beneath my hooves, I drag away the tamarisks!"*

Around them the walls of the Hospice quivered and flowed like mud, twisting into strange patterns, coming alive in answer to that call. Prussian soldiers heard that cry and turned to fire into the spectral being. But the bullets passed through it and Enlil laughed, an unholy sound that wrenched the souls of all who heard it.

Olaf grunted as he felt something tug at his chest and looked down to see a spent bullet un-peel from the torso armour, pop out and drop to the ground. He felt a sharp pain and knew a great bruising would come out of it. He sat heavily on the ground beside his wife.

But Enlil bellowed again. He raised aloft his lightning staff and from it came forth jagged blades of light that smote the Prussians like a storm. They fell to the ground, score upon score of them, and

Bejikereene screeched one more time. *Your spears are carried off by*"
"*!the wind*

The apparition only turned his head and grinned at her. With flames issuing from his open mouth, Enlil raised the lightning rod and charged into the *agora*. His head brushed the bottom of the landing above, for Enlil was now five times the height of a man and still growing. Bejikereene and Olaf watched him go, feeling that the world had uprooted itself and was walking to Babylon, as the saying went. After a time Bejikereene hauled herself wearily to her feet.

"Where are you going woman?" demanded Olaf.

"I don't know Olaf, but we must follow. That's the way out."

Shaking his head, Olaf stood on shaky legs. Bejikereene was already moving, though bullets stung the air around them. Stooping low as he could, Olaf followed his wife through the smoke and detritus of battle. They passed dozens of dead Prussians before they made it to the relative safety of the first abandoned barricade and hunkered down, bullets howling over their heads.

"Madness to go in there!" Olaf shouted, but Bejikereene's face was fierce. "Madness to be here at all Olaf, but here we are."

She laid a hand on his shoulder. "This statue is alive now, and we're both responsible for't. My mother always tole me clean up my own mess, and that's somethin' you oughta take on board, ya great lunk."

Olaf knuckled his eyes. "Aright woman, but be careful," he said, almost chuckling at the futility of that admonition. When he looked up Bejikereene was already scrambling over the barricade.

"Wait!" he bellowed and climbed wearily after her. Mercifully the shooting seemed to have slowed and he made it over without being hit. Clambering down the other side of the tangled mess he peered through the smoke. Bejikereene's receding form was limned against the glaring light of what looked like an ongoing explosion.

As Olaf looked closer he realised the luminous eruption was in fact the apparition that had escaped from Bejikereene's pouch, now grown twenty times larger and wreaking the kind of havoc you might expect from a regiment of artillery. It was dealing lightning bolts that zapped twenty soldiers at a stroke and the pitiful gunfire they were returning did not seem to affect that grinning monstrosity one whit.

Olaf shouted after Bejikereene but could not hear his own voice. Instead he forced his legs into a trot, cocking the *Securité* weapon and adding his own fire to the battle, dispatching one enterprising Prussian who sought to shoot Bejikereene from behind. He redoubled his pace, groaning with fatigue, but determined to catch up to his errant wife and effect their escape from this inferno.

Then another door opened way at the other end of the *agora* and a gigantic machine emerged. This was a two-legged monstrosity like the thing Olaf had fought in the bald man's laboratory, but again about ten times bigger.

It's right arm pulsed and a blur of flame and smoke issued forth, crashing into Enlil. But the god bellowed in what Olaf recognised as mirth and replied with a surge of lightning that arced across the chamber and smashed the machine back on its haunches.

"Gods and devils," muttered Olaf. "I hope you've got some remedy for this turnout, Mister Chance."

# 27

# Ever Becoming

In the ruins of the Womb of Time, an enormous web of mycorrhiza sprouted from under the bloodied and burnt fungcrete floor. A thousand times faster than any plant can grow, its hyphae multiplied and snaked through the foundations.

Cellular biota swelled and thickened to make roots, split the pavers and weave upward through charred timbers, the ashes of the fungal mainframe and bodies of jaegers and *Securité* mangled by bullets. Millions of tendrils ran into gaping wounds, threading themselves amongst dying nervous systems, using bodies and blood as fuel to sprout stronger tendrils that fused together, spurting up the fungal walls of the Hospice.

These rapidly extended, sprawling through the basement chamber that housed the Womb of Time. Out of it new tendrils continued to grow, travelling up through the superstructure of the Hospice and into the Hall of the Exposition. From above the Hall, the Hospice sent down a billion tendrils of its own fungal mycorrhiza.

In the hall of the Exposition the body of Julie Brown had been laid on a pallet. Three medical technicians fussed around her, but their expressions were grim. Tubes inside their instruments glowed as they laid first one, then another on the body, attempting resuscitation, searching for vital signs. Finally the chief medic looked up at the others and shook her head. A *Securité* sergeant spoke into a communications device and her troopers watched as the two techs reverently laid a sheet over Julie Brown.

But at that moment a wave of mycorrhiza came flowering out of the floor, another descended from the roof and both engulfed the body. The two streams met and became entwined. Within them motes of information transfused into ever-growing wells of data, self-replicating, learning.

The med techs and *Securité* backed away nervously as Julie was shrouded in vegetable matter and her flesh began to be absorbed. They watched an organic process as old as the earth recycling her physical matter. Soon the body was consumed, replaced by a pulsing mass of new organisms that sent out fresh shoots, sending information back and forth between the Earth Entity and the superstructure of the Hospice.

In a makeshift office in the heights of the Hospice, seated at a table adorned with neat stacks of paper and a small, intricate steel sculpture, facing a window with a bedazzling view of adjacent mountain peaks, Doctor Amordule was tracking the process through the chimera lens, visible in a screen set into a wooden frame. Beside it a second screen fizzed with data, representing the progress of Julie Brown's transubstantiation.

The doctor was startled by a chime in her ceramic earpiece, alerting her to the arrival of an entity through the *Mēnōg* interface. Seconds later, Chance appeared in the doorway of a cabinet to Amordule's left.

He looked dazed and disoriented, but recognised Amordule and stepped forward into the room, cradling his right shoulder. "Good morrow, Doctor. I don't think I shall ever get used to this. Where am I now?"

"Good afternoon Chance. You are in my temporary office in the Hospice and you are just in time, if I may use that quaint expression, to witness probably the most extraordinary transformation in the continuum of this planet."

But Chance was bending over, groaning.

"Are you alright, Lieutenant Colonel?" she asked.

"Just stretching, Doctor. I'm afraid I'm on a surfeit of extraordinary things at this moment. But do tell, what are we about to witness? And may I have a stiff drink first?"

Amordule nodded at the second screen. "See there. The dataviz shows that Julie Brown has ignited her role as the Cosmic Shekinah; the nexus between humanity and the Earth Entity. Whisky in the decanter."

Chance looked on in horror as the singer's body was broken down and absorbed by the creeping white web. "She had to die to do that?"

"Julie Brown knew of this potentiality," said Amordule primly. "She embodied the Cosmic Shekinah, the office of the Womb of Time. She voluntarily embraced its vulnerabilities, in order that this very process should be able to be enacted. In any case, she is not dead but reborn within the Womb of Time. Her mind is now pure data, facilitating the Great Work."

"Not sure I'm ready for this," grunted Chance, gratefully gulping a rare whisky.

"You'll be fine after your refreshments," said Amordule. "There, on the table you'll find coffee. And a flask of that herbal concoction you found so efficacious. There is a water closet and a shower in yonder cubicle."

"Ah, splendid," said Chance. "You were expecting me then?"

"I was told you were in transit through a phase of the *Mēnōg*," said Amordule absently as she typed on a flat keyboard, absent any of the underlying mechanisms Chance would have expected to see. Pouring himself a large carafe, equal parts coffee, whisky and the miracle elixir, he disappeared into the adjoining cubicle, where water could be heard being energetically employed. After a while he reappeared, towelling his hair. He sat in a chair beside Amordule. "I don't suppose you have a pipe or any tobacco?" he said wistfully.

"In the drawer in front of you."

"Really? How marvellous."

The next few moments involved Chance enthusiastically arming the designated pipe, a venerable wooden implement probably, he thought, once used as a hashish *chillum*. Amordule pointedly looked at the window and he stood to open it a fraction, blowing smoke out through the crack, which howled with the strength of the gale outside.

"Now," Chance said. "Remind me of the mechanics of this Cosmic Shekinah?"

"Remember the Caduceus, the two headed snake of *khuti* I told you about?" Amordule continued typing as she spoke. "The same divine principle of gendered polarity applies. Just as the gods require a consort in order to complete the *khuti* circuit, humans require a female and male counterpart in order to make their *khuti* manifest, in order, as the Hermeticists put it, to manifest the ever-becoming one."

"Yes, yes, the ever-becoming one," said Chance. "But what, pray, does 'making *khuti* manifest' look like?"

"To put things, however temporarily, into balance. That is the objective of the Great Work, the ultimate project we all work towards, no matter how reluctant or unwittingly, to bring the universe into harmony. I like to compare it to the creation of a piece of art."

"How so?"

Amordule plaited her hands and gazed at the abstracted sculpture on her desk. "When a piece is completed and made whole there is for a while a feeling of accomplishment, a vindication of one's life on earth. Just so, imagination allied with emotion are the essential ingredients in the creation of a stable universe. Artistry integrates that formula, making *khuti* manifest, which is to say, creating that stable universe. But that is an individual emotion.

"On the macro scale, by which I mean as it relates to returning the whole of humanity to a state of balance, well, that requires bringing the long sundered emotional poles of male and female into harmony again. This is our paramount strategic objective, as determined by the Womb of Time's dynamic situation modelling. By reinstating the Cosmic Shekinah the female component will once again be written in the human narrative. Only then can the human component of the programme be run and the correct answers be deduced as to where the human race is headed."

Chance took another luxuriant puff. "How is the human race to deduce this, it being one inchoate mass of squabbling fools?"

"Tut, Mister Chance," said Amordule, waving smoke away. "Negative comments about our fatally flawed species are not helpful. Our best template is in nature, in which all things are in harmonic balance. Unfortunately most of humanity no longer recognises this. To bring us back to that understanding we must complete the cosmic circuit and that is the function of the Cosmic Shekinah, embodied in an individual - the performer Julie Brown."

"I see. And what is to become of Julie Brown in fulfilling that role?"

Amordule turned to face Chance, and now her eyes were sparkling with joy.

"She will essentially become a goddess, embodying the cosmic capacities of the Sumerian entity Inanna, as handed down to her priestesses and thereafter to gifted women who have occupied the role through ensuing centuries. They are women of extraordinary *khuti* - of compassion, bravery and fierce intelligence. In technical terms their rituals make the *khuti* of the goddess manifest and provide a bridge to the metaphysical realm. That bridge must be anchored to the source of humanity's *khuti* - the planet itself. Thus it is the role of the goddess in the Cosmic Shekinah to reawaken the Earth Entity."

"A kind of magneto generator then," mused Chance. "Remind me of the nature of the Earth Entity?"

"In essence an entity similar to the gods, but housed entirely within the earth itself. Known as Lord Ningindizha, though interestingly 'they' have two genders. They have no communication with the gods, apart from their self-professed guardian, Enlil.

Amordule pointed to the screen, now showing a microscopic close-up of the cell walls comprising Julie Brown's composted remains. They were vibrating, glowing with the immense power of a green cosmic fuse. "Like Enlil, they have no especial interest in humanity, apart from the species' role in their ecosystems. We as a species, on the other hand have an existential interest in them. Restoration of the Entity will multiply our *khuti* by many factors. As soon as they transfuse their essential data into the fungal cells of the Hospice we will activate the processes to annihilate the Skein and fast-track humanity's evolution into the *Mēnōg*."

Chance cocked his head. "But I thought you said the Hospice's data would be destroyed along with the Womb of Time?"

"That is what I had led Vehemple to believe and what I told you, in case you were captured and interrogated. But the Hospice is like a plant, in that it has no brain or central command module. Its organic structure has distributed processing systems, so they can't be destroyed, as long as any one component survives."

"Well, that is splendid."

"Indeed," said Amordule. "Now. Do you have a report on your activities along your *apeira*?"

Chance put down the pipe. "Well, the, er, god appeared. That was interesting. And a very large coal mine was put out of operation. There was some jubilation amongst the people I was arrested with. I think I can say the mission was a success."

Amordule nodded thoughtfully. "From what I have observed through the chimera lens I believe you may be right. But as you may have gathered, that was only one small factor in our defences. We are responding to attacks from within and without. The Hospice was thought invulnerable, but Vehemple's treachery has put paid to that notion.

"Prussian soldiers are within our very walls, where they are being engaged by a contingent of Ottoman soldiers under their Caliph, whom I believe you have made common cause with? Lastly the Prussians have captured our rail depot in Cristaña and sent a train full of soldiers into the subterranean station beneath this facility, where I believe they were only prevented from invading the facility by the random intervention of an unknown operator, who is in possession of an iteration of the idol. That is the current situation, which I think could be described as 'dire.'"

"In that case I'd better stop loafing about and get down to it," said Chance. "Don't have another shot of that marvellous elixir do you?"

"In the drawer, Lieutenant Colonel. But take it easy on that stuff."

"Very well," said Chance. "What of Kalyenka? Where is she?"

"I believe she is in the Citadel, which is under assault by the Prussians."

"Thank you Doctor. I hope I will see you presently." Chance hurriedly downed another carafe of elixir, tipped a non-existent hat to Amordule and left her office. Exiting the office he took an escalator down several floors. As the door opened he heard gunfire echoing through the Hospice, but levelled his weapon on an empty corridor.

Consulting his glow-chart he proceeded carefully towards the *agora*. A fierce battle had evidently raged through the building. All the animals had fled. Trees, columns and architraves were toppled, furniture smashed, walls scorched or burning. As he came closer to the *agora* Chance picked his way across floors littered with dead jaegers, *Securité* and janissaries.

Peering down through an atrium which spanned five floors he espied grey uniformed jaegers swarming along stairs and escalators, all seemingly headed for the *agora*. He followed them cautiously. They were gathering in ranks along a concourse below him, but Chance detoured well around them, to a point where his glow-chart showed an auxiliary stairwell behind a security door.

His rooster pass opened the door and he ran down the stairs, passing a family of terrified foxes. The door opened in the rear of the *Securité* defence. They were behind barricades, their backs to him, firing at waves of oncoming Prussian troopers. Alongside them he recognized the baggy pantaloons and *bork* hats of the Caliph's janissaries.

Ducking low to avoid bullets hissing overhead, Chance made his way past tired and begrimed troopers, many of them wounded, till he found Rodriguez. The man's face was grim. He had a gouge in his cheek and a wound in his thigh. "Chance, you return at last. We have only a handful of troopers still living. The Prussians are relentless."

Chance laid a hand on his shoulder. "We need to hold on, Rodriguez. The *Sarhang* is doing his best to fight off the *Ljmmûm* in his spirit world."

"If he does not hurry there will be none left to defend him."

"For Devurrier then," said Chance.

"For Devurrier," smiled Rodriguez.

At that moment a Prussian jaeger who had crawled unseen through detritus and bodies lunged over the barricade and thrust a bayonet at Rodriguez. Chance shot the man, but more jaegers were leaping over the rampart and in the ensuing firefight Chance was hard pressed to survive. Another *Securité* died but five janissaries joined the melee and bested the Prussians.

Chance reloaded and turned to survey his section, only to see Rodriguez lying stricken on the ground. The Prussian bayonet had punctured his side, but he opened his eyes and raised a hand even as medics loaded him onto a stretcher. "Chance, this position is hopeless. Order a staggered withdrawal before it is too late. The Citadel must not be breached."

Chance cast an eye along the barricade, where those few unwounded were spread thinly along a long line. "I'll do my best to hold 'em while we withdraw," he said.

"Good luck, Chance," said Rodriguez, and his head lolled back as the medication took hold. "Withdraw to the Citadel in sections," Chance shouted. "One man to hold every twenty yards."

After that last charge the Prussians had pulled back to positions outside the *agora*, but Chance heard their officers bellowing orders. He cupped a hand to his mouth and shouted, "They're reforming and they have reinforcements. Watch your backs, *Securité*."

Gathering those wounded who could walk, the surviving *Securité* withdrew through the ruins, towards the mist-wreathed Chthonic Gates. Medics loaded up stretchers with the grievously wounded and followed, but behind them the janissaries were casting leery eyes at their retreating allies.

"*Beni dinle!*" Chance shouted to those men. ".*Gitme zamani* "

They only glared and looked at one another. "Where is your Caliph?" he asked, but at that moment heard a shout and looked up to see the Caliph approaching from the far end of the fortifications. The man looked positively cheerful, though his right thigh was bandaged and his face blackened by soot. "Ah, it is my friend Chance. Have you seen the woman doctor, Lady Amordule?"

"Yes, just now, upstairs. She directed me here."

"Such a beauty she is. I may accept her as a concubine. Yes my friend, so good to see you. I knew you would not miss a good fight. But I fear these Prussians have us on *kuzu çevirme*. We are soon to enter Paradise. Yet I am glad to die alongside such a warrior as you."

"Don't be too eager for death Caliph. We have to manifest the Ever Becoming One first."

"*Ne dedin?*"

"Never mind. We must retreat, my lord."

"Yes, I see it," said the Caliph. "I will order it, if only that I might see my sable lady again before I die."

He bellowed orders in Turkish and his janissaries moved out in good order, following the *Securité*. The Caliph watched to ensure they had safely retired and only a rearguard remained. But at that moment a mortar shell exploded, showering the defences with shrapnel and bodies.

Chance found himself lying stunned on a bed of sandbags. He felt blood running down his face and his ears were ringing, but could not feel any major damage. He looked himself over. Satisfied he had suffered no grievous wounds, he levered himself to his feet. There was no-one else standing along the line. Heart sinking, he looked down and saw the Caliph's broken body, lying dead against the parapet.

"*Tanrinla git,*" he muttered. "You were a good friend, for a short time."

He took up the Caliph's scimitar, determined to present it to his janissaries. But whistles and battle cries in German resounded. "Here we go then," he said, selecting rapid fire on his weapon. Firing a long burst towards the oncoming jaegers, Chance looked to left and right. No living men or women remained on the defences, so he turned and jogged toward the Chthonic Gates, where the last of the *Securité* and janissaries were filing into the purple mists.

Before he reached it Chance heard a mechanical crashing. He peered back into the *agora*, where something huge had appeared. Armour plated, bristling with weaponry, it resembled the flying automatons Vehemple had piloted, but was on an entirely different scale. It dwarfed the Prussians, who cowered away as it strode into the *agora*, spraying gouts of flame that incinerated them, engulfing the abandoned barricades in an inferno.

Gritting his teeth, Chance adjusted his weapon to load an explosive shell. He aimed and fired at the mechanoid, but the explosion did not appear to damage the thing at all.

Even as Chance reloaded he was startled by another apparition, appearing from the other side of the refectory. A flare of intense purple light preceded a figure seeming to flow upward from the ground. As it grew and took shape Chance groaned, recognising the distinctive entoptic eyes and elongated head.

He watched in fascinated horror as Enlil grew in stature, taking on the form of a titanic, vaguely humanoid body. Lightning kindled in his hand as he bellowed a challenge.

*"I am Enlil, storm of majestic splendour, who pillages the Mountains all alone; deluge, indefatigable serpent! Lord whose powerful arm is fit to bear the mace, reaping like barley the necks of the insubordinate!"*

There was more, but Chance's attention was distracted by the gigantic automaton, which was firing the cannon built into its arms. The shells crashed into Enlil but only seemed to augment his incandescent form. The god returned fire with a deadly accurate lightning bolt. Then he leapt and flew through the air at the automaton. There was a roar of colliding energies, and the machine crashed backwards against a pillar.

Flame billowed through the *agora* and though part of him wished to stay and observe this contest, Chance knew it was time to leave. He ran for the Chthonic Gates. Just before he plunged into its swirling vapours, Chance heard a shout. He looked back and saw the Baron Codrût Ancoulsis striding towards that titanic struggle, waving yet another iteration of the damned bloody idol.

# 28

# The Rampaging God

Ancoulsis tied his horse to a tree in a narrow forested gorge. The light was still good here in early afternoon, though heavy snow swirled through the overhanging branches. He glanced up to the spire of the Assassin, where amidst towering clouds a plume of dark smoke writhed. He gritted his teeth and cursed.

After a pause he unbuckled a fardel from his saddle bag, glancing inside to reassure himself that the idol's apotropaic pouch was secure. He heard an explosion close by, then the rattle of rapid fire. Ancoulsis had already avoided the patrols of several armies in his ride through the mountains, passing through charred forests full of dead men and horses. So far he had escaped detection.

In silence he prepared himself, tying cloak, pack and weapons across his back. After a moment's consideration he pulled the saddle off the horse and untied it, slapping it on the rump so the beast trotted uncertainly into the forest.

Ancoulsis watched it go, then began climbing the gorge. In the bright evening sky the ovate Murex Moon had risen, full and lucent, a shade of Byzantine violet. Indeed it was coming rapidly to its zenith. He was just in time, and at that thought he chuckled ruefully.

Soon the gorge levelled out and he was on a narrow path through thickset spruce and alder trees. Despite the moonlight reflecting from snowcapped peaks, gnarled branches of *krummholtz* occasionally tripped him up. Eventually he arrived at a blank rock face. He presented Jian Cong's talisman and a breach unfurled. Beyond it was a square-cut tunnel and set into the further end, the steel door of an elevator.

It opened as he approached and he stepped inside. The door slid closed and Ancoulsis felt a rapid ascent in his gut. Movement in the fardel demonstrated that his apotropaic pouch could not counter the radiation seeping from the Hospice. The idol was responding to forces not even Ancoulsis could anticipate.

The door opened. In the distance he heard the rattle of firearms, explosions, the slow howling of an alarm. He stepped forward warily, hearing shouts in Prussian, incoherent war cries in Turkish. He walked a smouldering corridor littered with shrivelled leaves and the burnt carcass of an opossum. Extinguishers were dousing a roaring fire in the chamber to his left. It looked to have spread from a blackened pile, where the bodies of several men were fused together by what must have been some terrible incendiary weapon.

Consulting his map, Ancoulsis climbed another set of stairs, noting that the numinous effects of the Hospice had further abated. That indicated severe damage to the fabric of the building and a probable decline in the influence of the *Mēnōg*. The *Sarhang* must be, as he suspected, in exile from the *Gētīg* and unable to shore up the damage. He climbed steep fire stairs, detouring through side passages to avoid soldiers or burning corridors, till he came to the level of the *agora*.

As he pushed open a doorway he heard a challenge. His eyes shrank, unaccustomed to the bright light of several torches. Ranged before him were several members of the Hospice Entheogen Academy, staring at him in silence. From a distance shots and explosions could still be heard, but this hall was strangely hushed.

"Baron Codrût Ancoulsis, you are trespassing in a sacred facility," said a woman he recognised as Sarantsatsral Yargui, a *Natugai* of the Mongolian people.

"You meddle in continuums with no regard for cosmic integrity and have endangered all of humanity by making us vulnerable to the Qliphoth," said the Yiddish necromancer Menahem Ziyuni.

"You will not be permitted to interfere with the Cosmic Shekinah," said Galyna Black Otter, the *Znakharka* of Ukraine.

"Turn around and leave this Hospice, ere we are obliged to eject you."

Ancoulsis said nothing.

"No, do not speak," said a voice he recognised as belonging to Jian Cong, though he could not see the Chinese sorcerer. "Continue to summon your demons. But do not expect success. We have been expecting you. We followed your journey through the chimera lens."

Menahem Ziyuni interjected. "Be careful Jian Cong!" For he had seen the Confucian *Shefu* swoop overhead and he knew that Ancoulsis was deadly dangerous.

But around Ancoulsis a shimmering aura formed. His eyes were closed and he was making a deep sonorous noise in his throat. The very air vibrated to his spell, but when Ancoulsis opened his eyes he looked about uncertainly.

"Your *apeira* shifting spells will not work here," said Jian Cong from the darkness. "We have blocked your sorcery."

"Very well," said Ancoulsis under his breath. "I shall be forced to call upon hierarchical powers." Uttering an invocation to Set-Typhon, he closed his eyes as the protective ward settled over him again. Then his voice erupted with power words whose timbre threatened the foundations of the Hospice.

"YOERBETH, YOPAKERBETH, YOBOLKHOSETH, YOPATATHNAX, YOSEORO, YONEBOUTOSOUALETH, AKITIOPHI, EREKESKHIGAL, NEBOPOSOALETH, ABERAMENTHOOU, LERTHEXANAX, ETHRELUOTH, NEMAREBAM AEMINA!"

Around Ancoulsis vast energies swirled, but the *khuti* web cast by the Seers of the Entheogen Academy overwhelmed them. They dampened and faded and Ancoulsis was left staring at the seers in consternation.

Jian Cong had settled to the ground, arms raised in incantation, but Ancoulsis, anticipating his attack, countered with a cantrip that hurled the *Shefu* backwards. Then, before the others could strike, he reached into his haversack and pulled forth a bundle of explosives. Hurling it at the Seers, he threw himself onto the ground as an explosion rocked the hall. An entire section of the Hospice collapsed upon them and under cover of the roiling dust Ancoulsis decamped. He made his way unerringly out of that wing of the Hospice, finding an entry to the top level. None pursued him.

As he strode along a broad corridor leading to the *agora* he came upon an extraordinary scene. A gigantic bipedal machine was marauding amongst the embattled soldiers, crushing them under its mighty steel feet and shooting missiles from tubes set in its forearms. Explosions rocked the huge chamber, fire ringed its high galleries and smoke billowed as extinguishers rained water down.

But from the opposite end of that enormous atrium a blinding amaranthine glow bloomed. Out of that conflagration appeared another towering figure. Ancoulsis recognised it instantly. Entoptic eyes blazing, the god Enlil arose and confronted the machine.

"At last," whispered Ancoulsis.

# 29

# A Commotion in his Pants

When the door of the elevator slid open, Black George could hear the roar and crackle of battle close by. Stepping outside he saw dead bodies in abundance, which heartened him somewhat. Prompted by the idol he floated, giggling, along a landing towards a staircase. All around he saw evidence of fierce fighting, but it was when he peered over the balustrades into the *agora* below that he witnessed the most astonishing tableau of all.

Prussian soldiers were scattering before the onslaught of Cockwattle in his giant tin suit. He was dealing some very impressive slaughter too, indiscriminately blowing up Prussians as well as Turks and the *tougrak's* own *Securité* troopers, who were sheltering behind barricades.

Buoyed by the startlingly paranormal effects of the blue *soma*, Black George failed to notice that Proko had scarpered when he left the elevator. The wife beater hied away, having failed to summon the courage to shoot Black George with the Kaiser's pistol, pocketed when he'd dived under the Dutchman's console.

Hidden by the invisible *tougrak* jacket, he stood some twenty feet away, hyperventilating. He kept telling himself to remember the sacred lady of his visions. If only she were here now to fill him with her calming presence. In any case, when Black George, howling furiously, set off down the stairs to the burning refectory Proko followed, clutching the pistol in a sweating hand.

For Black George in his delirium had decided he ought to ally himself with Cockwattle. No-one else in this madhouse seemed to have any idea how to take charge and Black George rather liked the Englishman's style - and the rockets in his forearms. As he pelted down the stairs, heedless of caroming bullets, Black George barely noticed a commotion in his pants, till a searing heat threatened to scorch his manhood.

Cursing, Black George pulled the idol from his crotch. It was pulsating wildly through psychedelic colour schemes. Furthermore its entoptic eyes were glowing, the lightning bolt was positively incandescent and the thing seemed to be growing in his hand.

"*I am Enlil, storm of majestic splendour!*" it cried and a lot of other things which Black George could not understand, his *soma*-addled brain being quite overwhelmed by the spectacle.

Even more astonishingly, he could have sworn he glimpsed through smoke the inn keeper from the Eagle's Nest. What the fuck was Olaf doing here? Crazier still, the man's wife was beside him. Reputed as the toughest bar room brawler in several valleys, she was toting an impressive firearm. As if that wasn't enough, the Irish soldier who Proko stole the idol from was also present. But that was not all.

Across the other side of that hall, tiny with distance, Black George saw a man who part of him recognised him as Ancoulsis, the Moldavian who advised the Karageorge. Could things get any weirder? Something was glowing in the Moldavian's upraised hand and a violet flame arced across the hall, where it met another blaze in the hand of the innkeeper's wife. Black George began to wonder if all this wasn't some rum-induced nightmare from which he would surely soon awaken.

But at that moment the idol in his own hand swelled by several inches, burning his fingers. He dropped it, but it stopped in mid-air, then levitated, growing in stature till it was filling the landing with a hellish purple glare. Black George looked around uncertainly. He almost felt that he was out of his depth. "Proko?" he said.

But Proko did not answer. The wife beater was watching from behind a nearby pillar, certain now what the Lady of Damp Shadows wanted him to do.

# 30
# Cold Flesh

General von Teufel came slowly to his senses. The pain was all consuming, but he opened one eye and forced himself up onto his knees. He froze, staring, for the Kaiser lay beside him and he was still, eyes wide open.

Teufel stretched out a hand to touch the Kaiser's shoulder. His hand trembled as he nudged cold flesh. There was no response. Dead? "*Nein, nein*, it cannot be. My *Führer*, you must awaken."

The general shook harder, though as a veteran of a thousand battles he knew a dead man when he saw one. Almost he broke down. There was moisture in his eyes, an emotion in his breast such as he had not felt since he was a *kinder*, being told by his mother that he was to go away to a military boarding school. Ach, the beatings, the ice baths, the endless running through blizzards. But that schooling had made Teufel, Supreme General Eric von Teufel, Knight of the Teutons, the man he was today. His face hardened. Abandoning futile gestures, he rose unsteadily to his feet.

Looking down at the Kaiser's body, he felt an urge to search it. "*Nein*, I am no grave robber. The Kaiser's body must be preserved untouched, for proper burial."

But the impulse was too strong. There might be something that needed to be kept safe, in case the body was violated by thieves, Jews or gypsies.

Teufel bent down, gasping with pain. He rummaged through the Kaiser's clothes, locating a bulky object. He extracted it, exposing a dazzling wash of violet light. There in his very hands was that cursed idol, throbbing with fiendish intensity. It should not be here. The Dutchman had it, *ja* and lost it, during one of his *töricht* experiments.

So how did it come to be in the Kaiser's pockets? Teufel's head reeled, grief conflicting with rage, for a new memory was surfacing. In it the Kaiser wrested the idol from Vehemple, who had stolen it. In response the treacherous Dutchman shot him and fled. Murderous swine! Teufel swore a silent oath as he gazed down on his departed Lord, hope of the Teutonic peoples. He would have his revenge.

That thought made him unutterably weary and he wished he could lie down and rest. His eyes closed and he tottered on his feet. But the idol had other ideas. Heat scorched his hand and a flurry of doubts assailed him. The Kaiser's voice upbraided him for cowardice. Teufel reluctantly opened his eyes, confirming his Lord was actually dead. But that only proved his vacillation. This would not do at all. The wounds in his chest and stomach were still leaking, but he was a Prussian warrior. He must get after that Dutchman and exterminate the swine.

Wait! He dimly remembered the Dutchman hovering over him with a needle, injecting him with something that temporarily restored vitality. Sure enough, there on the console was the syringe and a medicinal bottle. Teufel took up the instrument, pushed it into the bottle and depressed the plunger. It was half-full, enough to sustain his revenge.

He undid his collar and the first few buttons of his jerkin, pulled the blood-soaked under-vest away from his shoulder and stuck the needle into his flesh. Instantly he felt fire course through his veins and had to close his eyes to withstand the onset of dizziness. Taking a field bandage from his pouch he wadded it up and wedged it under his jerkin to staunch the flow of blood. After one more glance at his Kaiser and vowing silently to return, Teufel gritted his teeth against the pain and limped out of the room.

Confronted immediately by the baffling configuration of this accursed place, he felt a moment's despair, but the idol prompted the correct route through confusing turns and roundabouts. He stumbled on and found himself in front of a steel door. It was another of those electronically motivated chambers that could travel great distances within the building.

Teufel did not remember pressing the buttons, but seconds or hours later was slumped on the floor, being whisked silently up or down several levels. He woke from semi-consciousness to an insistent pinging sound and realised that the door was open. Emerging from the chamber, he espied several jaegers sprawled on broken furniture, smoking.

They leapt to their feet as Teufel shambled toward them. A dishevelled noncom with a bloodied bandage on his arm saluted, spitting out a cigarette. "General von Teufel! *Gott si Dank!*"

Teufel eyed him narrowly through the white mist roaring in his head. Words tried to form but would not make any sense. The men cast questioning glances at one another and the noncom put down his rifle. "Herr General, please, sit. You are wounded." He indicated a three legged chair propped on some rubble. The General swivelled his head and the room tilted absurdly. He coughed blood into his hand and wiped it on his trousers.

"Dead," he mumbled.

The noncom rushed forward to catch him. Assisted by another jaeger, he lowered the General onto the chair. Lighting a cigarette, he placed it on Teufel's lips and the General drew deep. The nicotine unfastened his eyes and he looked at the jaegers as though for the first time.

His voice emerged in a querulous whine. "Are you deserters then, that you are not engaging the enemy?"

The noncom saluted. "*Nein* my General. We are lost. This place is a maze."

Teufel lowered his head, trying to muster slippery thoughts. The cigarette helped. He took another drag. "You are?"

"Sergeant Höek, General."

"Rally your men Höek," he mumbled. "We attack the heart of this cursed place. Have you seen that filthy Dutchman?"

"Yes, Herr General. No Herr General, I have not seen the Dutchman."

"Shoot him on sight. *Nein*, capture him. I want him alive. Get me to my army. That way!" He pointed straight ahead, a direction prompted by the idol, whose image flashed in his eyes and bade him hurry.

Delighted to have orders, Höek turned on his men. "You heard the General! Put on your helmets! Fasten that collar, Dübelmann. Farger, fashion a frame from some wood. I don't know, find some! Use that painting on the wall. Cut it up man, use the canvas to support the General. *Raus!*"

Within five minutes General von Teufel was trussed up in a makeshift stretcher and being carried gently through the palace of the *tougrak*. Shots and explosions could be heard dimly in the distance. The little contingent collected more stray jaegers along the way and their march took on a more jaunty aspect. Heartened by the presence of their General, no matter how grievous his condition, the stragglers rallied gratefully and soon nearly a hundred troopers were escorting him. None dared ask where the Kaiser was and a rumour passed along the lines that the Dutchman had killed him.

A *medik* from the Alpenkorps regiment injected the sleeping general with a booster that contained a strong pain killer and amphetamines. Soon Teufel was propped on his elbows in the stretcher, growling orders.

The column came in sight of an enormous open space, built like an amphitheatre on a level below them, accessed by broad stairs. Battle raged there and smoke boiled up through the galleries of this mighty palace. Teufel ordered a halt.

The men eagerly checked and reloaded their rifles. The General was in a semi-conscious state, subject to intense visions featuring the idol. Convinced that the Dutchman was leading an offensive on Prussia itself, he had devised a plan.

"Sergeant!" he whispered. Sergeant Höek saluted and bent lower. "I am here, Herr General."

"Take this." Teufel pulled the idol from his jacket and gave it into the sergeant's hands. Höek stared in astonishment at the lustrous thing, which glared back through entoptic eyes.

Teufel beckoned with his chin and the sergeant bent closer. "If I perish in the battle, you are to return this to the homeland. And Höek?" The sergeant placed an ear close to the General's mouth. "See to our Kaiser. He is dead, upstairs. The idol will tell you where. Take him home also."

Höek stared wide-eyed. He nodded uncertainly. "Höek!" hissed the General and his voice became stronger. "Exterminate the *tougrak*. Capture the Dutchman and take him to Prussia for execution. Burn this hovel to the ground. Lead my men to victory!"

These were orders the sergeant could understand. He straightened up. "*Achtung!*" he bellowed. "Form up. Prepare to attack. Kill any *tougrak* on sight. Except the Dutch scientist. He is to be captured alive. When we reach the battle you, Farber and you, Dübelman, will remain with the General until we have subdued the enemy."

Höek marched to the head of the column, trying to ignore a voice in his head. The jaegers had all been experiencing those since they breached the walls of the *tougrak* fortress, but this one was different. The golden statue was ordering him to rush down the stairs and make his way into the chamber beyond, whose smouldering ruins were strewn with bodies and rubble.

Höek glanced desperately back at his general, but then his body seemed to take over. He looked on helplessly as his legs bolted and ran down the stairs. Behind him the jaegers broke formation and charged, but Höek was well in front, taking two stairs at a time. Shots howled around him and the smoke was choking but he shouted incoherently and ran on.

Ahead he could see a barricade, behind which *tougrak* were sheltered. Beyond it a colossal wall of purple mist, but something else was looming to his right. Monstrous, it roared like the engine in the factory where Höek worked as an adolescent. He slowed his headlong charge and gaped. That thing was made of steel, man-shaped, gigantic. Glittering with lights and spouting flames, it stalked the rim of the amphitheatre, smashing pillars, torching everything around it, killing jaegers as well as *tougrak* in its heedless romp.

Then Höek stopped entirely, for another tremendous apparition had appeared. Impossibly, it glowed magenta and Höek saw that it had the exact shape of the statue the general had pressed into his hands. He held that thing in front of his face and it leered, gleaming ever brighter till Höek dropped it with a shriek. But it did not fall to the ground. Suspended in the air it began to rotate, expelling a gout of purple flame that spurted across the room and joined with its gigantic doppelgänger.

There was an explosion, incinerating Höek, engulfing his oncoming jaegers in a fireball. General von Teufel and his stretcher bearers were immolated and reduced to ashes. But before them the idol was expanding, making a noise like all the howling winds that ever scoured the mountains, and across the *agora* a bandit chief, two innkeepers and an ancient Moldovian sorcerer watched their iterations of the idol join Enlil in unholy communion.

# 31

# The Data will be Galvanised

Chance groaned, sensing he had entered a new reality. Lying on a carpeted floor, his head ached abominably, eyes shut tight against an insistent, glaring light.

He heard a voice that sounded like Kalyenka's, easing through the fog in his head.

"Lie still," it soothed.

"Ah, Kal," he moaned. "Would that it was truly your voice."

"Ah, but it is."

He gradually opened his eyes, a feeling as of stripping a blood-soaked bandage from a dried wound. Kalyenka's dear face was above him, haloed against the light. She smiled.

"Which Kalyenka am I looking at? And what happened to your face?"

"Kalyenka Menscheivr, whom you met just five days ago. And I had a little accident, but I'm fine."

"Then I am home."

"Soon, my love."

"Where are we now?" he asked weakly.

"That is a little difficult for me to describe," Kalyenka said gently. "I had best leave it to the *Sarhang.*"

Chance raised his head further and saw that indeed, the mild countenance of the *Sarhang* was gazing at him from a screen behind Kalyenka.

"You are inside the Citadel, in a vector of the Hospice," he said. "Well, it is technically inside the building, but exists within the *Mēnōg* for all intents and purposes. Here we are safe from immediate attack in the mundane world and mostly hidden from the *Ljmmûm.* Some good news. Your escapade was successful. Enlil was evoked by

237

the activation of his idol and nullified the Qliphoth's *khuti* blockade. Their *egregore* is no longer able to penetrate the defences of this Citadel."

Kalyenka sat on the floor and eased Chance's head into her lap. She stroked his forehead. "You've done very well my darling," she said. "But this is too bizarre. I keep seeing you in the weirdest scenarios."

"And I you," he said. "It is truly the strangest story yet."

"Regard my painting, if you wish to see strange," she said.

Chance stared at the canvas on the wall. It was overwhelming, a masterful compendium of abstracted shapes and figures, encompassing vivid characters in a thousand scenes entwined. He recognised divers historical figures engrossed in battle or pastoral tableaus. All these variegated spectacles were somehow harmonised, creating a panorama of immense and compelling synchrony. But his eyes focussed on a vignette in the lower foreground, two naked bodies entwined.

"Is that me? And that is you?"

"Yes," said Kalyenka. "Part of the tale of the impossibly tangled world leading up to this moment. The painting is not quite finished. I call it 'D'Angel Moon', because it will be a D'Angel Moon when the work is resolved."

"I'm not sure I want it to resolve," said Chance, gazing up into Kalyenka's eyes.

"That will do children," said the *Sarhang*. "I'm afraid we are running out of time."

Kalyenka guffawed. "Oh really Doctor?" She turned back to Chance. "Don't be concerned. Time is the one thing we've got plenty of in here."

"Well I'm afraid that's no longer true," said the *Sarhang*, and his screen surrendered to a vision of a grotesque grey cloud, shot through with veins of bilious poison. "We are now surrounded by the Skein. Which means the exterior of this Citadel is in the grip of subjective time. It has enabled Cockwattle's consciousness to be housed in one of Vehemple's monstrous creations. He is at large within the Hospice and making his way to the Citadel. We must act immediately to forestall him."

"Enlil is doing a fine job of that," said Chance. "I just saw him manifest about thirty foot tall and whale the blazes out of a gigantic automaton in the *agora*."

"So you did," said the *Sarhang*, replaying that event on the screen. "And Ancoulsis is here too. I might have known he'd bluff his way past the Seers. That makes things even more interesting."

"You didn't know of Enlil's new manifestation?" said Chance.

"He's not omniscient darling," said Kalyenka.

"No I'm not," said the *Sarhang*, reappearing on the screen. "And if he weren't in my own Hospice I wouldn't see Enlil at all, because of his causality fields. But the presence of Ancoulsis is equally disturbing. He and the *Ljmmûm* may bring us undone yet."

Chance sat up, though his hand remained locked in Kalyenka's and he made sure he could still smell her warm, womanly scent. "Presenting for duty *Sarhang*, though you'll have to direct me. I have no idea how to tackle the present situation."

"Fortunately I do," smiled the *Sarhang*, indicating a young Asian man in the painting, sitting at a desk before a shimmering screen. "I've been arranging a diegesis with a talented fellow in an epoch a little further along, contemporaneously speaking, from your escapade at the coal mine in Australia. That successful mission, by the way, enabled me to deploy a two-way continuum with this gentleman as the locus point. Our collaboration will engage the *Ljmmûm* of his epoch in a singularity wherein we can confront and, theoretically anyway, destroy them. Kalyenka's painting has become the contextual background of this scenario."

Chance looked at Kalyenka. She shrugged.

"Would you care to elaborate in less technical language?" he asked the *Sarhang*.

"Apologies my dear boy, I was thinking out loud. I have concocted an offensive stratagem, the details of which I will soon make clear. We have the advantage that the Citadel of the Hospice still runs on *Mēnōg* time as it were - which means events happen as I will them. I am coordinating it so that my attack will commence just before the Skein envelopes the Hospice - the fulcrum upon which so much depends. This will occur at precisely the zenith of the Murex Moon."

"Forgive me if I play devil's advocate *Sarhang*," said Chance. "But is this timeline a little optimistic? What I just saw out in that *agora* looks rather like the last stand of a doomed rebellion."

"Yes, you could be forgiven for thinking so," said the Sarhang sombrely. "But there are other factors at play here. Some of my stratagems have been confounded, it's true, and we've merely mitigated the *Ljmmûm*'s onslaught. But Kulan's desert sortie has impaired their offensive powers considerably. That bought us the leverage to get you into the Qliphoth blockade. And we do need to buy more time, in order for Julie Brown's transubstantiation to be completed."

"Time?" said Chance. "But I thought time was an illusion?"

"Pay attention, Lieutenant Colonel. The Skein has infected this Hospice. We are now operating on subjective time, and it is running out. We need a circuit breaker. We have no choice but to make an all-out attack on the *Ljmmûm* in the Skein.

"I believe they are not yet aware that their blockade has been broken. But that may be academic if they manage to destroy this Citadel. We have come to the penultimate moment. The enemy is knocking at the doors."

The *Sarhang* opened the chimera lens to show Kalyenka and Chance the interior of the Citadel, where the survivors of the

*Securité* and the Caliph's janissaries were being tended by Hospice staff. The next scene showed a battalion of Prussians arrayed outside the obdurate walls of the Citadel. Five field pieces were firing directly into them, *through* the Chthonic Veil, but though the walls were scored with shot and dynamite, they showed no signs of yielding to the bombardment.

"Where are the rest of the Hospice staff?" asked Kalyenka.

"Some have perished in the attack, some as you can see have made it into the Citadel. Most have gone into emergency bunkers, as is standard procedure. They will be safely ensconced in the mountain, or else evacuating via tunnels to the outside world."

"Do you know if Doctor Amordule is among them?"

"I just saw her," said Chance. "In her office, when I returned from the, er, future. She sent me out to help defend the *agora*."

The *Sarhang* switched off the chimera lens. "The good doctor is coordinating our various spheres of operations. And she has given me the signal to launch into the *Mēnōg*, where through individual vectors we will penetrate the Skein. Are you ready Lieutenant Colonel? I have another carafe of the medicinal beverage you have found so rousing."

"Splendid. After a shot of that you may consider me ready."

"It is on yonder table. You seem ready enough, wielding that golden scimitar."

Scimitar? Of course. Chance felt the pommel of the Caliph's blade against his thigh. He tapped it cautiously to make sure it was real.

"Real enough," said the *Sarhang*. "And a powerful talisman now that the Caliph has perished and his janissaries, temporarily at least, are on our side. Now. We will each be entering the *Mēnōg* as energetic profiles animated by our own wills. Both of us will perceive things rather differently, but essentially we will be operating on vectors determined by our own experience. Remember that the Skein virus will also warp your perspective. But once we have confronted the *Lịmmûm* on the ground I have chosen, this will come down to a struggle of *khuti* against virus."

"Can you describe to me specifically what we're facing?" asked Chance, one arm around Kalyenka's shoulders. "I now have some experience of the *Mēnōg*, but it seems to be different every time I go in there."

"It is. Which means I cannot describe what form our enemies will assume. I can, however, tell you how we shall confront them."

"Please do," said Chance.

"Essentially we'll need to create a chain of energy," said the *Sarhang*. "I'll go in first to shield you from the worst of the *Lịmmûm's* attacks. Zhāng Sān will back me up, his dreaming modules acting as an interface between our consciousness substrates. The key target will be Cockwattle himself. He has designed the architecture of the Skein around his psyche. Once he is taken down the various substrates of the Skein will unravel. Lieutenant Colonel, you've been the closest to Cockwattle, so we'll trust that your dreaming senses are able to hone in on him. Kalyenka, I will ask you to remain here, to fine-tune your painting in close collaboration with Bitgaram, my young Korean friend."

"But I wish to be in the fight," said Kalyenka.

A shimmering eidolon of the *Sarhang* appeared in the painting, which seemed to have grown around them so Chance and Kalyenka were immersed in its depths.

"Your painting has become manifest in the *Mēnōg*," he said, and the very fabric of the work rippled and moved with him. "That makes you a formidable entity in your own right. To a Qliphoth in the Skein you will be as a frightful armada bearing down upon them. But your painting and our collaboration with Bitgaram are absolutely essential to our success."

"It is?" said Kalyenka, standing to look deeper into the myriad layers of her work. "But Augustine, painting is not a collaborative exercise. It is a solitary occupation."

The *Sarhang* led her deeper into the work's shifting terrain, where she could see an interlacing network of webbing *inside* the Skein's bitter shroud. "And it will remain so Kalyenka. The process will be purely intuitive, responding to transmissions as is your technique. The only difference being I will have opened the chimera lens so the transmissions will be coming from a scenario within the Skein, which Bitgaram has devised."

"I am rather confused," she said, backing away from the stench of the virus. "But I shall just keep working in that case."

"I should rather like some clarity too," said Chance, who had followed them into the painting and stood marvelling at its multifarious dimensions.

The *Sarhang* pointed to a mountain valley, where Kalyenka and Chance could see themselves walking. "Let me explain. Think of the scenario we have devised as a melodrama from the theatre. Though the *Ļimmûm* are actors in disparate performances from different eras, I have contrived to have them all appear in a single scene from this play. Kalyenka's painting will constitute the staging and scenic effects, thus controlling the emotional context which determines the outcome of the scene. The major difference being that this scene will take place within a specifically designed strata inside the Skein and its repercussions will be immense for both *Mēnōg* and *Gētīg*."

"I shall be honoured then," said Kalyenka. "But please, are we alone in this? Are not any of these entities from the *Mēnōg* willing to help, considering this Skein virus threatens their existence?"

"The Sephiroth have been persuaded to join our affray," said the *Sarhang*. "Once they realised what this struggle entails for the *Mēnōg*. That is no small matter. You must remember these entities deal with the fortunes of many other worlds, not just ours. They're at the intersection of several energetic planes of existence.

"Equally as trenchant, we have Kulan's devastating assault upon the Skein, effected with the assistance of a cohort of desert musicians from among his people."

"Yes, I painted them here," said Kalyenka, studying four figures in a vast landscape, their rock and roll *egregore* rupturing the Skein.

"These are heady concepts, Augustine," said Chance.

The *Sarhang* inclined his head. "Once you've encountered the *Mēnōg* nothing is ever quite the same again. But that's alright. Your brains are designed to deal with them. They've just never yet had to before."

Chance cleared his throat. "Augustine, before we launch, might Kalyenka and I have a moment alone?"

"Certainly. Do hurry though. Outside, subjective time is closing in."

With that, Chance and Kalyenka were in a garden, surrounded by tropical plants, above them a cerulean sky.

They kissed deeply, then pulled apart. After a languorous pause, Chance sat on a teak bench, carved with arabesque tendrils and spiralling stems. He pulled Kalyenka onto his lap. "What do you make of all this Kal? Are we really these different people scattered across time? Not that I doubt the *Sarhang's* word, but right now none of it seems quite real."

Kalyenka tenderly kissed the bruising on his face. "None of the things I have seen in my past incarnations seem real, Sebastian, Lafayette, Hoche, whatever your name is. Nor does this garden, which I'm sure only exists in the *Sarhang's* capacious brain. Except that being this close to you now seems as real as anything else in my life."

"For me also," said Chance. "Are we in love then?"

"Seems that way. Whatever that means." Kalyenka touched a finger to his chin. "I know that being with you fills me with hope and joy. Though I can't help feeling we've been corralled into this emotion by all the lives that preceded us, that we are merely a device used by the cosmos to further some end. The situation even comes equipped with a readymade expression, whose origin I cannot pinpoint, but which seems to embody us as universal templates, or something."

"What is that expression?" he said.

"*We are of the same breath, you and I.*"

"Yes, I have heard you say that, in my visions."

"And I you," she replied.

Chance gave Kalyenka a long look. He seemed on the verge of tears. All the events and traumas of the recent past were converging with the enduring anguish of his embattled life, as well as those of his other lives and the ongoing tragedies of the human condition he had witnessed in his adventures. They all came to a head, now that he had allowed this vulnerability, this *agape* for the woman who was so close to his soul. He clenched his eyes and his jaw, and eventually words filtered through, though he scarcely seemed to move his lips.

"I have done terrible things in my life, Kalyenka," he said. "I was a soldier of the throne of England, performing horrific deeds in its name, until I ..."

Chance reeled. Kalyenka had slapped him. Shocked, he blinked through real tears and saw that her eyes were fierce. "It does not matter," she said. "I have seen some of them, Lafayette. Some of the *very* bad deeds. But I have also seen the many good things you have done."

"You have? What things?"

"It does not matter," she said, glancing away. "The *Sarhang* has his ways. But it does not matter." She leant forward till her nose was touching his.

"As long as you do terrible things to me," she whispered. "Some of them, anyway."

"I'm afraid I must intervene now," intruded the *Sarhang's* voice. "Enlil has manifested in the *agora* and it seems the Qliphoth are about to join the party."

The garden had vanished and they were once again in the room with Kalyenka's painting and the eidolon of the *Sarhang*, who blinked at them with affected innocence. He continued speaking without pause.

"When the Murex Moon is peaking we'll initiate the melodrama. The aim is to engage the *Lịmmûm* until the Cosmic Shekinah comes into play and activates the Earth Entity, thus destroying the Skein and the *Lịmmûm* manifest in that space. Time for us to go, Chance. Look for the place where you last saw Cockwattle in person."

"Wait," cried Chance, once he and Kalyenka had disentangled. "How do I direct myself? Every time I go in there I seem to have no control of my destination."

"You will yourself onward, just as you will your limbs to walk," the *Sarhang* replied. "The data will be galvanised by your very intention."

"Act as a shaman does," grinned Kalyenka. "Proceed boldly, but with caution. And dream, just dream into it."

With that Chance was surrounded by a novel manifestation of light and fury. He felt blinded and bereft, for Kalyenka was no longer in his arms.

# 32

# As Above, so Below

"It's an interactive 4D porno game!" said Bitgaram in disbelief.

"What is?" asked Jae-Won, taking a bottle of Kickapoo from the fridge.

"This thing the *Sarhang* has me coding. It's basically a modified version of GangBang, the second most popular game in the US. Ultimate deviant sex role-playing stuff. Complete sensory immersion, the ability to have orgies with any number of other virtual participants. It's used by the American elites, though of course they all deny it."

Bitgaram clicked a key, enhancing an image of an elderly Caucasian, naked, obese, lying prone in a lavish cocoon. "They're fully hooked up in private consoles, sensors implanted so they feel *everything* in the immersive game space. No restrictions on what you can do."

Consecutive images of cartoon villains, monsters of popular imagination bearing exaggerated sexual organs, engaged in riotous orgy.

"Their avatars can be anything, as wild as their imaginations. Demons with giant penises seems to be a favourite. GangBang violates the laws of all US states, not to mention their precious Bible, but it's an open secret that they all use it. Paedophilia, coprophagy, necrophilia. The Epstein scandal was the tip of the iceberg. It's all been hacked and released online. Put lots of politicians and evangelists out of favour, sent some to jail."

Jae-Won put the bottle down, staring in horror at the screen. "God, that's horrible Bitgaram. Why are you cooperating? This *Sarhang* guy must be some kind of yakuza."

"No I don't think so," Bitgaram said. "I've talked with him a lot. He knew all about what we did to the PPP website, said it was brilliant. He's got some righteous line about 'redressing the evils of autocrats'. I figured he was working a sting on corrupt politicians and oligarchs. So I knew what he was proposing was not strictly legal. But I didn't know it was the scaffold for a 4D snuff movie when he sent me the grid to work off. I redesigned the mesh with high grain fidelity. Ultra-res polygons for geometry mapping."

"Amazeballs."

Bitgaram rubbed his eyes. "Sorry." He swivelled his seat around to look at Jae-Won. "You look pretty tonight. Thanks for coming in." Jae-Won smiled wryly. Her corduroy jumpsuit was embroidered with yellow daisies that set off her green dyed hair and prominent nose-ring, but she considered it a work outfit and hated feeling like a *jalanghae boida*.

"Thanks *jagi*," she said. "You look much better out of those adolescent metalhead rags."

Bitgaram's all-black outfit had been superseded by track pants and a purple cardigan with white offsets that Jae-Won said had hip-hop/surfer chic. They were in the Jeobchog graphics studio. It was late at night and all the other employees had gone home. Bitgaram was logged in for overtime and his Tsunami Z10,000 was hooked up to Jeobchog's database, downloading his finished designs. It beeped to remind him to refresh dataviz and he turned back to the monitor.

"Look how fast that mesh is populating," he said. "The *Sarhang* has overlaid this crazy painting as the game environment, even though he says he's never done game design before. And it's not just terrain texturing. The painting functions like some new breed of CPU. It's both software and processor, controlling the narrative of the game."

"But how did he get such a complex platform into their system?" said Jae-Won, despite herself.

"He's made the Tangerine Believers security algorithms, which are the best in the world, look like something you'd find in a coolmath tablet. And he's exploited them to turn the crypto-data system on its head."

Jae-Won took a gulp of Kickapoo. "What do you mean?"

"So it's like a form of cryptocurrency, which in theory is only processed once, 'cos that's how it works. But what if you could duplicate the transaction simultaneously, so it seems like one transaction but concealed within its coding is another, almost identical version, only with subtle differences? That manipulates the next coding exchange and so on down the line, so each transaction is slightly more warped than the one preceding it, till you've exposed enough to make a complete recoding on the other side of the ledger. Impossible, right?"

"Yes," said Jae-Won. "It invalidates all the security protocols the blockchain system was invented for. It's literally impossible."

"That's what I thought. But not if you're the *Sarhang*. He's already done it. He calls it the 'peer group pressure' algorithm. The security codes for each member of this business network - the *Sarhang* calls them the *Limmûm*, have to be validated in every transaction. But that's the system's greatest weakness - because it's a peer-to-peer network he's introduced an old trope to it - peer group pressure."

"How does that work," asked Jae-Won.

"The window to legitimise a data transfer has narrowed. If it's not approved within .00046 of a second, *any* transaction will fall through. The *Limmûm,* all seventy million, six hundred thousand and forty seven of them, are performing billions of transactions a second, so they don't want that system to malfunction. It's too big to fail. So the millisecond it passes the majority of their validation tests, the algorithms wave it through. These *Ljmmûm* don't want to let their other business partners down, that would bring on some kind of revenge, 'cos they're all very uptight people."

Jae-Won was silent. Bitgaram opened a can of self-heating coffee. "Check this out. It's the painting I told you about."

He was pointing to the top half of the screen, where above green lines of coding a three-dimensional grid was populating a bizarre landscape. Bo-Bae stared with widening eyes. She had studied art, been to MOMA in New York, but she could not place the style or topology. The detail was bewildering, infested with creatures - human and animal, inhabiting surreal landscapes.

"It's kind of Boschian," she said. "But also postmodern. It's fantastic. Why have I never seen this before? Who's the artist?"

"The artist isn't credited," Bitgaram said. "The *Sarhang* said it would compromise her identity. But I'm concerned with how it's translated into the immersive environment. The graphics processing is best I've ever seen. Look at the resolution, it's incredible. And it's animated, constantly moving around. Motion blur uses 500GB per node. Data's dense, man. That processing would suck a city dry."

"All this for a porno game?" said Jae-Won. "Seems like overkill. Looks like a government platform to me. The ray tracing acceleration is really high-end - how do you know it's for interactive porn?"

Bitgaram grinned. "The *Sarhang* had me design templates for the avatars he wants to introduce to the game, but he wants them left them blank, so they can be modified to suit the preferred characteristics of whoever inhabits them. But I had to know what the scalar and spatial parameters were, so I can transcode them. I looked up the standard code rendering toolkit and the only place these scan-line renderings are used is in illegal interactive immersive 4D porno games like Gangbang, where you can fornicate in real time with other avatars and battle other players for the right to select the object of your desire.

"The designs are done by these dark-net companies that specialise in child porn, snuff movies and torture bondage. So I asked the *Sarhang* straight up what he was doing. He just messaged me back."

Bitgaram clicked on a messaging board and increased the font size so Jae-Won could read it from where she was sitting.

*"Greetings Bitgaram. What does lolz mean? I keep meaning to ask, because you punctuate so many of your sentences with the expression. As a student of linguistics I'm fascinated by the etymology of your slang.*

*"As to your forebodings regarding the locus of this project, you are right to question me. Yes it is indeed working in 'shady territory' as you put it, but that is a necessary evil. This is the favoured terrain of the people I intend to call to account; you would call them Republican politicians, evangelist ministers and disaster capitalists.*

*"Though their nomenclature is international they are predominantly based in the USA. The deviant Skein-derived entertainments they favour are merely a sideline to their criminal activities, but I have found this predilection to be the vulnerability that brings them undone, precisely because they do not expect an attack to come from the Skein."*

Jae-Won lowered her glasses and looked at Bitgaram. "He writes like my Literary professor at University did."

"Yeah I don't know what he's saying half the time."

"What's this Skein he talks about?"

"I think he means the internet."

Jae-Won frowned at the screen. "So this game is definitely a modified version of Gangbang?"

"Yeah. It's got the exact same coding and players log in the same way."

"But surely they don't all use it at the same time?" said Jae-Won. "How does this *Sarhang* intend to catch them all out?"

"He said something about isolating their continuums in a fixed temporal field. By which I think he means he aligns them contemporaneously, so that no matter when they've used the game, he's able to compress or limit the temporal variations and bring them into line in a networked continuum. He called it continuum harvesting. It's impossible, obviously. But he says he can do it."

"Well, what's the point of it all?," said Jae-Won. "Assuming what he's saying is true, what does he do when he's got all these *sseulegi* in the network?"

"That's when the games begin. He'll introduce his own players, who will take the bad guys down."

Jae-Won frowned. "But these people, the Republicans, evangelists and Tangerine Believers are shameless. They've already been exposed as brazen hypocrites. Everyone knows they're just crooks who pray on TV to hoover up money from naïve rednecks."

"Not in their own country," said Bitgaram. "They only have one news outlet and it's just constant propaganda. Which is what they're trying to introduce here. The PPP is gonna let 'em too."

Jae-Won put the empty Kickapoo can on the console. "But even if they are exposed as pedophiles and deviates, what good will that do? It won't get them kicked out of power. They'll just deny everything and move on, tell more lies which all the stupid Americans will believe."

"Yeah I know. But the *Sarhang* seems confident this game will really change things. Not just here and in the US but all over the world. And beyond. He said something like 'as above, so below.'"

"Beyond? What is he, a religious nut job too?"

"I don't think so," said Bitgaram. "He seems more like a mad scientist."

"Well I hope he knows what he's doing. Things couldn't get much worse and we're running out of time."

Jae-Won's worst fears had come to pass. China having invaded Taiwan and Japan, the USA had declared war. Nothing had happened yet, but both sides were poised in deadly stalemate. Though propaganda painted them both as beacons of freedom and enlightenment they were equally repressive regimes, ruled by ideology and armed force, squabbling over the remnants of a world devastated by typhoons, tsunamis, earthquakes, floods, famine and drought.

The buzzer rang. "It's Bo-Bae." Jae-Won pressed the button that opened the street door and on the security relay Bitgaram saw his sister enter. "She looks worried," he said.

When Bo-Bae came into the studio she was in tears. "Have you heard? The American internet is taking over tonight. They're going to wipe out K-Pop."

"Don't worry Bo-Bae. We're nearly finished here," said Bitgaram. "I've got the VR synched up. That internet system changeover won't take effect right away anyway. Jeobchog is hooked into Defence contracts. There's no way they're gonna let them lapse till the new system is properly in place, otherwise we'd be exposed to hacking by the Chinese."

Jae-Won had her arms around Bo-Bae. "When can you launch?"

"As soon as I'm finished the *Sarhang* said to press go. He says it doesn't matter about the timing, he can synch into it as soon as it's ready."

"But what about all his other players?" said Jae-Won.

"He says he can do more of that continuum splitting, whatever that means, so they all join the network simultaneously. He seems to know what he's doing, so I'm just going with it."

"Well, is it ready?"

"Nearly," said Bitgaram. "The avatar templates are on standby and the environment texturing is almost finished. But I got the idea that the artist was working on the fly and making real time adjustments and could do that after the game had started."

"Why haven't you started then?" said Bo-Bae.

"I was waiting for you to get here."

Bo-Bae stamped her foot. "Launch it, now."

"Ok, chill, sister." Bitgaram typed an adjustment to the coding and pressed enter.

# 33

# A Fulcrum of Cosmic Energies

Vania peered up at the matrix of *gutta-percha* webbing woven through Cockwattle's ball room. Beneath his snoring body was a bank of flickering monitors, sprouting cables which ran into the webbing. Above him, between two chandeliers dependant from the embossed copper ceiling was the aperture Ancoulsis had described.

"You will see it somewhere above the installation," he'd told her, just before they parted at the hotel. "A small but distinctive aperture in which there will be a pulsing light. This is the nexus of Cockwattle's machine, a fulcrum of cosmic energies. If the idol is placed within it a feedback cycle will immediately begin and quickly go critical. By that time you will want to be well out of the building, for the eruption that follows will incinerate everything within the mansion grounds."

In the ballroom Vania jumped, startled by Cockwattle's voice. "At last, Vehemple!" he said. "Sure took your fucking time. Are you ready to begin the process?"

Vehemple? Who was that? Vania pulled out her poniard, ready to plunge it into Cockwattle's throat. But he was still dangling harmlessly in the webbing. His eyes were open now though, staring straight ahead into a bright light. He had not seen her. Screwing up her eyes against the glare, Vania saw he was intent upon a glowing screen that was attached to his harness. She edged around the *gutta-percha* web and glimpsed what looked like a mirror, lit from within, upon which glimmered the face of an ugly, bald man, speaking.

She could not hear what he was saying, but Cockwattle replied. "Pay attention you Dutch blockhead. Have you taken control of the

*Sarhang's* hovel? Have you managed to overcome the obstacles that seem to dog you?"

The man's reply was drowned out by the noise of machinery. It increased in pitch as lights flickered across the central console. Sparks scattered from gaps in the insulation and Cockwattle began to titter in that aggravating manner which Vania recognised as manic glee, usually employed when someone else was in distress. Oh, how she had wished to stab him, so many times during the past weeks when she heard that sound.

"You will repay me many times for this, Codrût Ancoulsis," she vowed silently, but the machine noises came to a crescendo and Cockwattle raised his head, grimacing as though in great pain.

Then his head slumped onto his chest and he was still. The machine vibrations subsided, lights rippling with less intensity. Was Cockwattle dead? No. Vania could faintly see his paunch wobble as he breathed.

She took out the idol from its pouch inside her shoulder holster. Its entoptic eyes glittered with unusual intensity. Vania fancied she heard words in some archaic tongue and saw a flash of light in her mind's eye. Shoving it back into the pouch, she crept forward till she stood beneath Cockwattle's sagging body. One lunge with her poniard and he would be gone. But her curiosity was afire now.

Suppose she *were* able to climb the web and place the idol in that aperture? The alarm had not been raised yet. She would still have time to get down and gut Cockwattle before his guards got to her. A surge of adrenalin encouraged that emotion. With a grim smile Vania commenced to climb.

It was difficult work. The *gutta-percha* was slippery and loose enough to defy purchase. But she had climbed the walls of her father's palazzo often enough. When she was young and had been out all night she could scale it in ten minutes. The trick to not falling had been to refuse to accept gravity, to find a crack where there was none, to will herself upward to her high bedroom window.

Now she found a way to ease her right foot along, into the seat of tension in a loop of cable, enough to hold her weight while she shifted upward and snagged fingers in the next section and then the next. In this way she inched herself up this slippery, swaying scaffold.

She came level with Cockwattle and looked over at his flabby frame, imagining the millions of people that had suffered for his greed. The temptation to slit his throat was almost overwhelming, but still there had been no alarm. Plenty of time. She continued climbing.

Just then she heard the voice of Cockwattle's portly butler Jagannath, from somewhere in the room below. "Goodness heavens," he cried. "What is going on here?"

Vania craned her head around. Jagannath was surveying the tangle of cables and the inert body of his master. He had not seen her yet. She hoped she would not have to kill him. She liked the man. He was a jolly fellow who gossiped incessantly as he served Italian inspired Indian delicacies, tempering the chilli heat for her delicate stomach, smiling as he ladled out exquisite gravies or sweetmeats, served her vodka in a crystalline goblet. She knew his family were captives in the compound, that he was under a strict contract and that he would suffer if he did not betray her.

But Jagganath must have heard the web of *gutta-percha* creaking under her weight, even over the hissing static of the console, for he shrieked. "Missus de Mezzanotte! What are you doing up there? Please to come down immediately. The master will be most cranky if you spoil his experiment. Oh please, come down before you disturb him."

Vania ignored him, concentrating on climbing those slithery cables. Twice she slipped and thought she would fall. She saw electricity sparking from the cable joins and knew that if she touched one of those raw wires her mission would be over.

Jagannath's voice went up an octave. "Miss Mezzanotte! I have been instructed by Lord Cockwattle. If anyone enter this rooms without express permissions they are to be executed. This is not something I wish to visit upon your person. Please to come down at once."

Vania glanced back, her stomach churning. "Jagannath, you must leave the compound at once," she shouted. "Something bad is going to happen here and I would hate to see your or family harmed."

"Yes mistress, something bad is going to happen," said Jagannath, wringing his hands. "The master is going to be very angry, with you and with me. I shall be beaten soundly. But if his guards find you here they will shoot you, sure as eggs cooking."

"I have something important to do," gritted Vania. "Your master is an evil bastard and he must be stopped. Go Jagannath, go now. Get your family out."

Vania kept climbing, one handhold at a time, as the web of *gutta-percha* swung more violently. Her right hand slipped when a connection snapped, spraying her with sparks. She hung, dangling by the other hand till she was able to hook her leg around more cables and gradually put her weight upon them. She found another handhold and hauled herself into a better position.

Jagannath retreated, calling shrilly for help. Vania heard another voice, but concentrated on the cabling, which became more difficult to find purchase on the higher she climbed. Then she heard the distinctive snick of a rifle bolt.

She glanced behind. A soldier had entered, his weapon held at port. "There," shouted Jagannath, pointing up at Vania. "But can you not climb up and bring her down?" he implored. "She is the special guest of the Master."

"Shut it, pandy," snarled the soldier. "Orders is orders."

Vania glanced wildly around. The soldier had settled his rifle on his shoulder, aiming at her. "Come down missus," the soldier shouted. "I'll only tell you once."

But Vania closed her eyes and found another grip, crawling up the last few yards through the swaying web, thinking wryly that now she truly was the Spider. She heard the crack of a shot and found herself dangling upside down, caught in the web. More like a fly than a spider, she thought, but wondered why she could not move. Her leg had gone numb and she heard the soldier shouting. Looking up she felt blood drip onto her face.

"I have been shot," she thought. How curious that it does not hurt. But she could not use that leg to right herself and climb higher. She tried again but it would not respond. She felt herself slipping back down through the web. A wave of despair nearly overwhelmed her but then she heard a voice, like a storm over the walls of Genoa.

*"I am Enlil, storm of majestic splendour! Hero whose awesomeness covers the Mountains like a south storm; who makes the good tiara, the rainbow, flash like lightning; grandly begotten by him who wears the princely beard; dragon who turns on himself, strength of a lion snarling at a snake, roaring hurricane; great battle-net flung over the foe!"*

Vania saw the god riding through the heavens, lightning flashing from his hands. She gasped, exulting in his power. His entoptic eyes were turned on her, staring through her soul.

A fierce passion arose in her heart. *"Kal Ibben! Biz eyni nefesdeyik!"* she cried, though she did not know what it meant. Somehow she found the strength to move her leg and this time there was such agony that she cried out. Summoning every mote of courage and ardour she possessed, Vania seized the *gutta-percha* to drag herself upright. Though stars shot through her vision and sweat coursed from her body, she clambered higher.

The idol spoke to her again, formless words that left Vania in no doubt as to what she must do. She heard another shot and this time felt a punch in her side as though she'd been struck by a lumpen hammer. She did not need the idol to tell her to keep going and as she climbed the last rung of *gutta-percha* she took the pouch from her bandolero and the idol from the pouch.

The idol's eyes flashed with purple fire but even as Vania stretched her hand toward the aperture she heard another shot and grunted at the impact. Then the idol was glowing bright, high and far away, freed of her grasp. But Vania was not looking at it any more.

In its place was Kalyenka's face, vivid and smiling. *We are of the" "same breath, you and I* she whispered and Vania too was smiling when she heard the final shot.

# 34

# Antimatter

Vehemple powered his exoskeleton into the battle, aiming bursts of hand-wheel fire at any targets that presented themselves. Though Prussian soldiers died as plentifully as Turks and *Securité*, it was of no moment. It was essential that he make it through to the Citadel, ensure the final destruction of the Hospice and the elimination of the *Sarhang*. Cockwattle appeared to be advancing that agenda in the *groot verkeerslicht*. Flames and smoke mostly obscured Vehemple's view of the *Securité* defensive fortifications but he was confident they were finished.

Flicking up a dataviz screen on his goggles, the Dutchman saw that the metaphysical integrity of the Hospice was under severe threat. A counter showing the number of living *Securité* personnel had dropped below thirty. The puzzling presence of six individuals not associated with Hospice personnel was also registered. They included the innkeepers from the Eagle's Nest, two local bandits and a Moldavian troublemaker. The Irish soldier Chance was present also, though he seemed to be retreating towards the Chthonic Gates.

But amidst the tumult of battle Vehemple beheld further disturbing anomalies. Each of these intruders was in possession of an iteration of the damnable idol, all of which were discharging electromagnetic emissions, converging on an apparition which dataviz classified as an aberration of scientific principles and hence impossible. The apparition seemed to be a macrocosm of the idols of Enlil, for it housed identical electromagnetic infrastructure and as they merged, all iterations of the idol ceased to independently exist.

This monstrous agglomeration of energies, which Vehemple refused to recognise as Enlil himself, eclipsed even the rarities usually circulating through the Hospice. It could not be measured on the sensors in Vehemple's exoskeleton. If neither his unparalleled intellect nor his apparatus could identify this phenomenon, it must be an illusion.

Nonetheless this hallucination was battering the *groot verkeerslicht* into a barely functional state with electrostatic discharges not unlike lightning. Its entoptic eyes illuminated the *agora* with a ghastly ultraviolet ambience against which even the raging wildfires and piles of dead jaegers paled.

Vehemple's exoskeleton contained limited instrumentation, however there was an inboard spectrograph. Booting that up, he scanned the electromagnetic structure of the Enlil entity. Roughly operating as a helix, the fixed axis of its power radiated in anthropomorphic form, limbs dependant upon quantised connectors operating under universal laws, yet relying on localised physics to exert mobility. Examining those ligaments, Vehemple was struck by an idea.

Patching his visual capacity into the *groot verkeerslicht,* he could now observe Enlil from Cockwattle's perspective. He spoke into the microphone at his chin. "Lord Cockwattle!"

There was no response.

"Cockwattle, do you hear me?"

"What? What? Who is that?" The man's voice was tremulous, hopeful. A roaring sound in the background.

"It is Vehemple. Behind you."

"What? I am not blinding anyone you fool. Blasted Dutchman. It's you who has stitched me up. What in hell's name is going on? You said I would be facing some rump security, not this ghost demon!"

"Never mind. Be calm and listen. Examine the panel in front of you."

"What? Hammer the flannel? What are you talking about you idiot?"

"*Nee*, the panel. From where you have been launching the missiles."

"What of them man? I've been shooting them off like ninepins. But this purple ghost, this fucking monster, it is defeating your automaton. You fool Vehemple, you have failed me again."

"Be silent man," said Vehemple. "Quickly. Look to the bottom of that panel. I can see it myself. There is a switch there. Flick it down, then aim the left arm of the automaton at the apparition. When you have a clear shot, press the black button above it."

But a flash of white light obscured his vision. "Aaaaaaagh!" Cockwattle's scream pierced Vehemple's ears. He bucked his head, upsetting the control arm so the exoskeleton reared and nearly fell. Teetering with its own momentum it staggered toward a barricade draped with scorched and broken bodies.

Cursing, the Dutchman squinted through flaring afterimages and steered the exoskeleton clear. Smoke engulfed his eyes but he managed to steady the machine and reposition his microphone.

"Cockwattle! Can you hear me?"

"Yes, yes!" came an answering shriek. "That abomination is hitting me with lightning. Lightning, Vehemple! Your precious machine is on fire. Get me out of here you fucking ingrate."

"*Zwijg!*" Vehemple roared. "Listen to me Cockwattle. We shall return fire with its very own weapon, if you will just do as I tell you."

Static filled Vehemple's ears. A repeated clicking sound, then Cockwattle's voice. "Very well Dutchman, I have flicked the switch. The machine is damaged but I think I can raise the arm. There."

Vehemple's view through the cupola was restored. He glimpsed the entity in the distance, a phantom shape in violet. The arm of the *groot verkeerslicht* came into view, extended towards it.

Cockwattle pressed the button and a bolt of shaped electricity shot forth and struck the entity. It was momentarily obscured by an ectoplasmic explosion, then Vehemple could see Enlil had been flung back towards the Chthonic Gates, its helix structure losing a high degree of cohesion.

"*Uitstekend*!" he shouted. "Now, do it again." But he could see that the discharge had severely depleted the *groot verkeerslicht's* batteries. It would take a moment to recharge. In that moment Vehemple's view of the entity glitched and was replaced by a darkened space.

Vehemple realised he was looking through Cockwattle's eyes into the ballroom in India where the man was transmitting from, his body suspended in *gutta-percha* webbing. To his left he saw a soldier, elevating a rifle. But Vehemple detected vibrations from above. He elevated Cockwattle's head to see a golden-haired woman, dangling in the webbing above. Though badly wounded by rifle fire, she was stretching forward to place an idol into the signal processor.

"*Nee!*" shouted Vehemple, willing the soldier to fire again. The man obliged and the woman grunted in pain. Nonetheless she managed to insert the idol into the processor, where it glowed a vibrant purple. Instantly Vehemple's sensors began to overload and a high pitched keening erupted from the machinery. There was another blinding flash as the screen whited out, then Vehemple was seeing through the *groot verkeerslicht's* eyes again.

Shaking his head, he peered through smoke and flame at a vague shadow moving through the *agora*. He cranked up the contrast on the machine's eyes and realised he was witnessing the entity reassembling itself, coming to its feet, poised to hurl the lightning.

"Cockwattle!" he shrieked, but vision blanked and Vehemple was back in his exoskeleton, reeling away from yet another explosion.

# 35

# Horse's Legs and a Woman's Breasts

Flames rocketed through the capacious galleries and corridors of the Hospice. Once filled with life and song, now they fumed in a vortex of smoke and the glowing embers of fungcrete and charred trees.

In the long hall approaching the *agora* an entire vaulted ceiling had collapsed, mounds of debris piled high against the walls. But a section of that detritus began to bulge and heave, then rubble showered convulsively into the air. From under it emerged the seers of the Entheogen Academy, seemingly unharmed by Ancoulsis' explosive attack.

They dusted themselves off and eyed one another grimly.

"That Ancoulsis is a cunning wretch," said Jian Cong ruefully.

"We should have anticipated his wiles," said Menahem Ziyuni.

"No point in recriminations," said the *Natugai* Sarantsatsral Yargui. "The moment is in flux and we are in grave danger. Julie Brown has entered a state of *Metis*, activating the Cosmic Shekinah, but the Earth Entity has not yet responded. Ancoulsis cannot be allowed to endanger the process."

"I will go to assist Julie Brown's transubstantiation," said Galyna Black Otter.

"I will determine whether Jörmungandr the Midgard Serpent has released its tail from its mouth," said the Völva Yrsa.

"I will ensure Ancoulsis does not further compromise this facility," said Jian Cong.

"Very well," said the *Natugai*. "We should tackle our respective targets and afterwards meet to debrief, if only by telemetry. The *Sarhang* needs to know whether the Hospice is secure and the Cosmic Shekinah evolving as ordained. He is already embroiled in battle with the *Ljmmûm*."

"And the Qliphoth are responding to Cockwattle's summons," said Menahem Ziyuni. "They are trying to breach the Hospice defences as we speak."

"Go then," said Galyna Black Otter. "And luck to you all."

The seers dispersed, but Menahem Ziyuni raised his heavy brows at Zhāng Sān. The dream engineer paused.

"Did you notice anything odd in Jian Cong's behaviour?" asked Ziyuni. "I observed that his alacrity in our ambush of Ancoulsis was at odds with his misgivings as to our strategies. I also intuited he was not using his full powers to counter the Moldavian's *magikal* sorties."

"Yes," said Zhāng Sān. "I felt there was some incongruity with his enthusiasm. Also his attack was repulsed without any great difficulty. It did occur to me that he was pulling his punches. Wait, I will call up his profile."

The Vietnamese savant closed his eyes and after a moment reopened them. "Yes, his dreaming modules are telling. He recently furnished an unknown party with details of a private retreat in the Altai Mountains. And there is the matter of a Chinese *siheyuan* ideogram, prominent in his dreaming, which resonates with some form of talisman. The third *fántǐzì* stroke on one flank of the character is sloped upward, in a manner which betrays hidden meanings. It is clearly a coded signal. Upon closer examination it concurs with a recent dream signature of the Baron Ancoulsis. It would appear that Jian Cong is in collusion with the Moldavian."

"It is true then," said Ziyuni. "He has betrayed us."

They caught up with Jian Cong in a charred entrance to the *agora*. Through that architrave a purple light flared. Menahem Ziyuni extended his energy and closed the door in Jian Cong's face. The *Shefu* wheeled around.

"Is this some ill-timed jest?" he demanded. "What in the ancestor's name are you doing? Do not hinder me. I must prevent Ancoulsis from destroying the Hospice."

"Your sham no longer deceives us, Jian Cong," said Menahem Ziyuni. "We have discovered your treachery. I order you to surrender yourself."

"Such nonsense," roared Jian Cong. "Do you think to question me, *Shefu* of the Middle Kingdom? I am beyond your petty authority."

"You are unmasked, Jian Cong," said Zhāng Sān. "We have evidence of your conniving with Ancoulsis. Surrender. The other seers have been notified and are returning to help restrain you."

But Jian Cong raised his staff as if to strike. He held that posture, his face undergoing an almost comical series of contortions, as might be expected of an uncloaked conspirator experiencing mental cogitations. They went from chagrin to umbrage through incredulity and disenchantment before resolving into an expression of resignation that preceded a cynical wheeze.

"Very well you boneheaded *shá bi*," he said. "But do not expect to apprehend me. I return to my home now. Remember that the Middle Kingdom is ancient and its patience infinite. You can expect to encounter me again." With that he raised his staff and leapt into the air, disappearing with a flash and whiff of sulphur which Zhāng Sān thought rather bombastic.

"He has gone back to China," said the dream engineer. "It will not be possible to extradite him."

"Quickly then," said Menahem Ziyuni. "Let us go to prevent Ancoulsis from more mischief."

They entered the *agora*, where a wall of purple flame limned the titanic forms of Enlil and the *groot verkeerslicht,* engaged in a ruinous melee. There they also saw Ancoulsis, tiny in the foreground with his back against a pillar. He had extracted the idol and Vania's manuscript from his haversack and placed them on the ground before him. Further along the *agora* was the unmistakeable bulwark of the Chthonic Gates, before which purple mists swirled in agitation.

Ancoulsis saw the Seers enter the *agora*. He had also observed Vehemple's exoskeleton prowling around the battlefield and decided he must end this scenario now. Summoning all his powers, Ancoulsis sought Vania through the *Mēnōg*. Through his fourth eye he saw her in Cockwattle's mansion in Bombay, climbing a web of cables. Suspended beneath her was the inert body of Cockwattle and lower still, a soldier unlimbering his rifle. Coming level with a signal processing box at the top of the web, Vania extracted the idol from a holster at her breast.

"Now Vania, now!" he shouted but she did not hear him through the ethers. He saw the soldier fire his rifle and the bullet strike Vania in the side. "No," he groaned and began to chant, calling up cosmic energies to assist her through the *Mēnōg*.

Alerted to this emission of magik, Enlil turned his head and beheld Ancoulsis. The god's laughter was thunderous.

Even as Ancoulsis continued to chant, an effulgence of ruinous, sickly light flared behind him. A rupture opened in the middle of the air and a series of grotesque figures emerged from it. Misshapen they were, agglomerates of negative cosmic energy. Encountering the rarefied atmosphere of the *Gēttīg* they took on horrific forms, the demonic profiles associated with their old tenure on this planet.

One had the body and legs of an arachnid surmounted by three heads; that of a bullfrog on the left and a tomcat frowning on the right. On its central head was the countenance of a dispossessed Duke, wearing an outsized crown.

The next monster bore a lashing serpent's tale, but its body was that of a wolf, its eyes that of an owl. Flames spouted through its snarling fangs.

There was a hideous beast with horse's legs and a woman's breasts, topped by the head of a cackling hyena. More vile beings boiled from that void, and at their coming the earth itself seemed to shudder. Foul odours surrounded them, gouts of flame and icy gales heralded their ominous tread.

Hearing the rancour of their approach, Ancoulsis turned and his face became ashen. "Qliphoth!" he wailed and redoubled the fervour of his incantations.

"I am Shemhamphorash," said the spider with three heads. "And I have come for thee Ancoulsis, who left the door open to let us in."

"I am Bael," said the wolven snake-owl. "And I have come for thee Ancoulsis, who thought to provoke us with thy tampering, who left the door open to let us in."

"And I am Agares," said the third, in the form of an old man riding a crocodile, with a goshawk riding on his arm. "I have come for thee, Baron Codrût Casimir Ancoulsis, who left the door open to let us in, to reward thee for releasing me into the river of manifest *khuti*."

"Jian Cong, I summon you to assist me," Ancoulsis cried, but he heard only the voice of Menahem Ziyuni. "Jian Cong has fled back to his Middle Kingdom. Desist from your evils Ancoulsis, and surrender."

But Ancoulsis placed his hands on the idol. "Enlil, I summon thee," he cried, and looking into that place where all magik derives he saw the face of Enlil laughing and in that instant Ancoulsis knew his journey to China had been observed by the god.

And Ancoulsis saw that upon returning from China he had been distracted and failed to subsume the energies released by his sorcery. Through that cleft the Qliphoth, who had long sought to ensnare him, found his *apeira* and had now come to claim him. Enlil knew it too, and now he laughed at Ancoulsis and left him to his dire fate.

For at Ancoulsis' feet the idol trembled, then flew through the air towards its master. Enlil received it, it dissolved into his form.

He swelled, incandescent, illuminating the *agora* in a brazen purple glare.

The *groot verkeerslicht* charged but Enlil buffeted it aside. Crashing to the ground, its cupola cracked, revealing the graven face of Cockwattle. The machine struggled upright again. It raised a golem arm and a missile smashed into Enlil. The explosion was transformative, obliterating the *agora*, but when the fiery vapours dissipated, the god remained. Enlil howled in exultation and hurled the lightning.

The bolt sheared an arm from the *groot verkeerslicht* and falling, it launched a missile from its forehead. But the missile flew awry and though its explosion boiled through the *agora*, the machine could not rise again to fight Enlil, and the lights pulsing in its limbs began to dim.

But Ancoulsis saw no more, for Shemhamphorash had seized his arm and threw him into the abyss, and he vanished into fathomless reaches of the *Mēnōg*. So it was that Ancoulsis did not see the Qliphoth go to the succour of Cockwattle in his *groot verkeerslicht*, nor did he see Vania climb the final rungs to the top of the cable web and insert the idol into its aperture. For Ancoulsis had been cast into that void where the Qliphoth dwell, and his *khuti* was extinguished.

Only Zhāng Sān and Menahem Ziyuni recognised the significance of these events, for their trained eyes saw into the summonings Ancoulsis had enacted. They saw Vania's valiant act release the glamour laid on Enlil's idols and his might redoubled as all its iterations, brought into this place by Ancoulsis, by Bejikereene, by Teufel and by Black George were completely absorbed into his manifestation. They saw Cockwattle's manor detonate in a conflagration that consumed an entire suburb of Bombay and annihilated his body.

They saw that Enlil's rage and exultation were great. He beat the Qliphoth back and again turned the lightning upon Cockwattle, smiting the *groot verkeerslicht* a mighty blow that crushed its carapace, and Cockwattle's data was sucked away.

But the Qliphoth, seeing that Enlil had arisen in all his wrath and power and that their patron Lord Cockwattle was banished, all fled. They fought each other to leap back into the void, though Enlil caught Bael and Agares and entrapped them in the palm of his hand, and ever after they were known as the Fingers of Enlil, for he wore them as rings which he used to dazzle his enemies whenever he encountered them in the reaches of the *Mēnōg*.

# 36

## Mere Theatrics

It was almost a familiar sensation now. Being enveloped by the penumbra of the *Mēnōg* at first swamped Chance's feeling of self; he became nothing, then everything, then he was gazing around at a fresh source of novelty. He was drifting through a vastness beyond seeing, beyond thought. Plumes of colour emanated around him; discharges of cosmic energy spiralling through a void where he twisted, helpless.

Occasionally, *beings* rolled by. Composed of light, sound and *khuti*, they bore no recognisable form. Incomprehensible, yet undeniably real. Chance did not even bother; he concentrated on maintaining integrity of thought, coherence of self, lest he shatter into a billion particles, lost in eternity.

He appeared to be cycling through some membrane that clung, viscous to his scrambled imagination. Remembering Kalyenka's recommendation (how was he even able to think in the absence of an organic brain?) he willed himself past it, became a dream where he was inviolate, a robust facade of resolute identity. He focused on Kalyenka, on the *rasa* sensation of her smell, but that was a trap, for the ambient became pornographic, breasts flowering around him in a garden of sensuality.

A slow gasp, basking in unutterable sensations of pleasure. Kalyenka, naked, regarding him from above her opened legs. Her vulva was impossibly pink, an invitation that hardened Chance to a point of recklessness. He longed to touch her, to tell her his lust had depths, but instinct warned him and he remembered this was not her demeanour. Though she could be wanton, she was subtle.

Something was playing on his imagination, mining his deepest urges, using them to distract him from his path. Ha! It was the

Skein, infecting his resolution. He tore his mind from Kalyenka, concentrated on his experiences with the *Lịmmûm*. They bloomed in his memory, hundreds of wicked men encountered in escapades across the globe. He sought their presence but they scattered, luring him on to further distractions.

"Concentrate," he told himself. He ransacked his memory for the moment he had been physically closest to Lord Cockwattle. He recalled the man's distended eyes and florid face, the attacks on the aircraft and in a sumptuous chamber in Cristaña (and here he hastily deflected away from the image of Kalyenka naked) and was instantly sitting at the rearmost table of a grand banquet room in Monaco. Cockwattle stood on a dais at the front of the hall, addressing hundreds of the wealthiest plutocrats in the world; the foregathered magnates of his Royal Armourers Association.

"And that, my fellows, was the point at which I swooped in and made another billion off the broad, sweaty backs of the gullible peasantry of Kenya," Cockwattle chuckled.

On cue, his esurient audience applauded. They sat at finely appointed tables guzzling delicacies, quaffing exquisite vintages and regaling each other with rare tales of their vulturine exploits. Though they wore extravagant watches, rings and cufflinks inlaid with sapphires, pearls and diamonds to bespeak their status, they were quite safe from predation themselves. Ranged around the hall were squads of mercenaries in red tunics, their flat, dead eyes monitoring the room.

Using miniature field glasses, Chance scanned the high walls. He saw elephant tusks carved into grotesque sculptures, an elaborate catafalque displaying the skins of flayed slaves, plundered statues, ancient carpets and gold embroidered *kilims*. Finally he was gazing at a huge, ornate wooden cabinet behind the table hosting the guests of honour. He recollected that on his last dream visit this cabinet held an iteration of the idol of Enlil. It was no longer there.

Chance allowed himself a wry smile. His mission to the Australian coal mine must have nullified this iteration of the idol, removing it from both *Mēnōg* and *Gēttīg*. He wondered what Bebop thought when he disappeared, in the middle of their journey to the protestor's camp.

A renewed bout of cheering returned his attention to the ballroom, where Cockwattle was concluding his speech. Icy blue eyes protruding, the man hunched over his bulging cummerbund, one hand idly resting on the head of a nubile young woman who sat, semi-naked, the nipples on her pert breasts pierced and rouged, eyes arranged into adoring complacency beside him.

Cockwattle raised his goblet of brandy aloft. "And furthermore, my most delectable competitors, underlings and pretend friends, let us never forget we owe it all to the good graces of our unwitting friend Enlil."

He waved his free hand at the cabinet, but something in the expression of those in the front row made him falter. He turned around, observing the empty space that had held the idol. Cockwattle glared at the butler who stood by the cabinet but the man only blinked, his face reddening. "Where is it you fool?" Cockwattle demanded.

"I, I do not know milord," the butler said.

Cockwattle uttered an inhuman shriek. His fists crashed on the table and he cocked his head, as though hearing a voice from within. While his mercenaries came to attention and lowered their weapons, Cockwattle's eyes roamed the room. They settled on Chance.

"YOU!" thundered Cockwattle as he rose from his table. "Get that man," he squealed, pointing and the soldiers surrounding the stage broke ranks to charge at Chance. Having already established there were no exits unguarded, Chance stood slowly, raising his hands. But just before they reached him the soldiers slowed to immobility.

"I'll take it from here, Mister Chance," said a voice and the *Sarhang* was beside him as the grand banquet hall dissolved. They were sitting on stools around a cracked wooden table in a tiny hut made of daubed clay. Chickens rustled in the shelves atop the stove, pecked at crumbs under the table. Small charms tinkled in a slight breeze. It was hot and the air smelt faintly of shit. "You've done very well, locating Cockwattle so quickly."

But Chance's eyes were drawn to a tiny, ancient woman sitting across the table from him. Her hair was long and grey, eyes tiny slits amidst epicanthic folds. From his time fighting amongst the Basque warriors during the Carlist Wars he recognised that unique genetic trait as belonging to the Euskadi, ancient peasant stock of the mountains of northern Spain. The old woman sipped on a cup of hot herbal tea, muttering to herself as her gnarled fingers threaded string through feathers tied around a stick.

The *Sarhang* said something in a guttural dialect and she looked up, eyes gleaming. "This is Agnolia," said the *Sarhang*. "She is the person with the most *khuti* you have never heard of. During the Spanish Inquisition, Agnolia was a housekeeper in the mansion of Inquisitor General, Tomás de Torquemada. She discovered the names of hundreds of women condemned to torture and execution for alleged crimes of witchcraft. Under Torquemada's nose she alerted many of them to escape into the mountains - until she was caught out and herself died a gruesome death at the hands of the Inquisitors."

Chance bowed his head and Agnolia's face folded in a wan smile. Finishing with the crude talisman, she stood and arranged it on Chance's fatigue cap. Peering at him with eyes like a raven, she spoke to him.

"She says it is a potent charm to protect you from the Evil Ones," said the *Sarhang*.

"*Eskerrik asko, Amona*," Chance said, but she stared blankly.

"The dialect she uses is an ancient one," said the *Sarhang*. "The Basque language is antediluvian, but the persecution her people endured led them to develop dialects alien to all others."

"Thank you Agnolia," said Chance. Rummaging in his pockets for his pipe, he turned to the *Sarhang*.

"I have a question for you Augustine. How is it that Cockwattle is rampaging through the Hospice and yet we are able to confront him in his continuum at an earlier time? Last time I looked things were not going so well for us in the *agora*."

The *Sarhang* had taken off his glasses and basked in sunshine leaking through the ancient cottage walls. "The peculiarities of the Skein mean that Cockwattle's invasion of the Hospice leaves him vulnerable. He has entered a field of objective time, but your presence at the banquet a decade ago provides a juncture in the Skein's subjective time field through which we can trace him. Think of it in the same manner as the fact that you're wearing your fatigue cap, though you lost it in a gust of wind atop the Hospice."

"I'm sure that makes some kind of sense," said Chance.

"The same kind of sense that enables the next stage of our gambit," said the *Sarhang*. "Allow me to review. The Skein's temporal anomalies are working in our favour as much as against us. Though Enlil has destroyed Vehemple's mechanical golem, Cockwattle's consciousness was not extinguished with it. It was sucked back into the Skein, where, as his body has been destroyed in some conflagration, it progressed along its *apeira* to his next manifestation in my Korean friend Bitgaram's continuum.

"There Cockwattle appears as a disgraced ex-President of the United States, a mountebank and grifter whose brazen effrontery and shamelessness found its perfect manifestation in that amoral time. Using a continuum harvesting process, I ensnared him as he participated in an artificial orgy in the Skein."

"A what?"

"The stratagem Bitgaram and I devised creates a critical juncture where the Skein meets the *Mēnōg*. Now that you have exposed Cockwattle, I have a direct line to his *apeira*. Along that *apeira* he indulges in a particularly sordid Skein simulacra. I exploited the Skein's peculiarities to isolate his *apeira* in a fixed temporal field, aligning him contemporaneously with other *Ljmmûm* of his epoch. Their avatars are projected into what they think of as a battlefield simulation. Instead they have no choice but to join us on a battlefield of my choosing which is, in effect, Kalyenka's painting."

"Ah, sound," said Chance. Failing to find his pipe, Chance was reminded of the flask he'd abandoned on his recent escapade. "Though I really have no idea what you're talking about. One last thing now. Was Ancoulsis following me when he came into the *agora*? I had his flask with me when I went into the future, but I left it behind when I recognised its coat of arms."

"An inspired decision," said the *Sarhang*. "If you still had his flask on your person, Ancoulsis may well have been able to prevent you from escaping into the *Mēnōg*. But no, he was not following you. Rather he sought Enlil, to enact the last phase of his plans."

Chance sipped from a cracked earthenware cup Agnolia had poured for him. He made a face at the bitterness of the brew. "And what plans are they, if I may ask?"

"That is a long story, for another time," said the *Sarhang*. "Now, if you are ready?"

The cottage vanished and Chance stood with Agnolia and the *Sarhang* in long grass on the downward slope of a valley between two mountains. A small stream marked the centre of the valley, whose opposing slope was embroidered with a riot of summer flowers. Chance recognised the place where he had given Proko the idol of Enlil, during their march to the Hospice. He also noted that the Caliph's golden scimitar was sheathed by his side.

The *Sarhang* was wearing a somewhat martial-looking black coat and a navy blue mariner's cap. Above them the sky was a fathomless blue and the white mountain peaks cordially remote. For a moment it felt very peaceful. Then a great howling went up from the forested slope opposite them.

Through the trees emerged a menagerie of huge demons, rippling with muscle, harnessed in armoured protuberances and prosthetics, bristling with whips and mauls. They bore a selection of elaborately curved and bejewelled swords, axes and spears such as only a puerile imagination could conjure. Growling and flexing, they paraded for each other, trampling trees and bellowing incoherent challenges as they pawed the earth.

One enormous beast with a single Cyclopean eye ripped out a conifer and hurled it like a javelin across the valley at the *Sarhang*. It stuck quivering in the ground twenty feet away.

The *Sarhang* sniffed. "Mere theatrics." But theatrics appeared to be the point. The *Ljmmûm* swung their weapons with gusto, chopping down imaginary soldiers and howling exultantly.

"Do not be overly impressed," the *Sarhang* said. "What we are seeing is merely the manifest egos of the *Ljmmûm,* as filtered through their avatars in a gaming simulation. They believe they can disconnect from this game at any time, but in actuality they have allowed themselves to be duped. Bitgaram is controlling the coding and they cannot escape till there is some resolution. Meanwhile, they have been sundered from the Skein by Kalyenka's painting, so the coding that created their scary costumes is degrading. See there, even now their imaginations are failing and their true nature emerging in these avatars."

Indeed, the *Ljmmûm*'s complex disguises were slowly fading, exposing a pot belly here, frail arms and a balding head there, the sagging physiques of men and women devoted to gluttony and indolence.

Before the *Sarhang* finished speaking there was a commotion downslope. Out of a roseate mist appeared hundreds of individuals arrayed along the banks of the stream. They wore a variety of period costumes, from Greek *klepht* and *armatoloi* battle armour through Hungarian hussar accoutrements to gowns of Parisian chic.

"Who on earth are these people?" asked Chance. "Some of them look rather familiar."

A broad smile creased the *Sarhang's* face. "Such is the power of Kalyenka's work that she has summoned the eidolons of prominent revolutionaries from the epochs she fought in. They are the people who stood against the tyrants of Europe in a thousand conflicts."

"Among the farmers and tradespeople you can see officers from the Greek uprising against the Ottoman Empire. The generals Yannis Makriyannis and Athanasios Dia stand alongside female rebels Manto Mavrogenous, patroness of the Hellenic cause and Laskarina Bouboulina, the only female naval commander, born in a prison in Constantinople.

"Kalyenka's compatriots in the Hungarian War of Independence include her friend Júlia Szendrey, the poet who married Sándor Petofi. She is urging caution to Lieutenant Mária Lebstück, who was 18 years old when she cut her hair and fought as a hussar, her adventures later enshrined in an opera. And there stands the fascinating Júlia Bányai, known as the Woman with the Sword. An excellent tactician, she was an adroit linguist and actor who employed her skills as a spy, uncovering many of the strategies of the Holy Alliance. She is in animated conversation with 'Father' Bem, the General who fought in Poland's uprising against Tsarist Russia and later led the Hungarians at Székelykeresztúr.

"Looking quite poetic there is the Croatian Serb General János Damjanich, who destroyed the Austrians at Szolnok. Like Count Lajos Batthány, he was sentenced to death following the defeat of the Revolution. He is discussing the weapons of the oncoming *Ljmmûm* with the engineer and journalist General István Széchenyi and with General György Klapka, who led the heroic defence of Komárom."

"Who are those women dressed entirely in black?" asked Chance.

"They are Polish intellectuals called 'the Enthusiasts', whose mourning weeds bear testament to the occupation of their nation by the Russians. Among them is Paulina Zbyszewska who attempted to assassinate the Tsar, and the writers Anna Skimborowicz and Kazimiera Ziemiecka.

"Wearing the distinctive tall black *kalpak* on his head is the Wallachian hero Tudor Vladimirescu, stalwart alongside Hüseyn Gradaščević, the Dragon of Bosnia. With them are the Armenian freedom fighter János Czetz and the Bulgarian poet Dobri Chintulov. And there, deep in conversation with British anti-slavery activist Anne Knight and the Irish writer Anna Wheeler is the French novelist and adventuress George Sand, whose hairstyle was considered rather radical for her day. I believe Kalyenka had a passionate fling with Aurore, as she preferred to be called."

Chance raised his eyebrows and the *Sarhang* touched his forearm delicately.

"Forgive me. I am sometimes indiscreet and forget the niceties of human relations. I have been too long in the *Mēnōg*."

Chance chuckled. "Kalyenka's passions are what draws me to her. I could not erase them even if I wished to. I would prefer to join her in them. But tell me, who is the tall woman who gesticulates and frowns so much?"

"That is the German author Louise Dittmar, founder of the *Welt-Bewegung* movement. She is expounding to the French unionist Pauline Roland, arrested for feminism and 'debauchery'. Listening on is Kalyenka's painting tutor, Maríe Demachy, who was killed in the July Barricades, and Lord Brougham, the English slavery abolitionist and prominent politician."

"By god I know Brougham," said Chance. "You must too. He is a member of the Pale Conduit. And I have to ask, but how will these people fight such an awful collection of monsters?"

"Their weapons are their *khuti*. Deployed in dreaming modes that becomes surprisingly powerful. Observe."

Now the *Ljmmûm* were charging downslope, absurdly exaggerated musculature rippling as they swung their weapons, rejoicing in their avatar's strength and virility. A darkness came over the battlefield and the monsters smashed through the stream, churning the earth with heavy hoofs and clawed paws.

But from the army of freedom fighters rose a shimmering rampart of purple brume, shot through with threads of gold. The *Ljmmûm* crashed into it and became enmeshed, swinging their weapons wildly. A chorus of hoots and squeals arose as they blundered about, blinded.

"They are expending their power," said the *Sarhang*. "That is our great hope. They are committed now, and they cannot see that the narrative is changing shape around them."

"For the invasion of the Hospice has stalled. The Prussian Kaiser is dead, his army destroyed and the Citadel has defied all attacks. Vehemple's treacheries on the *Gēttīg* have failed. But the *Ljmmûm* can still defeat us here. If the Qliphoth arrive before the Cosmic Shekinah can awaken the Earth Entity, they may yet overwhelm us."

Agnolia said something in her ancient language and pointed at a maelstrom swirling above the mountain peaks. Out of it dropped a gaseous bundle that disappeared in the trees.

"See, Cockwattle has entered the fray," said the *Sarhang*.

An enormous, bloated creature tottered into view. Orange in colour, it was girdled all about with scaffolding and wires that scarce held in its ponderous gut. Its artificially enlarged phallus was cradled in steel prosthetics so it stood erect like a mummified spear. The creature came raging onto the field, squalling hysterically, careful to keep a screen of acolytes and guards well in front of it.

The *Sarhang* chuckled. "Cockwattle is presenting here as he appears in Kalyenka's painting, which has somewhat distorted the Herculean figure of his avatar."

"I see Kalyenka has added some subtle touches," said Chance. "The nappies on the orange one are a touch of genius."

But in front of Cockwattle a void had manifested, disgorging dozens of beings so odious that Chance had to look away. Negative waves of energy somehow made coherent by alien intelligence, they were debilitating to look upon. "What in the name of fortune are they?" he cried.

"Our worst fears are confirmed," said the *Sarhang*. "They are the Qliphoth, the Husks of Eternity. They have managed to breach Kalyenka's painting through the treachery of Ancoulsis, and they have found their way into our scenario."

"What exactly are they?" said Chance.

"You have already encountered one - Azriel on the Moon. They are creatures of pure entropy, native to a mysterious region of the *Mēnōg*. We cannot hope to face them. Now the tide of the battle will turn their way and the Cosmic Shekinah has not yet invoked Lord Ningishzida, the Earth Entity. I fear our struggle has been for nothing."

# 37

# All the Demons in Creation

Aloft in his exoskeleton, Vehemple squinted at the carnage in the *agora*. The *groot verkeerslicht* was irreparably damaged and aflame on the floor. His exoskeleton's sensors had also been disrupted by Enlil's ruinous lightning.

As if to confound Vehemple's analytical functions further, a number of other paranormal entities had also appeared. Redlining instruments in his exoskeleton confirmed a major irruption of the space-time fabric. Unstable antimatter fields presenting as coherent organisms were swarming around the conflict. One of them seized upon the Moldavian, Codrût Ancoulsis. The man promptly disappeared, becoming antimatter subsumed in a quantum field.

Vehemple reluctantly understood that the focus of this struggle had moved into the quantum sphere - not his speciality. He had dabbled in metaphysics on behalf of clients who desired nuclear weapons. But he had not contemplated the more numinous aspects of a pseudo-science he regarded as a realm for ninnies and priests. Now he wished he had paid more attention to this nascent sphere.

For it seemed to be undeniably evident that what he was witnessing was the full-blown manifestation of several dozen quantum entities. Furthermore, the most powerful of them, Enlil the titan with entoptic eyes had proven more than a match for the supposedly invincible *groot verkeerslicht*.

The blonde woman in Bombay had destroyed Cockwattle's web, sabotaging his neurological links to the *groot verkeerslicht*. The quantum entity's lightning bolts had finished the job. Vehemple's mightiest creation was destroyed, a tangle of inanimate metal on the floor of the cursed Hospice.

He groaned, for his sensors revealed that Cockwattle's consciousness had left the *groot verkeerslicht,* escaping into the Skein. Furthermore, Enlil was rapidly regaining strength and had chased off the other paranormal entities, which seemed to be primarily composed of dangerous antimatter. As they escaped into a quantum vortex, Vehemple's dataviz showed that Enlil's attention was now focussing on him.

This scenario was out of his hands. It was time to go. Vehemple reversed the exoskeleton, stepping over a clutch of dead bodies mutilated by flame and shot. He could see an escape route through the debris and flames, but at that moment a jaeger stirred in the rubble behind him. He took careful aim at the Dutchman's arm, protruding from its metal harness. The shot was inaudible against the roaring of the inferno but in his exoskeleton Vehemple flinched.

He glanced down in disbelief as blood filled his metallic sleeve and began short-circuiting its delicate instrumentation. Another shot penetrated the hood of the rear engine pack. Black smoke oozed forth and alerts sounded in Vehemple's earpiece. The Dutchman strode on but his machine was failing and caught fire before crashing to the floor of the *agora.*

Unbuckling himself and crawling out from the wreckage, Vehemple rose unsteadily to his feet. He slipped on blood, stumbled on corpses and burning wreckage, seeking a way out through the smoke.

He did not see Black George, who was rampaging through the outer arcade of the *agora,* gnashing his teeth and howling with unfathomable rage. The bandit chief had entered some realm where reason was superfluous and all that was left to him was this senseless gibbering fury at all things past and future. The demons in his head swirled around him, taunting, for he was surrounded by smoke and fire and every fresh draught of ash-laden air that filled his lungs only fed his wrath. But as he stumbled through the inferno he saw the unmistakeable silhouette of the bald Dutchman and that focussed his rage to a palpable edge.

Black George followed Vehemple through the gutted corridors of the Hospice, fingering his long blade, whispering threats to the spirits that haunted his charred soul. He stopped suddenly, squinting through the befouled air.

Vehemple had come to a wall of flame, barring his way out of the *agora*. Smoke roiled all around, choking him. He staggered left and right, determined to circumvent this preposterous anomaly, to make his way down the mountain and escape on his flying machine.

He glimpsed an elevator shaft through the fumes. A light above it flashed red, indicating it was operable only in cases of emergency. But Vehemple had long ago memorised the master codes to all means of egress within the Hospice. He stumbled to it, punched in the numbered sequence to open the door. The panel did not respond, so Vehemple produced a tool to override the mechanism.

But Black George sauntered up behind him, whistling a Moravian jig. In his right hand the wicked knife dangled. Vehemple turned to regard Black George with bleak eyes. "There is nothing for you here, bandit. You should evacuate these premises before the *Securité* arrest you."

"Oh, I have found all I need," remarked Black George, as his right hand, seemingly of its own volition, jerked upwards, ramming the blade into Vehemple's abdomen, where it continued with murderous velocity to bury itself in his spleen.

Vehemple stared at him, uncomprehending. "I am almost there," he said. "You cannot stop me now."

But he was falling, and pain rose to greet him like a monstrous ape, enclosing him in remorseless arms. Black George allowed the weight of the drooping body to release the knife from its wound and did not blink as blood jetted over his eyes. For a moment he stood there, in the dim realisation that no exoneration had come from that act and that nothing proceeded from any of the foul deeds he had ever encompassed and that all he ever brought to fruition was the contemplation of his own evil.

But as the rage began to resurface in his mind, Black George became aware that there was another personage close by. Billowing smoke warped and distorted the being so that Black George cringed, concluding it was one of the monsters he'd just escaped. Then it shrunk again and he grinned, for he was merely facing Proko. Must be high time for that little bastard to perish too, though maybe Black George would draw that execution out a while. Make the swine squeal.

"Maggot," he hissed through clenched teeth, and his fingers tightened around the handle of the blade, till he recognised a pistol in the wife beater's hand. Black George softened his rictus, sheathed the knife and stepped forward with hands outstretched. "Ah Proko, my friend. At last. I have been looking all over for you. Time for us to get out of this shit hole and back to honest thieving."

But even above the roaring flames Back George heard a shot. It punched him in the belly, all the breath went out of him and he fell backwards onto Vehemple's body, still trembling and twitching in its death throes.

"Proko," Black George muttered in disbelief. "You would betray your chieftain? Here, help me up. I'll overlook this one and we'll laugh about it later over whores and rakia. Come on, Proko you old devil. I'll make you my Lieutenant and we'll be rich eh? What do you say?"

But another bullet punctured Black George's chest and blood gushed into his mouth. He tried to speak but could only cough. As he drowned in his own blood Black George was overwhelmed by the *soma* he'd drunk, mixed with dimethyltryptamines released by his dying brain. All the demons in creation rushed to claim his black soul and haul it into the abyss. The last thing he saw on this *Gēttīg* was Proko smiling, as the wife beater put the gun to his own head.

# 38

# A Golden Compass

The *Sarhang* was interrupted by Agnolia, waving one withered arm at the battlefield. He replied in her dialect and touched her gently on the shoulder. She regarded Chance gravely a moment, then walked slowly downslope to join the ranks of the 48'ers. "It is her last stand," said the *Sarhang* gravely. "She will die as she has lived, in grace."

Music arose from the battlefield and Chance saw there a phalanx of musicians serenely plying zither, cellos, oud, tympani, violins, flugelhorns and kettle drums. Alongside them a young woman sang in a clarion voice.

"That is Ermengarde of Occitania," said the *Sarhang*. "The Qliphoth will find her a formidable foe. The musicians of the Hospice are also here, creating a wall of *khuti* to slow down the enemy.

"See now the Qliphoth are morphing into anthropomorphic demons of the cloven-hooved variety. That is for the benefit of the *Lĩmmûm*, who have conservative ideas about how they prefer their demons to manifest."

The Qliphoth descended upon the 48'ers and the Murex Moon was obscured by a cloud of pollution. Lurching into the wall of *khuti* the monsters swiftly rent it apart. They set upon the musicians and revolutionaries and the slaughter was great.

"This is a grievous blow," said the *Sarhang*. "For we are not yet ready and the Murex Moon is nearing its apogee. I will summon the Sephiroth now."

There was a swirl of energy fields and Aiwass stood beside them. His golden visor looked out on the oncoming *Lĩmmûm*.

"Finally we confront the Qliphoth," said Aiwass. "Yes, they are ripe for my revenge."

More of his kind appeared. Like the Qliphoth, the Sephiroth were composed of energies without form, but like Aiwass they began to assume human shape, armoured in fantastical panoplies, wielding swords and lances of light as they charged down upon their ancient foes. Tiamat was among them, the Glistening One manifesting as a dragon who roared and devoured those monsters who had conspired in her usurpment.

Aiwass rose into the air and flared up over the ranks of the Qliphoth.

"I am Aiwass, the Minister of Hoor-paar-kraat!" he declared and smote them with his staff. They made a hideous lamenting and flung carrion and offal, but the Sephiroth fell upon the Qliphoth like a hurricane and fierce battle was joined. Against the rage of Aiwass many Qliphoth were extinguished and sent back into their void.

But in the distance a storm front was rapidly approaching. "It is the Skein," said the *Sarhang*. "See how the *Limmûm* are heartened by it. Already their coding is becoming stronger."

Indeed it seemed that the Skein had reinforced the morale of the dark host. The tangerine-coloured Cockwattle and his *Limmûm* demons seemed to grow in stature and beat back the Sephiroth. The Qliphoth rallied and came on again.

"Never fear," said the *Sarhang*. "I had Bitgaram factor this into his design - it is the de facto cultural fabric of his epoch."

But the dark and loathsome shroud hung low over the battlefield and Chance felt the dread horror of its unnatural presence. He felt sick to his heart and lost all strength in his limbs. Despair almost overwhelmed him and the surviving ranks of the revolutionaries quailed under its fell sway.

Then a voice resounded through the gloom. In a deep baritone it sang; "Here I come in my pyjamas, striding across the plains of Anatolia."

The *Sarhang* whirled. "Hafiz! You scoundrel. I thought they must have killed you off. Where have you been?"

The face of the poet creased into laughter. "Ah my darling, they cannot kill old Hafiz. I am a being of starlight and song. Do they propose to deconstruct the Universe? I have been in the wilderness, decanting the beauty of chaos."

From the ranks of the 48'ers Ermengarde sang in return and her voice carried like cleansing flames in a garden o'ertaken with weeds. The poet winked at her. He danced ahead, singing at the Qliphoth.

*"I am a Golden Compass - watch me whirl.*
*To the east and to the west, to the north and to the south,*
*In all directions I will true your course towards laughter and unity.*
*Watch me whirl into nothingness your fears and darkness -*
*just keep tossing them onto my golden plate."*

Dismayed by his lyrical onslaught, the Orange One sought to hide behind his minions. They in turn threw each other into the path of Hafiz's song and were sent howling into the abyss. Now only hundreds of the *Lįmmûm* remained, clustered around the Orange One, who gibbered and wet himself and sought to blame his compatriots for their dealings. But the Qliphoth fought on, striking lightnings of black dread against Hafiz. Though these smote him repeatedly, they shivered and fell away and he strode into their midst singing.

But now a new contender entered the fray - a grotesque creature waddling on multiple limbs of different lengths and seemingly of different biologies. It had a body moulded from parts of a reptile and parts of a goat and it possessed two human heads, both bearded and glum.

"Now we come to the true test," said the *Sarhang*. "That is Marduk the Unredeemed, the entity who betrayed Enlil. It is a chimera, manifesting as both Jesus and Mohammed. The asymmetrical limbs and torso are a reflection of the sophistry of its being. This monstrosity embodies all the hypocrisy and perversions of mankind, surmounted by the faces of two allegedly peaceful gods who are eternally at war. Their internal tensions have mutated and blighted its anatomy, this twisted beast of self-loathing and fraudulence. But it is nourished by the *khuti* of all the deluded humans who respond to its twisted message. That manifests as a great power in the realm of dreams."

Even as they watched, Marduk smote Aiwass with its dragon's tail and the Sephiroth spirit ignited with a purple flame that became a comet, racing back to his Moon. The Qliphoth fell upon the remaining Sephiroth with great savagery and it looked as though the battle was lost.

The *Sarhang* turned to Chance. "Now it is our turn to join the fray."

In his hand appeared a staff, whose head shone with the lustre of *Xerion*.

"How is that a weapon to kill demons?" asked Chance.

The *Sarhang* glanced down at the head of the staff, which bore an emblem of two serpents entwined. "Why, it is the Caduceus, staff of Trismegistus, also carried by Hermes and Iris, divine heralds. It is used to tear aside the veils of evil and illuminate the world with magniloquence. I have not used killing weapons since I was a child in the lands of men. Why would I start now? It is not how I defeat evil. My weapons are jurisprudence and morality, long years of study and contemplation. I wield them as a herald of light and compassion."

The *Sarhang* tapped the staff and it made a high musical note. He grinned at Chance. "Perhaps this will all have been for nothing, but somehow, Lieutenant Colonel, I feel that something will always come out of nothing. Artistry is an end in itself."

With that he cried aloud, "For the Dashtur Rashin!" and charged into the battle, where the light from his staff made the *Limmûm* monsters squeal and writhe away.

Chance looked to his own armaments and saw that all he held was the Caliph's golden scimitar. He stared soberly at the oncoming demons and thought of the *Sarhang's* words. He had neither artistry nor muse to uphold and he wondered how he would fare in this metaphysical milieu where thoughts and imagination seemed mightier weapons than swords or firearms. At least since being awakened to the beauty of art and nature he had fought valiantly in their service and as he had nothing else to hand, he figured that therefore the scimitar was as good a weapon as any other for him to wield.

So he drew the scimitar of the Caliph and bellowed "Kalyenka!", for she was the object of all his love and desire. She was his talisman and the thought of her strengthened him as he charged down into the battle. Leaping the stream at the bottom of the valley he slashed the thigh of a Qliphoth demon and stabbed another in the eye. Turning on him with savage glee, a third monster raised its great maul and swung it, a glancing blow that flung him to the ground. The beast loomed over him with its weapon aloft and Chance thought of Kalyenka and that it was finally his time.

But just then a mighty wind arose and the Moon broke through the clouds and its light was stronger than hope. Lightning crashed in the heavens and a mighty voice bellowed from the mountain tops.

"*I am Enlil, destroyer of the Elamites! There is lamentation in the haunted cities where I have visited my wrath. The Tigris and the Euphrates will brim forth in deluge when I call upon them. I will make the mountains anxious and you, Marduk, will feel the lash of my lightning!*"

Taller than the mountains, Enlil descended on a cloud and smote Marduk with prodigious lightnings. His entoptic eyes flashed as he cried out. "*Just as Humbaba cursed Gilgamesh and Enkidu, I curse you Marduk and all your Qliphoth and all of your* Limmûm. *I will cut off your head and take your lungs and make a gift of them to the Lord of the Good Tree.*

*"Your temples will be despoiled like an evil wind. I will rip out their foundations, strike them with the adze, kill the worshippers within it, turn that city into a deserted city. When would you restore its ancient property? Its possessions will be carried off by the wind! I will turn the city which used to be there into a city no longer!"*

"You are a mere statue," scoffed Marduk and the poisonous spines on his back rained like stones from a hundred catapults. But Enlil merely deflected them and reaved the Qliphoth as the wind reaves a field of corn.

"Ha!" cried Enlil. "You think it is chance that my effigy travelled so far, changing hands as often as a wine jar? No, you confused vessel of all the disquiet carried by humankind. Through all these *apeira* I have been edging closer to my goal. When Gilgamesh presented me with cedar I knew it to be a false gift, for cedar is the symbol of his treachery and treachery is on the lips of you and your minions. You and these Qliphoth (he spat the word) who have no *khuti* and merely suck on the void, parasites on the teat of the Universe."

Enlil's spear of lightning pierced the side of Marduk and the beast bellowed in rage and pain. On the talons of one mighty hand winked the rings of the ensnared Qliphoth, Bael and Agares and these Fingers of Enlil gave him added power so that his lightning seared through Marduk and the beast was nearly extinguished.

But Marduk squirted poison at Enlil from its fifth eye, located above the carbuncle on its second forehead. And it was Enlil's turn to howl, for the poison scorched his leg through the greaves made for him in the E-Kur. So Enlil drew forth his war axe and cut one of Marduk's limbs away as he taunted the fell beast.

*"A deluge dashing the hoe on the ground shall be invoked! At its front shall be the storm of my axe, at its rear it shall be a shield. Its overgrown hair shall be a harrow, its back shall be flames. Its*

*countenance shall be a malevolent storm that enshrouds heaven and earth.*

*"The glint of its eyes shall be lightning that flashes far like the Anzud bird. Its mouth shall rage with a blazing fire that extends as far as the nether world. Its tongue shall be an inferno, raining embers, that sunders the Land. Its arms shall be the majestic Anzud bird that nothing can escape when it spreads wide its talons!"*

Then Marduk reared up, and the talons on its longest limb raked Enlil from chest to groin. Enlil fell, and the sound he made impacting upon the earth must have been felt in the nether-worlds. Marduk pounced upon him and summoned all of its strength to despatch Enlil with a killing stroke, but in that instant Marduk discovered that all its strength had gone.

And it looked inside the void from whence it came and discovered that its *khuti* source, the prayers of the deluded *egregores* who worship Jesus and Mohammed had dried up. For somewhere within the Skein a hole had been opened, and its power drained like water from a bath.

And Marduk saw a blind Clever-man, chanting in a place where Marduk could not reach. Beyond him four *Anangu* men wielded musical instruments under desert stars. And the music they played poured through a portal of the Skein, and out of that portal drained all the *khuti* that had sustained Marduk with great strength.

And then Marduk was silent. The Murex Moon shone amaranthine and its light suffused the sky. For Inanna had come.

# 39

# Stone Trees and Flower Mountains

There was a moment when it all became clear. She was Inanna and she was Julie Brown. She was The Seated Woman and she was Kali and she was Xiwangmu, Eternal Goddess of the West and she was the oceans and the sky. She was the trees in the forest, water dripping from a blade of grass, she was ancient stone buried deep under the soil. She was the volcano and she was the frogs and the wolves and the bees and the mist that smoked in the morning. She was the goddess and she was Julie Brown. She was the Cosmic Shekinah and it made the shape of a rainbow.

Julie Brown stood up, if standing it could be called, in this realm where her bearings depended on the way she felt about them. An eye opened within and she saw a succession of women embodying the fabric of the Cosmic Shekinah. She saw the Dashtur Rashin, Olympias, Ermengarde, Harriet Jacobs, Nellie Griswold Francis, Isobel de Olvera, Sue Higginson, Harriet Tubman, Emily Kame Kngwarreye, Truganini.

These were the women who manifested *khuti* to safeguard the emotional and physical bonds between humanity and nature. Who understood there is no duality in that relationship and any difference is purely imagined. That nature is the Lord of the Good Tree and the Madre, that the duality in this Entity was encompassed within the planet that was its bones and its flesh, its guts and its eyes and ears and genitals and brain.

Julie Brown who was Inanna looked at Lord Ningishzida and saw a snake of rainbow hues entwined around a tree, contemplating its old home.

Then she saw close by a man with a face as ancient and joyful as the ocean. Kulan smiled. "We got him. Took some wakin'. He a good sleeper. But then, he a woman too, so extra hard to wake up." His laughter shook the walls of her temple till Inanna was forced to laugh too. "It is strange to laugh," said Inanna. "But it is good to laugh, on the way to Eternity."

Kulan looked up at the sky. "You got some funny constellations here *sista-girl*. That one look like an emu with his head on backwards."

He gestured to the skies. "We almost there *sista-girl*, or maybe I should call you Aunty. Lotta good work been done already, and I know you still getting used to this thing you become. You always been it, you just didn't know it. But the Rainbow Serpent's awake and that means we can start to regrow the place."

Kulan looked into the face of Inanna. "I'm going deeper now," he said. "Whole lot to explore in this place. Kinda different seeing it *from* the desert stars, looking back the other way." And Kulan walked away into the *Mēnōg* and was no more seen in the *Gētīg*.

Yes, there was a thing that had to be done. Inanna looked into the *Gētīg* and she saw the foul murrain that infested it. She entered that cursed Skein and sought till she found the precinct where the *Lįmmûm* were gathered and Enlil was there. But Marduk also was there, and the Qliphoth, for even those abominations were part of Eternity, and could be sundered from it no more than any other part.

But they were engaged with evil men, the *Lįmmûm* who stole the Boat of Heaven and sought to usurp her domain. Inanna began to sing, a golden ululation that calmed the battlefield. Her voice rang clarion over the bleating of the *Lįmmûm* and they shrank away from her.

Inanna descended upon them, and her light horrified them and they tried to flee, but they were trapped in the snare of the *Sarhang*. And their bodies housed neither *Ka* nor *Ba* and their *khaibet* was ascendant, so they had no *khuti* to take them into the *Mēnōg* and they could not join the ecology of souls and contribute to the Great

Work. Thus was the essence of the *Lịmmûm* made un-manifest. And Inanna struck terror into the Qliphoth so they scattered and fled back into their voids. But they took the *Lịmmûm* with them, and those fools vanished forever.

And Inanna looked upon Marduk and she saw that he was made of wroth and stone.

And she looked upon Enlil and she saw that he was her lover.

And they both bowed, Marduk in fear, Enlil in reverence. But Inanna laughed, for The Lord of the Good Tree was also among them. She was a serpent and a tree and grew out of everything and she, he, they, the Lord Ningishzida had already begun to grow through the Skein, destroying that virus with the power of new life.

And the Skein was rent apart and dismissed on solar winds. That virus could not flourish, now that the ecological compact had been restored. And because Marduk was non-compostable, a reeking midden of despair, it perished in that new growth and was dissolved into the void. New lands grew in its place, stone trees and flower mountains.

And Inanna looked upon the Lord of the Good Tree and she blessed they and she went out into the lands and returned justice to the people. Enlil resumed his place as the guardian of nature and he watched from the *Mēnōg* so that miscreants should not threaten his charge. And Inanna returned to her temple and watched from that high place. And she welcomed her people into the high gates and held the hand of the women and held the hands of the men and joined them in breath.

Under the gaze of Inanna her children Zithembe and Noxolo ascended the rainbow, half-human, half-*etemmu*. They showed the way for the others. And another baby race went tottering into the stars.

*Like a young man building a house for the first time, like a girl*
*establishing a woman's domain, holy Inanna did not sleep as she*
*ensured that the warehouses would be provisioned;*
*that dwellings would be founded in the city;*
*that its people would eat splendid food;*
*that its people would drink splendid beverages;*
*that those bathed for holidays would rejoice in the courtyards;*
*that the people would throng the places of celebration;*
*that acquaintances would dine together;*
*that foreigners would cruise about like unusual birds in the sky;*
*that even Marhasi would be re-entered on the tribute rolls;*
*that monkeys, mighty elephants, water buffalo, exotic animals, as well*
*as thoroughbred dogs, lions, mountain ibexes, and alum sheep with*
*long wool would jostle each other in the public squares.*
*She then filled Agade's stores for emmer wheat with gold, she filled its*
*stores for white emmer wheat with silver; she delivered copper, tin, and*
*blocks of lapis lazuli to its granaries*
*and sealed its silos from outside.*
*She endowed its old women with the gift of giving counsel,*
*she endowed its old men with the gift of eloquence.*
*She endowed its young women with the gift of entertaining,*
*she endowed its young men with emotional strength, she endowed its*
*little ones with joy.*
*The nursemaids who cared for the children played the* aljarsur
*instruments.*
*Inside the city* tigi *drums sounded; outside it, flutes and* zamzam
*instruments.*
*Its harbour where ships moored was full of joy.*
*All foreign lands rested contentedly, and their people experienced*
*happiness.*
*"That the orchards should bear syrup and grapes,*
*that the high plain should bear the mašgurum tree,*

*that there should be long life in the palace,*
*that the sea should bring forth every abundance:*
*May An not change it.*
*The land densely populated from south to uplands: may An not change it.*
*May An and Enlil not change it, may An not change it.*
*May Enki and Ninmaḫ not change it, may An not change it.*
*That cities should be rebuilt, that people should be numerous,*
*that in the whole universe the people should be cared for;*
*O Inanna, your queenship is sweet, return to your place.*
*May a good abundant reign be long-lasting in Urim.*
*Let its people lie down in safe pastures, let them reproduce.*
*O mankind plant your seeds and rejoice,*
*raise up the princess overcome by lamentation and crying!*
*O Nanna! O your city! O your house! O your people!"*

# 40

# D'Angel Moon

In her makeshift studio in the Citadel of the Hospice, Kalyenka had one eye on the shade of a janissary's trousers, the other on the oils she was mixing. The painting now stretched across an entire wall to accommodate the trousers amidst a bloody profusion of matters cosmic and mundane, as in the Hospice the aftermath of Vehemple's defeat was being played out.

Kalyenka looked away from the gathering corpses in the *agora* to Bitgaram's gaming module, where Chance was embroiled in melee alongside the *Sarhang* and the idol of Enlil, grown to titanic size, was taking on a monstrous abomination with two maddeningly familiar faces. Kalyenka increased the length of Chance's scimitar and shuddered when it split the head of a loathsome monster attempting to eat him.

She saw her comrades from a dozen revolutions perish under the dread onslaught of the Qliphoth and she wept, till she was jarred out of that emotion by the horrible deaths of Vehemple, Black George and Proko. That scene too was horrendous, but the fates of these men conformed to the symmetry of the painting, for the evil they had perpetrated throughout their lives was its own reward and that was un-exonerated death.

But the transmissions were still coming from another place, and they sang of Vania. It seemed so long since Kalyenka had any intimation of her friend's whereabouts but now she saw her on the canvas, climbing an outsized arachnid's web.

Kalyenka wanted to cry out, to warn Vania she was surrounded by great danger. That much the transmissions told her, though she could not identify what form that peril took. Nor could she communicate her fears, for she knew the transmissions were one way, delivered straight onto canvas. She looked down at her hands, which carried on independently depicting Vania's progress.

They trembled as they painted Vania's final scene. And in that last moment when Vania's eyes were locked on hers, recognition bloomed in them. Her mouth opened involuntarily but there was another shot and Kalyenka realised that the ghastly noise she could hear was the sound of her own grieving.

Then that scene was blotted out and Kalyenka sensed that Vania was gone too. Her eyes welled with tears for her friend. But she knew Vania had become *etemmu* and would live forever.

Kalyenka painted the form of a tall woman whom she recognised as the Dastur Rashin Shanahnaz Shahzadi and her nose twitched, for she had caught the scent of *khadib* oil. Then she saw the *Sarhang* was alongside Rashin and Kalyenka knew they had found each other, somewhere in the reaches of the *Mēnōg*.

She painted Doctor Amordule, dear Adhira, who had evaded all attackers, defended the Citadel staunchly and would take over the running of the Hospice now that the *Sarhang's* work was done. And Kalyenka realised that the *Sarhang*, Augustine D'Angel *had* gone, and his tale was over.

She saw Ermengarde in her painting, cleaving the Qliphoth with great skill, and singing as she worked. She saw Marie Demachy, whose unnerving eye for detail helped her defeat demon after demon.

She saw Hafiz, who wrought devastation amongst the Qliphoth with his distillations of cosmic truth, which held far greater potency than their dread entropy. And as she delineated his shining eyes she heard his voice chanting from afar.

*I have learned so much from God*
*that I can no longer call myself*
*A Christian, a Hindu, a Muslim, a Buddhist, a Jew.*
*The Truth has shared so much of itself with me*

*that I can no longer call myself a man, a woman, an angel,*
*or even a pure soul.*
*Love has befriended Hafiz so completely*
*it has turned to ash and freed me*
*of every concept and image*
*my mind has ever known.*

And she knew that Hafiz would continue to chant truth as long as there were people alive to try to match his beauty in their pursuit of the Great Work.

With the defeat of the *Lịmmûm* Kalyenka saw Bo-Bae, Jae-Won and Bitgaram's world become a little safer. The ocean's currents were mightily disturbed and the polar caps much diminished, but now that the ecological compact had been restored and the *Lịmmûm* vanquished, measures were put in place to remedy their ravages. Nature was restored to pre-eminence and Bo-Bae's country voted out its autocratic rulers, planted ten billion trees, gave living rights to its rivers and lands and began the slow process of ecological recovery.

The home of the Tangerine Believers, the tyrannical and crumbling rogue state infested by Christian *Lịmmûm*, charlatan inheritors of the Crusader's mantle had retreated into itself, there to bicker and shrink while the good people in it overcame their morbidities, assisted by the Cosmic Shekinah which resolved intractable issues between men and women, between white man and black. The *Lịmmûm* among them found they could no longer preach false texts and expect anyone to listen, while women and men abandoned their games and embraced the strength of the Ancients.

Over Cristaña the moon had reached its zenith, a purple ball towering over Gobruk, and its radiance encompassed everything in the painting, influencing all that took place under it, as it was in the old days before humans abandoned themselves to the lesser beings within them.

The Skein was unravelled and that virus excised from the *Mēnōg*. The computers of its devising were reduced to their component parts, so they could not challenge the living fabric of the Great Work, the ecology of souls and the *khutiverse*.

In the high foreground of the painting Kalyenka saw a rainbow. And Inanna appeared, who became the Cosmic Shekinah, and embodied the bridge between male and female that preserved their bond with nature, and she ensured that the quantum pact was complete and the world could go on in harmony with a universe that was ever becoming, as it headed toward union with itself, the Supreme Being.

Kalyenka painted twin children, babies really, who had been elevated into holy beings suffused with light. Hybrid creatures, part-human and part-spirit, they were a new breed of being, making a bridgehead for the rest of humanity to follow.

They walked with sure feet and looked with sure eyes as they became elevated into the *Mēnōg*. Their wisdom was already great, infused with the substance of their parents and bolstered by the manifest *khuti* that comprised the Cosmic Shekinah. The legacy of intergenerational trauma that bred anger, suspicion and hate was banished from their souls, and they were *tabula rasa*, freed of the anxieties that tyrannised their ancestors.

Then Kalyenka's gaze returned to the *Gēttīg* and saw that finally there was a respite from war, though nations still marshalled their armies and coveted each others possessions. But the armies had lost their surety and their leaders were doubtful, for they knew that the world was somehow different. And Kalyenka felt that too, and she felt that the Great Work was being done, though she did not know what form a new world would take. But she knew that the painting was finished. That much was certain.

# 41

# Sifting Through the Ashes

Bejikereene and Olaf stared at the charred remains of the Eagle's Nest. After witnessing the ruin of the Hospice they had not been at all surprised when they reached their home at the top of the mountain.

Soldiers had burnt their inn to the ground after looting everything of value. The church was gone, as were most of the houses. Invaders had destroyed the well, defecated in the streets, left behind broken carts, empty ammunition boxes and the carcasses of the dogs they shot. Worst of all they burnt the inn to ashes, leaving only hearthstones poking out of the rubble like embarrassed sentries.

But once they'd stopped staring and Bejikereene squeezed out a few tears, both realised they didn't really care that the old place was gone. The ideas that the Hospice had let into their heads made its loss seem trivial. There was too much to be done to worry about the old ways.

Bejikereene was already sifting through the ashes of the Eagle's Head, categorising and reassembling, beginning the work she knew must be done. Though her nose wrinkled at the sour tang of urine and smoke, she was planning a redesign based on what she'd seen in the Hospice. No reason not to plant mandala flower beds amongst her cabbages, nor to dismiss the notion of an energy-efficient rammed earth low-rise with an ironic asymmetrical façade maximising natural light, in place of the old inn. She couldn't think where she'd come by these notions, but they seemed to make sense.

Olaf sat on the bricks of the hearthstone, leaned his chin on his fist and contemplated. One glance told him the soldiers had not lifted the bricks in the floor, so his sausage and pickled vegetables and much of his store of beer and wines would be safe. That meant they had food to see them through the next stage, whatever that was.

Lazlo was fossicking through the ruins of his bakery and the other villagers were returning one by one, hushed and awestruck by the abrupt cataclysm of their world. Soon Olaf would talk to them, or rather, he thought, let Bejikereene do so. Meanwhile he would work out how to best organise them all for travelling, something that somehow seemed inevitable, though again he had no idea where they were going. Or when.

Their return from the Hospice had taken three days. After stumbling out of the burning ruins they'd limped down the mountain, passing dazed and bewildered soldiers, some of whom they gathered up and helped negotiate the steep forested slopes. Bejikereene nursed two badly burned Turks, leading them on the back of a mule Olaf rescued from a ravine. Along the way they accumulated fifteen more soldiers of varying nationalities, most of whom were wounded, all glassy-eyed and shell-shocked.

They'd left the soldiers in an abandoned farmhouse, promising to come back with food and water as soon as they were able. Those ragged men would soon heal with good food and rest. Bejikereene opined that they would make excellent workers in the cause of some project she felt was imminent, if yet unknown. In the meantime the soldiers might settle in the valleys and work the land that the bandits had scared all good folk away from. Olaf did not argue with his steely-eyed wife. He too felt an implacable optimism, despite the devastation all around them. Bejikereene voiced it as they approached the village.

"Something has changed Olaf. I can feel it. I don't know what, and don't give me that look. Something has changed, and for the better. The world is different somehow. We were part of it, us and that crazy talking statue, which knew all the old words from my parent's books. And that soldier we helped out and the witch woman, who I always said ain't no witch at all, but an artist."

"Yes my love," said Olaf, and he touched her on the arm. She turned to him and he smiled, and her eyes glazed with tears. Their lips touched and they regarded each other as if strangers met on a dark night.

But they had not spoken of what they saw in the *tougrak* place. Not yet. It was still a potent horror swirling in their minds. Bejikereene kept reliving Enlil's visitations, his glowering entoptic eyes, the spectral commands that seemed to come from afar but at the same time from deep inside her head. Forever after she renounced the trappings of Christianity and practiced only the rites of Ahura Mazdā. Her prayers always paid homage to Enlil, along with admonitions that he should never trouble her again.

Olaf kept his own counsel. On the way home, walking through the violet mist that suffused the mountains he'd observed strange emanations; half-formed creatures that were there yet not, but seemed to gain fidelity by degrees. Voices and eerie cries wafted through the forest, shadows flitted through the boughs of ancient trees. Olaf came to regard these apparitions as manifestations of a hidden truth; along with the revelations of the Hospice they comprised evidence that things had indeed irrevocably changed.

He had always suspected there was more going on than what he saw on the surface of this world. The Bible spoke of these things as the province of priests alone. But Olaf doubted whether priests knew any more about it than he, long having concluded that their words were mere plaster over the void, coded messages which encouraged the greed of those who thought they were better.

Now he knew for certain there was a whole other world beyond this one. Something so fantastical, so absurdly different that it was impossible to understand. And the thought gave him hope.

Soon all the villagers would return from the caves up on the mountain top. They would no longer be afraid of the *tougrak*, because from now on, things were going to be different.

# 42

# Wax Batteries

Above alpine meadows the sun broke and basted a billion trees. Heather and brambles, grasses and saplings awoke, sparkling in defiance of the long night. Photons sparked photosynthesis from thirsty sap. Their energies ricocheted through stem and root, across untold billion stamen and cells, a vast battery of unimaginable power. Flowers sparkled, raw effusions erupting from green fuses barely able to contain them.

Elk stirred, ermine and egret. Exhausted after his night's prowling, even a fox cocked an eye as the crimson tide came flowing down his den walls. Bees rose, tawny hordes gathering the energies to stoke their own wax batteries. The entire population of the mountain range shuddered in fulfilment, replenished by that golden torrent.

Neither in the camps of men was it cursed, as hangovers took root or rot took hold in gun-blasted wounds. Despite their afflictions, even the dying felt some absurd and intangible hope.

The officers were gone now, or stripped of insignia sat with their cannon fodder around campfires, marvelling at the sweet breath of the earth, freed of hectoring orders and the imperative to kill. Despite the hangovers and the wounds something had changed forever, and there was a sense among these survivors that the rising tide of joy would not be curtailed by some calamity, that they would not be shot as deserters or whipped for straggling. That they could make their own way home, and that things were going to be different there, too.

All eyes were turned to the stronghold upon the mountain. There, at the fulcrum, peace reigned. The moon was sleeping, skies flowering like the blue tamarisk. The vile smokes and effluent of war had been washed away by something far greater, something so profound that these battered and bleeding men could not speak of it.

They looked away from the impervious Assassin, stared at one another and none stirred when a deer ambled out of the undergrowth and gazed at them silently. One by one the men stood up and limped away, through the forests and the valleys and slowly out of the mountains.

They were entering a vast world without end or beginning. They were striding to the lip of the universe, as ancient and new and nonsensical as Eternity itself. They were going home.

# 43

# War Stories

Chance ordered a fresh pot of tea and sat back as it sauntered toward him on a tray that had no visible means of support. "I will never get used to this," he sighed. But Kalyenka was walking out of the bedroom and he smiled. "Good morning my love. You look ravishing for a woman who drank so much vodka."

"Hush, rabbit," said Kalyenka. "Thanks to this new gravity I don't get hangovers any more."

"My old wounds don't seem to trouble me half as much either," Chance said. "Not even the one I copped from that Qliphoth creature, whose fangs were as long as your legs, but not half as shapely."

"Let's not swap war stories again."

"No, let's not."

"I'd rather hear about the giant coal mine in the future. What was all that about?"

"I don't really know," said Chance. "But I suspect I wish I did."

# GLOSSARY

*Agora* - A Greek meeting place or town square.

*Akh* - The collective components of the soul as realised by its intellect, enabling proper integration into the ecology of souls.

*Almarabi* - Wealthy Eastern merchants and *Ljmmûm* conspirators.

*Apeira* - Every sentient being occupies a unique envelope of *khuti* space, their measure of the *apeiron*. In effect these are individual continuums with which we negotiate the *khutiverse*.

*Apeiron* - The infinite space of the Cosmos.

*Ba* - The principal component of the soul, reflecting its personality and power, i.e. its *khuti*

*Caduceus* - Hermetic symbol of a two headed serpent entwined around a staff of wisdom, representing liminal and subliminal consciousnesses and the duality of all things. Gods and goddesses, men and women, animals and nature all follow this principle, relying on a gendered counterpart so their powers become manifest, fulfilling their cosmic function. The *Caduceus* indicates this duality. It shows that all things are in polarity - they must be made manifest with their opposite in order to work. Nuanced and preferred genders are included in this reckoning - the Cosmos is an inclusive arena.

Chthonic Gates - a liminal threshold, the boundary between seen and unseen worlds.

Ecology of souls - When human souls leave the *Gëttig* and progress into the *Mēnōg* they take their place in the ecology of souls, which constitutes humanity's place in the divine cosmos. They join the flow of nature moving towards its better self. For nature is about evolution; from atomic cells through biological metamorphosis to human beings, from there to a point where biology becomes no longer relevant, where we become pure *khuti*. The individual's quotient of *khuti* dictates their evolutionary progress in contributing to the Great Work.

*Egregore* - From the Greek word *egrégoros*, meaning 'wakeful'. Any significant grouping of aligned people creates a wavefront of psychic momentum known as an *egregore*. When the psychic energy of a population is aligned under religious mania or in the name of nationhood, particularly under the direction of a charismatic autocrat, an *egregore* can be highly dangerous.

*Etemmu* - Akkadian word for 'ghost', which came to mean the higher consciousness of the soul transfigured into divine light after death.

Force and Form - The two polarities of masculine and feminine, fire and water, which bind the physical cosmos together.

*\*Gēttīg* - From the Avestan tongue: The profane or earthly realm inhabited by humanity.

*Groot verkeerslicht* - outsized offensive automaton as devised by Vehemple.

Hermeticism - the oldest human scientific belief system.

Jeobchog - South Korean transnational corporation encompassing national defence and internet infrastructures.

*Ka* - The vital essence of a soul, that which is the repository of manifest *khuti*.

*Kal Ibben* - A powerful incantation adopted by the D'Angels and the Keepers of the Flame, a subset of the Zoroastrian cult. Both a key or opening spell and a protective ward. Also an excellent cipher, as *Lĵmmûm* are unable to pronounce the phrase. It requires a combination of *khuti and* cognitive understandings which they lack.

*Khaibet* - The physical shadow of the soul, that mortal part which enables earthly living, but cannot transmute through the Chthonic veil into the *Mēnōg*.

*Khuti* - The fire of the universe - a divine energy that is present in all things; an ineffable fluid flowing through the ethers and our mortal bodies. It permeates the universe, constituting what humans know as space and time, of which we are all indivisible parts. It also constitutes what humans know as soul - the immanent being inside each living creature.

*Khutiverse* - The intangible endoskeleton of the Cosmos, constituting the intermingled flow of time and space which manifests as *khuti* in the *Gēttīg*.

*Ljmmûm* - Sumerian word for a class of usurers and slavers. The primary cause of all human wars and misery, they are an ancient cabal of loosely allied merchants embedded in global economies. The richest people in the world today, the shadowy figures who control the economies of nations, who profit from war and famine, these are the living embodiments of that cabal. Focussed entirely upon material greed and power they have no fixed ideological, racial or denominational identities. Such is their intergenerational corruption that they have passed down increasingly corroded *khuti* DNA to their dynastic heirs, deficient in the vital components that allow soul transmission into the *Mēnōg*.

*\*Mēnōg* - From the Avestan tongue: The quantum or sacred realm which parallels our own. A scientifically verified shadow dimension, repository of the great mysteries, home to the entities variously known as gods, demons and other assorted monsters.

Metis - A state of cosmic grace, suspended between worlds, close to ineffable powers.

*Molka* - From *mollae*, Korean for secret, and *ka* for camera – meaning the illicit filming of women. It can also mean shaming for alleged infamy, a well-known tactic in an industry which thrives on scandals.

Quantum pact - The interdependent equation between humans and nature, the gods and the *Mēnōg*, which constitutes and guarantees the coherence of the ongoing *khutiverse*. Animals recognise it. They do not behave out of dumb instinct but are consciously enacting their roles through participation in the dance of nature, *working towards a specific end*. The most cogent victory of the *Ljmmûm* has been to swindle humanity into failing the quantum pact, by refusing to acknowledge that its salvation lies in reaching union with nature.

Qliphoth - Designated by Biblical terminology as demonic beings, these are necessary cogs of the cosmic machine - negative counterpoints to the Sephiroth. Nonetheless they are known as 'the husks that surround the light of manifest *khuti*', which translates as 'the beings which obstruct cosmic energies'. In ancient days they enlisted with the *Ljmmûm* to control humanity in exchange for rations of manifest *khuti*, drip-fed to them through organised religion. That role is resurrected in this epoch to assist the *Ljmmûm's* assault on both *Mēnōg* and *Gētīg* through the Skein.

*Rasa* - From a concept in the Sanskrit language conveying the essence of a feeling, which evokes an emotion in the correspondent. In the *Rigveda* scriptures *rasa* is described as 'the luminescent consciousness', which is expressed in the rhythm and emotion of an artist's work.

*Securité* - the Hospice defence battalion.

Sephiroth - The primary creative force of the *khutiverse*. In the Tree of Life, a Hermetic map of the *khutiverse*, the Sephiroth are designated as cosmic power nodes connected by pulsing conduits. Their opposites are the Qliphoth, the primary nullifiers, un-beings of the Void. In nature, which is to say, in the broader cosmos, everything exists in polarities. (See Caduceus)

It demonstrates that the universe is a mystery set up for the birth of what's known in Hermetic terms as the Ever Becoming One, which is the evolution of the united consciousness of all things. Just so, the Sephiroth exist to counterbalance the negative energy of the Qliphoth - and this function is in harmony with that cosmic equation. An interesting particular is that the Sephiroth and Qliphoth are also living entities of the *Mēnōg* (see Aiwass).

Skein - An analog technology that joins the physical world of the *Gēttīg* to the *Mēnōg* dimension of dreams and the subconscious, what we'll call the transcendental reality, enabling physical transitions between them. It mimics the fungal mycelium networks which interconnect all trees and growing things, allowing the transport of nutrients and information.

The topology of the spirit world has similar characteristics, in that like mycelium its networks are conduits for vast transformative energies. Seers, witches and prophets use these conduits to glimpse the spirit realm through the use of entheogens and magikal praxis, which require applications of khuti and applied emotion. The Skein enables the *Ljmmûm,* who are deficient in the *khuti* qualities which allow transition into the *Mēnōg,* to enter that realm.

However the Skein is a dangerously unstable technology. Because it was designed as a simulacrum of nature, it is in a sense, alive. But it lacks *khuti,* the essential ingredient of nature. It is essentially a form of virus, mutating and replicating itself. The viral mechanisms of the Skein replace the sub-atomic structure of the *Mēnōg* with a sterile counterfeit, so that it warps the very fabric of the Cosmos.

*Sûk* - An Arabic or Persian marketplace and cultural hub.

*Supreme Being* - The united consciousness of all things.

*Tjuringa* - The most sacred talismans of the Indigenous Australian *Anangu,* anchoring the earthly power of their guardian spirits. These are primordial stones carved with powerful stories, venerated for millennia. They correspond directly to entities living along song-lines, under the most sacred waterholes and mountains. Many of them, including the *Tjuringa* connected to the Rainbow Serpent were stolen by agents of the *Ljmmûm.*

*Tougrak* - pejorative slang for D'Angels. Origin unknown.

*Tuat* - Named after the terrain of the afterlife in the Egyptian Book of the Dead, the *Tuat* is a multidimensional map of the cosmos encompassing the area between continuum streams in which we experience life and what we mistake for time.

*Verkeerslicht* - remotely operated offensive automaton.

*Yazata* - The Zoroastrian tradition and Hermetic sciences posits every sentient being as having a counterpart in the spirit world, known as the *Yazata*. They are united with it after death.

*N.B. Authors note: Owing to a diabolical ruse perpetrated by the *Limmûm* through the Skein, the definitions of *Mēnōg* and *Gētīg* were deliberately confused in the first two volumes of D'Angel Moon. That subterfuge has been corrected in later editions and they are now correctly represented in this Glossary.

.

# Don't miss out!

Visit the website below and you can sign up to receive emails whenever Mick Daley publishes a new book. There's no charge and no obligation.

https://books2read.com/r/B-A-VSJC-ZMQAF

**BOOKS 2 READ**

Connecting independent readers to independent writers.

## About the Author

Mick Daley is a musician, journalist and house painter living in the Northern Rivers of NSW.

Read more at https://www.mickdaley.com.

Milton Keynes UK
Ingram Content Group UK Ltd.
UKHW042004281024
450365UK00003B/155